THE
CROWN
OF
LIGHT

STACEY MARIE BROWN

Cover by Dane at Ebook Launch (https://ebooklaunch.com/ebook-cover-design/)
Developmental Editor Jordan Rosenfeld (http://jordanrosenfeld.net)
Edited by Hollie (www.hollietheeditor.com)

ALSO BY STACEY MARIE BROWN

Darkness of Light
(Darkness Series #1)

Fire in the Darkness
(Darkness Series #2)

Beast in the Darkness
(An Elighan Dragen Novelette)

Dwellers of Darkness
(Darkness Series #3)

Blood Beyond Darkness
(Darkness Series #4)

West
(A Darkness Series Novel)

City in Embers
(Collector Series #1)

The Barrier Between
(Collector Series #2)

Across the Divide
(Collector Series #3)

From Burning Ashes
(Collector Series #4)

Crown of Light

Dedicated To:

To those of you who are already wondering…
The next one is coming!

And again to:

Coffee, Starbucks,
and the unknown hot guy from the Internet.

Crown of Light

ONE

"Kennedy!" My name rang through my head, chilling my heart. I didn't recognize the woman's voice but it felt so familiar it tugged at something deep inside. "Help her!"

With a skittering feeling up my spine, I spun around and gasped.

The Seelie Queen stood before me. She held a sword above her head as she loomed over Ember's rigid body, which lay on the floor.

"Ember!" I screamed.

Neither of them heard me. The blade swung toward my friend's neck.

"No!" I tried to budge my feet, but my entire body felt glued to the spot. Helpless.

The weapon came down on Ember's neck; a blood-curdling scream rang off the castle walls.

A white light blinded me.

Then everything went black.

Thump. Thump. Thump. Throbbing pain. It dragged me out of darkness, stabbing hot and sharp like *my* head had been cut off. The aching spread down my arms and jaw. My eyelids creaked open, lashes grazing my glasses. I blinked, slowly absorbing my surroundings. My heart thrashed against my ribs, the remnants of the dream slipping from my mind, but the terror still clutched my chest.

Where was I? What was going on? My head jerked around trying to make sense of the scenery. Cold throbbed off the cement walls, which were stacked with various-sized storage crates. The room was at least two stories high and just as wide, and the only light slipped in from a high window. *How did I get here?*

A pounding at the base of my skull brought with it flashes of memory: a cave. Greece. Sword. Strighoul. Ember screaming my name.

Lorcan.

Then darkness.

Panic fluttered at the base of my throat. I looked up at my hands tied to a thick pipe above my head. My mouth formed a shriek, but only a garbled noise came out. A cloth clogged my voice.

The rope scraped along the pipe, creaking with strain. My wrists tugged and twisted against the restraints above my head; the blood in my arms drained, pricking them with pain. I thrashed wildly against the cord with a desperate cry.

Lorcan had taken me. For what? What happened to my friends? Were they all right? We had discovered the final piece we needed to defeat Aneira. A throng of strighoul had attacked us in the cave where we found the Sword of Light, Nuada's sword—the one thing that could kill the Queen.

Then Lorcan's group had turned up and blocked our escape route. But he hadn't come for the sword. He came for *me*. It didn't make sense. If he was still working for her, why would he take me and not the one thing she feared and wanted the most in the world? How could I be worth more than a treasure of Tuatha De Danann, who were a race of godlike people gifted with supernatural powers?

My thin arms yanked on the rope, rubbing it against the metal until blood dripped down and soaked into my pants.

Kennedy, calm down. Think. Study your surroundings.

I squinted, my shoulder bumping my glasses higher on my face. The thin window at the top of the room let in a sliver of moonlight. The room was heavily shadowed, but I could see giant warehouse boxes. Vancouver was spelled out on one of them. Was that Vancouver, Washington, or Canada? No matter what, I was close to home. The sun-cooked mystic land of Meteora, where I had last closed my eyes, now lay across the world from me.

Taking in everything helped keep me grounded, gave me something to focus on.

What you know:

A.) You are close to home.

9

B.) Lorcan is holding you hostage.

C.) He definitely wants you for something. It means he doesn't want you dead. Not yet anyway.

D.) If they want you, it means there is room for negotiation.

E.) Or Lorcan will just torture you till you do what he wants.

I quickly shook "E" from my head, my heart drumming all the way down to my stomach.

The only thing Lorcan could want were my Druid powers, which I barely knew how to use. My skills were very minimal. Only a month ago I found out I was one of the last known Druids left alive. Aneira had systematically annihilated the entire race from existence, because Druids could not be controlled, and we were more powerful than her. Clearly, not me. I was nowhere near her level. Only a few were that strong, and she killed them all.

My parents smuggled me to Earth at the height of Aneira's genocide, hiding me with a human family to save my life. I grew up knowing I was adopted but with no idea I'd come from a magical Druid line.

Magic! My attention flew up to the rope, shifting myself on the hard cement. I grunted, my tongue flicking against the gag as my mouth tried to close enough to form words, desperate to try all the spells I knew. I really needed to learn charms that could unlock or untie.

There was one key difference between fae magic and Druid magic. Ours came from words, from drawing upon energy outside us, while fae had magic in their blood. We had to speak incantations to invoke our magic. Fae could shift, glamour, kill, and lure without uttering a word.

I choked on my saliva trying to shut my jaw enough to get words out on my tongue. Garbled noise hummed from my mouth. I did nothing more than drool on myself, like a teething baby.

Our magic had to be precise. We had to say the enchantments clearly and with meaning. I tried a couple more times, babbling and spitting. Eventually I gave up with an aggravated cry bellowing through the fabric in my mouth.

"Isn't it crazy?" A deep voice came from over my shoulder. I yelped, my sore head smacking against the brick. A figure sat on one of the boxes near me, one leg bent up, arm propped on it, green eyes flashing in the dim light.

Lorcan Dragen.

My heart thwacked against my ribs. *Holy nerf-herder.* How long had he been there? I knew dark dwellers were silent in sneaking up on their prey, but it was still unnerving for him to simply appear without my notice.

He was the kind of rugged good looking that numbed your brain and tongue, stealing educated women of all their logic. Standing about six two, broad shouldered with corded arms, large hands, and a body so built it rippled wildly beneath his T-shirt and jeans. To top it off, he gazed at me with ruthless yet disarming, sexy, piercing green eyes beneath a head thinly covered in stubble. He was built to intimidate and entice.

He reminded me a lot of Eli, his younger brother. They had the same mannerisms, the same intense eyes. It confused my brain to like one and despise the other. I had learned to trust Eli over time. But I was no fool when it came to Lorcan. He was not his brother, and I knew exactly what he was capable of, how cruel and twisted he could be.

"A powerful Druid can be so easily thwarted by a simple piece of cloth." A smug grin spread over his mouth, and he dropped his leg to the floor, leaning forward on the box with his arms on his legs. "It's hard, huh? To form clear words around a gag?" His mocking pity burned my pride, like tape ripped from flesh.

I didn't move or swallow. This was the man who had ordered Ian's death. My friend's dead eyes haunted me and tore at my heart every day. Ian was Ryan's cousin; I had known him as long as I had known Ryan. I missed him so much. I never told Ryan or Ian, but I had a crush on Ian since I was ten.

Now Ian was dead.

Samantha killed him, but Lorcan gave the order. He was also the man who slaughtered Ember's real mother and would have destroyed Ember if Lily hadn't taken Ember and run.

Lorcan had sided with Aneira and betrayed his family. He was the one who had kidnapped Ryan, Josh, Ian, and me. Three of us became prisoners to the Seelie Queen, along with Jared when he tried to save us. Josh, Jared, and I escaped, but Ryan was still there.

No matter how gorgeous Lorcan's physical form, he was evil to the core. And now I was his hostage.

I didn't speak, watching his every move.

"I'm not stupid. I know the second I unbind your mouth you will try to do a spell and run." He stood, striding slowly, like he was stalking prey and preparing to pounce. "I can't have that." He lowered himself to a squat in front of me, his gaze prowling over me. "We're at quite an impasse since I need your magic. What should I do about that, li'l Druid?" It was not a question but a taunt.

My back dug into the rough wall, pressing so hard my bones made a cracking sound. Blood rushed through my veins, clipping off my airways. His nostrils flared, and a glint flickered in his eyes. He knew I was terrified. Dwellers had sharper senses than almost all fae. He could hear my heart pounding, smell the fear pumping out my pores.

"I really hate doing this, but you leave me with no other choice." He balanced on his toes, his hands clasped. His words were calm, but I felt the threats under each one. My stomach coiled tight, waiting for his next sentence. "If you try a spell on me or try to escape...let's just say I know exactly the path your little sister, Halley, takes to get to school every morning. Samantha watches her very closely. There is a bit of forest she goes through...all by herself."

Oh god. Halley. Oxygen rushed out of my lungs in a whoosh. Samantha wouldn't hesitate. Her gorgeous face and girly style of clothing fooled you into thinking she was harmless. She was completely crazy and the most bloodthirsty of all the dark dwellers. When Lorcan's group kidnapped Ryan, Ian, and me, she was the one begging to spill our blood. More than anything, to hurt Ember.

"I also know when your father goes on his early morning runs and when your mother leaves her office." Lorcan leaned closer, his mouth only a breath from mine, warm air brushing over my lips and down my neck. He spoke low, his voice husky. "My link to Sam is instant. You try anything and they will be dealt with faster than you can get out of this room. Not hard to make any one of them disappear. You understand me, Druid?"

I did. Dark dwellers were able to communicate with each other through their minds, but they had to be in close proximity of one other to do it.

Liquid pooled at the back of my eyes, my throat constricting. His nearness mixed up my mind, like dice in a cup. It was nothing more than a game to him to unravel me. And it was working.

"Do you promise to be a good little Druid?" He pulled back just enough to look in my eyes.

Ember had explained that promises or oaths in the fae world were binding. You couldn't break them without painful consequences, until released or fulfilled. My own studies had revealed this didn't really work on pure humans, but if you had even an ounce of fae heritage or magic like Druids did in your blood, then it would affect you.

I blinked back the tears in my eyes and nodded.

"You know I need to hear you say it." He hitched up an eyebrow. "I'm going to take this gag off. I want the first word you say to be yes. No tricks, pet."

There was no question I would do what he asked. Ember and Ryan were the fearless ones, ready to buck the system. I wasn't. I was quiet and shy with a habit of saying things people found odd. But I was no hero, especially when my family was being threatened.

He slipped his fingers behind my head, knotting through my long brown hair. His green eyes fixed on me so intensely I had to glance away. Lorcan's physical looks, intensity, and his cruelty overwhelmed me. My body trembled at his nearness, wanting to be far away from him.

The bond behind my head loosened and my jaw cracked with relief when it felt a bit of freedom. He grabbed both ends of the cloth, slowly peeling it away from my mouth, his fingers dragging down my cheeks. His green eyes drilled into me expectantly.

I rolled my jaw, trying to close it all the way, finally able to swallow naturally.

"Let me hear the word." He grabbed my chin, holding it tightly between his fingers.

I gulped, letting the sound form on my tongue. "Yes," I whispered. "I promise." The weight of my agreement dropped down on me, heavy in my body. It wasn't painful, but the pressure stimulated feeling back into my legs.

Lorcan leaned back on his heels, a haughty grin hooked up the side of his mouth. "Now was that so bad?"

I narrowed my eyes at him. Too bad looks couldn't kill. He chuckled and rose to his feet. "So there is a feisty streak in there."

"What do you want with me?" It was hard to talk after being gagged so long, but the anger stirring underneath pushed the words out.

"You know what I want." He folded his arms, his muscles coiling under his black T-shirt. "What every man wants when a girl is tied up in front of him."

My heart smashed against my ribs, my legs pressing back into my chest painfully. Terror iced every cell.

Lorcan let out a deep laugh, his head tipping back. "Magic, pet." He smirked, slanting his head. "What were *you* thinking?"

I opened my mouth but nothing came out.

"Wow, li'l Druid, you need to get your mind out of the gutter." He clicked his tongue at me, then took a step, looming over me. "First, I would never need to take a woman who wasn't willing. They come to me. And I kill scum who force women. Second, you would never be the type I'd take to bed."

Relief washed over me but an unexpected flush of indignation rose up my cheeks. I was strangely insulted.

"When you hinted at doing something to Ember at the time you tried to kidnap her, was it simply a joke?" I pointed my chin up, staring him in the eyes.

"Words." He shrugged and bent over, getting back in my face. "The power of a subtle threat makes people do whatever you want. They react like fools." He raised an eyebrow at me poignantly. "They'll agree to anything. Right, pet?"

My mouth fell open, then slammed shut, anger grinding my teeth together.

"But the thing with me is you don't know for sure which words I say are the true ones." He inched closer, pressing my head back into the brick. "I could be lying, and I will kill your family without a thought. Or I could merely be making you think I would. Doesn't really matter now though. You already promised."

"You are despicable," I seethed.

He stood, laughing. "That is the only thing we know for certain here."

I jerked my head away, staring into the corner of the room. The shadows painted ghostly figures on the walls. I had so many questions, but all that mattered to me was the well-being of my friends left behind in Greece. Were they all right? What had happened to them?

"You had strighoul attack your own family." I shook my head with disgust. "What kind of person does that?"

"Me, apparently," Lorcan replied.

"You don't know what family means. Do you even know if they are all right?" I whipped my head toward him, fury burning away my fear of him. "Or don't you care at all? Are you that soulless?"

He stared down at me, his face expressionless. My inner clock ticked off the seconds, the tension in the room rising.

He inhaled, his arms curling over each other. His shoulders rolled back, his entire demeanor changed in a breath, and the beast skimmed his skin.

"My *family* is my business. I don't have to explain myself to anyone, especially to an inconsequential Druid."

The jab sliced across my chest, but I kept my head high. When I spoke, I kept my voice low but firm. "If I'm so insignificant, then why go through such a big production to take me?"

He lifted his chin higher, his nose flaring.

"Words." I narrowed my gaze on him, an understanding striking me. "You like to use them...to hurt, threaten, or intimidate, but your actions tell me a different story. You need me."

A flash of red bolted across his eyes, his feet stirring.

"I already promised not to run or use a spell on you. You have me. So please tell me if my friends are all right. Is Jared? Ember?" I pleaded.

He jerked his head away from me, strolling to the other side of the room. He rubbed the back of his neck, then his forehead. Had I made him nervous?

"I had Dominic check on them to make sure. The group that got split from you are all alive. Your boyfriend's fine." He stared up at the sliver of window.

I sighed in relief, my head dipping forward and leaning on my cuffed arms. Jared. He was safe. Thank goodness. "The others? Ember? Eli? Josh?"

"My brother's alive," he said without a hair of doubt. "Figuring Ember is too." There was something in his tone which brushed against my intuition.

"What happened? What aren't you telling me?"

Lorcan whipped around, ire clenching his fists. "There is a lot I'm not telling you." He strode to me, his body seeming to grow twice as big as mine, like the big bad wolf. "Enough questions. You need to focus on yourself. I will need your magic. And a lot of it. And you are nowhere close to the level you should be in order to help me."

"Is this about the curse Aneira put on the dark dwellers?" I nudged my glasses back up my nose with my hanging arm. My nerves were numb with lack of circulation. "Is that all you can think about? Yourself? There is a war coming and all you care about is getting back into the Otherworld?"

"Oh, this goes way past that," he sneered. "Getting back into the Otherworld is the least of my worries."

My eyes widened with surprise, once again feeling off kilter. Lorcan was exceptional at doing that.

"My life isn't the only one dependent on your ability to break a curse."

"But I can't break your curse. It is way beyond my level."

"You broke the one in the cave. The one guarding the sword."

"Only because it was cast by another Druid." I flapped my arms helplessly. "It seemed eager to have me there, like it had been waiting for another Druid to come along. And I barely did it. It was more like I nullified it."

He stared at me for a long time, irritation humming along his aura. "Then you will learn." He walked back to me and leaned over. "Get some rest. Your training starts first thing in the morning." His face was only an inch from mine. "And, pet?" he whispered. My eyes locked on his. He tugged something from his back pocket, his hands moving so fast I didn't realize what he was doing before it was too late.

Cloth prodded my lips apart as it slipped between my teeth. My jaw protested, clamping down as my cry drowned in the back of my throat. I shook my head back and forth, like a horse against a bit.

"Can't be too safe." He winked with self-satisfaction, tying it tight behind my head. "Especially with you. I'm thinking deep down this sweet exterior is nothing but a front."

My throat burned with unspoken rage at the smugness on his face. I wanted nothing more than to set him on fire. Too bad I didn't know that spell. Though Druid magic was supposed to be used for good, I was reconsidering my take on the dark side.

Lorcan winked and spun around, strolling to the doorway. He reached the open entry and turned back to look at me. "Oh, and, pet? Don't even wish for someone to hear your cries. They never will." He tapped at the wall and then walked out, leaving me in the dark, chilly warehouse alone.

I tried to swallow the sob building in my throat, blinking repeatedly. *You're going to get through this, Ken. It will all be okay.*

It was the first time I outright lied to myself.

"Wake up!" A jolt of pain stabbed up my thigh, digging into my lower back. I jerked my eyes open with a gasp.

The sun from the window haloed her, my vision clearing to take in the figure over me. The peace of my brief sleep washed away in a sea of flaming red hair, light blue eyes, and porcelain skin. Terror gripped my throat and clawed at the edges. She was dressed in tight black skinny jeans, and her long hair flowed loosely around her shoulders. With brown rider boots and a green jacket, she looked right out of a Gap ad.

Samantha Walker.

She had the appearance of an angel and personality of a malicious killer. She was the one who had slit my friend's throat. I watched Ian's life soak into the dirt with Samantha's laugh echoing in my ears.

Instant loathing and terror curled in my gut. Her boot kicked my leg again. A sharp, savory scent drifted from a styrofoam takeout container, and my stomach gurgled despite me. I had no idea of the last time I'd eaten. The thought of eating now made me nauseous, but in spite of everything, my tummy wanted nutrients.

"Lorcan seems to like taking in the strays." Samantha stared at me, her lips twisted in disgust. "He's captured you twice." She tipped her weight on one leg, tapping a finger against her lips. "Now, I thought Druids are these mighty seers who can see the future. You'd think with powers like that you would have seen him coming. At least one of those times."

I swallowed over the gag and turned my head, defensive anger rising to my solar plexus. The first time Lorcan kidnapped me, I hadn't known I was Druid. My magic was dormant inside. All my life I had episodes of speaking odd statements without my control, but they were rare. Now they were happening more frequently. Sometimes I stayed present and sometimes I didn't, but I had yet to have my first "full" premonition where I saw the future happening. Owen told me I came from an extremely powerful line of Druids, but maybe it missed me. I might be the dud.

"You can't even do some basic spells. That's really pathetic." Samantha shook her head. "You're worthless. Not sure what Lorcan thinks you're going to do for us. Personally I think getting you was a waste of time."

She lowered herself, balancing on her heels, the container propped in one hand. "Smell good? I can hear your stomach growling from here."

My gaze whipped to her then back to the window, watching puffy clouds drift across the slip of blue peeking through. *Keep calm, Kennedy. Breathe.*

One of my first lessons with Owen and Cole was centering myself. My magic came from outside me, but I filtered it through my core. It was a gage. The calmer I was, the more controlled and precise I was, though I had yet to really master it. In Greece, the fear of disappointing Lars or even Ember propelled me. Here I was struggling to find any trace of calm.

"Here." Samantha laid the container next to my leg, her voice sugary sweet. She pulled an orange juice bottle from her jacket pocket, placing it near me. "I know you must be starving. And so thirsty." When she opened the lid of the food, steam billowed out, twisting my stomach at the heady whiff of scrambled eggs mingled with peppers and potatoes. "Go ahead." She nudged at the box, her eyes wide and innocent, but a cruel smile twisted her mouth.

My arms were tied above my head, my mouth gagged.

Anything Samantha did was for her own pleasure. She liked torture most. "Not hungry right now?" she said, bouncing back up to stand. "Well, I'll leave it there for when you are." She moved toward the door, her steps halted as two men walked through the doorway. The last of Lorcan's clan—Dominic and Dax.

"Why do you always have to be such a bitch?" Dominic smirked, seemingly more amused than upset. He scared me. He had a wild unpredictability about him, like the beast skimmed the surface all the time. Tall with a ripped body, he looked Brazilian, with tan skin, dark eyes, and wavy brown hair. He was sultry and exotic. But terrifying.

Dax was Lorcan's second-in-command. He was also so beautiful it was difficult to remember he was an assassin. He stood over six feet tall, lean and built, with a close-cut haircut and milk chocolate complexion. His cheekbones and full lips would be the envy of most women. The brief time I had been with this group before being turned over to the Queen, he came across as the quiet, serious one. His eyes were always moving, taking everything in.

Dax looked over at me, his mouth pressed tight. "Lorcan ordered you to give her the breakfast."

"I did." Samantha arms flew back, motioning to the breakfast next to me. "I gave it to her."

"Samantha," Dax warned, his head tilting to the side.

"You're no fun." She folded her arms. "You both know as I do this is a joke. Miss Little Goody-Goody can't help us. She's barely out of an onesie. No way does she possess enough magic to break the spell on us."

"That is not for us to decide. Lorcan is willing to work with her to improve her ability," Dax replied. "Right now he gave you a simple order: make sure she got food and drink while he was away."

Lorcan was away? What was he doing? I wondered how far away from civilization we were. Did he say my screams wouldn't be heard because it was true, or merely so I would think it was true? I wondered what would happen if my magic aptitude wasn't up to his standard? Maybe he'd kill me.

"He didn't say I couldn't have some fun as well." Samantha grinned and marched back to the stack of boxes where she plopped down with a sneer directed right at me. But I looked away from her. In the daylight I could see the writing on the cases. The shipping address was Vancouver, Washington.

We were close to Portland, Oregon, a city I knew well. My mother took me to the famous Powell's Books every year. Books. Facts. The one thing we had in common. She would get us a hotel room, and it was the only time we were alone together. Halley never wanted to come. She said it was boring.

You can't run from him, Kennedy, remember? You made a promise. Then my brain clicked. There might be a chance. My body stiffened as the realization crashed down on me. I had only promised I wouldn't run from *him*. Not Dax, Samantha, or Dominic.

A loophole.

My heart slammed in my chest as Dax walked over to me, desperation clogging my head.

The only way I could get my head to work? Start a list.

A.) Wait till you are untied.

B.) Let them get comfortable. They will never think you are capable of escaping them.

C.) Make sure door is clear.

D.) Perform a spell.

E.) Run.

"D" was where things got a little tricky. What spell could I do? The revealing spell was the only one I felt proficient in doing with the little time I had to getaway. Not exactly the best spell for a breakout. The actual incantation would do nothing to them, but the power in the words might.

I had sent Ember face-first onto the ground dozens of times when I was learning. I only needed to knock them out or daze them for a bit to give me enough time to run.

It was a stupid plan. They were dark dwellers. I was me. But I had to try. I had no idea what Lorcan had planned for me, but it sounded more complex than merely breaking the spell on the entire clan that kept them out of the Otherworld. What if he was still working with Aneira? What if I was a trade? She could either kill me or use my powers against my friends. I couldn't let either happen.

Dax pulled a knife from his belt and sawed at the rope binding my wrists. "We know you can't run." His brown eyes drilled into me as if he could read my thoughts. I gulped, looking away.

My arms dropped away from the pole, the blood rushing back into them with spears of pain. My hands lay limp in my lap. He untied my gag, and my jaw throbbed as I closed it. I rubbed at my limbs and jawline to get feeling back into them.

"Eat," he commanded, nudging the food with his foot. Then he turned to the boxes next to Samantha. Dominic leaned against the doorjamb, blocking a clear path. The three of them chatted, but my focus was internal, my mind trying to roll around my plan, my fingers absently stuffing chunks of food in my mouth. I guzzled down the orange juice. They didn't let me have any utensils. Not surprising.

Are you really doing this? I knew all too well I wasn't brave like Ember, but I needed to channel her. *If you get away, Lorcan might do something to your family in retaliation.* Doubting thoughts coursed through my mind as time ticked uselessly by.

What if Lorcan's plans for you are ten times worse? What if he kills them anyway?

I wasn't spontaneous, and I didn't like the feeling when I needed to be. Why couldn't my seer ability kick in now and let me know what the future held?

To run or not to run?

Dominic moved toward his group of dwellers, all of them in conversation. No one paid attention to the waif of a girl in the corner.

This is a bad idea. You can't outrun them. Disappointment sagged my shoulders, the truth of my capture sinking in.

Then a peal of laughter resounded through the warehouse, ripping through all my logic and mooring straight into my heart. The sound of Samantha's laugh sent me straight back to the night Ian was brutally murdered.

"Please, don't . . ." Ember's cuffed hands were *clasped together as she pled.*

"Sorry, too late." Laughter bubbled from Samantha, who howled up into the trees with her giddiness. Her arm swung in a fluid motion across Ian's throat, the knife flaying him open as blood sprayed out in a fountain. A scream lodged in my throat as I watched fear widen Ian's eyes. Then he clutched at his throat and his body dropped, his life flowing out on the ground.

Ian's dead eyes floated in my mind while Samantha's mirth cackled in my head. That was all the trigger I needed. I no longer cared about logic or risks. I set down the food carton, my lips parted, the force of my words directed at them. I put all my emotion behind each syllable, and the spell flew from my mouth heading for them. Dominic's head rose just as it was slammed back. His body flew into Sam's. Boxes tumbled; one hit Dax and knocked him to the floor.

That was all I saw before I jumped up and ran for the door, my legs stiff from sitting so long.

The moment I hit the doorway, I realized the epic stupidity of this plan. But it was too late. There was nothing to do but go forward.

My legs weren't long and I'd never enjoyed exercise. Growing up, I read indoors while others played outside.

Funny what adrenaline will get you to do.

I sprinted out of the room, sailing down a corridor with multiple hallways dissecting off from it. I had no idea where the exit was, but my body moved like it knew. Maybe it was my seer power, but I turned and twisted down passages like I had my own inner GPS. In the distance I heard yelling, the dark dwellers already in pursuit of their prey.

So, so stupid! What were you thinking? I chastised myself. It was foolish and laughable that I hoped to escape three trained hunters. But my legs didn't stop. Pushing harder, I leaned forward, willing myself to move faster. My heart thumped in my chest, my breath straining against my lungs. *Go! Go! Go!*

I curved around a corner and my gaze landed on a brightly lit exit sign. Hope burst into my veins, and I pumped harder on the cement floor.

My side knocked into the door bar, ramming it open with my hip. I shoved at the heavy exit, slipping outside into a parking lot. Trees surrounded the lot, wrapping thickly around the building. I understood instantly we were not close to the actual town of Vancouver. We really were in the middle of nowhere. The warm late-summer sun draped around my chilled bones, almost mocking me. *Don't stop and don't look back. There has to be a main road somewhere. Flag someone down.*

My heels dug in and I sprinted around the side of the block building toward the front, following the road. It was there in front of me, and I could follow it out, but then my body turned for the forest. It seemed to have a mind of its own.

Bang.

A door slammed open behind me, and a voice yelled my name. Fear pirouetted in my throat as I took off. I reached the forest, the trees taking me in, cocooning me. I weaved through the twisted branches, curving and zigzagging, longing for the forest to protect me from the beasts hunting me.

A snap of a branch resonated behind me, and I cranked my head to look over my shoulder. The area seemed empty of anything threatening. My head started to turn forward when my body slammed into a wall. I bounced back, falling on my ass with a yelp.

Ignoring the sharp pain in my rear, my eyes took in what I collided with. Fear turned into pure terror. *No. No. No.* Here in this giant forest I had to run straight into him? Literally. What were the odds? I sucked in a gulp of oxygen. Like water evaporating under a hot summer sun, hope deflated out of me, re-pumping in with aching sorrow and terror. My chest throbbed with the knowledge I hurt the precise people I wanted to protect.

I was done. And so was my family.

Lorcan stood over me, his hands on his hips, his expression stone.

We stared at each other for a while.

"You guys can go back," Lorcan said. "I can handle it from here." His focus never strayed from me, his voice icy. I glanced over my shoulder and saw Dax, Dom, and Sam standing there. I hadn't heard their silent approach.

I gulped and faced Lorcan again. I never swore. Not for any moral reasons, it simply wasn't allowed in my house growing up. I got used to never doing so, but at this moment only expletives crossed my brain. Dread pooled in my abdomen and curdled.

The three dwellers slipped away as quietly as they arrived, leaving me alone with their alpha.

"Lorcan, I-I…"

"Shut up," he growled.

My mouth clamped together, my teeth clanking.

He didn't move a hair, but I felt his energy explode over me, pinning me to the earth.

"Tell me, li'l Druid. How were you able to break the bond? Have you been hiding your true talents from me? Playing the innocent newbie?" His green eyes sparked with red. His body vibrated with fury.

"I…I didn't break anything," I replied, his words sinking in. "Wait. Can I get around a bond? Am I capable of doing that?"

"If you didn't break it, how were you able to run?" His lids narrowed, taking an intimidating step closer, ignoring my question. Terror pressed on my bladder.

I looked away. If I told him, all my cards would be played.

He reached down, clasping my arms, and hauled me to my feet. The power of his aura swamped me, almost suffocating me.

"Tell. Me. Now. Druid." He gripped firmer on my arms. "I have little patience...and Sam is all too eager to revisit your family."

I swallowed the knot in my throat. "My promise was only to not run from *you*. It didn't mean I couldn't run from the others."

Lorcan's gaze punctured deep into my eyes, his jaw grinding with tension. Then suddenly the side of his mouth lifted, a chuckle escaping him. He shook his head and smiled.

I froze in place, terrified of his change in demeanor, feeling like a fish caught on a line.

"Well, well..." His eyes glinted with mirth, his hold on me softening. "Li'l Druid is not as boring as I thought. You got some spunk under the nerdy glasses. Should have foreseen the brainiac would find a loophole."

"Boring?" I didn't care what Lorcan thought of me, but still, the insult nicked at old wounds.

"Sweet, timid as a mouse, monotonous. A *nice* girl." He spoke the last description like it was an insult. "Exactly the type Jared would like. Dull as hell."

"Excuse me?" My back went rigid, irritation gluing

my vertebras together like mortar. "How dare you!" I sputtered. "You don't know me, and you clearly don't know Jared very well."

"Oh, I know my nephew better than you might think." That annoying smug grin tipped up his mouth. "Why are you getting so upset?"

"Because you called me boring...and *nice*."

"You don't want to be called nice?"

"No...yes."

"Which is it?"

"No. Not the way you mean it," I floundered.

Lorcan's smile widened, and embarrassment heated my cheeks.

"I know an insult even if it's dressed up in a polite declaration." I glared up at him. "I went to high school. You don't know cruel until you've attended one of those," I shot at him. I didn't get angry a lot, but when I did, watch out. Lately I had been experiencing a lot of new emotions. Awareness of my Druid powers brought fire into my belly. A fire I liked and was terrified of at the same time. "Believe me, those girls could teach you a thing or two about torture." My rant sprayed from my lips, falling on the forest floor, billowing up into silence as it hit.

Lorcan glowered at me, his gaze darting between my eyes, a smirk still playing on his lips. The longer his stare hung on me, the more I twisted with unease. His eyes penetrated you, eroded through to your soul. I did not like his closeness or the intimacy his regard brought. I turned my neck to the side, breaking away from him.

"If you are going to punish me, then do it. But please, if you have any soul left inside, please leave my family out of it."

"But hurting your family is the only way you will learn." His statement yanked my head back to him.

My eyes widened. "No. Please," I begged.

He dropped his arms away from me. "You won't run again?"

"No." I shook my head. "I swear."

"You already did that. Look how well it stuck." He lifted an eyebrow. "At least I will cover all my bases now. Tricky witch."

"I am *not* a witch." I huffed through my nose. I had knowingly been a Druid for only a few months, but there were things that felt embedded in my bones. Being called a witch was one of them. Witches were human with no actual magic. They recited spells and created potions but only used the power of the mind, not actual magic.

What I read in the books Cole gave me long ago was that Druids were once witches. The gods grew fond of a group of them and gave them true magic, extending their lives and influence in the fae world. That was when the fae started to fear their power and turned against them, mostly because of the Seelie Queen. It literally became a "witch" hunt to find and kill all Druids.

"Sensitive, aren't we?" He folded his arms. I really wanted to rub that smile off his mouth.

"How about I call you an overgrown kitty with an attitude problem?"

Lorcan snorted, his head falling back, a deep laugh detonating up to the branches above. His honest amusement unsettled me. A lot. He was not supposed to be a normal person. He was the bad guy, and I wanted to keep him in that box.

"*Touché*, li'l Druid," he said through a few fluttering chuckles. "I will let this little jail escape go, but you will never do it again." He leaned closer to my face. "Right?"

"Right." I nodded furiously.

"You want to know about another loophole—on my side?" he whispered, conspiratorial, his mouth only an inch from mine. "You can't run from me, remember? So, anytime you try..." He tilted his head. "You run directly to *me*."

I sucked air through my nose, leaning back with the weight of the truth. Of course, this was the reason I smacked straight into him in this vast forest. Why my body acted like it knew where it was going. It wasn't my seer ability helping me. It was the bond. No matter what, I could never escape. It would betray me and bring me right to him.

I felt tears of hate and anger stab at the back of my eyes, but I gritted my teeth to keep them back. He would not see me cry. But if powerful Druids could break fae promises, then I was going to find out how.

Whatever it took. I would not be bound to Lorcan forever.

THREE

Lorcan walked behind me the entire way back, shadowing me, producing an itchy restless feeling along the back of my body. My thoughts kept circling back to Ian. This man was the reason Ian was dead, why his family would never know what had happened to him. To any of us.

From the day Lorcan kidnapped me the first time, I had never been able to return home to my family. That was now more than four years for them. I couldn't imagine the worry, fear, and heartache they felt each day I didn't come back. Ryan's family had double the despair between him and Ian. And Ian would never return home.

My future had always led me away from my family as my Druid abilities slowly leaked out. But not without a goodbye, and not completely. Their grief and my sorrow were Lorcan's fault. Blaming him, hating him for it, gave my despair a target.

Samantha made my soul blacken with abhorrence. The moment Lorcan and I entered the building, she greeted us, her eyes bright and her feet bouncing.

"Who gets punished first? Daddy or little sister?" Samantha licked her bottom lip, and her gaze landed on me with evil glee. "Sister would be easy, but Daddy would be more fun."

Acid burned up my esophagus, clumping at the back of my throat.

"No one." Lorcan's hand pressed into my lower back, pushing me forward. I jerked away from his touch. He dropped his hand and motioned with his head for me to continue walking.

"What?" the redhead exclaimed, her eyes widening as we walked past her. "She tried to escape. She needs to be taught a lesson."

With speed my eyes couldn't discern, Lorcan swiveled, grabbing Samantha by the throat and shoving her against the wall.

"Are you questioning me?" Lorcan's voice was even, almost soft, but the underlying threat beneath each syllable vibrated under my feet.

Samantha's nose flared, her eyes flickering red. Every second that passed, Lorcan's energy radiated heavily in the room. She lowered her eyes and then her head.

"No, Alpha," she managed through gritted teeth.

"Do not step out of place. You are the lowest ranked here. You obey. Never question my decisions. You got that?"

"Yes." She kept her eyes on the floor, but the single word sounded as if it were being torn from her throat.

I had seen Cole and Eli both go into alpha mode. It was scary, but Lorcan truly terrified me. Maybe because deep down I knew neither Cole nor Eli would hurt me. It might be stupid to think you could ever completely trust wild animals, but I did them.

I did not trust Lorcan. Neither the man nor the beast.

Lorcan dropped his hand and backed away. "I want you to go scout for our next location. We need to keep moving. We leave here before dawn," he ordered. "Go."

Samantha lifted her head, pushing off the wall with a nod. She turned to leave and her gaze caught mine. Menacing hate flickered across her face, sending waves of fear through me before she looked away and stalked out of the building. My knees locked in place, her animosity stilling me.

I knew she detested Ember and would kill her given the chance, mostly because Samantha had wanted Eli. Had thought he was hers. Yet Eli clearly chose Ember. You couldn't be within a thousand yards of those two and not know they were meant for each other. Samantha did not see it that way.

Now it looked like I might be next in line on her list. I realized what she was capable of. I needed to watch my back.

Lorcan grabbed my arm and tugged me back to the room where he had tied me up. Dax stood at attention next to a duffle bag set on one of the large box containers.

"Dax, go join Dom. We can't let our guard down for a second. Cole and Lars will be coming for her the moment they regroup," Lorcan commanded his second. Dax gave a nod and walked out. A long broad sword lay strapped to his back, and a gun was sheathed on his hip.

"They're really all okay?" I rubbed my arms, the chill in the large room dimpling my flesh. I was still dressed in the green cargo pants and black tank top I'd worn in Greece. I was dirty, bloody, and my head still throbbed from where Dax knocked me out.

"You mean is Jared all right?" He unzipped the duffle bag pulling out a book so thick and big it could have crushed a small child. The magic pouring from the pages trickled over to me. I could feel its power calling to me, bringing me to it.

"Of course I'm worried about Jared," I said absently, my attention on the book. My legs moved to it without a thought. "He's my boyfriend." My boots hit the box and I stopped, reaching out to touch the old leather-bound cover.

"Wait." Lorcan grabbed my hand before my fingers brushed the book. The title was worn off the cover. "You can't simply grab a fae book. You need to understand it first. How it will react to you specifically."

I hated to admit he was right. Fae books were alive. The words inside boiled with magic. They all had different levels of energy. This one buzzed my body with life, beckoning me to dive between its pages.

"Why me especially?"

Lorcan glanced over at me, still clasping my hand.

"Because this book holds every Druid magic spell known. Your family created a lot of them."

"My...my family? Do you know who they are?"

Lorcan let go of my fingers. "What do you know?"

My lips pinched together, not liking the way he turned it back on me. Trusting Lorcan was like believing two parallel lines would intersect. Was never gonna happen. And I felt every word I said he would somehow use against me, against my loved ones.

"What?" Lorcan snorted. "You think telling me is giving me a leg up somehow?" He inclined toward me, his signature smug smile ghosting his mouth. "I don't want to waste time, like we are doing now."

Tugging at the ends of my hair, I exhaled and decided informing him of what I knew couldn't hurt me. I hoped.

"I only know what Owen told me. He thought my heritage stemmed from Cathbad's line. They were the mediators between the mortal world and the gods, straddling both planes. Aneira feared them the most and had them all murdered." I rubbed my palms against my pants. "When I researched the name, not much came up. Simply that his line became influential leaders, scholars, seers, and healers. Extremely clever in the ways of war. They were called on by the gods and became the favorites and they were given true magic and extended lives."

"You sounded like you just regurgitated a textbook." Lorcan rolled his eyes.

"Sorry if I like facts and knowledge." I put my hands on my hips. "I know how it might make someone like you uncomfortable."

"I think li'l Druid is getting a bit lippy for her own good." Lorcan's eyebrow tipped in warning. I didn't bow to his expression. "If Owen is right, which he usually is, and looking at the time frame of when you came to Earth and when the Druids were killed, I'd say you're the prodigy of Keela and Reghan."

My mouth parted, warmth trotting around my heart. The moment he said the names I felt a sense of familiarity, like their very names were sketched on my bones.

"My parents…" I whispered. "What do you know about them?"

"Not much. They were of the highest Druid clan. Extremely gifted in healing and seer abilities. I think they had two children, but both were said to be killed along with them."

"I had a sibling?"

"I don't even know if they were your parents." Annoyance flicked at the corners of his mouth. But I did. It was instinctual, like breathing. My heart recognized their names, bringing them in with an embrace. "Look, I didn't pay much attention to Druids…nor did I care what sex their offspring were…and I give even less of a fuck now. We need to get to work." He twisted to the book, pointing down on it.

"You don't know anything else about them?"

"Yeah." He growled over his shoulder. "They're dead."

I sighed knowing I would get nothing else out of Lorcan. As hungry as I was for any detail about my blood family, I was grateful for this information. It was more than Owen and Cole told me. And I had little doubt they could have easily concluded the same thing about my parentage. Why had they not told me? Why keep it from me?

I stepped next to Lorcan. The energy pumping off the book made my hands itch with anticipation. "How did you get something like this?" I sucked in a breath, staring at it. I could feel its excitement, wanting me to touch it. "Owen told me it was lost."

"Believe me, it was not easy." Lorcan's lip hitched up on one side. "Let's say it had been lost in a man's private collection for centuries. Now it's been *found* once again."

"You mean you stole it." I met Lorcan's gaze.

He shrugged. "Doesn't matter how I came about it. It was meant to be possessed by a Druid, not that weasel of a fae. Seriously, the man was a weasel. A shape-shifter."

I snorted, a gurgle of laughter escaping before my hand went to my mouth. Guilt and disgust at myself flickered in my belly, and I shot my gaze back down at the book. How could I laugh? I was a hostage, not enjoying a relaxing day with my friends. And I missed my friends so much. Ryan. Ember. Jared. Even Josh and the rest of the dark dwellers had grown to be considered friends. I still wasn't sure about Gabby, but I didn't think she knew what it was to have girlfriends.

They were all somewhere out there. Hopefully safe.

My mind went to Jared, the last night in Greece together in the tent before everything went to hell. How we argued. I wanted to do over so many things about that night. My heart ached I missed him so much.

Lorcan had taken me away from him. Away from all of them. My jaw locked down, my back stiffening with a new wave of resentment.

"You want my magic and need me to do spells," I said stiffly. "Let's get started."

He watched me for a bit, as though noting my change in demeanor and trying to determine what it meant, then nodded.

"Okay, but you need to go slow. I have no idea how it will react when you touch it. It's been locked up a long time, so it's more eager than you to be felt up again."

I rolled my lips together, ignoring his insinuating pun. "Fine." Slowly I reached for the book, my fingers shaking with anticipation. The book vibrated on the wood, moving toward me. It was like the moment before you hug someone you hadn't seen in a long, long time, but they were so familiar to you it was like you had never parted.

My fingertips brushed the surface. Energy soared up my arm in piercing abundance, as though I'd touched an electrical fence. White light flashed behind my eyes, ripping my sight from me. I no longer felt my body or recognized time and space. I existed but was no longer present.

Flash.

I stood out on a bluff overlooking a scarlet field. Blood rained down from the sky, streaking my face in red gruesome tracks.

"You can save them," a woman's voice sounded behind me. I whirled to see a tall, stunning creature with long red hair and violet eyes. She was so breathtaking it was hard to behold her. She was also familiar, but I knew I'd never seen her. "It's you, Kennedy."

"What do you mean?" It didn't seem to faze me that she knew my name.

"The end is coming. Blood will paint the ground. It's you who will stop it."

Flash.

Skyscrapers of rock rose around me, monasteries bloomed from the tops like mushrooms. White clouds billowed; the earth went dry and crusted from the intense heat that beat down on the ground. But I couldn't feel it or smell the distinct rich soil in that part of Greece, in Meteora.

"Nooooooo!" A guttural scream rattled through me. Ember stood there. Eli was crumpled on the ground. Next to Ember stood Aneira, the Seelie Queen. "Eli!" Agony twisted Ember's features, her body was bent over, her arms cuffed.

That's when I saw him gasping for air, blood seeped from his throat, watering the dry dirt. He was dying. *Oh god, Eli!* I tried to move to him, but my body wouldn't let me. I let out a frustrated cry, desperate to help, to protect and heal my friends.

Ember continued to howl; tears ran down her cheeks. My heart felt like it was being ripped in half as I watched her, unable to do anything. A gurgling noise behind me drew my attention. I glanced over my shoulder. My chest clenched, squeezing out the air in my lungs.

"Cole?" Owen hovered over his brother. The leader of the clan was crumpled on his knees, his hand wrapped around his throat. There was no blood, but Cole gripped his throat as if it had been cut.

A sensation tugged my attention away from them.

Lorcan lay on a patch of green grass surrounded by trees. The area reminded me of the Pacific Northwest in the States instead of Greece. He also clutched his throat, gurgling with pain.

The brothers are marked for death. The thought curled around me.

Somewhere in my brain I understood I hated him, but my vocals screamed his name. An anguish I couldn't decipher tore at my heart. "Lorcan!"

His head turned to me like he heard me, his eyes meeting mine. A smile hinted on his mouth, then his body went limp. Life seeped out of his body, leaving his eyes cold and dead.

"No!" I shouted. A grief so deep dropped me to the ground, everything bursting white.

Flash.

My eyes bolted open, and I gasped for air. I lay on my back, a figure leaning over me. My brain jumbled and hazy, still reeling from what it had seen. I felt panicky and couldn't understand the objects around me. Nothing made sense. Instinct sent fear pumping through my body. I sat up, my gaze moving around frantically.

"Kennedy, calm down. Breathe. You're okay." The man next to me stroked my arm, then my back. My eyes darted to him. I was scared but also strangely comforted by him. I blinked a few more times. He was familiar to me, but I couldn't recall his name. Nothing felt real, as if I were not tethered to the earth.

"Is this real?" My voice quivered, reality still bopping away from my grasp.

"This is real, li'l Druid. Take a deep breath." His rumbling voice was soothing. He rubbed the spot between my shoulder blades. "Feel my touch. Concentrate on that."

All my attention went into those two things: my breath and his strokes on my back, which felt so good. Slowly I settled back in my body with every breath. With every inhale, the dream vanished from memory, slipping through my fingers like water, but reality filled its place.

Warehouse.

Lorcan.

Kidnapped.

Book.

With a swoop everything came back to me. Lorcan's touch became vexing. I moved away but turned to face him.

"You okay?" He stayed on his knees, his expression guarded.

"What happened?" I glanced up at the book. It sat on top of the box, appearing innocent and harmless. It didn't want to hurt me. It was simply too much magic flooding my system at once.

"Well, you went stiff, your eyes rolled back in your head, then your head started spinning, pea soup sprouted from your mouth, and you talked of the devil

45

before you started crawling the walls like a crab." Lorcan rose to his feet.

"*The Exorcist*? Really?" I narrowed my eyes and glowered at him.

"Too soon?" He reached out his hand to help me up. I took it but let go the moment I was on my feet.

"Lorcan..." I sighed.

"Not really far off from what I said. Minus the puke and crawling the walls."

"And the devil talk?"

"Well, you did scream my name." The side of his mouth hitched up. "Same difference, right?"

I couldn't fight the smile wanting to break free. It once again only riled my anger, and I folded my arms. "Anything else?"

"Yeah, you said some really freaky shit about the end coming. That blood would paint the ground and..." He rubbed his stubble.

"What?"

He lifted his head, his tone unemotional. "That the brothers were marked for death."

"Brothers..." My mouth fell open, slivers of my dream brushing the edges. "You and Eli..." I vaguely remembered seeing both of them. And Cole...but I was no longer sure if I actually had. I only recalled blood everywhere. And dead, empty eyes.

"I am not touching that thing again." I shook my head. "Worst nightmares ever."

"It wasn't a dream." Lorcan's head slanted to the side, his hands going into his pockets. "It was a vision.

I've been around long enough to see a Druid go into one. You've never had one before?"

"Not like that." I stared at the innocent-looking book again. "I have 'episodes' where I say things I can't control. Sometimes I don't remember...but this...no, I've never experienced anything like it." I shivered as a chill ran down my limbs. "Was what I saw real?"

"I don't know. What did you see?"

I bit down on my lip, rolling back through the ambiguous glimpses. The more I tried to grab for them, the more distant they became. "I'm not sure. Eli was dying, so were you...I think. And I may have seen Cole also."

He lowered his head and stared to the side.

"It's more a feeling. Loss, agony, devastation..." I shook my head.

"Your abilities are growing." He pulled his hands free, letting them drop to his side.

"I don't want to go through it again."

"Tough," he replied. "You're a seer, a Druid. It's part of your powers. And I need you."

"Why?" I rubbed my arms with agitation. "What is so bad about being on Earth? Is it really so horrible you'd murder my friend, kidnap me, and betray your family to leave it?"

He clamped his mouth hard. "You have no idea what you are talking about."

"What part did I get wrong?"

"This has nothing to do with being on Earth," he growled.

"Then what?"

"Not your concern right now." He spun back to the book. "You're going to work with this book until you come to an understanding. We need the spells that are inside so you can practice. And I don't want you passing out every time you turn to page one."

A wave of rage crashed against my ribs. *Stay calm, Ken. Keep centered.*

My emotions were heightened from whatever Druid puberty I was going through, but Lorcan could invoke a storm in me. With one look or word, I wanted to hit him.

I'd never hit a person in my life. Lorcan might be my first.

<center>~~~~~~</center>

"Again!" Lorcan rubbed the dirt off his pants, getting back to this feet, the strain of the day wearing on his features. How many times had he been tossed into the brush, cut by rocks, tree limbs, and prickly plants? I wasn't surprised.

I was a mess: sweaty, pounding head, starving, and so exhausted it was hard to stay on my feet. He had me working on one spell for five hours and had become my guinea pig for the last two. The first half hour I could not deny the thrill of slamming Lorcan to the ground over and over, only a minor retribution for all the horrible things he had done. But in honesty, it had lost its appeal some time ago.

I did not seek vengeance. Anger only created more anger. And I couldn't live full of hate, except when he rolled back to his feet and demanded another go.

"Lorcan, I need to stop." I bent over my knees sucking in a breath, strands of my tangled hair sticking to my face. After a week in Greece without a proper shower, all I dreamed about was the sensation of water trickling over my skin, washing away all the grime.

He had moved us deep into the woods next to the warehouse, Dax and Dom patrolling around us. Samantha had yet to return from her mission, but with the sun inching closer and closer to the horizon, I knew she would soon.

"One more time." He rolled his shoulders back, sucking in through his nose. "You don't have it yet."

I shoved my glasses back up my nose and stood tall. My voice was raw from belting out a defense spell over and over. It surprised me this was the first one Lorcan wanted me to learn. I would have thought he'd have me go straight into training on a spell-breaking curse. The moment the book and I came to an understanding, it let me unseal it but blasted through my nervous system, which it did apologize for. It was overeager to be opened again, especially by a true Druid. Lorcan flipped past all the fortune, love, and healing spells and turned right to a basic defense spell. It basically flung anyone within a twenty-foot radius away from me, flattening them on the ground and stunning the assailant for a good thirty seconds. Enough to get away.

The words had to be clear and precise, half the time they fluttered to him and barely pushed him back. A handful of times I had gotten him good. The more exhausted I grew, the less those times happened.

"You have to be able to do this, no matter how tired you are. It needs to be second nature."

"Not on the first day."

"You don't have the convenience of taking your time." He put his hands on his hips. "The war is coming."

"I thought you wanted the war," I accused. "Isn't it why you kidnapped my best friend to trade to the Queen? To start the war?"

Lorcan folded his arms, his chest puffing up. "I never wanted the war. That was what the Queen wanted her for. To me, Ember was a means to an end. Collateral."

"You truly are awful," I whispered.

"I'm not going to say sorry for what I did." He widened his stance. "Ember was nothing to me, my family was everything. I did not know what she was to Eli at that time. He had yet to claim her, or I would never have touched her."

"Very nice of you."

"I'm not nice." His deep voice rumbled between us. "And I won't apologize for kidnapping you for my own gain. The first time you were only a faceless human I knew I could use to control Ember."

I locked my jaw, sorrow burning in my throat. "That's all we were to you. Objects." My voice wavered, fatigue letting down my barriers. "But you killed a friend. *My family.* Someone who was everything to me." The dam broke, the hurt and grief seeking release.

Lorcan glanced away.

"And I don't believe family is everything to you. I think *you* are everything to *you.*"

Lorcan's head jerked back toward me.

"You say what you do is for your family...but then you hurt and betray them at every turn." I kept my gaze locked on him. "Do you know how much Jared idolized you? Loved you? You broke his heart!" Mentioning his name brought a flood of emotion to the surface, tears breaching my lids, thinking of Jared's goofy smile, his warm hazel eyes.

Lorcan moved quicker than I could track. His fingers clasped around my arms and shoved me back into a tree, knocking the wind out of me. Fury built behind his eyes, vibrating his body. He loomed over me, his eyes red and vertical like a cat's. Fear gripped my throat like fingers, and I went still.

"You don't know me. You have no idea what I think or feel. What I've been through." He snarled, pressing me back until the bark dug into my scalp.

A tear slid down my face, and I turned to look at him. "Then tell me."

His lids tapered. "I don't have to tell you anything. I don't give a damn what you think about me."

I stared into his eyes, staying silent.

"I don't," he grumbled, pushing away from me. "You are just some little girl I need something from. That's it."

My reaction did not change.

"Shit!" He ran his hand over his head, turning away from me. "Don't stare at me like that. It's fuckin' freaky."

My mouth opened without my order, the words flowing off my tongue without a conscious thought, my mind drifting. *"You hide behind masks. Different. False. Soon you will not be able to find yourself beneath the facades."* I jerked, my mind snapping back into place, and I slammed my jaw together with an audible click. I couldn't control when stuff happened like that.

Lorcan gaped at me, his shoulders rising with every intake of breath, eclipsing the forest with his presence. His rage stirred the atoms in the air, and energy affronted me from every angle. He lurched forward, toward me. My lips parted to articulate the defense spell, but it stopped in my throat, a warning telling me to stand my ground instead.

His boots came flush with mine, his red eyes meeting mine. I held my chin up, not letting myself flinch at his nearness. Tension boiled in the tiny space between us. His chest surged against mine as he breathed in. I didn't move, didn't break away from the hostility in his eyes. Our gazes locked in a match.

He exhaled with a snort, like a wild animal. Green flashed in his irises and his eyes broke away from mine with a grunt. He stretched up an arm, curled his hand into a fist, and punched the tree above my head, raining bark on my head. Then he turned, with shoulders curled forward, swept up the book, and strode out of the forest back toward the warehouse.

Once he slipped out of sight, my body slumped back against the tree, my lids shutting with a mix of relief and fatigue that ran deeper than my body.

The sun dropped below the tree line and left a slight chill creeping into late summer. I tried to push off the overwhelming loneliness I suddenly felt. I wanted to go home, crawl in my bed, and hear my dad cooking dinner while my mom talked to him about her day. I wanted to hear my sister blasting her annoying pop music from the room next door. Ryan opening the front door, like it was his house, greeting my parents, and running up the stairs to my room. I missed the smells, the comfort of being loved and safe.

I understood I would never have it again. Not that scenario. At "Camp Dweller," as Ember called it, I had a family: Jared, Ember, Lily, even the dark dwellers. But I missed Ryan. He was my home. The person who knew me inside and out. We'd been friends for so long I didn't remember a time without him.

And I had to leave him in the Otherworld, as Aneira's prisoner. I understood why. He was sick, really sick. He hadn't been conscious for days. There was no way we could have gotten him out. Neither could we secure Ember's stepdad, Mark, who was locked away in another part of the castle, or West, a dark dweller, who was chained down in Aneira's dungeon.

No matter the reasoning, it didn't take away the guilt and the horrendous shame your soul held knowing you left your best friend behind to protect yourself. I knew he would have wanted us to go, to get away when we could, but it didn't matter; I hated myself. And every day I worked on my magic, I thought of Ryan. I needed to become strong enough in my abilities to help get him out of there. I would not be at peace until I did so.

I wiped at the last of my tears and straightened up. "This is no different, Ken," I said to myself. "Lorcan's using you, so use him right back. Learn everything you can. Let him train you to be the fiercest Druid you can. Then kick all their butts." I smiled, letting my pep talk seep in, already feeling the strength of my words. "Do it for yourself. But most of all, do it for Ryan." I looked down at my boots. "I love you, Ry. And I am coming for you."

The declaration gave me something to hold on to. A reason all this was happening. I would no longer shed a tear or back away from doing a spell one more time. Ryan had always given me strength, and even now he could.

I pushed off the tree, tilted my head up, and marched to the warehouse, ready for whatever was ahead.

"Damn, the little annoying witch came back." Samantha sighed, falling back against the wall, her scowl grazing me. "I was hoping she got eaten by a rabid squirrel or something."

"Sam," Lorcan warned as he pulled containers from a backpack onto the top one of the crates. The aroma of food reached my nose and fell heavy into my empty stomach, making it shriek.

"What?" Sam batted her lashes at Lorcan, shoving off the wall and walking over to him, grabbing one of the takeout boxes. "She's the size of an acorn. Wouldn't be hard for one to take her down."

"What did you find?" Lorcan ignored her and opened one of the cartons. My stomach growled at the sight of six tacos lined up inside. Mexican food was my favorite. I wasn't sure if he happened to know it because of his previous stalking sessions or it was coincidental. I didn't care.

"This place will be buzzing with employees tomorrow, and we need to be long gone." He held out the dish and a bottled water for me. I didn't hesitate to snatch them from his fingers. Then I retreated to the corner of the room and sat down where I could watch them but keep my back guarded while I ate.

Samantha sat opposite me. "There's a place along the coast near Siuslaw National Forest. An abandoned house. Way off the track of humans."

"Good." Lorcan nodded. "We'll head there right after we eat."

Only half listening, I stuffed in another taco. I was never much of an eater, but since "the change" when I acknowledged my Druid powers and started using them, I couldn't eat enough. Magic burned a tremendous amount of energy, and I had started doubling my food intake back at Camp Dweller. Now I felt like I could triple it. I hoped no one else wanted a taco.

Footsteps resounded over the concrete. Dax and Dom returned from their posts. "We need to leave. We heard a car a mile down. I think it's heading here," Dax stated.

"Shit," Lorcan grumbled. "Someone might have reported us. Coming to check it out." He rubbed his shaved head, a tic he did often when he was frustrated.

"Probably heard you two in the forest." Dominic smirked, tossed a food box to Dax, then took the next one. "I swear Dax and I kept checking in to be sure you two weren't actually having sex instead of training."

A taco dropped from my hand as I made a mangled noise in my throat. Heat instantly overtook me, pinching every nerve in my body with overwhelming sensitivity. Nausea gripped my stomach; my gaze went to Lorcan, who stood stiffly, scowling at Dom.

Dom popped his head up. "What? Dude, I've heard you having sex. You're loud. It sounded like whatever you two were doing. Animals rutting or dying."

"Not funny." Lorcan moved to the bag, shoving in the last container. His eyes darted to me then back to the bag as he shook his head. "And thanks for ruining my appetite, fucker."

Chagrin sizzled my cheeks. The thought of having sex with me made him lose his appetite. Not that it hadn't destroyed mine as well, but it still stabbed my ego. *Are you serious, Ken? Lorcan finding you repulsive is a good thing.* The feeling was mutual.

"Let's go." Lorcan lifted the bag onto his shoulder. The other three snatched up their packs, stuffing their food away, and headed for the door. Lorcan curved back to me, but his eyes wouldn't meet mine. "Move."

I snapped the food box closed but rose so slowly a sloth would have beaten me.

"Kennedy, I'm not kidding," he growled, taking a step to me. "I will throw you over my shoulder."

"Or knock me out again with your gun." I was healing, but the back of my head was still sore and crusted with dried blood from where I'd been pistol-whipped.

"Dax hit you; I didn't." He curled his fingers, beckoning me forward. The sound of gravel crunching under tires broadcast the approach of a vehicle.

"Same difference." I brought the box to my chest, holding it like a security blanket. "He doesn't do anything unless it's on your order."

"Actually, he did it all on his own," Lorcan snarled, his boots moving toward me. "Now get your ass moving, or I *will* order him to knock you totally out this time. Hell, I'll do it myself."

"It's only a human coming—I thought you murdered those for breakfast." My words opposed my calm, soft tone.

"Dammit, Kennedy!" He reached for my arm, yanking me into him. He snatched the food box from my grip and tossed it to the ground.

Reflections of headlights flickered from the small window. I was playing with fire. I couldn't run from Lorcan, but what if I was found and taken away from him? Was that another technical loophole? There was a good chance I would then be putting human lives in danger. They'd kill the humans before they let me go.

A car door slammed.

This time I willingly went when Lorcan tugged me. He hunkered us down behind a wall as the click of a key turning over in the lock sounded down the hallway. "This way," Lorcan whispered, pulling us the opposite way.

The door creaked open, light blazed down the corridor. "Hello?" a man's voice called out. "If anyone is here, you better get out now or I'm calling the cops."

Lorcan snorted at the man's declaration. We continued to slink down another hallway, his footsteps silent, while mine pattered against the concrete floor.

"You're trespassing and I've got a gun and I'm not afraid to use it," the man bellowed, his voice sounding closer than I thought it would.

Lorcan curved around a bend leading us to an exit on the far wall. His hand tightened around my arm as he started to jog to the door. Halfway there shots rang out and zipped past my head in a whoosh before pinging off the walls. I let out a yelp.

"Stop!" the man yelled. I looked over to see a bearded, heavyset man pointing a gun at us. "I will shoot you."

Lorcan growled, pulling me into his body, his arms covering my head.

"I said stop!"

Bullets rang out in an explosion, rushing at us and embedding into objects around us. Lorcan hauled me toward the door, huffing. His elbow slammed into the release bar, wrenching me through the door to the outside. The late evening had obscured anything past the tree line. Darkness called us to veil ourselves in its cover.

The man's voice was a blur of noise behind us as we ran straight into the forest. Lorcan did not stop and pushed us past the entry of the woods, snaking us around trees and brush and taking us deep into the woodland.

I tried to keep up, using my adrenaline to continue moving.

Finally Lorcan slowed down, grabbing a tree. It was then I saw the dark stain soaking his shirt.

"Oh my god." I went to him, my hand hovering over the hole in his side. "You've been shot!"

"Yeah, no shit." He blew out a heavy breath and turned to look at the wound. "Damn, I have to get the bullet out before I start to heal." He dropped his bag, ripped open the zipper, and dug inside.

"What are you...?" I stopped when I saw him produce a small medical kit. I wouldn't have been surprised if each of his people had one in their bags. Being a dark dweller was a hard business, especially on the body.

"I need you to get it." He opened the lid, digging out a knife and what looked like long tweezers.

"I'm sorry, you want me to what?" I gaped.

"Get the bullet out." He sighed with annoyance. "Don't tell me you're squeamish of a little blood."

"No." I frowned. "I've never dug into someone to retrieve a bullet. Sorry...not in my repertoire."

"Well, guess what, Girl Scout? Tonight is your lucky night."

"You know being good isn't an insult, right?" I folded my arms, still feeling like it was.

Lorcan nipped at his bottom lip, making him look like the bad boy full of naughty plans. The type most other girls would trip over their tongues to get closer to.

Thank goodness I was not that girl. I liked the geeky boys, the ones with bigger brains than muscles. Jared was the exception because he also was such a nerd for computers and comics. Not that I didn't enjoy his six-pack.

"If you live inside the lines, you won't know the true pleasure of life."

"I think I'm doing just fine." I held out my hand.

He chuckled and placed the tweezers in my hand. "Try those first."

I nodded.

He grunted as he took off his shirt. My eyes drifted away from the sight of his sculpted torso. I wasn't dead. I saw the magnificence of his physique. The man had a twelve-pack. A deep V-line and indents peeked out from his low-riding jeans. His appearance was equal parts of a masquerade: he was fae—alluring, but he was also a killer.

He dug back in his bag and retrieved a flashlight, clicked it on and held it on himself to show the bleeding wound.

"Where are Dax and the others? Can't they do this?" I gripped the tweezers.

"I sent them on." He jutted his chin to his side. Since I never heard him say the command, he must have ordered them through their link. "It's only you and me. I'll walk you through it."

"Done this before?"

"Many times." He ripped a disinfectant towel out of the package with his teeth and handed it to me. "Now hurry, I can feel it closing up."

I wiped around the wound and took a deep breath.

"Just do it."

I braced my hand on his stomach, feeling him flex under my touch, then I leaned over, getting in line with the gash. I used one hand to pull away the skin, opening the healing wound; the other went in with the tweezers.

"Don't be tentative; dig in there."

Biting my lip, I pushed the tool in with a sickening squelch, following the bullet trail.

Lorcan grunted, his grip on the flashlight quivering.

"Keep it straight," I ordered, digging in deeper. The shadowy light was already making it difficult to see.

"Yes, ma'am." His voice was strained, but I could hear humor behind his words.

I hoped the bullet would be close to the surface. Of course it wasn't. My glasses slid down my nose, and I nudged them back up with my shoulder, losing my grip on his slippery skin, jerking the long tweezers inside him.

Lorcan growled with pain.

"Sorry."

"I'll get them next time for you. Don't do it again. Please."

I resumed my digging, beads of sweat tickling my hairline as I worked.

"Extremely surprised this hasn't made you vomit or pass out yet." He readjusted the flashlight, angling the light better for me.

"That's because you have a preconceived notion of me as some squeamish, fragile little girl," I replied, my glasses slipping again. "Glasses."

He pushed them gently back up my nose. "So do you."

I lifted my lashes to look at him, his finger still touching my frames. Our eyes connected, and a jolt kinked my lungs, squeezing my airways. A buzzing sensation speared my chest, and I snapped my gaze back down, concentrating on what I was doing. Disgust climbed up my throat, dragging along anger until they reached my cheeks, branding them with heat.

He dropped his hand and stayed quiet for a while. I spotted something silver deep in the wound when he spoke again.

"I didn't mean for him to die," he said low and rough, pulling my attention.

"What?" I peered at him.

"Ian. Your friend." He cleared his throat. "Whatever you think of me, I don't kill for fun."

I froze, the tweezers grasping the bullet.

"He was supposed to be used as a threat. You all were. I never planned on hurting him. Or actually turning any of you over to the Queen. Things got out of hand." He stared past me, keeping emotion empty in his face. "I knew Ember would volunteer to take your places."

I couldn't find my voice to speak. Or move.

"Samantha has always been unpredictable. Especially when it comes to Ember. I should have seen it coming. But in honesty, even if I knew, I'm not sure I could have stopped her." He shrugged. "But I wanted you to know. He wasn't supposed to die."

The information yanked my emotions around like a kite in the wind. I didn't know if his declaration made me feel better or worse. That Ian could still be here, living his life, only mashed my heart more.

My lids fluttered and I choked back the grief clawing

up my throat. I turned my head back down to the wound. It had stopped bleeding, the skin trying to mend around the surgical tool. My fingers squeezed down, the grippers locked around the bullet, and I yanked my arm back in a smooth pull.

"Fuck!" Lorcan bellowed, sucking in a harsh breath.

I held up the tweezers. "Got it."

He made a grunt-snort, his eyes darting to me. "Think you enjoyed it a little too much."

"Maybe," I said softly, dropping the bullet into the dirt. What was it about him that invoked such a strong reaction in me? In the moment I had enjoyed causing him pain. To generate even a sliver of hurt I felt losing one of my best friends. But it didn't come close to bringing Ian back. Or changing anything that had happened.

I cupped my hand over the reopened hole, gushing with fresh blood, and started to chant. It was automatic for me to want to heal the hurt. Energy filled up from my feet, the earth giving me power, and I pushed it out through my hands with my words. The flesh knitted itself together, covering the tissue, veins, and muscle. The skin was bright pink, but his own healing powers would ease it in moments.

"There." I stepped back.

Lorcan stared down, then back at me. "Thank you." He wiped the crusted blood over the scar with his T-shirt then tossed it in the bushes. Fae never had to worry about cops finding and doing DNA tests on their blood. Fae blood always came up inconclusive.

"Time to get going." He grabbed his bag, pulling it onto his good side. Catching my eyes on his naked torso, he glanced down then back at me. "Don't want to dirty a new shirt. Only have one left." He herded me forward.

"Speaking of clothes, I need new ones." I gestured at my bloody, sweaty, filthy top. "And a shower."

"We'll find a shower at the next place. And I'll have Samantha get you some clothes."

"No." I shook my head. The thought of her picking out clothes for me, touching anything, only revived a fresh image of Ian's blood gushing over her hands.

"Fine. I will," he grumbled, whacking a tree branch out of the way. "There should be a door right up here."

I had gone through fae doors when entering and exiting the Otherworld previously. The sensation was odd, like walking through film or gelatin. Humans normally couldn't see them, except if you were a seer or "sensitive," so I wasn't surprised to see a wavering of energy ahead of us. The air glimmered and rolled, the negative and positive particles rubbing against each other.

"Don't want to lose you in there." Lorcan grabbed my wrist. "Or for you to get any ideas."

"I couldn't run anyway, remember?"

He shot me a look and lifted an eyebrow. He didn't say anything, but he didn't need to. I recalled Ember telling me the bond she had to Lars broke once she was in the Otherworld, which might have been the real reason Lorcan held on to me. The bind didn't work in the Otherworld or in the hallways connecting the worlds. There I could run from him.

Something to add to my list of things to remember.

But would I even risk it? My family...my little sister. Lorcan might say he hadn't meant for Ian to die, but he sure didn't get upset when Sam killed him. And she would certainly have no problem slaughtering my loved ones.

At this moment I actually didn't want to run. Not until I could master some of those spells in the book secured in Lorcan's backpack. When I knew I could keep my family safe and save my sleeping friend from an evil queen.

God, Ryan would love how dramatic that sounded. I grinned to myself. *Such a drama queen.*

Lorcan pulled me through the door, our bodies disappearing into thin air.

He guided me through the doors quickly. The evening had given way to early dawn light. Time had sped by on Earth, while it felt only like minutes to me. Time worked differently in the Otherworld. I tried to understand it mathematically, but it didn't seem to have any logic or reason. When I had returned from Aneira's castle the first time, almost four years had passed on Earth when it only felt like a month. Four years of my life—gone. I went from eighteen to twenty-two in a matter of weeks.

I assumed my family thought I was dead. They probably mourned my loss and tried to move on. I doubted I would even recognize my little sister anymore. She was twelve the last time I saw her. Now she'd be turning sixteen.

I longed to look for them, to see how they were, even knowing I could never let them see me. My presence was no longer safe, my life no longer meant to be part of theirs. It hurt my heart so deeply, but I would always put them first. And even if they didn't know it, it was better for them to think me dead.

Growing up I always knew I hadn't belonged. Not because I was adopted. My parents made sure they never outright showed favoritism to Halley. But deep inside I sensed I didn't fit. I was different. I simply didn't realize how much.

"This way." Lorcan motioned me to follow him.

The salty, fishy scent of the ocean tangled in the breeze and curled in my nose as I trailed after him through the heavy brush. The forest was thick with dewy fog, and a sudden chill rose on my skin. The distant sound of waves crashing told me the Pacific Ocean was close.

Siuslaw National Forest was only four hours away from Olympia, but I had never been here. My mom only liked trips to tropical places that were all inclusive. She considered camping torture. Roughing it was if the resort ran out of umbrellas for her drinks.

I loved her, but she was not a "fun" mother. My dad was when she wasn't around, but it was rare he'd do anything even slightly spontaneous, afraid of upsetting Mother's routine.

Lorcan shoved through brush, the forest giving way to a clearing and a white two-story house backed up against another part of the forest. The house was built close to a bluff, the ocean only a half mile from the deck steps.

It was still dark, but the closer we got to the place, the more rundown it appeared. Chipped paint peeled off the wood in chunks, the deck sagged, and the windows were all boarded up.

"Home sweet home." Lorcan pushed at my lower back, directing me up the rickety steps. He opened the door and ushered me into the house. I stepped in, a moldy odor knocking into my senses. I rubbed at my nose as if I could get the smell out of it. In the living room rotting floorboards creaked under a mildewed rug. An ugly brown sofa sat in the middle of the room, which looked like it had been here since the house was built.

"About time," Dominic yelled from the kitchen, drawing my eye to the next room. The three dark dwellers waited in the kitchen, each gripping a coffee mug. An avocado-color retro-style light hung from the middle of the kitchen over a round wooden table, where grocery bags sat on top. Four farm-style wood chairs circled it. The small kitchen was wallpapered in a yellow, flowery print, which was peeling away like the paint outside.

"Smells like Samantha's cooking." Lorcan wrinkled his nose, likely at the musky rug odor as he strolled into the kitchen.

"Shut up." She glared at him, taking another swig of her drink.

Coffee... I licked my bottom lip, the smell of coffee beans making its way to me. Growing up in the Pacific Northwest, Starbucks' capital, it was in your DNA to love coffee. Ember, Ryan, and I always met at a cool coffee shop and talk for hours.

Now I realized how innocent and uncomplicated those days were, even though we thought the opposite at the time. The stuck-up Kallie Parson and her group were the bane of our existence...now we were fighting for the lives of humans and the survival of Earth.

"The shower works." Dax nodded to the stairs next to the kitchen. "But no hot water."

I cringed. *Of course.*

"The gas is off, so no stove either. Only thing working is the microwave," Dominic grumbled, opening the door to it, placing a mug inside. "Not that any of you assholes knows how to cook except me anyway."

"Somehow, chief, you will have to work in these conditions." Lorcan shook his head with humor, stepping farther into the room. "You guys check out the vicinity?"

"Yeah." Sam hopped up on the counter, her feet dangling. "There is nothing for five miles on all sides of us."

"Good." Lorcan nodded. "I need an area I can work with Kennedy and be assured no hikers or rangers will interrupt us."

The microwave beeped, and Dominic grabbed the mug out of it and handed it to his alpha. Lorcan cupped it in his hand and leaned against the counter.

"Dax, I want you to find out anything you can on the others. See if they are back yet and if they are looking for her." He jerked his chin to me.

Dax nodded.

"Sam, I want you to patrol the property. Dom will join you when I get back." Lorcan took a drink of his coffee, my mouth watering at the smell. My nose sensed it was not the cheap, crappy kind. The aroma coating my tongue was deep and rich.

"Get back?" Samantha set down her cup. "Get back from where?"

"Not your business." Lorcan pushed off the counter and strolled over to me, his face stern. "I won't be long." He held out the cup of coffee to me, my hand instinctively taking it from him. The moment I did, he turned back to his clan. "While I'm gone, I only want Dom in the house. He will watch over Kennedy until I'm back." His eyes burrowed into Samantha.

"Are you fuckin' kidding me?" Her mouth dropped open, getting his meaning. "You don't trust me around the mouse? What do you think I'm going to do to her?" Blue eyes went from Lorcan to me; a glint of mischief ran through them. "Swat her around?"

"Not for you to question my orders," Lorcan replied evenly. "You just follow them."

A glimmer of a smile hinted on Samantha's mouth, her gaze hard on me. "Of course."

In that moment I knew I was in trouble. I felt she'd find ways to be cruel. Creative ways so Lorcan wouldn't notice.

It felt like I never left high school.

<center>~~~~</center>

Lorcan walked me up to the second floor, locating the only bathroom in the house. The rising sun filtered through the window, glittering the bathroom in light.

"Here." Lorcan tugged a towel from the cupboard. They smelled like dusty mothballs, but there were at least towels still here.

"It's going to be freezing, but at least you can get clean." He set down a bottle of shampoo, a razor, and he grabbed body soap out of one of the grocery bags. "I'll be back soon." He turned to exit.

Lorcan was leaving me? Fear hit me, causing me to rush after him without a thought.

"Where are you going?" The words fumbled from my mouth, and I grabbed his arm.

He narrowed his eyes as he looked down at my fingers clutching him with desperation.

I pulled away, curling my hands around each other. *Why did I do that?*

"I will be back soon," he said, stepping out of the room and shutting the door. The quiet of the chamber engulfed me as his footsteps disappeared down the stairs.

A strange loneliness and fear rushed over me. My legs itched to follow him, anxiety buzzing in my lungs. I ran to the door, making sure it was fully closed, hating there was no lock.

I had made my decision to stay, not like I had much of a choice. But I would not look for ways to run. I would use this bad situation and learn as much as I could. However, my resolution didn't take away the emptiness I felt at not being with Jared, Ryan, Ember, or my family. They were who I needed, not Lorcan.

I was alone. Scared. I had read about too many people who had been kidnapped developing affection for their captor. Stockholm syndrome.

Lorcan was a murderer. A horrible, revolting person. I needed to remember that. He could play whatever role he wanted, tell me whatever he thought I wanted to hear, but I would only see him as a butcher.

A beast.

FIVE

The shower was painful, the icy water stabbing at my skin like needles. But the filth from my time crawling in the caves of Greece still coated my skin. Blood and sweat covered me like an extra layer of skin. I gritted my teeth and finished washing my hair the best I could. I tried to shave, but the razor slid over the goosebumps on my legs and stung like hell.

When I felt I had enough of the first layer of grime off, and my teeth chattered so loudly it echoed in my head, I got out, wrapping my body in the old, smelly towel.

I stepped up to the mirror and stared at the reflection. I looked different. I couldn't explain how exactly, but it already seemed like I had matured in the last few days. In my dark brown eyes, I saw a girl way older than her twenty-two years. I had shed the skin of a child and become a woman.

I always looked younger than my age. Freckles speckled my nose and cheeks, and my brown hair reached my waist. My petite frame resembled a child's body more than a woman's. But I had always been an older soul. The Druid in me showed signs early on, always seeing deeper into people's souls when most people my age were pretty shallow. Still, I had been sheltered and kept safe with the love of my parents, a home, friends, no real worries.

Even though I had missed four years, I felt I had lived them all in the past few weeks. I'd experienced things most never would in a lifetime.

And the hormones I thought I bypassed as a teenager were hitting me hard. Staring into the glass, I untucked my towel, observing my body. I was so used to being teased for being flat, it took me by surprise to notice my hips were wider, and my formerly small breasts were apparent. I would never be a woman with huge breasts or butt, but this was a big change for me.

The slight curves captivated me. I felt older. Sexier. I touched my breastbone and slowly moved down, skimming over my skin. I had never been really sexual. I never fantasized about a boy touching me...and certainly hadn't touched myself. I grew up thinking masturbation was wrong. Not that my parents talked about sex to me. Ever. It was suppressed in my house. Sex or sexual feelings were wrong. Dirty. Bad.

Ryan and Ember talked openly about it, but I never engaged in the topic, feeling weird I didn't feel the same things they did about sex.

Even with Jared, fear kept me from ever crossing the line. Yet since discovering I was a Druid, my attitude had progressively shifted. The more we kissed, the more I started to desire him, but we never had sex. He tried to nudge for more, but something always stopped me. It was the source of our argument the last night in Greece.

I knew everyone assumed we were having sex because we slept in the same tent, but Jared and I did no more than mess around, our bottom halves always clothed. And that scarcely happened since most of the time I passed out after Lars overworked Ember and me trying to get the location of the sword.

I inhaled sharply as my fingers trailed over my breasts and down past my stomach. A tightening gripped between my legs. A need built in my stomach, something I had briefly felt with Jared before fear stopped me. This time I didn't want it to end.

My lungs drew in swallow breaths, my body starting to tremble, my cheeks flushing. But I hesitated, feeling ashamed to continue.

I could hear Ryan's voice in my head. *It's natural! Jesus, girl, if you don't, one of these days you are going to snap in half because you'll be so rigid.* I knew he was right. It was biology, but it didn't ebb my shame.

I pushed past my mortification, not letting myself think, my hand finding its way down, my fingers moving. *Oh my god...* Pleasure swelled so powerfully into me I gripped the sink with my free hand, my other one moving faster and deeper. A groan escaped my throat and I tried to ignore the embarrassment I felt at hearing myself respond like that. To turn this away from me, I pictured Jared. I felt even more awkward seeing his face as if he would be shocked at what I was doing. It made me want to giggle instead, breaking my mood.

Then another image slithered into my thoughts, his form pressing into me from behind, his deep voice in my ear. I quickly shoved it out, forcing Jared back in, but he easily slipped out again, the other's face returning.

No! I screamed into my head, closing my eyes. *That's disgusting!* But my body burned hotter at the wrongness, pulsing and squeezing, driving me past the point I couldn't stop. A moan emerged between my stunted breaths. My thoughts had run away from my control, positioning the figure behind me again, imagining him grabbing my hips, opening me up wider for him, taking me to a new level. His hand built me higher and higher until I cried out.

Noooo! I tried to push it away again, but it was too late. My body clenched at the picture, an explosion popped behind my lids, and a cry crossed my lips. I no longer felt I was in my body, like a vision, but a thousand times better.

A euphoric high smashed inside me, locking my muscles, and holding me captive for several moments before I crashed back to Earth. I gripped both sides of the sink to keep myself standing. Another blissful sensation washed over me. It was amazing. I could see why everyone chased after this.

With every second after, the embarrassment crept in. I inhaled a shaky breath and lifted my lids, my flushed face tilting up to the mirror. I froze, air catching in my throat. Green eyes blazed in the mirror behind me, sparks of red flickering at the edges.

Lorcan.

Oh. God. No. Panic and humiliation splashed over my cheeks, horror gushing like a river in my chest. I snatched up my towel, wrapping it around myself, keeping my back to him.

He stood in the doorway, unmoving, his face stone. We stared at each other, neither of us speaking. The air in the room sputtered with tension.

I couldn't move or breathe, straddling the line between fear and unbearable mortification. No doubt he had seen me naked. How much did he see? Did I say anything? Acid filled my stomach at even the idea I had hinted his name.

Now the moment was over, the notion I had pictured him not only disgusted me, but made me infuriated with myself. I felt dirty, appalled, like I needed another shower.

His chest moved up and down, his fists clutched around a bag, crinkling the plastic. He didn't shift, but the room sizzled with magic, like the beast was about to appear, packing the space with apprehension.

"Here's some clothes. Should fit," he finally spat out, tossing the bag on the floor, glaring at me. "Put them on and meet me outside in twenty. There's food for you in the kitchen." He grabbed the doorknob and slammed the door, the house shaking on its foundation.

I stood for a few seconds before I dropped my face into my palms. The first time I had ever done that and I got caught. *What possessed me to do it anyway? Especially now. Here, under the roof with them. What is wrong with you, Kennedy?*

After a minute, I turned, grabbed the shopping bag, and peered inside. Clothes and other items I needed were crammed inside. Lorcan actually did what he said he would. He went and got me stuff. The gesture infuriated me. He was awful. We all knew it. So why didn't he ignore my wish and have Samantha run the errand? It seemed beneath him to do it himself. Lorcan held his alpha title with arrogance and pride. But he went shopping for me because I didn't want Samantha touching my clothes? Why did he care if I got upset? What was his end game? Why show me kindness when he held my family members' lives ransom?

The bag was full of shirts, sweatpants, jeans, sweatshirts, undergarments, a backpack, and toiletries. Even tampons. I slipped on underwear and a sports bra. They fit perfectly. Then I dressed in a pair of gray sweatpants and a black hoodie. I wanted to be covered, displaying no skin.

He had already seen enough.

Nature and nurture were fighting inside me. I was taught to view the naked body as shameful. It wasn't that my parents said it explicitly, but they communicated it in the way my mom would turn her nose up at a girl wearing something she didn't deem appropriate and their rule that no one should ever be nude in the house. But my Druid side felt exhilarated without clothing. Free.

Nurture still won out, the humiliation caking my insides as I slipped back on my boots, brushed my teeth and hair, then headed downstairs.

Thankfully the kitchen was empty. A hot egg sandwich and sliced apple sat on a plate, a bottled water next to it. Hunger pushed away my chagrin. Sitting at the table I consumed the breakfast with haste, barely letting the food hit my taste buds.

Come on, Kennedy. Grow up.

    A.) You are a twenty-two-year-old woman.
    B.) It's natural.
    C.) It's time to stop being embarrassed of your
       sexuality.
    D.) Go out there and act like nothing happened.

Making a list always calmed me. I felt like I could deal with things, see them clearly in my head. With my trusty list giving me strength, I stood, pushed back the chair, grabbed the water, and moved out of the kitchen door to face a girl's humiliation like a woman.

<p style="text-align:center">~~~~~</p>

For the next five hours, Lorcan's mood was abrasive, bordering on cruel. He barely looked at me and didn't say a word about what he observed. My own mood went from being embarrassed to mad. He didn't let up and forced me to do the defensive spell over and over until I was in tears.

At the fourth hour he finally introduced a new invocation. This one was kind of like the one Lars had me do in the cave—challenging another spell so the two nullified each other. It only worked on menial enchantments. It was the baby spell for what I figured he eventually wanted me to do. I was surprised he started me at the basic level and hadn't forced me to jump a few levels to get there faster.

"I don't care if you've done something similar with Lars; you need to have the basics down to build on them. You need a solid foundation," he snapped as he

79

walked up behind me with the book. "Now, do it again." He held the book out for me to read, his face twisted in a scowl.

"Can I have a break?" My body felt limp, and I craved a nap.

"No," he barked.

Exhaustion had frayed at my patience till nothing was left. "Stop being a jerk." I swung to him. "Why are you mad at me? I'm doing everything you ask of me and doing the best I can."

"Not good enough."

Blood vessels strained; my teeth clamped together. Damn, he could make me so furious. But he wasn't the only dark dweller who was obsessed with getting back into the Otherworld. They all were. Because they were barred.

My head jerked to Lorcan. But…we did enter! Confusion filled me, knocking loose something I should have realized a long time ago.

"Wait." I tilted my head, my eyes widening with awareness. "You can get in and out of the Otherworld," I accused, my head shaking in puzzlement. "You took me there. Your whole group can use the doors…" My sentence bled into the air. "I don't understand. Why do you need me so badly then? You are free of the curse, right? You can go to the Otherworld."

His head snapped to me, our eyes meeting, but he quickly swung away from me, running his hand over his head. "Not exactly."

"What does that mean?" I tossed out my arms. "You said you wanted me to break a curse. Why go to all the trouble to kidnap me when you are already allowed back in? Makes no sense."

He whipped around, nerves along his jaw twitching, and stomped up to me, forcing me to backpedal. His figure loomed over me; his nose flared. "Be careful," he rumbled, energy bouncing off him. All sense of humanity evaporated from him, the beast humming underneath and ready to strike, to kill. "Do not forget your place here."

Terror lumped in my throat. Struggling to swallow, my eyes could not move off him.

"You are not here to question. You do what I say if you want your family to stay safe."

"Only true cowards use innocent, defenseless people to threaten someone." The words spilled out like they had a tendency to do sometimes. "But I guess I shouldn't be surprised."

He watched me, the air growing thick and unstable between us. I was terrified of him and of what he could do, but I kept my chin up, trying not to let my voice quiver. He took a small step closer to me, his expression menacing. He moved like I was prey, taking in each nuance, every beat of my racing heart.

"Take a break, but after lunch we are starting again," he spoke, his voice low and deep. Then he walked around me and toward the forest.

I watched him storm away, his shoulders taut, fury wafting off him.

"Where are you going?" My voice floated to him.

"For a run," he snarled, his eyes flashing to me over his shoulder. "Is it okay with you, *witch*?"

The brutal tone slapped me across the face, and I blinked back emotions coming to the surface. I rammed my reaction down, hoping Lorcan didn't catch it. It was because I was tired, not because he could ever hurt my feelings.

He stopped, and his gaze fastened on mine. His pupils elongated, red spreading over his irises, sending fear into my veins. He curved around, moving faster than I could blink. His boots hit mine. I sucked in, wanting to stumble back, but instinct held me in place. His body stood barely an inch from mine, his beast vibrating at his skin, stretching his shirt and curling his back. His eyes became completely red, a rumble rocking his chest and hitting every nerve I had from my toes to my head.

We stayed there, the heat from his body assaulting my skin. His breath was heavy, slithering down my neck. My heart thumped in my chest, the line between life and death almost transparent. At any moment he could kill me. This thought burst forth a surge of stimulation, emphasizing every one of my senses. I felt alive.

What the hell? My body felt out of my control, hormones knocking against my skin like bugs trapped in a glass jar. Wanting out. Desiring something.

Lorcan let out a ragged huff. He closed his eyes, inhaled, and then swung away from me, disappearing into the forest.

It took me a few minutes to move from my spot, the odd moment slipping away and the real world settling back in. I felt ill. My mind conjured up Jared. I had nothing to feel guilty over. The notion that was even a passing thought was too revolting to even contemplate, but seeing my boyfriend's face in my head gave me comfort. Like a safe place.

Relocating myself to the kitchen, I pushed the incident away and focused on making myself a sandwich. It was strange to be a so-called prisoner but have free rein to move around the house. It messed with your mind, creating a false sense of comfort with your captors. As I finished my sandwich, Dax came barreling into the house, crashed the door, his eyes scanning the room.

"Where's Lorcan?"

"Went for a run." I wiped my hands on my napkin and swiveled to Lorcan's second. "Why?"

He ground his jaw and headed for the side door, ignoring my question. His movements were jerky and agitated, and dread simmered in my stomach. I got up and followed him out.

Dax halted in the yard, his face stern as he looked out toward the forest. A strange buzzing drifted over me, like being next to a radio tower. I was pretty sure Dax was communicating with Lorcan. I had experienced the sensation around the dark dwellers before.

It was a full minute before leaves wrestled and Lorcan came bursting out of the woods, holding his garments. Not wearing them.

Oh... My... Impulse took my eyes to the ground, but they flashed back up, not able to look away. His physique was almost unreal, like a work of art...and massive. Heat burned my face, my eyes darting again to his lower region. *Holy crap.*

At Camp Dark Dweller I had seen plenty of naked men, mostly Eli and Cooper. I got embarrassed at first seeing the guys in the buff, but after a while it didn't bother me as much. Let's just say they were all extremely well endowed. And taking in Lorcan...the Dragen brothers were especially impressive. Frightening even.

I clenched my fist, mad I even noticed. *It's Lorcan.*

I had seen Jared with his top off or in underwear several times, and he was nice to ogle, but for some reason observing Lorcan stirred my insides, making me uncomfortable, hot, and agitated.

"When?" He tugged on his jeans, covering himself. I let out my breath.

"They'll be in this area in less than an hour," Dax replied stiffly.

"What's happening?" I asked.

"They have help from the Unseelie King." Dax continued to ignore me.

"Fuck." Lorcan shook his head, pulling on his T-shirt. "Cole?"

"And Cooper. It's always gonna be a problem."

"I know, but it also will be a problem for them. We can stay one step ahead."

"What's going on?" I bounced between Dax and Lorcan. I was kind of surprised Ember and Eli weren't part of the search. It didn't sound like my friend. She'd be the first one to come for me. *Where was she? Was she okay?*

"You are a hot commodity, li'l Druid." Lorcan shoved his feet in his boots and hustled to me, gripping my arm. "Come on, grab what you can. We leave in five minutes." He yanked me into the house.

I stumbled into the kitchen after Lorcan. "How do they know where we are?"

"We're dark dwellers, and even though we split, we still have a connection. It will take a bit, but as long as we're on Earth, they'll be able to find us. And we'll always be able to feel them coming when they get close."

I had a search party. My mind and body didn't know how to respond. First came a rush of relief and happiness. But at the same time, their search would be futile if Lorcan could always sense them coming. And even if they got me back, could I leave? Would I be able to physically walk away from Lorcan because of the bond?

Dom and Samantha burst into the house, their eyes meeting Lorcan's, and nodded. They picked up their bags and started filling them with food we could carry. Lorcan led me upstairs and retrieved his backpack off a twin bed in the first room. I hadn't slept in so long and couldn't deny I had been looking forward to sleeping in a bed tonight.

Lorcan went to the bathroom where I left the shopping bag and dug to the bottom, pulling out the new canvas backpack. He stuffed all the things he bought me inside, zipped it up and tossed it to me.

"Time to go, li'l Druid." He watched me. "Don't get any ideas. Call me a coward, but remember your family is merely a door away." The threat hung heavy in the air. "And Sam is eager to act."

My lids lowered in a glower, and I nodded. I could never let my guard down. I detested him.

SIX

The backpack banged in rhythm as my legs tried to keep up with Lorcan. He maintained a steady pace through the forest when he came to a dead stop, my body smashing into the back of his with a thud.

"Ow." I stumbled back, rubbing my nose, feeling like I had collided into a boulder.

"Shhh." He held up his finger to his mouth, his gaze zigzagging over the forest. I stiffened with worry. Dax and Dom hovered at his side, their heads tilted, listening. Sam trotted up behind me. Her presence made me press closer to Lorcan.

Lorcan took a deep breath, his muscles moving against my hand.

"That's not Cole." Samantha smacked her lips like she was tasting the air.

"No. It's not." Lorcan growled. The vibration from his throat pulsated down my spine.

"What?" Nerves wound around my gut. "What's going on?"

Lorcan took another deep breath and swore.

"Do you think it's merely by chance they're in this area?" Dax gripped the knife on his hip. "Why else would they be here?"

Lorcan glanced over his shoulder at me, back to Dax. "They're a little miffed I jumped the line in Greece?"

Dominic snorted.

"Lorcan?" I hissed, forcing his attention back to me. I didn't understand what they were talking about.

"Strighoul."

Panic stuttered in my heart. "What?" Images of long needlelike teeth, patchy skin, red eyes. Strighoul were creatures like a cross between a vampire and a ghoul. They were cannibals. Their favorite meal was fellow fae, absorbing the magic of whomever they consumed.

My path had crossed with them before. In Greece. Because of the man standing before me.

"Well, aren't you old friends?" Ember would have been proud at the sarcasm dripping from my sentence. "Maybe they want to meet up for a barbeque or something."

"Doubtful." Lorcan's eyebrow lifted, a slight smile coming to his mouth. "Unless we're on the menu."

Chilling cries cracked through the trees. We all swiveled in their direction. They were a lot closer than we thought.

"Shit." Lorcan grabbed my hand and tugged me to the left.

The others split off, stripping out of their clothes as they ran for the enemy, while Lorcan steered me the other way, running faster than my legs could move.

"Lorcan!" I stumbled, falling to the ground, my hands skating over the rocky earth. "Owww."

Without hesitation he swept me up in his arms, wrapping my legs around his middle, my body pressed to his front. "Hold on." He looped my arms around his neck, taking off at full speed. I hated being carried, especially by him, but I could never have matched his pace. I squeezed my arms and legs tight, holding on to the loop of the bag on his back as he tore across the woodlands.

It wasn't long before the friction of my body moving up and down his produced a thought in the back of my mind. The abrasive jolting forced little puffs from my throat. The image of us having sex careened into my thoughts, knocking out anything else. Hot and relentless. Fire scorched my stomach and dropped lower.

Stop it! I wanted to bleach my mind the moment it came through. *How disgusting am I? What is wrong with me? Why would I even let that thought cross my mind, especially at this time?*

Jared's smile plundered in, and Lorcan's touch became so disgusting I could hardly breathe. "Let me down." I needed to be far away from him, stop the bugs from skittering under my skin. "Now."

"Not yet."

"Yes. Now!" I shoved away from his chest. His eyes burned into me, but I couldn't look at him.

"I can still smell them." He grabbed my back, trying to keep me secured to him.

"I don't care." I wiggled, letting my legs go so he had no choice but to drop me.

A noise came from his throat as he released me to the ground. I immediately turned, continuing our forward motion through the brush.

"What the hell happened?" He grabbed for my arm.

I slipped away, marching faster.

"Kennedy?" My name rumbled up through my shoes into my body. "Stop."

I didn't.

His fingers circled my bicep and spun me around, slamming my body back into his. He held my arm in a death grip, his eyebrows furrowed. He was too close.

"I can feel your anger." His voice was low, almost sounding like a question. "It surged out of nowhere."

I bit down on my lip and tried to back away from him.

"I know you hate me." He clutched me tighter against him. "But that was different..."

Humiliation marinated in my belly, stinging my cheeks. I felt sick. It might have been normal for a hormonal girl to think about sex. But not for me and certainly not with him. I loved Jared. And Lorcan was a brutal murderer and to even have thoughts like that was wrong. Disgusting and wrong on so many levels, but mostly because deep down a part of me was turned on at the idea.

I jerked away from him and took one step.
An explosion popped in my head, everything going white.

Flash.

"Now, Asim." The Queen motioned for the little boy to touch Ember. Ember's lips parted as an unspoken word formed on her lips. The beautiful boy placed a finger on Ember's wrists and her body jolted as if she'd been electrocuted, the word dying on her tongue. Her eyes widened, flashing black, the demon side consuming the whiteness. She jerked and twitched, light and sparks dancing off her skin. Her backbone went straight, her body seeming to grow with power and dominance. A low menacing cackle slipped from Ember's mouth, her expression turning haughty and confident, as if she feared nothing. The girl I knew was gone, replaced by someone who looked like her but was cold and cruel.

Lights overhead popped, the room sizzled with electricity that found its way to Ember, pumping her with more energy.

"Another one," the Queen yelled over the buzzing in the room, hiding behind my friend. Asim sets another finger on Ember's arm.

Any last surviving light shattered. Her body went rigid as electricity coursed into her, making its own power source. A bolt of fire wrenched from Ember, hitting the glass, then bounding back into Ember. She flew up into the air, tearing away from Asim. Aneira shrieked as the rod of energy splits through Ember's stomach into her own.

Ember screamed; the pain in her voice dusted my heart with ice.

Pain. Agony. It reflected on her features like it had been molded with clay. Tears leaked down her face, her mouth open.

Then in a pop, the energy dissipated.

Both women slammed to the ground.

I wanted to run to my friend, to hold her in my arms, heal her. My feet wouldn't move.

The Queen's soldiers rushed to her side, fussing over their leader. I tuned her out, unable to leave my friend. My seer-self picked up on a deep vacuum throughout her body.

Ember's powers were gone. She was empty.

"What happened?" She clutched her stomach, sitting up, but the horror on her face told me she already knew. "What did you do?"

The Queen smirked. "I told you, Ember, I learned how to transfer your powers to me without using blood."

Flash.

The room snapped to another stone area, a chamber in the Seelie castle. A body slumped on the floor not far from me. I moved closer, reaching down to roll it to face me. The woman's body flopped over, and dead brown eyes stared up at me.

A chilling cry broke from my lips as I pressed my hand to my mouth.

I stared down at... myself. Glasses rimmed the empty gaze. Then suddenly the mouth curved, jolting me back.

"You failed."

Flash.

～～～

I screamed, my eyes tearing open to a pitch-black room. I didn't understand where I was...who I was.

Scared. Paralyzed.

The images flickering through my head felt as real as the room around me.

"Kennedy, it's all right." A man's voice came through the darkness; a body moved to mine. The bed I was in squeaked as he climbed in next to me. "Breathe."

My gaze darted around as my vision adjusted to the blackness, seeing more shapes and outlines. Moonlight allowed me to notice a one-room cabin. Kitchen. Sofa. Table. More people. Three. They stared at me from where they lay on the floor, sofa, and chair, as terror rattled my uneven breaths.

Afraid.

"Shhh." Large hands brushed over my head in soothing strokes.

Everything felt unreal, like if I reached out and touched it, it would pop like a bubble.

"Kennedy," the man next to me demanded. "Look at me."

My lashes lifted to his.

Green.

Familiar.

Lorcan.

"Is this real?" I whispered.

"It's real." He pulled me into his chest, his hand still running through my hair, calming my racing heart. The sound of his heartbeat was like my tether, pulling me back to Earth.

"Prove it."

His finger trailed over my ear, tucking a chunk of hair behind it, the tips of his fingers squeezing my earlobe, sparking a jolt of pain through me.

Real.

I sighed, shutting my eyes, and burrowed deeper into his chest. Every time a vision took me, I had this deep-seated fear it would keep me this time. Trap me in its walls. Forever.

"I hear your heartbeat. I smell...spaghetti?" Actually I smelled him. A manly, woodsy smell with a touch of fae, sweet and wild. It was intoxicating. "I feel your fingers on my back."

"What are you doing?" he muttered into my ear.

"Making a list. It's how I calm myself. Been doing it since I could speak." I rubbed my cheek against his shirt, the images of what I had seen still hovering. "In visions I can't smell or feel pain. This is how I understand this is true." But I could sense others' pain.

Ember no longer has her powers. I squeezed my lids closed, speaking so low I barely heard my own words. "Aneira has Ember's powers."

"What?" Lorcan pulled back, searching my face.

"She did some spell...I don't really remember. All I know is Aneira has them...she wants to destroy Earth. I-It was...so much pain." I shuddered and Lorcan pulled me into him, sweeping his hand through my hair in soothing strokes.

He held me for the next minute, rubbing my back. The warmth of him, the power of his arms around me, made me feel so safe.

Safe? Lorcan? He was the last person who should inflict any feelings of security. He was my enemy. I could not forget that.

As if a light flicked on, flooding in the bright light of reality, I jerked away.

"Thank you," I mumbled with annoyance, moving back against the headboard.

He nodded, glancing away.

"What the hell?" Samantha's voice came from the sofa. She sat up, her bright blue eyes darting back and forth between Lorcan and me.

"She gets visions," Lorcan grumbled, pushing off the bed. "It takes her a minute to come out of them. To understand where she is."

"I don't think that is what she was referring to." Dominic snorted, stretching out on his side on the floor, his elbow propped on a pillow, a blanket barely covering his naked body.

Lorcan's lids lowered, his arms crossing over his chest.

"Shut up, Dom." Dax laid in one of the reclining chairs, his hand rubbing his face. "She's the kid's girl...don't start."

The mention of Jared forced me to peer down at my hands twisting on my lap.

"Just making sure we don't have a repeat of Eli." Dom shot over his shoulder at Dax. "Look what trouble that fuckin' abomination caused us."

Fire shot up my back, propelling me from the bed. "Excuse me?"

"Oh sorry. Did I hurt your feelings, little witch?" Dominic returned my glare. "I don't care if she is your friend. She has caused nothing but misery. Tore our group in half. And because of her we are now headed for a war."

My mouth dropped open.

"Dom…" Lorcan warned.

"Ember didn't do anything," I yelled. "You guys did it. You divided your own family. Don't blame another for your own selfish actions. And the war was always coming. You guys lit the fuse. If anyone should be blamed, it should be you."

Dominic was on his feet, his shoulders rolled forward in fury. Samantha leaped from the sofa, coming up next to him, her eyes wide with fervor.

"Want to say that again, *witch*?" Dominic leaned over and bared his teeth, his eyes glowing red around the edges. "I dare you."

"Stop!" Lorcan moved between us, pushing me behind him. "Back down, Dom."

Dominic's gaze was latched on me, his teeth growing into daggers.

"I. Said. Back. Down!" Lorcan's voice boomed, his body enlarging in the small space, his authority pulsing.

Dominic licked his lip, his eyes still on me.

"That's. An. Order." Lorcan growled.

Dax had gotten up and moved in next to Dominic, pulling him back. "Time for a run, man."

Dom finally turned his head, his shoulders unclenching. He nodded and let Dax lead him out of the cabin.

"You too, Samantha." Lorcan tipped his head for the door. "Do a circle around the cabin."

She bowed her head to his request, shooting me a glare that could have melted metal.

When the door snapped shut, Lorcan rounded to me, his arms crossed. He stared down at me, expressionless, giving me no idea if he was angry.

The intensity of his gaze made me wiggle around.

"You have a death wish?" he asked.

"No." I gripped my hands together. "But I will defend my friends. Especially when someone is wrong."

Lorcan's eyes went back and forth between mine. Slowly the side of his mouth curved up and he shook his head. "Be careful. Dom is the most feral out of us. Doesn't take much for him to snap. And Sam is close behind."

I pinched my mouth together, knowing I had acted without thinking. Very unlike me.

"But you were right."

"What?" My head bounced up, my eyes wide.

"I used to blame Ember too. Hated her. Detested the way Eli lost his shit around her and couldn't see past her. Thought I was doing all of us a favor getting rid of her. But..." He leaned his weight on his right leg, smoothed a hand over his head. "I see it now. Everything I did—" He let his sentence drop, scrubbing a hand over his face. He grunted and moved around me, heading for the small refrigerator on the other side of the room.

"Everything you did, what?" I tracked him as he pulled out a beer from the fridge.

"What's done is done." He popped it open and took a swig. "Can't change the past."

I strolled over to him, the light from the moon illuminated half his face. "Why did you go to Aneira?"

He leaned a hip against the counter, facing me.

"At the time I thought it was the best way to go, directly to her. Lars couldn't break the curse on us, and he would only take Ember, my only leverage, off the table. I couldn't have that. Nor did I want a war. And when I found out she was Aisling's daughter, the dae niece of the Queen...it was my ace in the hole." He took another long drink. "I thought I could threaten Aneira to spill the truth of what really happened all those years ago."

"But it didn't work out like you hoped."

"Not even close." He made a genuine frown. "Never underestimate how low someone will go to hide the truth."

My hand moved without my permission, swiping the can from Lorcan's fingers. His eyebrow bent up, crinkling his forehead.

"I learned to never underestimate evil." I took a long glug. When Mom wasn't around, my dad would let me have sips from his beer. I grew to like it, the taste reminding me of those small moments we shared.

"Did you just steal my *last* beer?" His irises danced, humor twitching his lips.

"Yep." I took another gulp and smiled back.

"Guess you were right."

"About?"

"Never underestimate evil." He crossed his arms, grinning at me.

~~~~~

When the visions had taken me, Lorcan picked me up and relocated us to some vacant cabin over the border in Canada. It was a tiny seasonal hunting/fishing bungalow, likely personally owned and by a man. It was sparse and rundown, leaning toward dirty, with hunting and fishing magazines, pictures, and kitschy "art" around...if you called a singing fish on the wall art.

The one-room cabin was so remote it unsettled me. I'd never been so far away from a town or city. At least with this group if something happened or we needed an item they could use the Otherworld doors to travel quickly.

Lorcan was still on guard, muttering about how there was nowhere we could truly hide. Cole would always be only steps behind us. We stayed there for a few days before moving to another place. We took up a pattern of moving every two to three days. Sometimes I had my own room, but most of the time we sprawled between one or two rooms. Lorcan usually gave me the area or bed farthest from Dominic and Samantha. Their disgruntled attitude toward me, behind Lorcan's back, grew each day.

The one thing Dominic loved to rile me about in front of Lorcan was Jared, constantly teasing me about having nerd sex or how neither of us had a clue what we were doing. He wanted a rise out of me, but I never gave it to him, choosing to stay quiet and let him get bored with my non-reaction. He was a bully, just like the dozens I had dealt with in school. It seriously had been ten times worse in junior high. Dom was low on the terrorizing scale.

Samantha, on the other hand, was efficient and incredibly skilled in tormenting. She did it secretly. Finding me alone coming from the shower or in the hallway, she would only smile and mention my family.

"Your dad looked so cute today." A malicious smile spread over her mouth. Beautiful devil. "He flirted with me in line at the café. I don't think he's getting any at home. We sat and talked for hours." She clicked her tongue.

My nostrils flared, and I pinned my lips together.

"He wore this adorable bow tie." She ran a finger across my chest bone. "You know, the one with the brown gavels all over it."

I sucked in a sharp breath, my heart constricting in my chest. She was not lying about seeing him. I knew exactly what bow tie she was talking about. Halley and I gave it to him for Father's Day one year. It was hideous, but he wore it all the time with pride. He said it was his favorite gift.

Tears pricked behind my lids, the grief of missing my family, the pain I caused them, thinking I would never see them again.

"Next time I 'happen' to run into him," she leaned in closer to my ear, "I think I'll take him to that quaint little hotel by his office. We'll get acquainted. He definitely needs it."

"Leave him alone." Her threats were not empty. She would do it. Play with him, destroy his marriage…all to hurt me.

"Oh, I don't think that's what Paul wants. He seemed quite keen to continue our conversation."

I hated the way she said his name, the intimacy in it.

"What do you want from me?" I blinked back the tears. "I'm doing everything you ask me."

"Yeah, you're such the *good* little girl. So obedient. Dull. I have no idea what he sees in you. You are definitely not his type at all."

"You don't know what Jared's type is," I spat, the knife sinking in right where she wanted it.

She smirked. "I wasn't talking about Jared." She turned and sauntered down the hallway leaving me open mouthed and staring after her.

SEVEN

The weeks passed, the end of summer bleeding into autumn, a chill mounting in the air. Every day, whether rain, fog, or snow, Lorcan took me outside to work on my magic, attune myself to detect another's energy, and sense what another person wanted from me, without them saying a word. Lorcan was impossible to detect, his shield strong, but I was getting better at listening to the others' intentions.

I couldn't deny I was feeling much more confident, spells coming easier to me, every one of them making it more likely I could help Ryan, and assist in the coming war. I still had a long way to go, but Lorcan pushed me and convinced me I was capable.

"Never doubt, li'l Druid. It's in your blood. You just have to know it here." He rubbed my beanie. We were now high in the mountains in Montana somewhere. I liked the soft sounds of wet snow droplets dripping off leaves and drumming the earth of the surrounding forest. "Don't let the voices cripple you."

"We're talking metaphorical voices, right?" I glanced up at him. His green eyes peeked out from underneath his own black beanie. It was below freezing, and he had on a puffy jacket over a Henley shirt with jeans and boots. I was swathed in layers of shirts, sweaters, a jacket, gloves, scarves, and boots.

"With you?" He chuckled, tugging my hat farther over my ears. "Probably not. There are vast facets and dimensions in there."

"It's like the Syfy channel in here." I tapped my forehead and grinned.

"With a black hole that sucks in what I teach you, never to be seen again."

"Shut up." I shoved my arm into his stomach, which felt more like nudging a cement wall.

He laughed, snapping the spell book closed, turning away from me.

"Are we done?" An unexpected stab of dread swarmed around my chest like bees. I didn't want to think about why. "Don't you want to do the spell again?"

"I thought you might like to have a break today. You've been working really hard."

Strangely, I didn't want a break. Training with Lorcan had become the best part. I enjoyed the lessons, even looked forward to them.

I shoved my hands in my pockets, staring at the ground, white flakes landing on my boots. I shouldn't like it. I should be hating every minute being held captive by Lorcan, away from my friends, my boyfriend...

"Ken?"

"Yeah...thank you." I wrenched my feet loose of the ice blocks and trudged toward the cabin through the two feet of snow on the ground.

"Hey." Lorcan reached out, grabbing my arm. "Why are you upset?"

"I'm not." I shook my head.

"Kennedy." He turned me to fully face him. "I know you...that is not a happy 'no school day' face."

"You don't know me. This is my face when I'm excited."

He tipped one eyebrow up.

"What? I liked school." I tossed out my arms. "I'm a freak. What can I say?"

"That's true." He nodded. "But you're wrong. I *do* know you."

I glanced sidelong at him. I could never admit I enjoyed hanging out with him. It was demented. Sick. *You are only using him. Getting what you can so you can get Ryan. That is what is keeping you going.*

Thoughts of rescuing my friend from the Otherworld really did push me harder every day, but it wasn't the only thing anymore.

"What's wrong?" he asked softly.

"Everything," I mumbled.

"Are you missing Jared?"

My head snapped back to him. It was the first time

he had outright asked me about Jared. Even worse, I hadn't been thinking about Jared.

I rubbed my gloves over my face, only smearing snow around.

"Hey." He pulled my hands away, brushing the clumps of ice off my cheeks.

"Yeah...of course I miss him. I miss all my friends. I hate not knowing if they are all right. If Ryan..." I shifted my weight to one leg. "But that's not—it's not why I was upset." I took a deep breath. "I like working on my magic. It used to feel more like a chore, but something's clicked lately."

"And you get off on the high." Lorcan did his half grin, which could melt even an iceberg. "It's okay to admit. Magic does that. It's almost as good as sex."

I lifted both eyebrows.

He leered at me, wiggling his eyebrows. "I said almost. Believe me, nothing is better than sex, especially when you do it right."

"I thought it was like pizza."

"It's always good, yeah, but with some, it's..." His gaze moved to the side. "Probably shouldn't be talking sex with my little nephew's girl."

No, we probably shouldn't be, and normally the topic of sex would make me blush and try to change the subject.

Normally.

"Why? Is it more amazing with some? Do some people have special tricks they can do?" I had neither of those.

Lorcan turned back to me, his gaze intense.

"Chemistry," he rumbled. The oxygen coming into my lungs seemed to falter.

I gulped, struggling to swallow, as if I'd eaten an entire container of peanut butter. Staring up at him, I felt frozen on the outside, while inside a fire raged and I ran in circles screaming, but not trying to escape.

A.) Hormones. It's only because the chemicals in your body are on the fritz.

5.) It's not Lorcan. You'd be reacting like this if it was anyone...anyone with abs, a rear end, and face that insanely hot.

D.) What the hell am I making a list about again?

1.) Jared. You miss Jared.

I did. I missed him a lot and loved him. But in that moment all I could feel was Lorcan's hand clutching my arm. His grip sent jolts of electricity through my veins, causing them to short-circuit and make me brain dead.

Lorcan's gaze dropped to my mouth. My head spun, making me dizzy. I couldn't get myself to move. If anything, it was as though he was pulling me into him and I had no control. A black hole.

Then with a jolt, he grunted and shoved away from me, jarring me out of whatever trance had overtaken me. It was like being tossed into a snowbank and finding sharp rocks underneath the powder.

"Take the rest of the day off if you want." He had already started walking, his back to me. "We're leaving first thing in the morning."

I stared after him, his figure disappearing for a long time before I moved.

My mind rolled with questions but none my gut would let me answer. I felt confused and unsure, which I hated. That was why I was prepared for every situation. I studied and researched till I was sure and secure in what I was doing. Every moment with Lorcan was a test I couldn't ever prepare for because it constantly changed.

I leaned my head back, letting the flakes tickle my face as they landed, my eyes taking in the white clouds, the branches of trees. Around me the falling snow muted the sounds of the forest.

Most mornings before we started to train, I meditated. Centering myself allowed the seer to come out with more power to control it.

I took in a deep breath. Suddenly the tree branches disappeared as blinding light detonated across my eyesight.

Flash.

Dungeon.

Bars lined each side all the way down a dark, narrow corridor where I stood. Dirty, damp hay covered the floor, soaked with liquids, water or urine. Chained bodies hung from the walls, but none I recognized.

"About time. Light turn on." A strange jerking voice rolled down the walkway knocking into me. I jumped, glancing all around for the source. "Fire needs a light."

I stayed quiet, my eyes still wandering the dark, foul place. My heart thumped in my chest. Somehow I knew the voice was talking to me.

"Light bright or out like night?" A squawk snapped my head up higher. Was a bird talking to me? It did kind of sound like my aunt's cockatiel. The same speech pattern.

I took tentative steps down the path. I halted when I saw a short and stocky creature, ugly with a huge bubble nose and eyes, wearing tattered, grimy clothes. A troll. He was putting new hay into a cell. This one had a spiked collar hanging from the wall, blood still crusting the spikes.

"Knock. Knock." The voice cracked, and I followed it to a black raven sitting on the troll's shoulder. "Nobody home."

"What?" I stared at its black, beady eyes, watching me with its head tilted. My visions had never interacted with me.

"Fire out. Now light dim."

"Hey." Did I just get insulted by a bird?

"Only together you will burn." It tilted its head to the other side and squawked. "Prophecy true. You. Her. Grimmel know."

"I'm sorry, but what are you talking about? And who is Grimmel?"

"Light. Baby fire." He walked across the troll's back as the troll leaned over, spreading out more of the fresh hay. "She needs light. You need fire. Both need the false night."

I rubbed my temple with frustration.

"Light return to darkness. Or all lost. Gone. Bye-bye."

With his last words I felt myself shoved back, everything going black.

Flash.

~~~~

"Turn on the water in the bathtub," a man's voice boomed, and I turned toward it like a beacon of light. Swimming through the murk I searched for the speaker. I wanted to find the man, his voice drawing me to move. "I need to get her out of these clothes."

"Fuck, man, her lips are blue." Another man joined the first, his voice a murmur. Sounds of rushing water. Where was it coming from?

"Get out," the first man said. His timbre so familiar and seductive, my arms and legs kicked faster toward the glow above me.

"She's unconscious, so she won't know if I see her naked...like I care."

"I said get the hell out."

"Whatever, man...but you need to stop this shit right now. Don't lose your way too."

A growl hummed in the air, vibrating something deep inside me.

"Look at you. You are guarding her like I'm going to fuckin' attack your mate."

"Don't even go there, Dom. That couldn't be further from the truth."

"Sure." The sound of a door slammed.

"Come on, Ken," the man mumbled in my ear. He was so close.

Burning pain besieged my body, exploding like

knives over my skin. I screamed. My lids and mouth flew open.

Pain.

So much pain.

"It's okay," a voice spoke in my ear. "I'm here."

Struggling to suck in air, my teeth chattered violently, clanging against each other.

Bathroom.

I was in a bathtub.

Arms around me.

"Focus on my voice," the familiar voice said.

My body couldn't stop shaking and twitching, and he struggled to hold me.

"Take slow breaths, li'l Druid."

Lorcan.

The comfort of him behind me relieved my struggling lungs; I eased back into him. The warm water continued to rise, threatening to flood over the side. A foot stretched to the faucet and shoved it off.

"Reeeaaal?" I trembled, my teeth still clacking.

"Real."

"Shooow meee."

Water sloshed as he lifted his hand, stroking it over my head and down to my ear, pinching till I felt the prick of pain.

I exhaled and leaned back farther into him, my tremors ebbing.

"I-I hear the drops from the faucet. I smell soap. The generic, cheap kind. I feel…" Oh my god. Awareness of myself, of my naked body and the one behind mine, pressing into me.

Also naked.

And I felt all of him at full attention.

I jerked forward, twisting to look at Lorcan.

"You…you're naked." I shivered. I wasn't sure if it was from being cold.

"I am. It's pretty standard when people take baths." Lorcan placed his arms on the rim of the tub. "You were going into hypothermia. You hadn't returned in an hour so I went to look for you. Found you under an inch of snow."

There were no soap bubbles to hide his physique under the clear water. My eyes couldn't seem to stop themselves from glancing down. My already departed breath stumbled, hitching in my chest. Oh wow.

My cheeks flamed, along with other parts of my body. I hated it. I didn't like not being able to control myself, my reactions.

"It's impressive. It's all right to stare. I get that a lot." He shrugged.

"Wow. Hello, ego. You sure your head can fit in this room?" I shook my head.

"Which head?"

I groaned and splashed water at him, making him laugh.

"Relax, Kennedy. It's just a dick. I'm sure you've seen one before." Lorcan slanted his head as though he was asking.

I had. Being friends with Ryan, I saw plenty on

cable and in movies. But none of them were like Lorcan's. And so close. His entire body caused me to stir.

"Wait." His mouth dropped open. "You haven't taken the kid's out of the packaging yet?"

"Don't be crude." Embarrassment lashed me.

"How old are you?"

"Don't be a jerk."

"No, I'm really asking." He pulled himself higher, staring at me.

"Technically I'm twenty-two...lost a few years being prisoner in the Otherworld." I glared at him, my accusation centered on him. "But before I left I was about to turn eighteen."

"By eighteen, you still hadn't touched one?"

"No." I couldn't look at him, my shivers zigging sporadically down my back. "I wasn't the girl guys liked."

"Well then, those guys were idiots." He leaned back with a huff.

My lashes snapped up to peer at him, stunned by his words.

"But you and Jared never...?"

"Why are we talking about this?"

"Sex. It's natural, Ken. You get so uncomfortable when it's brought up, which is why I never mentioned the fact I saw you pleasing yourself that morning."

Oh. My. God. Could I drown myself? Please? I just wanted to dunk my head beneath the liquid and dissolve like bath salts.

"See? Look at you. You want to drown yourself right now, don't you?"

Dammit.

"Why does it embarrass you so much? You call yourself a nerd. You should know the science of a human body, its biological needs."

"You're not human."

"Yeah...we're even hornier." He laughed. "And you aren't totally either. You know, Druids were exceedingly sexual beings. I heard many rumors they had ceremonies to appease the gods by having group sex on Samhain and Beltane."

"Gross."

"Why? Because they are free with their bodies? Don't treat sex like it's wrong or something to be ashamed of."

"It's how I was raised." I sighed as my hidden internal thoughts rose to the surface. "But I feel the Druid in me wanting out." I waggled my head. "Not for group sex or anything...that...no. But there is a divide in me. Sensations I never had before."

"You crave sex?"

I nodded.

"So why didn't you with Jared?"

"I don't know. Something always stopped me." I batted at the water, the temperature dropping to lukewarm. "Crippling fear."

"Hmmm." Lorcan rubbed his head, glancing away.

"What?"

"Fear is fine, but *crippling* fear?" He placed his arm back on the ledge.

"I'm psychologically screwed up. Be honest. It's okay, I can take it."

He chuckled. "You're not. You're just a little uptight. And what's funny is I don't think you really are underneath."

"Why do you say that?"

"Because you haven't tried to hide your body from me while we're in here." He motioned toward me. "When you're not thinking about it, you are very comfortable in your skin. The problem is you overthink things."

Now I felt naked in a whole new way, completely exposed. Finally my brain registered I was sitting with Lorcan in a bath, bare.

"See, you're overthinking now."

"I can't help it." Awareness of my unclothed body only highlighted his. My eyes roamed around trying to find a place to land.

"Kennedy?" His voice was deep, stirring heat in my stomach. "Look at me."

I inhaled, locking my jaw together, I turned my head to his eyes.

"No. *Look at me.* Don't be ashamed by wanting to look."

Fear choked me, but I forced myself to gulp it back, hurtling past my comfort zone and lowering my eyes. Taking him in, I battled chagrin and worked not to turn away.

The more I viewed his physique, the more sensations

swirled inside. I bit down on my lip. I wanted to touch him. I wanted to know how it felt in my hand.

The other Kennedy, the impulsive, free one, took over. I scooted forward, my fingers reaching out.

Lorcan snatched my wrist. I inhaled sharply, my eyes locking on his. Red sputtered through the green; his jaw locked. His playful mood was gone.

Neither of us said a word, my chest heaving against my ribs. He licked his lip, then slowly lowered my hand back into the water.

Bells and warnings bounced against my brain trying to be let in, but none of them broke fully through. I felt so out of my body, like someone else was doing this. The pads of my fingers brushed the tip of him, and Lorcan sucked in a slug of air through his nose. I didn't know if I was even breathing anymore. The feel of him utterly intoxicated me.

He kept hold of my wrist but let me move freely. I ran a finger down the length and then wrapped my hand around. I felt him twitch, thickening under my palm. I moved up and down, stroking him.

"Fuck," Lorcan whispered so hoarsely it was barely a word, his hips jerking slightly.

My heart pounded and heat throbbed between my legs; a need I never experienced before clouded my head, setting my body on fire. I wanted—I wanted more.

"Hey." The door banged, rattling on its hinges. Dom's voice broke through. I jumped away, my back ramming painfully into the faucet. "I made soup. Dax is already scarfing it down. Better hurry if you want to get any."

"Yeah." Lorcan cleared the heaviness in his throat, scouring his face. "We'll be right there."

Dom's footsteps went back down the hall. I didn't move. My gaze had shifted to my toes under the water. *What did I just do?* Acid filled my stomach, torching and corroding.

Lorcan swore again, but this time his words dripped with contempt and fury. He heaved himself out of the tub, the water splashing out the side. He ripped a towel off the rack and without even a glance, stormed out of the room, slamming the door so brutally the frame cracked. He stomped down the hall before another door banged, shaking the house.

A sob curdled in my throat, and I grappled for breath. I felt disgusted. Shamed. Guilty. Dirty. My mind kept throwing up images of Jared. All the sweet moments we had, the tender way he looked at me. The hurt in his eyes if he learned what I did. The torture was too much, tears broke out, hiccupping in my chest.

Whatever was going on with me needed to stop. This was not me. I didn't do stuff like this. I was so off kilter and confused lately. I was disintegrating, bits of my former self tumbling out into space. The visions, being kidnapped, missing my friends and boyfriend—it was all contributing to these insane behaviors. Right?

I was not attracted to Lorcan. I had been curious. Nothing more.

That was the only answer. I wouldn't accept anything else.

EIGHT

The vast empty space chilled my bones. My aching muscles shivered. I was exhausted, my body still recovering from a reduced body temperature and heart rate. I went to bed right after dinner, rolled into a ball, and fell sound asleep.

When Lorcan woke me, it felt like I'd scarcely closed my lids, and my body ached like the time Ember talked me into taking a boot camp class. Still haven't forgiven her for that one.

We didn't speak till later in the morning when we moved locations. It was only the basics like: "Do you have everything?" or "Stay close." His mood was neutral, which frustrated me more than a display of emotion. I couldn't figure him out. Just when I thought I had, he would do something to change my opinion again. I wanted him to be cruel. It would be easier for me to loathe him in return. He never seemed to do what I wanted.

"Come on." He steered me into our new lodgings with a hand on my shoulder. Samantha had found an empty building near Idaho or Wyoming. It didn't really matter to me where we were anymore. All the places were blurring into a collection of nondescript accommodations, vacant cabins or warehouses, always situated next to a forest to disappear into if need be.

Stepping through the large space, I spotted several filthy mattresses, which probably had rats and bugs living in them. But besides the empty bottles of booze scattered around, there wasn't much else. Samantha said this one was used as a "safe house" for fae. Smugglers and pirates used it a lot, trading black-market items.

"I'll do a run on the south side." Dax addressed his alpha.

Lorcan nodded, his gaze darting over the room with unease. He was nervous. His feet and hands fidgeted. His nervousness made me uneasy. "Dom can circle the other way. Even though this is supposedly a safe house, there is a main Otherworld door not too far from here in the Grand Tetons."

"You think we should leave?" Dax adjusted the knives strapped to his back, glancing around like we were about to be attacked.

Lorcan pinched his mouth together, then slowly shook his head. "We'll stay tonight, but no longer." He turned to Samantha and instructed her to get supplies and return swiftly.

She nodded and left, Dom and Dax following behind her. The silence curdled and clotted the air like sour cream.

"Let's get to work," he said, his voice echoing off the rafters. My gaze roamed over him as he strode for the door, his back taut and hunched forward.

I had *touched* him, been naked in a bath with him, and now he'd put me in some kind of box and shoved me away. The memory was there, brushing the edges, but I wouldn't let it out in the full light of day. It felt as if I really analyzed what transpired, it would blind me...or kill me.

I wanted to forget it. Why couldn't today be the one time he gave me a day off? I needed space from him, from what happened.

"Now, Kennedy," he grumbled over his shoulder, walking through the door.

I sighed and followed him out. This was going to be a long day.

~~~~

"What the hell is wrong with you today?" Lorcan scratched his scruff, his lids narrowing on me. "You had this spell down yesterday."

I brushed my hair off my face with annoyance, sweat dampening my forehead. "I'm trying."

"No, you're not," he huffed, stomping up to me. "Are you trying to piss me off?"

"What? No."

"Is that what this is about?" He loomed over me, his arms folded. "Get back at me? You all pissy because of what happened?"

My mouth parted, the shock of his blunt words transforming sharply into fury. I shoved up my glasses, gritting my teeth. "As much as you'd like to think the world orbits around you, it doesn't. You think everything is about you." My finger went to his chest. "You are the most self-absorbed, egotistical, narcissistic *asshole* I have ever met!"

He blinked.

Silence.

Uh. Did I just tell off a dark dweller? I never swore, but wow had that felt good.

He tilted his head, watching me. Nerves along his jaw twitched. The high from my outburst wilted like a drying flower.

Crap. He was angry. "I'm sorry. I didn't—"

"Stop," he cut me off, leaning farther over me, the side of his mouth hooking up in a grin. "You *did* mean it. Don't take it back. Do not apologize for what you feel." His eyes glinted with humor. "And it was frickin' hilarious. You swearing? Kinda hot."

I inhaled. "And deserved." I glared at him, my arms folding into a barricade between us.

"That too." He smirked and stood straighter. "Maybe now you can actually do some magic? Got that gigantic tree out of your ass you've been growing since last night."

"What?" My mouth dropped. "Me?"

"Stop overthinking it, Ken. Nothing happened." He let his shoulders drop back.

"Nothing happened?" I held out my arms. "In some cultures what I did would get my head chopped off."

"And in some it's how they say hello."

I snickered. "And what culture is that?"

"Uh. The dark dweller one." He grinned.

I started to laugh, the tension chipping away. His smile widened, and he put his hands on my shoulders, shaking me, loosening my muscles. "Better now?"

I nodded, exhaling the rest of my hostility. It wasn't in my nature to be mad at people. It stressed me out.

"Okay, let's get to work. I want to advance the challenging spell, eventually get you into breaking spells. Samhain is coming; we have no time to waste."

Lorcan and I worked till I was so tired he had to spoon-feed me dinner. I passed out straight away, drained from the last couple of days and grateful for the darkness to cradle me.

~~~~~

A hand fastened over my mouth, jolting me out of sleep. A dark figure loomed over me. A scream gurgled in my throat, fear shooting up my veins in a rush of adrenaline.

"Don't make a sound," a familiar voice whispered into my ear.

I blinked a few times until the initial shock eased enough to make out the vibrant green eyes staring down at me. Lorcan. Tension throbbed off his taut silhouette in surges. I instinctively nodded, sensing his anxiety, though my mind rolled with questions.

He grabbed my arm, helping me to my feet. His body heat soaked into me as he pulled me in tighter to him.

"The Queen's men have found us." His lips brushed my earlobe, sending a shiver down my neck, but I jerked to look at him. "We need to run."

The Queen? My eyes widened with questions and terror. How did they find us? Why would they come looking for us anyway? Was she after Lorcan for betraying her?

In the distance a squeak of a door from across the building opened and terror gushed up my throat like a hose.

"Shit." Lorcan grabbed my hand, swung me around, and tugged me toward the opposite end of the building. At a bang to our right from a side door, Lorcan twisted in a different direction. I glanced over my shoulder and bit down on my lip to keep my gasp inside.

More than a dozen men dressed in the Queen's tunic tunneled through the door, each one holding some kind of weapon: bows and arrows, sticks covered in spikes, swords.

The door where Lorcan pulled me whipped open, stopping us dead in our tracks. Soldiers poured through. Lorcan's head circled around frantically. They came at us from every exit.

Trapped. Dread locked my chest. My brain sought order in the jumbled chaos.

A.) Fight.

B.) Negotiate.

C.) Pee my pants.

Sadly option C was looking like the most likely as the guards descended on us. Lorcan growled, the vibration sending shock waves into my hand. His shoulders rolled forward, his jacket straining, his body growing into the beast.

Dark dwellers were killers, but I didn't think he could take on forty soldiers holding fae weapons.

"No." I squeezed his hand. "Stay with me. Please," I pleaded.

His gaze snapped down to me, pupils vertical, irises flashing red. He inhaled through his nose and turned his face back to the men, his chest pushed back.

Through my fear, I felt relief. Happy he agreed to stay by my side. It was natural for them to fight. To kill. This had to be going against every impulse.

It was in that moment I realized my enemy had become my ally. An unsettling thought. But my hand stayed clutched to his, needing his presence.

My brain wondered briefly where Dominic, Dax, and Samantha were, knowing they took turns keeping guard at night. It was odd for all them to be missing at once.

A brown-haired fay moved up to us, a smirk on his face. Fay were the elite group of fae, and like a typical fairy, he was beautiful: crystal clear violet-blue eyes, clean shaven, high cheekbones and a cleft chin with full lips. But I knew beauty was only surface deep, especially with this man. I had met him before when I was prisoner. He was the captain of the guards, the general only under the First Knight, which used to be Torin's role.

"Quilliam." Lorcan's voice broke my train of thought, returning my focus to the moment. "I'd say it was good to see you, but we both know that would be a lie."

Quilliam's lids fluttered.

"But it seems you have missed me." Lorcan dropped my hand, moving in front of me. I glanced over at the men behind me, only about six feet from touching us. "Or does the psychotic bitch desire me back? I've heard she likes beasts in and out of the bedroom." Lorcan clicked his tongue. "Still in a guard's outfit I see. Not enough for her, Quilliam?"

He growled. "I may not wear the uniform now, but I am really her First Knight."

"So just her plaything, then. It's okay, you can be honest here."

"That pubescent human boy, Josh, has no idea he is playing a fay game. He's her toy. Soon he will find out she's only been using him. Stroking his ego so he'd turn on his own friend and steal the sword right from under them."

What? Steal the sword? Josh was her First Knight? My brain couldn't unravel Quilliam's statement. Josh had been with us in Greece. Helping us. He was Ember's friend and sort of mine. He'd been held captive with me in Aneira's castle. Granted, there was something I never completely trusted about him. He seemed way too enthralled with the Queen even when she was holding us prisoner. But it didn't make sense. Would he really betray Ember? She had trusted him.

"Josh stole the sword?"

"Delivered the damn dae along with it. You guys lost…as usual."

Oh my god. Ember was taken back by the Queen?

"And how giddy I got when Her Majesty sliced your brother's throat right in front of me."

Lorcan jerked and something flashed in his eyes, like he was recalling a memory.

"Dead...those few minutes before that disgrace brought him back were almost the best of my life. Only would have been better if it was you."

Lorcan sucked in. A strained expression flinched a nerve in his cheek. It flittered quickly over his face before it was gone again.

"So that's why you are here? To kill me?" Lorcan cocked an eyebrow. "Is that the biggest your dream gets? Fuckin' pathetic, Q."

Fury blotched Quilliam's cheeks. With his right hand, he gripped the handle of his sword, which hung from his left side. He took a step. Then a smile curled his mouth, chilling my bones as effectively as the snow that nearly killed me the other night.

"Neither Her Majesty nor I could care less about you, dweller." Quilliam tilted his head, his gaze roaming over me. "I came for her."

Me?

Lorcan stiffened, slowly craning his neck to look at me, then back to Quilliam.

"But the Queen *does* request we kill you." Quilliam took another step, forcing Lorcan to press back into me. "But only because you are in the way of what she really wants. The Druid." His piercing blue eyes dug into me and terror shot through my body.

Like a finger curled around my lungs, I felt my breath halt in my chest. *Oh. My. God.* She knew about me. What I was. How she found out I wasn't sure, but if Josh was under her thrall, it was most likely him. He had been there every day when I trained at Camp Dweller. He knew what I was.

The sound of Quilliam unsheathing his sword hit my eardrums. Lorcan's body curled, his stance widening, a roar tearing through his teeth.

It was like someone hit the play button. Everyone unfroze and in a blink came for us. My gaze snapped to the armed soldiers heading directly for Lorcan, going first after the true threat.

Fear caught in my throat, freezing me. Banging noises splintered across the room as sleek black beasts burst through each door, coming behind the groups of fay, attacking.

Hands grabbed me from the back, my throat belting out screams, my body wiggling violently against the Queen's men. I was no fighter. Not like Ember. But adrenaline kicked in, my elbows smashing into anything behind me.

"Ken!" I heard Lorcan yell, trying to get to me, but weapons swung for him, creating an obstacle course between us as he dealt with the abundance of men on him. He didn't fully shift to his beast, but I saw his hand curve into claws, his nails slicing through a group like a cheese plate.

Screams exploded from the edges of the fay. The other dwellers shredded flesh and crunched bone, working their way through the throng.

We were still outnumbered.

I stopped my struggle at the sensation of steel across my neck. A huge knife with ridged edges pressed against my throat. "Don't move, Druid. She said she wanted you alive but didn't say if it was barely." A beautiful voice resonated in my ear from behind, his brutal words contradicting the tone.

A bellow rang out, men parted enough in front of me to see a knife dig deep into Lorcan's side.

"Lorcan!" I screamed, watching blood squirt out in gushes. The sword bit at my neck as I tried to move to him.

"No, you don't." The fairy behind clutched the back of my neck, dragging me away. Away from Lorcan.

Something snapped inside me. I didn't even think. The defensive spell came to my lips as easy as breathing. Latin words shot from my lips with venom. Power bubbled around the sound and burst forward like an atomic bomb, rushing the air out with explosive force as it slammed into everyone orbiting me.

Bodies bent over like they had been sucker-punched and flew back, sliding, rolling, and crashing into equipment, walls, and each other.

I gaped, shocked at what I did, at seeing everyone on the ground. A ring of figures circled me, as if I were the center. The sun. It was a few seconds before they started to stir.

Kennedy. Run. A part of me thought about running. Even from Lorcan. But another part, a larger one, didn't want to leave him. I needed him. *It's because of the promise. I couldn't run from him, anyway.* My brain came back, my own words sounding defensive.

"Lorcan!" I bellowed, my legs already turning for the nearest door. He jumped up, stumbling a bit, as if he still wasn't sure which way was up.

Quilliam grunted and rolled to sitting, shaking his head.

I had no time and sprinted over to Lorcan, grabbed his hand, which thankfully was back to human shape, and yanked him behind me. He slowed at seeing his clan on the ground.

"Dax!" Lorcan beckoned to his second, his legs still wobbly. Dax's beast shot up to his feet, their eyes connecting. The buzz of energy told me Lorcan was speaking to him through their link.

I pushed through the door, leading out to the crisp evening, the night still far from dawn. The moment we were outside, Lorcan took the lead, his legs moving faster than mine.

He didn't say a word as the door clicked shut behind us. I turned thinking I'd see Dax, but no one followed. We were only about a hundred yards away when I heard the screams.

Shrieks of death. Dark dwellers feasting on fairy flesh. I didn't ask what Lorcan ordered Dax to do. I didn't have to. The Queen was going to lose a lot of men tonight.

In the stillness of night, we ran through the darkness, my hand still wrapped in Lorcan's.

The Queen was hunting me. The game had changed.

~~~~~

Lorcan didn't want to chance the doors, afraid they'd be crawling with the Queen's soldiers. We ran until he had to carry me, pushing until the sun hovered at the horizon. We only paused long enough for me to help heal his deep stab wound faster.

Stacey Marie Brown

He found another vacated fishing cabin somewhere in the Rocky Mountains. It was tinier than the first one we had been in, with only a bed and lounge chair in the one-room cabin.

"I was really hoping the Queen would never find out about you." He tossed his backpack on the single bed. "Shit, this complicates everything. We have to keep moving. We can rest till the sun goes down. Then we move out."

I sat on the bed, exhausted, but my mind buzzed with what happened.

"Where are Dax and the others?"

Lorcan walked to the fridge and opened it.

"We're splitting up for now. With the Queen out for you now, we need to keep an even lower profile. We're stealthy, but we hold a lot of magic. Altogether, I'm afraid Aneira will find us easier." He grabbed a can of Coke, frowning at it. "Of course we had to find the one cabin whose owner's a fuckin' teetotaler."

I knew it was not my fault, but I felt being the "last-known Druid" was a huge burden to everyone and everything I touched.

"I'm sorry." My hands twisted in my lap.

Lorcan's neck cranked to me. "Why are you sorry?"

"Having to split with your family." I sighed, glancing out the window. "When you took me, you didn't know what you were getting yourself into, huh?"

"Kennedy." He said my name like a scold. "Look at me."

I rolled my head his way.

"Do you hear yourself right now?" He strolled over.

"You are apologizing to the guy who kidnapped you for making *his* life inconvenient." He cracked open the soda, took a swig, and raised an eyebrow.

"I've hit a new level of pathetic, haven't I?" I cringed, touching my forehead.

He crouched down, pulling my hand away, his face even with mine.

"You are not pathetic. You are extremely sensitive and kind. Probably too much so." He glanced back and forth between my eyes. "And you probably know by now I'm the kind of guy who likes things a bit difficult. There isn't anything I won't battle or do to keep you safe."

"Wow," I whispered, my voice failing me. "My Druid magic is incredibly grateful. Glad I get to come along with it."

A ghost of a grin hinted on his mouth as he stood, handing me the soda can.

"Rest. I'll wake you up when we need to leave."

I gripped the can and nodded, watching him head for the front door, probably to keep watch like my very own guard dog.

"And Ken?" He swung the door open, stepping out. "I said there wasn't anything I wouldn't do to keep *you* safe...not your magic."

He slammed the door, leaving me gaping at the closed door.

NINE

When I woke up, the sun grazed the horizon and shadowed the tiny cabin. Noise from the bathroom drew me out of my slumber. The door stood open, and I pushed off the bed, my feet padding across the wood floor.

I came to the doorway and stopped. Lorcan's unclothed back faced me. Droplets of water sprinkled across his skin, like he'd scarcely gotten out of the shower. Tattoo and muscles rippled as he tugged on a T-shirt. His back was so defined and strong, but my gaze caught on something else crisscrossing his skin. I had seen him naked several times but realized I had never really observed his back in detail.

Deep scars lined his back in rough trenches, like barbed wire had been dragged across his skin over and over. Ridges, valleys, and healed wounds varied. My hand went to my mouth too late, as I'd already gasped.

Lorcan jerked his head to look at me. When he saw me, his body stiffened. He tugged his shirt down, covering his scars, and turned away from me. He said nothing, leaving my mind bustling with curiosity.

"What are those from?" My voice softly bounced around the walls.

"Being a dark dweller is tough on the body." He shoved his dirty shirt in his bag on the sink. Something in his tone, the way his vocals strained at the end, told me he was lying. Or at least not telling me the full truth.

I pressed my lips together, the room filling with silence. It grew around us, expanding into every crevice. My mother instilled the habit of stillness in me; it was unconscious now. Silence would pressure anyone to confess or babble eventually, trying to fill the void. The longer you were quiet, the more likely the other person would talk. She did it to those on the stand in court, to me, my sister, and father when she knew we had done something wrong.

I waited patiently, pretty sure he was aware I sensed he was keeping something from me.

He sighed, zipping up his bag, then dropped his head forward with irritation. "It's nothing you need to know about."

"Why?"

He snorted. "You don't want to know about half of things done to me or I've done. I'm a killer, Kennedy." He swung around, his eyes narrowed. "Do you expect you are going to dig and find a diamond in the rough with me? You're not. I'm as bad as everyone thinks...and I'm okay with that. So stop thinking I can be redeemed or some shit." He lifted the bag on his shoulder. "Come on," he mumbled, pushing past me, entering the main room.

"No," my voice rang out, halting him in his tracks. "I don't believe you for a second. You can tell yourself whatever you want. Others might believe it, but I don't."

"Haven't you heard actions speak louder than words?" he said over his shoulder.

"Exactly," I responded. He'd done nothing but protect me, risk his life to defend mine. He'd helped me grow as a Druid, demanded me to be my best, and pushed me past my comfort zones. Ian still twisted in my soul, but Lorcan's confession that he hadn't meant to hurt him eased it a bit.

He wasn't all good; not even close. I was fully aware of that. His crimes were far too great, but I still couldn't stop my feet from shuffling forward. My hand reached for his shirt, tugging it up.

Lorcan's muscles constricted, but he didn't pull away, which encouraged me to continue. Being this forward was so unlike me. Time in his presence, and the more he challenged me, gave me a new confidence I had never held. Normally someone like him would have made me nervous and insecure, but instead I stepped up, facing his strength with my own.

My hands pushed up the fabric higher, displaying the channels and ridges of scarred flesh. My heart sank like a floundering ship. He had been whipped. The lashes across his back were too numerous and straight in their design to be anything else. Acid curled around my stomach, sizzling at the edges.

Lightly, I touched his skin, causing him to jerk under my touch, but he still didn't move away. His breath hitched at my contact. Slowly, I began to trace the wounds, the tips of my fingers gliding down each one like I was finger painting.

His muscles flexed beneath his skin and grew hot under my hand, stealing the air from my lungs. My mind became blurry, so I did not recognize the shift in the room or the way my heart pounded in my chest. Heat rose through my belly to my face.

Stop touching him. Stop touching him now. Logic demanded of me, but my fingers continued to follow the rough, traumatized skin.

Lorcan's head twisted even more to peer at me over his shoulder. I felt his green eyes piercing me, scorching. I couldn't meet his gaze; I knew there would be a question in it. One I could not answer. Tangled sensations I was not ready to acknowledge clogged my chest.

"Tell me," I whispered.

Through my lashes, I watched his Adam's apple bob as he swallowed, his hands squeezing into fists.

"Please." The word was barely audible.

He sucked in a raspy breath, his shoulder blades shifting under his skin. I was consumed by the sudden desire to spread both my palms across his back, to feel and explore every taut muscle in his back. His jeans hung low enough to see the definition of his lower back as it dipped to his rear.

My throat tightened, and tingling heat poured over me in waves, making me dizzy. Squeezing my lids shut, I fought back the need to keep exploring, going past where the scars were, and way beyond where I should. I had already stepped way over the line with him, and I couldn't figure out why. Why I kept finding myself here. Why I was drawn to him, wanting to touch him.

"Ken..." Lorcan breathed out, jolting my eyes open. The way he said my name, the thickness in his throat, zapped me like an electrical fence. I yanked my hands away, stepping back.

Our shallow breaths bounced off the walls, echoing in my ears. Like being tossed in a freezing lake, clarity shocked me back to reason. Worms of guilt wiggled into my chest. I crossed my arms.

"They're from the Queen." Sadness clipped his tone.

My head shot up. "What?"

Lorcan's gaze collided into mine. "What I told you earlier was true. I was never really in cahoots with Aneira. I planned to use her, but I underestimated her power and how she could control me. Her glamour is nothing I had experienced before." He shifted around to face me, running a hand over his shaved head. "And let's say she didn't take my deceit kindly. Not that it would have stopped her anyway. She enjoys torture like it is sex."

"She did that to you?" I gulped.

"Personally and repeatedly." Lorcan folded his arms, keeping his gaze on me. "She's known to keep her victims locked in her chamber so she readily has them at hand to abuse when the urge strikes her."

"Did she...lock you up?" My body grew heavy at the idea of Aneira hurting him, doing other things with him.

"No." His expression grew dark. "Because I wanted her to."

"What?" My mouth fell open. "You wanted her to torture you?"

"I wanted to be in the castle." He rubbed the scruff along his jawbone and looked away from me. "I needed to get my brother out. To save West...shit." He dug the heels of his hands into his eyes. "West is there because of me. Because he trusted me, like he always did. She caught him, told me to take Ember or West would get the punishment of my failure." Lorcan sucked in a shaky breath.

"That's the reason you took Ryan, Josh, and me? To get Ember...so you could save West from Aneira?" *Holy shit.*

Lorcan's mouth compressed as he glanced away from me, the truth written all over his face. Another wave of understanding thumped down on my head. His actions were wrong, trading Ember to be Aneira's prisoner instead of West, but I understood. Desperation to get his brother and his family free of the Queen's brutality had driven his actions.

Lorcan stood in front of me, but it was as though a different guy was in his place. My eyes opened wider to his character.

"I let him down. He trusted...believed in me." A shudder ran through Lorcan. "Knowing what she did to me... I can't imagine the pain he is going through. What she's doing to him. What will happen to him being on the Light side too long...the curse..." Anger clipped his words and he swiveled away, pacing the room.

"Curse?" I tilted my head. For some reason I didn't

think he was talking about the one which barred them from the Otherworld.

"I'm not sorry for abducting you. For trying to get him free from her. I was only thinking of my brother." He shook his head, his voice going cold. "But things didn't go the way I hoped."

"Why did she let you go?"

Lorcan gave a humorless chuckle. "Because what she did was far worse."

My chest and throat knotted until I could barely swallow. Ember never said, but she hinted enough at what Aneira did to Torin. Not solely physical abuse, but mental and sexual. Sick, demented stuff.

"Did she...?" I cleared my throat, not knowing how to finish the sentence.

"Fuck me?" Lorcan curved up his eyebrows.

I nodded, not able to look at him.

"No." He curled his hand around the back of his neck. "Is it deeply twisted to feel slightly offended? What, I wasn't hot enough?" He held out his arms, trying to lighten the mood.

I couldn't help the laugh bursting from me. "I don't think that was the issue." I shook my head, my long hair jiggling around my face.

Lorcan was past hot. He stopped you in your tracks. The exact type of guy I didn't even have to avoid because I did not exist on their radar. Lorcan was eons more attractive than the models I saw in magazines— sexy, rugged, primal, raw, and untouchable.

Jared was the only one of the brothers who was half human, which made him feel more real, more tangible, as if he were tethered to the earth. The man who stood before me was not. He was far out of my realm or the next one over.

He dropped his arms, the brief amusement deflating from his face.

"What did she do that was worse?" I asked, afraid of what he would say. What could be worse than being tortured and raped?

Lorcan lifted his head, grief flickering through his eyes. "What no one knows, except my pack, is not only did Aneira ban us from the Otherworld, but she cursed us from returning. If we find a way through the doors and go back...our own world will kill us. Dark or Light side, it tears us apart. Rips the dweller from our body. It's slow and utterly excruciating. It is what's happening to West right now."

"Oh my god." I touched my throat. "So even though you can go through the doors, you can't stay? But West... he has been there this whole time."

"Yeah. I know." Agony flicked at the corners of his eyes.

"What will happen to him?"

"I don't know. The fact he still is alive. More than a day or two and the pain becomes so unbearable it feels like my essence, my beast, is being torn from my body. The magic is thick."

I understood what he was saying, but I needed to grasp its power for myself. Research the facts. "Can I?" I wiggled my fingers. "See the curse?"

He nodded, opening his arms.

My tongue curled around the invocation, the revealing spell coming easy to my lips. The magic knocked into him, but he stayed in place, absorbing the burst. The magic swirled around him, exposing the dark enchantment under his skin. My seer sight took in the thick, greasy fog tangling through him, climbing his spine like a vine, alive and pure evil.

My mouth fell open. I had never seen or felt anything so strong and malicious. The Queen's signature was stained all over it.

"Every day West spends there, it literally is shredding his soul from him. His beast. It's why I fought to stay, to be down in the dungeon with him. To save him or take his spot. Aneira saw through me and let me go."

I cocked my head, aware Aneira was not the type to simply let him go. Not without making sure he suffered for his duplicity.

Lorcan smirked unhappily.

"What did she do, Lorcan?"

"What you see. It's not only one curse, but two. She afflicted me and my bloodline. If one of us dies, the others follow." Sorrow rolled his jaw and reflected in his irises. "Said it was only fair. I killed her family, she would take mine away."

"Eli," I muttered, feeling his grief deep in my bones. The hazy glimmer of a vision I had brushed against my mind. Eli's throat cut...Lorcan dying. "I think I saw that. In a vision...but why did I see Cole as well?"

An odd grimace wiggled his mouth.

"Because it wouldn't only be Eli."

"What do you mean not just Eli?" My eyes widened. As far as I knew Eli was Lorcan's only living relative. Lorcan began to wander around, his shoulders tight and defensive. He was not someone who talked about himself or anything, really.

"Lorcan?" I took a minuscule step forward.

"Why do you care?" He whipped around, startling me. "Have you put some Druid spell on me that makes me blab to you like a teenage girl?" He hugged himself as though warding himself against me. "I don't need to tell you shit. You are my prisoner, not my fuckin' therapist."

The Kennedy before would have slunk back, quivering under his wrath. Only a few weeks ago, he could turn me into a butterball of fear. When did it stop? I didn't remember, but his outburst only made me suck in a deep breath and take another tread closer to him. "If you feel better paying me as your therapist, then go right ahead. I'm comfortable taking your money."

His gaze snapped to me, roaming over my face before a grin cracked his mouth. A soft chuckle rumbled out as his smile grew over his striking features. The way his eyes roamed over me, glinting with mischief, ignited flames in my belly, boiling logic right out of my head. Nervously I tucked a piece of hair behind my ear, staring at the floor.

I had never been that girl. I rolled my eyes at girls who became giggling messes around a cute boy. Especially because normally the boy was dumb as a brick and said the stupidest stuff. But the girls would flip their hair and laugh at whatever he said. It made me cringe. The guy whose favorite subject was PE was not the boy I liked, always preferring the one working on experiments during lunch. The geeky one who liked science and math. It was why I fell for Jared. He was so geeky and sweet. He was gorgeous, but his nerdiness kept me from really noticing. We were a perfect match.

So why was my heart pounding in my chest now? Why did heat swell in my stomach and dip between my thighs? I was in love with Jared yet Lorcan was primal. It was natural to feel the abundance of sexuality bounding off him. To be affected. It was chemical. A scientific reason my body reacted to his.

Then why didn't you ever feel this way around Jared or any other dark dweller? A voice taunted me. *Why does the graze of Lorcan's fingers stir desire through you?*

I gritted my teeth, pushing the thoughts from my head.

His hand lifted, tucking another strand behind the opposite ear.

My lungs constricted.

Dammit squared.

I should not react this way. Stepping back, I strove to put distance between us. It was the only way I seemed to think clearly lately.

Not backing down, I folded my arms, returning to the subject. "What do you mean not only Eli?" My gut already sensed what I felt was coming, but I needed him to say it to me.

He smirked, bobbing his head like he understood why I backed up. "Not going to let this go, huh?"

"Nope."

"No one knows." He stroked the back of his neck again. "I'm not even supposed to know, but my father's cheating ways were blatant. He stopped even hiding it from my mother. She didn't seem to care as long as she stayed the alpha at his side." He rubbed his face—a habit of his. "I followed him one night. Saw where he was going. I was really young, but I understood enough the sounds coming from the hut. My father had sent out his second-in-command, her husband, earlier that day on a mission."

Lorcan moved across the room. "I overheard them talking about Cole. My father said something like he was happy Cole had taken after her so no one would know. It was like a punch to the gut. I knew Cole was his. I kept the secret, pretending he had no connection to us. As a kid he really didn't look like my father…but he also didn't look like the man who was supposed to be his real father. Years went by and, as much as I tried to deny it, it was in the way my father treated him, little jabs from my mother, and the continued affair with his mother. Cole shared little mannerisms so much like my father.

"And I hated Cole for it. Like it was his fault." Lorcan twisted his fingers together. "I've blamed and hated him my whole life, especially when we were banned here and he became our leader. My loathing was sealed when he chose Eli over me as his second."

"Are you sure? Cole, Owen, and Jared look—"

"Like their mother," Lorcan replied. "Their father was blond with bright blue eyes. None of them resemble him."

"Is Owen your half-brother?"

"No. I don't think so." Lorcan stuffed his hands in his jeans. "When Eli was just a baby, I woke up to my parents fighting. She mentioned his 'other' son. Not plural. I knew she wasn't talking about either me or Eli. I don't think their affair started till after Owen was born."

"Wow." I ran my hand over my hair. "No one knows? Not even Eli or Cole?"

"Cole might sense it, but I don't think he knows for sure."

"Don't you think they have the right to know?"

"Why?" He shrugged his arms. "What would it change? It would only screw them up. Eli has our parents on a pedestal; he idolizes them. He never saw the truth. When they got killed, Eli seemed to forget every awful thing our father ever did. How cold and unfeeling our mother had been. She had simply looked away every time Father's rage got the best of him and he came after us."

"He beat you?"

Lorcan laughed, running a chill down my spine. "Not all these scars are from the Queen."

"He beat Eli too?"

"No." Lorcan's chest rose as if he were ready to defend an attacker. "I never let the bastard touch him. I would make certain his wrath pointed to me. Every time. I could take it. Eli was only a kid."

Shock held me in place. The man everyone hated because he was cruel, selfish, and unfaithful to his brethren was not the person before me. This man guarded his younger brother from abuse, taking it himself instead. His defiance to Cole was from years of hurt, carrying a truth only he knew. I saw a boy who didn't know how to handle all the secrets and pain he kept inside, lashing out in all the wrong ways. A casualty of something out of his control. Mistakes and deeds done by those who should have loved and protected him. Instead he did the protecting.

"I do not want to take that away from Eli. Our parents are dead. Why not let him remember them in a good light? Nor will I destroy Cole's life. He never needs to know. It would only hurt him."

"That is not for you to decide. You can't shield Eli forever. He needs to know, Lorcan. He needs to understand everything you've done for him. How you've protected him."

"No."

"Why?" I bellowed. "Why are you determined for them to think the worst of you? You are not the man they believe you are."

His jaw clamped, fury setting his shoulders.

"You know what I think?" I didn't give him time to respond. "You prefer them thinking you are heartless and spiteful. Then you don't have to face your own feelings. To acknowledge how hurt you feel, how angry you are...resentful."

"Of course I'm resentful of Cole. My father was leader, I was next in line. I was older...I should have been the next in command. But everyone wanted Cole in this new world. The bastard baby who took my role."

"That's not who I was taking about."

"Eli?" he sputtered. "You think I'm resentful of Eli?"

"Yes. And not because Cole picked him for his second. That only iced the cake for you."

"Shit," he spit out. "You really are a fucking therapist. So tell me, wise one, tell me why I'm a dickhead. Please. I can't wait to hear."

"Because you took every hit for him, sheltered him from your father's wrath." I took a step toward Lorcan. "And how did he repay you? He thinks your parents are saints, while you hold the scars and his animosity."

His body expanded, his shoulders expanding, filling the room. "Watch it," Lorcan seethed through his teeth, barely controlling his rage. I gulped as his boots hit mine, leaning closer. "Eli never knew, and I don't begrudge him. I envy his innocence."

"Emotions don't care about logic. Your mind thinks one thing while..." I placed my palm on his breastbone. "Here? It can't help but feel hurt. You took the abuse while he got by scot-free. And now he looks down on you while he holds your parents high on a pedestal, and Cole too."

Lorcan's body vibrated with anger, his breath choppy, flaring through his nostrils. I was scared, but I locked my legs and backbone, not cowering away from his lethal gaze.

He grabbed my arms, pushing me against the wall, making me gasp. The dark dweller leaned over me, his lips so close breath tickled down my neck as my pulse jacked up. This terror lumping in my stomach had nothing to do with him harming me, but my heart hammered in my chest, unable to move or retrieve oxygen.

Lorcan tipped closer to me, stealing all my air. His mouth grazed my cheek, dipping to my ear. "You can keep digging. You aren't gonna find a good man underneath," he whispered huskily, forcing me to gulp. "I kill with desire. Fuck with violence. I'm exceptional at both. Don't for one moment think I'm anything more, li'l Druid."

In a blink he was gone. My skin suddenly chilled from the absence of his body pressed against mine. He strutted over to his bag, picked it up, and proceeded out of the cabin without looking back.

I couldn't move as my lungs tried to catch their breath.

A spurt of anger flamed up my back. I hated the way he could twist me. It wasn't right. I shouldn't be reacting to him so strongly. Everything was wrong with it. He was vile, and I needed to stop looking and see what everyone else saw.

Jared was waiting for me, worried sick. I would not indulge this need to figure out Lorcan. I huffed and grabbed my bag.

The moment he left the room, I realized I had been so caught up with finding out Cole was the Dragens' half-brother I hadn't asked about the other curse Aneira put on him.

If one died...they all died.

"Lorcan!" I called after him, my feet following him outside, running to where he stood. "Wait."

I came to a screeching halt, terror syphoning my oxygen as the scene before my eyes turned into a full-blown nightmare.

Oh. My. God.

The strighoul had found us.

Dozens of them stood before us, their razor teeth glistening from the moonlight. Each dressed in a montage of clothing, some with boas and costumes, others looking like homeless yuppies. The clothing would have been amusing on humans, but it only enhanced their frightening, wild, and boorish appearance.

Strighoul were the bottom feeders of the Otherworld. They primarily lived off consuming fae. Humans didn't give them as much of a rush, but they weren't choosy when the pickings were slim. They didn't only suck blood, they dined on you like a steak. While consuming the flesh and organs, they took on powers or energy from their victims.

Not a welcome sight at all.

"The only reason I can think why you're here is either you have a crush on me and simply can't admit it. Or…" Lorcan's arms spread out, pushing me behind him. "You're still working with the Queen. You're still her bitch?"

Queen? Why would the strighoul be working for the Queen? And what did he mean by *still*?

"Don't hide that tasty morsel from me." One of them stepped forward. He was dressed in a faux fur vest with a worn long-sleeved shirt underneath, Bermuda shorts, and cowboy boots. His hideous scarred face, patchy skin, and sharp features looked like Dr. Frankenstein had put him together. His red beady eyes landed on me, roving down my body salaciously. He licked his lips, rubbing his belly. "She might be tiny, but I can tell from here she'd be the best dinner I've had in a long time. Gourmet."

"You aren't going to touch her." Lorcan's body went rigid, his hand pushing harder into my thigh. I didn't budge, the need to stand beside him was stronger than my desire to let him shield me. That didn't stop the almost paralyzing fear dripping in my stomach like a coffee maker. There were dozens of them and two of us. He couldn't protect me from all of them as they horseshoed around, trapping us.

"I'm not?" The leader smirked, flashing his teeth again. "It's only you, dweller. I think I can take you."

"I still like my chances." Lorcan's thumb circled in soothing motions against my thigh. I was pretty sure he was unaware he was doing it, but it steadied my galloping heartbeat a bit. "Remember, I know what you assholes are capable of. Especially a third-rate strighoul like you, Hovek. You get a promotion, or did you just dress up for me again?"

"Fuck you, Dragen." The strighoul furrowed the place on his face where eyebrows should have wrinkled. "I should have killed you in Greece. You and your brother would have been the highlight of the job."

Something about their conversation didn't sit right with me. Lorcan had hired them to attack *us* in Greece, right? Why would the strighoul kill their benefactor?

"Missed opportunity." Lorcan shrugged.

Replaying the scene of the cave in my head, my head jerked up to look at him, my mouth dropping open. I felt as startled as if a bolt of lightning struck me. Here was another revelation about Lorcan I knew in my soul. My seer saw past all the masks. The truth dangled before me.

"You didn't hire them to attack us?" I stuttered over this new truth. "Did you?"

Lorcan glanced at me, his jaw rolling, his eyes telling me to be quiet.

Hovek let out a howl of chilling laughter. "You think we were there because of him?" He motioned to Lorcan, his lip curling up in a snarl. "This piece of crap couldn't offer us anything we'd want...except you. Or the dae."

I couldn't break my gaze off Lorcan. Was anything I believed about him true?

"Not the time," he muttered.

"But you didn't—"

"No." He gritted his teeth. "They were already there.

I jumped ahead. Used the opportunity to my advantage. But I didn't hire the strighoul to hurt my family. They were there on the Queen's orders. Not mine."

"Holy shit." Twice tonight he had me swearing.

All of us had it so wrong. We assumed Lorcan had set us up. We blamed him. Granted, he still used their attack for his benefit, but the truth was vastly different. When I accused him, he took the blame. Didn't steer my view of him. He let me believe he was capable of something like that. He let everyone think the worst of him at every opportunity.

Lorcan turned his attention back onto the strighoul, spreading his feet in a wider stance. "Tracking down a human and a predator that can rip you into shreds isn't something you would do…unless there is a huge benefit in it for you. The Queen pulling your dog collar again?"

"You're right. We don't work for free. Neither did the dark dwellers at one time…when you used to be highly regarded." The flesh-eating monster chuckled, a chilling noise, like metal grinding against metal. "But we all know she isn't any ordinary human." He pointed at me. Anxiety iced the back of my neck. Bile crawled up my throat.

Heat curled off Lorcan, his nails digging into my leg like a pitchfork. I could barely feel the pain, adrenaline pumping so hard it numbed my body. It actually centered me and stilled the panic fluttering in my lungs.

"I promise you unimaginable pain if you touch her," Lorcan growled, his voice sounding less human.

"To taste that flesh. To tear into her. A *Druid*," Hovek said the word dreamily. "That kind of power…" A glaze coated the leader's eyes, his tongue slithered out, swiping over his hundreds of needle teeth. The group around us stirred, smacking their lips and grunting with the urge to gorge on me.

My head darted around, my lungs clenching with frantic breaths. He could do a lot of damage in a short period of time with magic like mine.

"The price for her head and the other girl's…" Hovek rubbed his hands together. "The reward is worth forgoing eating her right here."

"The other girl?" I heard myself stammer with a sinking feeling.

"The dae," Hovek snarled. "Vek, our new leader, is hunting her right now."

"Vek is in control?" Lorcan scoffed. "That's a horrifying thought."

"That fucking dae killed Drauk, our old leader in Greece," Hovek sneered, sending shivers through my skin. "She did me a favor."

"Loyalty is essential with you guys."

"We're as loyal as you are," Hovek jabbed back.

"Why don't you run along now? I promise I will only kill half of your group." Lorcan pulled his claws from my leg, jolting me. His scythes grew longer. Threatening.

Saliva dripped from Hovek's mouth. I swallowed, feeling the other strighoul creeping closer. "We don't stop till we get what we want by whatever means necessary. Your group used to understand and live by the same creed. Now you're simply purring pussies leashed by one." He nodded to me.

"Come here, Hovek, and I'll let you stroke my back." Lorcan's frame bent forward, his T-shirt ripping in two. The lethal spikes on his back shredded the fabric.

"I may have to keep her alive for a bit, but the Queen said nothing about you." Hovek gnashed his teeth.

The air snapped with energy, which I felt to the tips of my toes. A screeching battle cry came from one of the strighoul who had a tiny tuft of hair on its head. The women and men looked so much alike I couldn't tell if it was a girl. Didn't matter. He/she wanted to capture and eat me anyway.

A deep growl rose from Lorcan, his body shifting just enough to give him razor claws and deadly spikes on his back, his eyes blazing red as the strighoul sprang for us, wailing.

Then my sight flashed a blazing white. Bursting colors ignited my brain, driving me to my knees.

NO! But the visions didn't give me a choice when they came.

Flash.

A scene appeared before me. A dark forest. The trees felt familiar, as did the moss coating the rocks, and the way the fog curled around the forest bed. It was home. Piercing shrieks twisted me around as dozens of strighoul ran straight for me. Like I wasn't there, their forms slipped through me, charging past. I cried out and swiveled around to see where they were headed. Instantly I recognized the outline of a girl holding a knife, ready to fight the monsters.

Ember!

The strighoul had found her. Just as they found Lorcan and me.

The scene jumped forward to Ember's body lying on the ground. A strighoul straddled her, strangling out the last bits of life. Blood dripped off his broken mouth onto her face. Ember's jet-black hair with red streaks billowed around her head. Two different-colored eyes stared up at the sky. Life dwindled from her gaze.

She was dying.

I tried to get closer, but my visions only let me observe.

The rest of the group inched forward to help finish her off. A cry bubbled up from my throat but was drowned out. A roar broke through the night, trembling the ground, bouncing off in surround sound, echoing inside my head and out. A black sleek mass barreled through the strighoul and leaped toward Ember's body. Eli's beast moved over her protectively.

"Kennedy!" My name wailed through the air. I jerked my head toward the sound.

My arm burned, like hundreds of fire ants had begun to bite me. I looked down, seeing blood gush down my arm.

"Kennedy. Snap out of it!"

I turned to look at Ember, but she was gone. The scene around me vanished like a burning photograph.

My name rang out again, jolting me back into reality with a gasp.

Flash.

It felt like I had been slapped so hard my body rang, jolting me back into reality.

Strighoul surrounded us. Lorcan slashed through groups of them at a time, but one had reached me, its teeth driving into my arm. I screamed. This was definitely real. I felt every dagger in its mouth breaking my skin, burrowing deep into my flesh, the smell of blood pooling up my nose.

"Just a nibble. Only a tiny nibble." It manically laughed over and over.

My body went in defense, the chant came to my lips without even a thought, spurting energy in a huge dose.

The strighoul's teeth ripped out of my skin as they were flung back. Everyone except me went flying. Lorcan crashed into a group of strighoul, his body lost in the heap of killers.

"Lorcan!" I screamed as teeth and hands clawed at the dark dweller, his howls beating at my chest like a gong. His body was sucked deeper and deeper in the sea of flesh eaters. Like a mix between *Jaws* and a zombie movie, I watched in horror as they devoured him.

My lips rolled to spout the defending spell again, when a deep roar quaked the night and rocked me back on my butt.

Sleek black fur, red eyes, and paws bigger than my head slashed through the horde veiling the beast. Hacked parts of heads, arms, legs, and chunks of flesh spurted out, dropping on the ground, splattering with a sickening heavy wet sound as the beast tore out of the mass.

"Holy..." He was massive and pulsated with tremendous power and fury. The man was gone. He was all animal and would kill without thought. But he was also magnificent. Beautiful in the most deadly way. The beast leaped from the dead bodies, his black fur shining with blood. He curved around, backing closer to me; his eyes remained on the strighoul, a growl vibrating his throat.

The handful of strighoul stopped in their tracks. Lorcan snarled and moved forward like he was going to attack. The group retreated into the trees, but I could still see them, their red eyes watching us from a safe distance.

I scrambled to my feet, tucking my bloody arm to my chest. It pulsed like it had its own heartbeat, but there was no pain. Or I didn't feel it. I actually felt strangely light. My head buoyant, drifting up to the sky, dragging my body along like a kite tail.

Lorcan huffed, drawing my attention to him. His eyes locked on mine. They were still red, but flecks of green splintered through. I saw him then, the man behind the beast. The one who made me feel safe. His nostrils flared as he looked at my arm.

I looked down.

I shouldn't have done that. Blood normally didn't bother me, but my arm wasn't merely bloody. The strighoul's teeth had shredded it. Tendons, muscles, and matter stuck out of my arm, displaying bone underneath.

My head spun, vomit rose up my throat. I didn't even notice when my knees crashed into the dirt, but I knew I had.

"Ken," my name came out garbled as Lorcan shifted back, a naked human body replacing the beast.

In human form he was still a beast. But in a completely different way. Naked Lorcan was just as frightening. He was enormous. Like monster size.

And so, so hot.

"Thanks..." Lorcan crouched down, brushing hair away from my face and straightening my glasses on my nose. "You must be really losing it, li'l Druid, because I know you would never talk so blatantly about a man's package like you did." His eyes glinted. "Especially mine."

Holy shit times a thousand. Had I said that out loud?

"Yes, and you said that out loud too." He grinned, tearing a piece of my shirt and wrapping it around my wounded arm. Then he encircled me in his arms and grabbed his dropped bag. "You're too high to heal yourself right now. You've lost a lot of blood and the toxins from the strighoul's bite are really going to affect you. You are going to be hallucinating for a bit."

My body rose in the air as he stood, keeping me close to his chest. Everything was a contrast between hazy and sharp. Objects came to life. The trees moved like they were talking, the bugs flying around hummed so loud I burrowed into him to block them out.

My gaze drifted up to his face. His strong jaw locked with determination, his hold on me tight as he rushed us out of the area. Cuts from his face wept down over his stubble.

His skin pulsed, an aura around him flamed with colors in beautiful pigments I had never seen before. Even the darkness surrounding him was alive, pulling me in...*like a black hole*. And I wanted to jump in.

He was so beautiful. Visceral and brutal. I longed to be consumed by him, to touch him again. I watched a hand reach for his face. A cerebral part of my brain understood it was mine, but I had no notice or control of my body. Purely emotions. Want.

Fingers traced his jaw, running over to his lips. His gaze lurched to mine then back up, a muscle twitching along his mouth. The colors around him flamed in reds and oranges. Watching them like a firework display, I noticed slight hints of green and blue at the edges.

"Ken," he muttered, his lips pinching together.

God, his mouth fascinated me. His lips were perfect. A billow of heat rolled through me realizing I longed for them. On me. Kissing me...everywhere.

"Ken...stop." He growled, his lids squeezing shut before he let them open again. "Don't think you'd feel the same if you weren't high."

Was I talking out loud again?

"Yes, you are, but it wouldn't matter." He grunted, lifting me higher in his arms as he walked us through the forest. "I can feel and smell you."

Feel me? Smell me?

Lorcan licked his lips, propelling another wave of desire through me.

"Being this close, I can tell when you...are..."

Horny.

Lorcan let out a scratchy laugh.

Oh hell. I vocalized that too.

"Yep. And I'm finding it quite amusing." He peered down at me, a mischievous grin on his mouth. It was a smile that could drop you to your knees.

A tiny voice told me I should be embarrassed. Humiliated. But the sensation never came. His heartbeat banged against my ear, a drum. The harmony against my ear grew stronger. His body was music to me.

"Shhh," I hissed to all the things around me. "I hear music." I leaned my head against his heart. A thundering rhythm filled my ear. "Oh, I love this song." I sighed, feeling the beats spike through me like they always did, filling my body with hunger. Hunger for passion, lust, desire...

I felt him chuckle against my ear, adding another instrument to the orchestra. "Sleep, li'l Druid."

Beethoven's Symphony No. 5 came alive in my head, swirling with colors and movement. It was one of my favorites. Every year my family went to the Seattle Symphony and heard the orchestra bring his work to life.

But this time Beethoven came with images of fanged monsters and evil queens on stage acting out a play in front of a full audience. Blood painted and dripped from the theater walls, coating everything in deep crimson.

While Lorcan made love to me on the piano.

ELEVEN

My lids bolted open, and I shot up into a sitting position, my heart fluttering like a hummingbird. My mind swirled with images of Lorcan over me, rocking. The ecstasy he caused me burned bright in my head, heating my body with utter mortification.

I blinked repeatedly. Oxygen sprang out of my lungs like I had tried to sprint a mile. Or a quarter mile. Exercise wasn't really my thing. A streetlight from outside barely broke through the coated glass, leaving the strange room in heavy shadows. *Where am I?*

"Hey." Lorcan's voice sounded next to me. A hand touched my thigh, making me jump away from him. My hand scoured the floor, where I found my glasses and shoved them on my face. They were familiar, something I could anchor to, giving me clarity of sight and mind.

Lorcan's shape sharpened in front of me. He crouched next to me, dressed in his last pair of jeans and T-shirt, his eyes bright and soft on me. Even with both of us dressed, I felt naked and exposed, as if he could see what my mind had conjured up. The way he had made me feel in my hallucination.

"It's okay. You're safe."

Safe? I didn't feel safe around him. My dream twisted in my gut like a snake, strangling my air as shame, guilt, and anger rose up my esophagus.

Jared. How could I dream about having sex with someone else? Things I couldn't imagine my own boyfriend doing to me. The details, unbelievably real, brewed a heady concoction of disgust at myself. At Lorcan.

"Kennedy?" He moved closer and reached out for me again.

"Don't. Touch. Me." I crawled away, bumping over the backpack he had put under my head to sleep, and hit my spine against the wall. My eyes adjusted to the darkness, giving definition to objects around us. Boxes and large containers filled the area. An exit sign glowed dimly in the distance.

One more warehouse of some kind. Just another place to hide for the night before we moved on, adding to the endless string of forgettable places we'd stayed in while on the run.

"Guess we're back to you hating me." He looked away, smirking. "Instead of begging me to fuck you."

"Wh-wh-what?" My mouth dropped open. Did he actually say that? Had I...? I was on fire, right? Was this a case of someone dying from internal combustion?

It was possible, right? I kind of hoped so.

Bits of the dream came back to me. My need for him as his hands and mouth explored my body. Licking, sucking, kissing. Pleading with him to take me. To fill me. *Oh. My. God.* My hand covered my mouth.

"Yes, Ken, you *begged.*" He snickered, his green eyes glinting.

Humiliation burned my skin, stirring anger. I was glad it was so dark. If he could see my chagrin, it would only make this worse.

"I was drugged. I didn't know what I was saying." I curled my fingers into fists, my shoulders bristling to strike back.

Lorcan tilted his head, a cocky smirk on his face. I wanted to slap it off. To fight his smug attitude with harsh words.

"How do you know I was begging *you?*" I jabbed. "You weren't who I was dreaming about."

Hello, lie.

Lorcan's gaze focused on me with the intensity of an ocean wave about to drown me. A knowing smile slowly curled his mouth.

I wanted nothing more than to vanish. Was there a spell for that? I needed to learn it if there was. It would be enormously useful right now, because in his eyes I saw the truth.

I had called out his name. I struggled to swallow, and I glanced to the side. "Oh."

"Don't worry, li'l Druid, I won't taunt you...too much."

"Such the gentleman."

"I think we both know I'm not." He stood, sauntered over, and hauled me to my feet. My jacket scratched along the cement wall, my body trembling at his sudden nearness. He leaned over, placing his hand on the wall by my head, his mouth a few inches from mine, his voice low and husky. "Nor would you want me to be."

My lungs tightened. He inched closer, amusement behind his eyes.

The jerk was playing with me. Having fun because he *thought* I was an easy target. Little, naive, timid, insecure Kennedy. My palms smashed into his chest, jarring pain up my left arm, but I ignored it, shoving him again. He stepped back, raising his arms in surrender, letting me move him.

"Don't mess with me, Lorcan," I seethed, biting back the stinging from my wound. "Upsetting a Druid is not a bright move. I'll soon be able to turn you into a toad."

His lips parted as if to say something.

"And before you say you're disappointed I couldn't come up with something cleverer, how about I turn you into a large itching sore on a troll's ass? That sound better? Just. Try. Me." I pointed at him, feeling puffed up and ready to smack him. I was never one for physical violence. Ever. *Until* I met him. It would hurt me way more than him, but it might make me feel better.

Lorcan's jaw rolled, holding back the laughter I saw in his eyes. I saw something else, another emotion there which flushed warmth low in my stomach, sending my gaze to the far side of the room. I folded my arms in a huff.

"Ow." A jolt of pain ran up my crudely bandaged arm. "Crap! That hurt."

"Let me look at it." Lorcan stepped up to me, reaching for my arm.

"No." I glared at him, backing away. "I'm fine. I'll heal it."

"Ken." He sighed. "Let me look at it. You may be different, but you're still human. If it gets infected... Well, I'm gonna have to chop it off," he teased.

"Shut up." I waggled my head, feeling a begrudging smile tilt my mouth. He cradled my arm in his grasp, spreading his legs to lower his height. Gently, he unwrapped the cloth from my lesion, parts of it sticking painfully to the dried blood, tugging at the wound and hair on my arms.

"Owwww." I ground my molars together.

"Come." He didn't even give me a choice, leading me down a hallway. Flicking a switch, the room buzzed with fluorescent light, revealing a unisex bathroom. Lorcan's hands slid under my arms, lifting me swiftly onto the counter.

"Lorcan—"

"Be quiet." He turned on the tap and wet some paper towels. Holding my arm, he pressed the cloth to the sticky blood. He didn't speak, his fingers working gently over my skin.

I felt like an exposed wire, every nerve volatile and overly aware of him. The dream kept his touch like electrical charges in my brain.

"I can do a spell," I whispered. "Heal up the wound."

Lorcan's eyes flickered up to mine. His gaze stole other words from my tongue and moored them back in my stomach.

"You can after I clean it out." He loosened the last bit of material, exposing my injuries. His touch was light as he sponged away all the blood. "But you might not even need to."

All I could do was stare at my arm. Some of the holes were still red and raw, but no longer could you see the bone. It appeared to be healing.

Without a spell.

"I don't understand. How can…?"

"You're human, like I said, but being a powerful Druid has its perks." Lorcan tossed the ratty piece of shirt in the garbage. "When the gods gave Druids their powers, along with longer lives, they gave you the ability to heal faster as well."

My free hand went to touch the closing gashes, unable to comprehend.

"Uh-uh." Lorcan snatched my fingers with his, waggling his head. "Doesn't mean it can't get infected. We're gonna have to keep it clean and watch it, but your immune system should start closing it up."

"I heal like fae?" I pushed my glasses up my nose, ogling my arm.

"Not as quickly but closer to fae than human."

"But-but…I never have before."

"Your powers are getting stronger every day." Lorcan bent down, rummaging in the cupboard below. He grabbed a small first-aid kit and popped back up. The box contained bandages and disinfectant wipes.

"Owen said I was blocking my Druid abilities before. My brain would not allow the magic to come through because it went against how I was raised."

"And now that you are aware, they're coming at you like a speeding train. It will take time to develop how to handle them. Some take years to fully settle in."

I nodded. I was already struggling with how to control the abundance of magic I felt inside with my amateur skills. The guerilla-style learning I'd done in Greece had almost broken me. Lars demanded so much from me and most of the time I failed him. But every day I was growing, learning a bit more.

Lorcan had been as hard on me, but now I understood why. "That's why you want me."

His neck jerked, his gaze snapping to mine.

"I, I mean my magic." Heat rushed to my cheeks. "I'm the only one who can break the curse she put on you." Truth hit me like a whack-a-mole. "It isn't about having me as backup or breaking the curse to get back into the Otherworld. Not really. It's about Eli and Cole, isn't it? This is about you wanting to protect them. Saving West from losing his beast."

Lorcan's jaw twitched. He focused on my arm, dabbing it with the disinfected wipe. "How do you know it's not about saving my life? Maybe I don't want to be tied to those fuckers if they die. Or losing my beast?"

"Because." My voice barely came out a whisper. "I know."

A blaze hit Lorcan's eyes, his shoulders rolling back. "You. Know. Nothing." His focus on me became like a laser. "What did I tell you earlier? Stop trying to find the decency in me. I'm a dark dweller. There is no good. And I'm the worst of them all. Because deep down I'm only out for me."

"No," I spit back. "You're not. It's just what you want everyone to think. You care, Lorcan. You probably care more."

A storm stirred in his muscles, which writhed under his skin. "Then you are a fool."

Hurt burned down my esophagus, my fingers white knuckling the counter. "Don't."

"Don't what? Tell the truth?" His hands slapped the counter on either side of me, his body curling like he was about to attack.

Like a trapped animal, my muscles locked down, my lungs straining to claim more air. The sizzle at the base of my back told me this wasn't from the kind of fright you get from your life being threatened. This was from something far scarier.

"Damn, you're like a baby lamb. Naïve, sweet, and adorable."

"Don't tell me, you're the lion?"

"No." He snarled. "I'm the fucking beast. You know how I know I am only out for myself?" He tilted his head, his features hard and cruel, but something truly frightening smoldered underneath. "That I couldn't give a shit about anybody else's feelings…including yours?"

"How?" The word was barely audible.

It was a split second, a halted moment in time. His gaze lowered to my mouth.

Then everything combusted.

His fingers roughly grabbed my jaw, yanking us together, sliding into my hair. His mouth crashed down on mine.

I should have stopped him. Pushed him away. But the thought never came to me. His lips, consuming me with need and desire only awakened my own.

Flames, like a Bunsen burner being turned up to high, lashed at my insides and fueled me. Desire ignited like a spark in gasoline. A small gasp escaped me as his lips parted mine, his tongue grazing my lips.

Responsible, logical, timid Kennedy was gone.

My legs wrapped around him, pulling him into my body, my hands sliding up the back of his head, deepening our kiss. He growled, pressing with fevered need into me. He gripped my face tighter, inhaling me. I no longer cared about breathing. Air was only one more thing between us. One hand pressed into my lower back, demanding my body to be nearer, his other hand ran up my thigh.

We still weren't close enough. My hands dropped from his face, finding their way under his shirt, skating over his ripped torso.

He growled and grabbed my legs, tugging them snugger around his waist. I could feel him hard against my thigh and stomach as he moved against me. His hands progressed over my body, awakening my nerves.

If any bit of reason was still hanging on, it let go, disappearing into the pit of lust. Clothes felt heavy on my skin. I wanted them off. I wanted his off. I never had been so forward. So desperate. I had little to almost no experience before Jared. And our making out was sweet and timid. Clumsy hands and bumping noses, but it was on even terrain. We both were shy about discovering each other. And it really hadn't gone far. My underwear never came off.

But Lorcan was not shy nor a novice when it came to women. He was on the other side of the spectrum. Way, way out of my league.

I *was* a lamb. But this lamb had a case of rabies or something. I was wild, feral, and frantic.

My fingers clawed at the button of his jeans, popping each button open with a single tug. He wasn't wearing any underwear. The sharp memory from when I saw him naked and stroked him only fueled me. My head grew dizzy.

"Fuck," he rumbled hoarsely when my fingers grazed him, breaking off the kiss. "Kennedy?"

Hearing the question in my name let a trickle of reality in. And I wanted nothing to do with it. He felt so good. I wanted it to continue. For once I didn't want to think or analyze or create a list of the pros and cons. I just wanted to give in to the hunger inside.

I shoved his pants over his hips. Was I really going to do this? He knew I was a virgin. What if he stopped because of that? Fear dribbled in my lungs, but I pushed past, letting my fingers brush over him again.

He sucked in harshly, tipping himself into my touch. "Ken?"

I didn't answer; I didn't dare speak. The bubble we were in was so fragile I knew my voice would break it. My response was to nip at his bottom lip, tugging it between my teeth.

169

Whatever barrier Lorcan was trying to put back up crumbled into dust. A rumble vibrated off the room and his hands slid through my hair again, yanking back my head as his mouth recaptured mine. This time it held even more need.

But it also was filled with resolve. The decision was cast. Neither of us was going to stop.

Trepidation squeezed at my lungs, a voice deep in my gut trying to be heard. But the chemicals in a body outweighed any good sense.

His touch skimmed up my shirt, his thumbs gliding over my bra, dipping underneath the fabric. *Oh god.*

Sense. All. Gone.

My hands curled around the hem of his shirt, pulling it up. *Yes. I want this.*

Then everything disappeared like someone snapped their fingers. My vision disappeared in a blaze of white. My body and mind separated, and I could no longer feel or comprehend existence.

Pictures began to roll into my vision.

Flash.

Ember lay on a bed with IV tube running from her arm into the person sitting in the chair next to her. Eli's head is bowed forward, his face twisted with agony, his voice harsh but low.

"When I was dying, you probably didn't think I heard you, but I did. I will give you the same inspiring words you gave me. Don't you dare fucking die on me, Brycin. Don't be so damn pigheaded, either. If you really want to piss me off, you'll live. Being alive, so close to me ...and I can't have you. That will punish me enough. More than you dying on me. And I know you love to get under my skin. Torture me." He laid his forehead on her leg, his shoulders sagged with anguish as a deep rumble crawled from his throat.

Flash.

Jared picked me up and whirled me around. His laugh was full of happiness, his face so open and pure. "I love you," he muttered against my neck.

Flash.

A cry swung my head around. A gasp caught in my throat.

An arrow headed straight for my face. My scream echoed through the air.

Flash.

I was standing in a field. Dead bodies were sprawled and shredded in lumps for miles. *Tap, tap, tap.* The sound of blood dripped off leaves, saturated the ground, echoed in my ears like each one was a cannon. My gaze lowered to something tickling my feet. A scream slammed into my chest. Everyone I loved and cared for lay in a heap around me. My white dress was covered in gore, my bloodstained hands trembled as I peered down on them.

Panic ballooned in my chest; tears burned my eyes.

A squawk of a bird jolted my head up. A raven was perched on one of the dead bodies with its intelligent gaze on me.

"Grimmel," I breathed out, not feeling entirely alone.

"Darkness and light. You must decide. Only one can be." It cocked its head.

"What are you talking about?"

"No one knows."

"Is...is this the future?"

"Maybe," it responded. "Maybe not."

Helpful. "Why do I have these visions if I can't do anything about them?"

"Change destiny. It is you."

"I don't understand."

"Clearly." Grimmel fluttered his wings. "Every decision changes another. You change all."

"How?"

"Be the light."

I had no idea what the bird was talking about, but I sensed a heavy burden on my shoulders.

"Fire needs light. Needs night. Fate in air." The raven took off in the sky. "Grimmel know. None listen."

"Wait!" I called out.

"Return light to fire. One cannot be without the other."

The moment he uttered the words, everything around me disappeared.

Lost in the void of nothing.

No body or consciousness.

Just darkness.

Flash.

Hundreds of strighoul, terrifying and ghoulish, stood around a burning building. The flames reflected off their pasty, patchwork faces, teeth chomping all together in a chilling drum sound.

Their leader let out a howl, and they took off running for the building.

A building I knew was in.

Flash.

TWELVE

"Fuck... Kennedy, wake up." A voice dragged me into awareness, forcing me from my sleep. My eyes fluttered open to see a man hovering over me, his brows furrowed, his mouth pinched. "I need you to focus. This is real. And we're *really* about to be dinner."

Fear. Panic. *Where am I? What is happening?*

He leaned over and tugged on my ear, pain lurching into my head.

I inhaled. Lorcan.

I blinked a few more times, trying to center myself. I was back in the room where we slept earlier. Lorcan must have carried me here. How long was I out? It was freaky what could happen to me while I was not present in my body.

He leaned in, grabbing my face. "Do you feel my touch? Hear my voice?"

I nodded. A bang hit the outside wall, and I jerked my head to the high window. Smoke billowed, flames kissing the glass.

Oh god. "Strighoul," I gasped, the images dancing in my mind. "They're here. I saw it."

"If you had any vision telling me how we got out of this, I'd love to hear it." He grabbed my arms, heaving me up to sitting. Standing, he slipped his backpack over his shoulders. "The strighoul somehow found us again. And they brought friends."

I stood and grabbed for my own bag. Since being on the run, the instinct to act was taking precedence over logic.

Run first, talk later.

I tore off after Lorcan, my strides gobbling up the space between us and one of the exits.

My heart thumped along with the pads of my feet as I tried to catch up. He stopped at the door, twisting to see where I was.

"Hurr—"

A loud crash interrupted his sentence. Glass shattered from overhead, shooting out like darts and raining down in razor drops. A strangled cry issued from my vocal cords as I wrapped my arms over my head and dropped. Just then a ball of fire skimmed close to my head, collided with a rack against the wall, and burst with life.

"Kennedy!"

The flames alighted on a shelf stocked with cans of paint and packaged rollers. The awareness of what it meant calculated in my head. Paint, and especially paint thinner, plus fire, equaled exceedingly bad things. But Lorcan's voice drew my attention.

"Are you all right?" Lorcan's skidded on his knees next to me, grabbing for me. Green irises examined my face critically, his expression tense.

"I'm fine." I held on to him, rising to my feet. Black smoke curled up from the plastic melting off the paint rollers. "We have to go. Now."

He nodded, twined our hands, and jogged for the door. He twisted the knob and glanced out.

Shrill shrieks arose from the night. A dozen strighoul screeched and bolted for the open door.

Lorcan slammed the door, twisting the bolt, securing the exit right before bodies thumped against it, trying to break in, their fists and nails raking down the door.

"You're trapped, dweller..." A nasal voice screeched from the other side.

Flames erupted outside the door, rising up to the high window above the entrance. My head darted around, smoke mushroomed from every window around the exits. "I thought the Queen wanted me alive? They're going to kill us!"

"Shit!" Lorcan smacked his hand against the wall. "Remember they're not bright, but I think they are hoping to smoke us out...or start a really big barbeque." Lorcan rubbed his face, a smirk lifting his lip. "You'd probably taste really good marinated in juices."

I tilted my head, glaring at him, heat curling over me. "Not the time."

"What? You're going to deny a dying man his last meal?" His eyebrows curved up, the implication clear.

176

My body flushed. But the image of Jared from my vision was still raw, dampening the heat. "This is not a joke, Lorcan. What are we going to do?" I threw up my arms toward all our blocked escapes.

"You think I was joking?" He snorted.

Okay, brain. Come on, think.

They'd surrounded us and half the place was already on fire. My mind ran through the options.

A.) Pick a side not on fire and try to run through the throng of flesh eaters. Hope we get through.

B.) I need a plan B.

My eyes rounded the warehouse, landing on a set of stairs leading to the roof. I groaned, already hating the idea. "Lorcan?" I pointed up. Smoke started to fill the room, forcing my lungs to spasm. We needed to hurry.

"Right behind you, little bird." He shoved me toward the stairs.

"Little bird?" I asked over my shoulder, my legs trying to take two steps at a time.

"Yeah." His boots pounded the metal behind me. "When you get really...*excited*...your heart beats like a hummingbird. You also make these cute little twittering sounds."

"Whaaaat?" A hodgepodge of embarrassment, desire, and anger clumped together in my stomach.

"You asked." I didn't have to turn around and see the smile I heard in his voice. He and Eli were so alike in ways. In the most tense, life-threatening situations, they acted as if it were all under control. Like they planned it this way.

Whereas I flailed about without a plan, squawking and flapping.

Like a bird.

Damn him.

My lungs heaved with coughs, trying to rid themselves of smoke. Lorcan grabbed me by the waist, taking me up the last couple of stairs and seizing the roof door. The knob didn't budge as he tried to twist it open. Locked. Perfect.

Lorcan didn't even hesitate as he rammed the steel exit with his shoulder. The lock snapped with one shove, the door flinging open. He thrust me out into the cool night air, which was laced with heavy spirals of smoke. I covered my mouth with my shirt, trying to lessen the gagging in my throat.

Lorcan scanned the area. His nostrils flared. He probably smelled each and every strighoul waiting for us in the forest below, while my brain wracked with spells I could try to conjure. None were very helpful. But the defense enchantment had always affected everyone around, and a mass spell would be extremely good right now.

"Lorcan." I shouted over the loud crackle of the flames. His eyes found mine across the roof. Without saying a word, he seemed to grasp what I was going to say. He nodded as if he could read my mind.

Oh please say he can't do that.

A chilling cry came from the forest surrounding the building, sending off a wave of disturbing bellows. Red eyes lit up the trees like Christmas lights and moved closer. Fire licked up one side of the building, jumping quickly to the other and curling to the roof.

We had to do this now.

He moved, placing his back against the door to the roof, knowing my spell had no boundaries. Out of the corner of my eyes, I saw him start to strip out of his clothes, stuffing them into his backpack. The awareness of what he had planned filled my head like a vision so clear it was like I thought of it myself.

He tossed his pack at my feet, and I scooped it up, pulling it over my arms across my chest, my own bag taking residence on my back.

The sensation of knowing his plan without a word rattled me, but I had no time to think of it. Another strighoul came out with a burning torch and chucked it through a window below us.

"Uh, Ken, hate to rush you, but this place is a storage warehouse for paint and paint thinner."

I knew exactly what would happen. If the flames hit the paint thinner? Big boom.

I lowered my head, lifting my hands, chants filling my mouth. We only had one chance. I had to be sure this one had a lot of steam behind it. I built each word on the other like blocks. I couldn't see him, but I could feel Lorcan stirring behind me. My body understood the moment he turned into the beast. I felt it happen. His presence took up every inch of space around me.

The chant spit over my lips, and I pushed the incantation out into space with a sonic blast. My eyes opened to see the trees and bushes heave backward like a hurricane had hit them. Squeals and screams bled through as bodies flew back.

Everything after that hit me like a train, fast and brutal. Lorcan's front paw curled around my body, his claws hooking my clothes. He wrapped me into his chest and plunged us off the roof. Midair he swiveled, his spikes aiming for the ground, and locked me against him.

I wasn't ready for the impact. Lorcan hit with so much force, his spikes cut gouges into the cement, and he lurched to a stop. As I flew from his grip, his nails ripped my clothes and skin. I smacked hard, rolling and tumbling painfully across the parking lot. The backpacks cushioned some of the impact.

He growled, leaping to his feet and rushed to me. I felt pain everywhere, but my brain was on escape mode and pushed it back. I fisted his fur, helping me rise to my feet.

Wails arose from the forest, sending more fear into my limbs.

"Oh. My. God." I looked over my shoulder as hordes of strighoul approached from the forest, snapping their teeth and pointing their long blades at us, singing out a chilling battle song.

Lorcan nudged me with his nose. I started to run. Logic told me to run the opposite way of the butchers, but I only made it a few feet when another group burst through the trees in front of us. Mid-step, I twisted, changing direction. Lorcan leaped for any that got too close, his claws ripping through skin like butter.

Lorcan shoved me onward, and I could feel him telling me to run, to get away while he fought them back. I didn't hesitate. My feet started clapping against the ground, taking me away from the building.

A crack of glass. That was the only warning.

BOOOOM!

The ground shook under my feet, I lurched forward, and my glasses were ripped from my face. I soared across the lot and tucked my head as I crashed back down, skidding over the gravel, burning and slicing my arms and legs. Again I was thankful for the two backpacks encasing me. They were a slight buffer for my torso, taking the brunt of the impact as I rolled and bounced over the asphalt.

It still felt as if a giant elephant stomped on me. Everything hurt, but fear for Lorcan forced me to look back. I squinted and tried to perceive shapes through blurred vision. Smoke, debris, and dirt coated the night making it impossible to see anything more than obscure outlines.

"Lorcan!" I knew I shouted, but my ears resounded with a dull ring, only picking up my muffled cry. I pushed myself up, every part of skin and bones ached. "Lorcan?"

Be all right. Please be all right.

I screamed his name over again, stumbling on my feet through the haze. Chunks of the building, some still burning, scattered around my path. I tripped, my boots squishing something underfoot. Peering down, I gagged. Guts. Bits of flesh carpeted the ground, bodies torn apart and dismembered by the explosion.

"LORCAN!" My voice shredded, hanging in the air. I hated not having my glasses. At every black indistinct mass, my heart stopped in my chest.

Then my stomach plummeted. A few yards in front of me through the wreckage, a huge form with black fur and razor blades on his back lay crumpled on the ground.

"Noooo." I lunged forward, falling to my knees before the beast. Blood seeped from hundreds of deep wounds swathing his body, but my eyes locked on the one carving his stomach. His entire midsection was slashed open, intestines, guts, and blood pooling out. "Lorcan. Dammit, Lorcan." My quivering hands cupped his muzzle. "You stay with me. You hear me?" Fae were hard to kill, but not impossible, and I really didn't want to challenge the theory. "Wake up," I shouted down at him, feeling the trepidation crawling out my throat. "You can heal, right? You need to heal!" I heard my voice going up several octaves.

A shriek in the distance sent ice through my veins. Some of the strighoul were still alive and looking for a fried dinner. I knew they'd even eat their own, taking whatever powers they could. Finding us here, vulnerable, would be like Christmas to them.

"Please!" I shook him. "Get up. We have to go."

The beast didn't move, its breath shallow. Fading.

"Please don't die." I bent over him, whispering. My throat clogged with tears, feeling helpless. "Don't leave me."

Lorcan's life was wilting away, like those flowers I had saved... Helpless Kennedy was suddenly knocked in the head and shoved out of my body. My back went straight. I was not helpless.

I was a Druid.

I could heal. Except all I'd brought back from death were flowers. Quite different from a massive beast.

"Dammit." I bit down hard on my lip, tasting blood. Another cry from a strighoul haunted the night, amplifying my anxiety. "Relax, Ken." I rolled my shoulders, starting to mouth the words. This was going to take more magic than I had ever used. More than what I used in the cave when I broke the curse on the sword. This was healing a life, taking energy from around me and syphoning it into Lorcan.

I shut everything out, closing my eyes and only concentrating on my words, my hands hovering over his stomach. Pressure slapped me down, hunching me over. Sweat tickled my forehead. I couldn't simply say the words, I had to feel them as if my soul was speaking instead of my mouth.

I imagined Lorcan's crooked half smile. The way his eyes glinted with mischief. The way he brushed hair away from my face or took my hand. The way he kissed me.

I put every emotion into my chant and forced the words through my teeth. I pushed till I had nothing left then collapsed onto soft fur.

My lids couldn't even open when I heard another cry in the air.

Snuggling into Lorcan, sleep took me prisoner, leading me away from awareness.

THIRTEEN

"Ken-ne-dy?"

I lurched up, my name clanging through my head, yanking me out of a deep sleep. The smoke was still thick, the building still smoldering and flaming, telling me I hadn't been out long. My head spun around, searching. My name felt so real, tangible, dragging me out of oblivion. My gaze landed on the body next to mine.

Lorcan was still asleep but back in human form and in the buff. His clothes remained in the pack circling my stomach, which probably had saved me from critical injuries.

But most of all, the gaping hole in his stomach was closed up. A scar lined the skin together in a distinct ridge, red and raw, but his guts were knitted back inside. *I did it!*

Relief exhaled from my lungs. "Lorcan?" I touched his face gently. The pop of flames and the unseen danger of strighoul hissed over my skin.

"Kennedy?" a voice boomed in the distance, the one which stirred me from my dreams.

My back went rigid, glancing over my shoulder.

"Ms. Kennedy?" a tiny voice called, much closer.

Inexplicable panic rushed into my veins. I knew the voices.

Cooper and Simmons. Searching for me.

If someone later asked me why I reacted the way I did, I would have no answer. Impulse took over and my gut ruled my actions. All I knew was I *needed* to move. Get away before I was caught.

"Lorcan," I hissed in his ear, shaking him. "Wake up."

His lids fluttered, his green eyes glazed before zeroing in on me with intensity.

"We have to go." I tugged on his arm, trying to get him to his feet. "Now!"

His lips turned white as he slammed them together, standing up with a groan. His pain would have to wait. Wedging my shoulder under his arm, I led him away from my rescuers.

Just a few weeks ago, I would have rushed straight for them, elated to be saved. Something had changed. Now my lungs fluttered with fear as I hoped to get away before they landed on this spot.

Lorcan normally took one stride to my two, but I had to drag him at a quick pace. He grunted, limping on one leg, trying to keep up. He jerked from me, picking something up from the ground, and shoved it in the side pocket of my backpack.

"Hurry," I hissed.

Grasping my desperation to get away, he upped his speed. Lorcan probably thought I was hurrying him away from the strighoul. Then his nostrils flared, and he slowed.

Crap. He smelled Cooper.

I interlocked my fingers in his and heaved him forward, desperate for him to keep moving. We got to the edge of the forest when my name rang out into the night, stopping Lorcan dead in his tracks.

Crap multiplied.

Desperation caked my throat. We needed to keep moving. They were so close. We were going to be caught. Anxiety danced at my feet as I tugged on his arm.

"Kennedy?" Cooper yelled out, the distance narrowing. "Lorcan?"

Lorcan glanced over his shoulder, his muscles stiffening at Cooper's voice. Then he looked back to me, down to our linked hands, and up to my face. His eyes narrowed with incomprehension.

"Come on." I tugged on him, but he didn't move, just grew cold and hard.

"No." Anger rumbled from his chest as he shook free of my hand. "I release you. You can go."

In an instant, the promise lifted off me, the pressure of the bond gone. Instead of freeing me, panic caged me. My feet didn't budge.

"Go!" he spat, flicking his head toward the voices.

"No." I wagged my head, lacing my hand with his. His puzzlement was palpable.

"Ms. Kennedy?" I whipped my head to the side. Simmons's tiny silhouette was outlined through the haze, flying in the air, every second getting closer to seeing us.

I snapped back to Lorcan's gaze, pleading. His hand tightened on mine.

That was the only response I needed. I whisked around and bolted into the forest. His breath came heavy and strenuous, but he followed me without a word, naked and hurt. We sprinted through the dense brush, weaving around trees. My heart thumped and my legs darted as if Cooper and Simmons were actually nipping at my heels. Adrenaline pumped through my system. We kept up the pace until my legs buckled.

"Stop," Lorcan's ordered. "You need to rest."

"No." I shook my head, forcing my feet to keep going. "We're not far enough."

"I. Said. Stop."

Glaring, I swung around to face him. Mistake. My eyes darted to the side away from his bare skin and well-endowed physique. Even without my glasses, it was not difficult to make out every detail. To recall every detail.

"Kennedy?" My name was stuffed full of questions. None of them I wanted to answer. Especially with him naked.

"Here." I pulled his bag from my shoulders and tossed it over to him. He caught the bag, unzipped it, and hurriedly dressed in his jeans and T-shirt.

The moment his body was covered, my shoulders dropped in relief. I could see every muscle through his shirt, but it was like a barrier. A layer of protection to keep me from doing something really stupid. Like I almost did earlier. Heat curled through me at the thought, spiraling to disgust and anger.

"Kennedy, look at me." Lorcan moved closer to me and I reversed back. "*Ken.*"

"What?" I folded my arms across my chest, my hand going up to adjust my glasses, not finding them.

"I said look at me," he growled.

I didn't.

"Are you going to tell me what happened back there?"

"Building blew up. I healed you, and we got away from the strighoul."

Silence penetrated the space, severe and concentrated. I fastened my lips together, trying to fight the human nature need to fill the space.

"We both know," he took another step, "that's not what I meant."

I backed up, my shoulder ramming into a tree, halting my escape. He moved so close in front of me I could feel the heat flush off his body.

"Why didn't you go to Cooper? I released you." His voice was low and gravelly, sending bumps over my skin. "You were free."

I licked my lips, still unable to meet his gaze.

His fingers clutched my chin, forcing my attention up. "Why did you stay? You could have escaped. Left me. Gone back to your life…to Jared." His eyes blazed, igniting my skin and sucking all thought out of my head. "I wouldn't have stopped you."

Pinpricks stabbed behind my lids. An unforeseen hurt twined around my chest as a flash flood of emotion careened into me.

Could he let me go so easily?

His gaze darted over my features, taking in my reaction, flickering with red.

Oh god. With utter clarity I realized I should have left. Not because I wanted to get away from Lorcan. But because I didn't. At all.

I ran because I wasn't ready to be without him.

He leaned over, grabbing something from the pack at my feet. Black frames wrapped between his fingers. *My glasses.* That was what he picked up when we were leaving. It was small, but the act gripped my heart even more. He understood how necessary they were to me. He unfolded them and slipped them up the bridge of my nose, my vision sharpening. The glass was scuffed and scratched, but I felt better. Complete.

His thumbs stroked my jaw. My heart pounded in my chest. The need for him to undress me and feel his bare skin on mine consumed me. It was like lightning, crackling the air between us.

"Kennedy." His hoarse tone told me everything. He knew, probably sensed, the lust zapping through my body. His hands cupped my face, desire sparking his eyes, which implored mine, searching for my answer.

And I wanted to scream yes. To give in to the yearning. To let emotion rule me instead of thought.

Sex had always made me nervous. Petrified actually.

But right then, I wanted nothing more. To have him so deep inside I couldn't breathe. To lose myself completely. To cry out his name. I trembled, my skin flushed, and my body pulsed with longing. The thump of my heart moved down my stomach, settling between my thighs. The sensation almost collapsed my legs.

A rumble came from Lorcan, his fingers sliding up my jaw, gripping my head with desperation. "Like a little bird," Lorcan whispered. His mouth brushed over mine, taunting me. There was no doubt why I had stayed with him, why I hadn't chosen to run instead.

The force building between us was too strong for me to let go.

His lips swept mine again. I wanted more.

My toes went up, and I drove forward, crashing my mouth against his, hungry and ferocious. He groaned, his hand clasping the back of my head, the other on my lower back, bringing me into him, his need digging into my hip.

His tongue skimmed my lips, parting them, deepening the kiss. I had never felt so wild and desperate. Each swipe of his tongue made me want more. My hands moved over his body across the wounds I healed.

White light burst into my head, jerking me back with a cry. *No. Not again!*

The outside world was gone.

Flash.

Jared paced the floor at the ranch house. "What do you mean you lost them?"

"I'm sorry, Jay. But Lorcan seems to be one step ahead of us." Cooper folded his arms. "They were there. It was hard to smell them through the burning flesh of strighoul, but they had been there. I don't know how long ago, though. We'll keep trying. We're not giving up on finding her."

"Let me go with you next time." Jared clenched his fists. "I hate sitting at home worrying over—"

"Jared..." Cole stepped up, rubbing his cheek.

"Stop treating me like a kid. I don't want to be home with a babysitter while you're trying to save *my* girlfriend. *I love her*, Cole. So much I can't sleep. To even think what Lorcan could be doing to her..." His lids closed briefly, agony sputtering over his features. "She's *my* mate. I want to help find her."

Flash.

I stood on a hill, the night sky exploding into hues of effervescent colors, illuminating the field around me. The earth vibrated under my feet, bleeding up into my bones. The energy in the air crackled off my skin. I took a step, the edge of the hill opening up to the valley below. I sucked in a breath. A thin veil held back thousands of warriors beating their feet and weapons on the ground as though I'd stepped into a modernized version of an ancient battle.

I could sense their need to attack, their taste for blood.

"Unite." With a flutter, the black raven flew down and clipped his nails around the boulder.

"Grimmel." I turned to the bird, his presence reducing my anxiety. "Thank goodness you're here."

"Why? Grimmel can't amend. Only light change."

"How can I change it? Stop this war from coming?" I glanced back down as a bolt of lightning cracked across the sky and splintered a hole in the veil between worlds; the castle became more dominant and clear in the distance.

"No stop. Only fuse."

"Fuse?"

Grimmel tilted his head, a strange sound clicking his throat like he was annoyed. "Fire and light are out. No activity upstairs."

"Ahh." I rubbed my temples in frustration. "Just tell me. Stop being so enigmatic."

"Light be bright. Brighter than fire." He squawked, his wings batting the air as he rose. "No time. Go. Land of Demon King. Must unify."

"Don't go!" I reached out to stop him from flying off.

"Turn. See. It is you. Light must unite." He darted over my head. I twisted, following his outline as it was absorbed by the shadows. My eye line dropped lower, and I stumbled back, my hand flying to my chest.

I stared back at myself dressed and armed for war. I stood a hair behind Ember, Eli, and Cole, but behind me was Lorcan and his clan. All the dark dwellers were back together, either in or out of their beast forms. We stood together.

United.

Flash.

I was in a small room, stone walls circling me, my intuition told me I was in the Queen's castle. The single object in the room hovered before me, igniting the room with a hazy light. Magic leaped off the object, snapping at me like a guard dog.

The Sword of Light.

"Grimmel found. Druid must retrieve." Grimmel's voice came from the dome window. "Only one."

I was so concerned about my friend's safety I'd forgotten that the Queen taking Ember probably meant the sword was in Seelie hands. Aneira would guard it with her life. Protect it with charms and curses.

I walked around the sword, sensing the impenetrable magic cording it. "I can't break that. It's too strong. I am not powerful enough."

"Then all lost. No hope."

He was like freakin' Yoda. "Grimmel, I'm nowhere close to being ready to fight it."

"Must. Grimmel says so."

"Oh, if you say so."

"So does King. Demon needs Druid." He patted his feet on the windowsill. "Time is up."

Flash.

~~~~

I inhaled sharply, my lids opening up. Hazy leaves and an outline of a person draped across my vision.

"Ken? My sight cleared, and Lorcan's face sharpened in front of me. "Hey." He brushed a strand of hair off my face. "You're back."

I knew him right away, the vision didn't cripple me this time, but I still felt unsettled.

"Real?"

He tugged my ear. "Real."

Images of my vision zoomed in and spanked me like a naughty child.

Jared's worried face hung in my brain like warning sign. *What the hell am I doing?* I was with Jared. He loved me. And I was kissing someone else. No, his uncle. I was not a cheater. I detested people who did so, not understanding how they could do that to someone they loved.

Crushing shame toppled on my chest. I shoved Lorcan away, darting around him, my hand on my chest, trying to breathe. *No. No. No. I can't feel this way. It's wrong.*

"What's—?"

"No," I gritted through my teeth. "Don't say anything."

"Ken, what did you see?"

Gathering my strength, I sucked in a gulp of air and swiveled back on him.

"I saw the truth." I lifted my chin, trying to build a wall. "This." I motioned between us. "Can never happen. I'm with Jared. *Your. Nephew.*" I got the reaction I was hoping for. Lorcan flinched, glancing away. "He loves me. I will not hurt him."

He stayed silent, his Adam's apple bobbing up and down.

"I still will help you break the curse. Save your brothers."

His neck snapped in my direction.

"I will work day and night. Whatever I can do…"

His muscles lined in a ridge around his ears. "But?"

I hated he knew me. "That is it. Nothing else between us," I pronounced. "And we will be going back to Lars's."

"What?" His mouth parted.

"My visions are growing steadily stronger. You know that. To have a chance in this war we must work together. Whatever your problem is with your family…it's nothing compared to what is coming for us. They need me. They need you."

"No." Lorcan's head shook as he ran his hand over the back of his neck. "No way."

"We have no other choice." I knew it was up to me to unite the groups. I had to.

"Yes, we do. We don't go." He wagged his head. "Absolutely not, Ken. There is too much bad blood between us. You think they would even let me come back? Cole or Eli would probably kill me on the spot. There is no way we could all work together."

"You're going to have to learn." I folded my arms with set determination. "Ember needs me. And your brothers need you. Lorcan, put your grudges aside for a minute. We can only win if we join them."

He huffed, exhaling deeply.

"Please. For me?"

His gaze shot to me, his head tilting in a "that's not fair" expression.

"I'm going. You can come with me or not. I have a responsibility. I will not back away and hide." I stared at him, desire for him churning in my chest. I didn't want to tell him exactly what Grimmel showed me. What I was up against. "But I really hope you will. I want you there. Your family wants you there. No matter what you think, you are blood. Eli loves you, and you love him. It's time to mend the rift before it's too late."

Lorcan moved around with agitated movements. "Dammit, Ken...how can you ask this of me?"

"Because deep down you know I'm right. You know what Aneira is capable of." I cleared my throat. "Plus, I saw you in my vision. You were there. All the dark dwellers were together again. Working as a team." I rubbed at the sleeves of my tattered sweatshirt. "Don't you want to make it right with your *brothers*? Both of them?"

"Both?" He cocked up an eyebrow. "You think I should tell them? About our parents."

"Yeah, I do. It's not fair to you or them. It wasn't your secret to keep. They need to know."

Lorcan let his head drop back, staring up at the sky.

"And you go back to Jared," he said softly.

"Yes." My throat choked on the word. "It's the only way."

Lorcan exhaled, squeezing his eyes shut briefly before nodding. "My condition if we do this is you help me break the blood curse *secretly*." His voice was clipped with formality. "I don't want anyone to know about it."

"Okay."

His eyes went to mine and sadness flickered in them before they grew impassive. "All right. Let's go find Dax, Dom, and Samantha. Then I will return you to where *you belong*."

The knot in my throat expanded. I gritted my teeth, forcing the tears away from my eyes and agreed.

FOURTEEN

It took two days to track down the rest of Lorcan's group because he still wanted to stay away from using Otherworld doors. Their link only worked within a certain proximity, like walkie-talkies.

The silence between us was painful. He kept his distance, never touching me unless it was to help me up a steep mountain or ridge. Every time he spoke, his formality clawed at my chest, but I swallowed back the pain.

It was the right thing. He was following my wishes to a T. When did some part of me decide to follow its own path, to reject what was right and long for what I couldn't have? *Only infatuation*, I told myself over and over. It will go away in time. It wasn't real. Jared was real.

My dreams seemed to be charting the same course as my instinct, though. Lorcan appeared in every aspect of my mind as I drifted off to sleep, curling my body against this raw desire. The torture was supposed to lessen by the day, but each time he caught me staring at him and snapped his gaze quickly away from mine, my frustration mounted.

"Lorc!" a voice boomed out as we walked up to a small cabin in the woods. Dax loped out of the door, heading for us. This was the only building I had seen for hours, and I would have missed it if Lorcan hadn't gone straight to it. It blended with the surroundings, melding with the mossy boulders and dense camouflage of trees. A great place to hide.

"Hey, man." They smacked each other on the back, giving a quick "bro" hug. "All good?"

"Yeah. We're good. Had Dom and Sam tracking the area for strighoul and the Queen's men. Clear here."

"Thanks." Lorcan nodded and steered me to the cabin. Dax frowned down at Lorcan's hand, which stayed firmly on my back.

I let Lorcan guide me, grateful for his presence more than ever, my shield from a pack of hungry beasts. Dax, Dominic, and especially Samantha only saw me as a means to an end. A sacrificial lamb.

Hate was not a strong enough word for what I held for the redheaded dweller. She was one person I could happily see gone. Dead. And I never wished for anyone's death.

"Don't worry." Lorcan's fingers rubbed my spine, and I focused on him. "I sent Samantha ahead. She's going to try to locate Lars's compound for us."

My mouth gaped. How did he know I was thinking about her? And he said us...like... I slammed the door down on the thought, cutting it in half. No. There was no us.

As we entered the cabin, Dominic stood, his movement predator-swift as he clasped his leader on the shoulder. "Lorc, glad you're all right." He was the most animal-like of the group. He moved with a slow, prowling grace, as if he were always hunting. Ready to attack.

My muscles tightened and my heartbeat picked up the instant he was near. Afraid he'd sense my unease, I examined the space, taking my attention off him.

The place was bigger than it appeared from the outside. We stood in a large living/dining area. Sofas surrounded a fireplace and a lush rug on the wooden floor. A long dining table divided the kitchen and living room. In front of me a wall of windows overlooked a creek and forest, with chairs arranged around the deck on the other side of the glass. To my right stood the kitchen and then a hallway, which probably led to bedrooms. A loft hung above the kitchen, a ladder by the table leading up to it. It was rustic and simple but nice. It would have been a relaxing spot. Romantic. If not for the company.

"Report." Lorcan stood in front of his men, one hundred percent alpha.

"We looked into what you asked. West is no longer being held prisoner." Dominic crossed his arms across his huge chest. "It looks like the Unseelie King and his men were able to get them out."

"Thank the gods." Lorcan's shoulders sagged and he rubbed his face. I could read the relief radiating off him, the happiness his brother was finally safe from Aneira.

Knowing Lorcan, he still hated the fact he wasn't the one to rescue him, but relieved just the same.

"And the other thing?"

Dominic frowned, his gaze sideswiping me. "The other prisoners are free too."

My head perked up. "Other prisoners?"

"Yeah, your chubby friend and *Emmy's* human daddy." Dom snarled Ember's name. I didn't care how he felt about them, all I heard was his statement.

"They're free? Really?" A smile broke over my face, my eyes ping-ponging between Lorcan and Dom. "They're home safe?"

Dom snorted. "Not exactly."

My smile fell.

"What do you mean? Are they okay?"

"Papa and Twinkle Toes will never be able to come home."

"Dom." Lorcan's voice was deep and commanding.

"You wanted me to check on the two new fairies, and I have no idea why." The glare from Dom told me he blamed me. "Why do we give a shit about them or if they ate fairy food or not?"

Invisible hands twisted my vocals. I shot a look of alarm at Lorcan.

He sighed. "If what Dom told me is true, your friend can never leave the Otherworld again. Once you eat fae food...you can't come back. He would die on Earth."

I sucked in a breath. Ryan would always be a prisoner, never able to come home or see his family again.

"They're all living together in a house on the Dark side. The fox, human daddy, your friend, his boyfriend, that asshole Torin, and his shadow, Thara."

Boyfriend? Did he mean Castien? Had Ryan hooked up with the fae soldier who watched us in Aneira's castle? He had been nice and protected us on several occasions from the Queen's wrath. I was glad he decided to change teams. He always showed Ryan extra care. My best buddy had a hot boyfriend. *Good for you, Ry.* About time he was appreciated.

"You found out...for me?" I peered up through my lashes at Lorcan.

Mistake. Red fury sparked in his eyes.

"No. I didn't do it for you. West was my concern. Your friends were an afterthought."

Silence blossomed between us, and Dominic smirked at us.

"What's the plan, boss?" Dax broke the tension, shoving Dom over as he stepped beside him. Both stared at their leader, ready for his command. "You wouldn't explain anything, and Sam wouldn't tell us where she was going."

Their link was so fascinating to me, how they could talk to each other in their minds.

Lorcan rubbed his mouth, then moved to the windows. He pressed his spine taller with authority. "We're rejoining our kin." He twisted to glance over his shoulder. "This fight is bigger than us. We all need to work together."

Silence filled the room. Then it exploded, and anger painted the walls.

"Excuse me?"

"What the fuck? Are you kidding me?"

"No. No, fucking way."

"You want to go back? To Cole?"

"Didn't we already try that shit and they said no?"

"Have you lost your mind?"

"This is joke, right?"

Dom's and Dax's shock ran over each other like colliding freight trains.

Lorcan's expression stayed even. "No. This is not a joke. It's anything but." He clamped his mouth shut and turned to face us, authority riding high on his shoulders. "I have sent Samantha out to find our clan. They have blocked the ranch from us, but a *little birdy* told me they are stationed with the Unseelie King." His eyes met mine briefly.

"What happened?" Anger rumbled in Dax's voice. "You wanted nothing to do with this war. We split from our clan, Lorcan. We are no longer welcome. Nor do I want to be."

"We chose to follow you...*I followed you.*" Dom took a step to Lorcan, a level of threat in his movement. "The plan was to be nowhere near the war when it came. What the hell changed?"

I moved without thinking, darting in front of Dominic and blocking him from Lorcan.

Dominic jolted to a stop, his eyes widening then tapered, lowering into slits. "Ah." A cruel smirk hooked his mouth, his eyes flashing with red. "I see."

Lorcan's heat blazed behind me as he flattened protectively against my back.

"I swear, you make one more step, Dom, and I will end you." His words vibrated into my spine.

"Holy shit." Dominic's head jerked to his alpha. "You didn't?"

"Doesn't matter," Lorcan snapped. "Changes nothing. You touch her and I will make certain it is the last thing you do." His presence seemed to fill the room. "I am still your alpha. My word is law."

Dominic held Lorcan's gaze, tension battling in the room before his lids lowered and he backed up. "You chose her over us?" Dax spoke softly.

"I'm not choosing anyone. I am making the best decision for all of us." Lorcan drifted away, his hand running over his head. "We are part of this war. Hell, we pretty much started it. It didn't go the way I wanted. That's my fault. I should have never taken Ember, especially when I knew she was Eli's mate. Anger ruled every choice I made. A true alpha cannot lead that way," he said without even a flinch of discomfort. "I will not apologize for my actions. They are done. We need to move forward. But I want to know..." Lorcan nestled himself between his brothers and me. "Are you with me?"

Dax and Dom both peered at the ground, shuffling their feet. A second passed. Then another. My chest filled with apprehension. What if they said no? What would happen?

Dax was the first to look up, his face stern.

"I am with you, Alpha."

Lorcan nodded, turning to Dominic.

Slowly Dom raised up and nodded. "I'm with you too, Alpha."

"Good." Lorcan smiled briefly. "It's not going to be easy. They will not want us back either, but we'll have to deal with our family quarrel later. This war will destroy us if we don't work together. I need to know you are one hundred percent behind me, which means being behind Kennedy. She is a part of this. A huge part. I don't want to question for a moment you won't protect her." He placed his fists on his hips. "You guard her like you do me. You listen to her like you would listen to me. Understand?"

I struggled to swallow over the knot in my throat. I was expecting to see beams of hatred and resentment laser into me. Instead Dominic and Dax glanced over to me, then back to Lorcan with open expressions.

"Yes, Alpha."

Lorcan nodded, his stern demeanor dropping away. "Okay, all we can do now is wait for Samantha to notify me. I want each of you to take shifts patrolling the area. The Queen has a major hard-on for Kennedy. We can't for one minute let our guard down."

"She's not the only one." Dominic snorted and went out the door, acting like no weirdness had happened.

Dax lifted an eyebrow at Lorcan and me before he followed Dom out to start patrol.

The door shut. Lorcan's neck and shoulders dropped at the click and he rubbed his face with a heavy sigh. The dominating chief faded, leaving the man I had gotten to know in his place.

Lorcan. Unguarded.

Clarity poured over me, opening my eyes. I was the outsider, the one who did not belong but the only one allowed to see the real person underneath. With everyone else he was a ruthless leader. With me I saw the hurt, the vulnerability, the man trying to guard his heart and hide his weakness. Love.

The realization strummed confidence into my bones. My boots knocked into his heels as I touched his back. The muscles flexed under my palm.

"Thank you."

"For what?" He jerked his head, his jaw locking down. The moment I touched him, the blocks piled up, and he moved away from me. "Nothing to thank me for. We have a deal. I keep you safe, return you to your loved ones, and you help me break the curse." He wheeled around, his face stone. "That's all there is."

"Lorcan..."

"What?" Anger nipped at his lips. "You going to tell me there's *more*?"

Yes was on the tip of my tongue, but I couldn't seem to form the word.

"That's what I thought." He smirked, incense flaming his eyes. "Jared is waiting for you."

For a moment breath left me as though Lorcan had stepped on my chest, crushing my heart and lungs. I frantically blinked away emotion.

"Take the bedroom at the end of the hall. Shower. Get something to eat." He motioned to the fridge, then went for the door.

"Where are you going?" My body and words moved forward with frantic desperation.

"Patrol." He tugged the doorknob.

My heart responded, spurting out of my mouth. "Stay."

He stopped dead in his tracks, the door half open. Gradually he twisted his head around to look, his lids narrowed.

Blood heated my cheeks, working down my neck. *Did I really just say that?* "I-I mean..." What did I mean? "It's only ...the place is empty and I'm not..." I coiled my hands together, trying to put together my thoughts. But I couldn't admit any of them out loud.

I shriveled under his silence and intense gaze. I knew it wasn't fair to want more of him. I had made my choice, but I wanted both worlds.

"Go to bed," he ordered. "You will be safe here." Then he left.

Humiliation and hurt tickled my eyes. I pressed my hand to my throat, where a painful lump had gathered. Biting down on my lip I forced it all back and turned and walked down the hallway to the last bedroom. I took a shower and got something to eat like he suggested, but I did it without thought.

My head and heart were empty of everything, easily letting me drift off into sleep.

Flash.

"You want me to talk? Fine." My own angry voice rang behind me as I swiveled around. I was standing in a tiny cabin staring at myself. Ember was squirming near the door, her eyes wide, biting at her top lip. "Why didn't you tell me about Ryan?"

Ryan's name causes a knee-jerk reaction. Why was I asking Ember about Ryan? And why was I so upset with her? I couldn't see it all over my doppelganger's image. The nerve in my cheek twitched, my teeth clenched, and a fire burned behind my eyes.

"I—" Ember stuttered, her guilty gaze drifting away from my copy.

"You kept the truth from me. Don't you think I had the right to know *my* best friend since kindergarten would never be able to return to Earth?"

"Ken…" I felt the heavy guilt laid over each letter of my name. I no longer cared about my dream-self or how she responded. I don't care. All I knew in the moment, without a doubt, was my best friend had been lying to me. She had known about Ryan for a long time and kept it from me. My seer realized it. The deception went back for months. Even when I was still at the Dweller Ranch, she knew and never told me.

Anger coated my tongue, and I wanted to strike out like a whip. How could she keep something like that from me? The thought of her doing it to "shield" me fused my ire. She must have thought I wasn't an equal in her eyes, but a child to coddle and protect from the bad, bad world. I did not want to be guarded or be cocooned from the truth. I was as much a part of this war as she was.

And he was my best friend. Part of my soul. Resentment sprinted up the back of my throat.

Flash.

Stone tunnel.

Dark.

Torin, Eli, Ember, the pixies, and I stood in front of a wall with torches. Eli and Torin were flush with each other, their shoulders tight, hands fisted.

"Stop it, both of you." Ember shoved at the men, pushing them a part. "We don't have time for the testosterone crap."

"No. You don't," another man's voice said.

My head jerked to see the wall swing open, a tall blond boy, dressed in the Queen's uniform stood on the other side.

"Josh?" Ember sputtered, her mouth open in shock.

"You seem surprised." A tight smile thinned his mouth.

Flash.

I whipped my head around.

An arrow headed for my face.

A scream turned into a shrill squawk.

Flash.

~~~~~

"Shhh." The bed dipped with weight, the pure darkness making it hard to determine reality. Was this still a vision? Was I awake? Asleep?

"It's okay." A deep murmur hummed in my ear, arms wrapping around me, pulling me into warmth. "I'm here."

My brain still couldn't figure out the truth. So many nights I had dreamed of Lorcan's arms around me. What if it was simply another delusion?

"Is this real?"

Lorcan tugged me in firmer against his bare chest. "This is real, li'l bird. You're at my cabin. Safe. With me."

"I need to know," I whispered, my breath heaving.

His hand laced through my hair, brushing it over my shoulder, his fingers pinched my earlobe till a jolt of pain zapped at my nerves. The tiny sting centered me, becoming the most welcome sensation. I squeezed my lids, exhaling.

I was here. It was real.

"Now sleep. I have you." His words wrapped around me like the coziest blanket, calming my beating heart.

He was really here, holding me. In the dark I continued to let a slice of reality not exist. Most likely everything would change tomorrow. Lorcan and I would separate, never to be alone together again.

I rolled over, burrowing my face into his chest, inhaling his scent. It was like an aphrodisiac. "Thank you for finding out about Ryan," I murmured, a sigh emanated from my body. I fell into his warmth, letting myself plunge into the black hole.

FIFTEEN

It took three more days for Samantha to find underground information into Lars's base. Even if you had been there, it was spelled to force you to forget. The security surrounding it was so secret and impenetrable, I didn't even want to ask how Sam found out.

During that time, Lorcan and I went from ignoring each other to laughing so hard when we tried to cook dinner together Dom and Dax stared at us like they wanted to toss us in the creek. Dax especially wanted to kill us when Lorcan and I got in a food fight, and Dax got caught in the crossfire. I still smirked at his expression when I bonked him in the side of his head with an inedible muffin.

"I can feel the protection spell. It's right here." I lifted my hands to feel the sizzling air shielding the demon's lair. We used up most of the day getting to the coordinates Sam had given us. We did not follow our urge to turn around and go the other way; we knew it was part of the spell on Lars's home. "It's so powerful." "Stay here till I know it's safe." Lorcan placed me behind a tree. I stayed only because I knew it comforted him. I had nothing to fear, but he wanted to be the first to interact with whomever came.

He took a breath and stared at the ground for a moment, like he was building himself up for what came next. Exhaling, he rolled his shoulders back and ran toward the enchantment. Lorcan grunted, throwing himself against an invisible barrier, his body rebounded back into the dirt with a brutal crunch.

I resisted the urge to go to him, gripping the bark of the tree. He picked himself up, brushing off the dirt from his clothes.

"They'll be here soon," he said to all of us.

From my time on the dark dwellers' property, I understood how spelled barriers worked. They directed humans away without them being aware, and if fae found the property, they couldn't get in unless invited or were part of the spell. Interacting with the barrier set off alarms, and they would know someone was trying to cross the property. Lars's men would be here soon.

It took them less time than I thought. As if I conjured them myself, Rimmon and Goran were at the boundary line with their weapons raised. It wasn't like Rimmon needed anything since the man was a monster, part giant or ogre. He was at least eight feet tall, dark, marred skin, bald, and scary. His hands were almost bigger than me. He could smoosh me with a finger.

Goran acted as Lars's right-hand man. He was built like he trained with special ops. He was shorter than Lorcan but so ripped it was almost gross. He stood stiffly. His blond hair was slicked back, his blue eyes directed at us with force.

"What do you want?" Goran gripped his blade handle.

"To speak with your boss. Or my brother."

"Our barriers are not open to you. You must leave."

"Not gonna happen." Lorcan shook his head.

"Leave. Or we will kill you," Rimmon said matter-of-factly.

Lorcan rubbed his hands together. "I think the King would be extremely upset with you when he sees what I have brought him."

I bristled a little at Lorcan's words. He made it sound like I was an offering. One he could bestow on the leader for rightful passage, and it was not my decision to come back, to do this together.

"Believe me, he will be very interested in what I have."

"And what is that?" A deep, silky voice emerged from the trees; the power behind it rattled my nerves. A man stepped out. Black hair, olive skin, familiar yellow-green eyes. *Lars*.

As usual he wore an impeccable suit. Today it was a gorgeous tailored gray-blue. The only time I had seen him in relaxed attire was in Greece. He held just as much power in cargo pants, but the suits matched his personality better. Unimpeachable both in looks and in power.

"You have nothing. She will come willingly." Lars clasped his hands together, his gaze darting to where I hid behind a tree. He slowly looked back at Lorcan, his eyes flashing black for a moment. "I do not deal with traitors. I kill and torture them."

Before Dax, Dom, or Sam could move, my boots crunched the brush underfoot as I strode beside Lorcan.

"And if you want me to work with you, you will not harm him." The force behind my declaration startled me, especially because I meant every word. "We work together or not at all."

Lars tipped his head and watched me with those unnerving eyes. "Ms. Johnson, you surprise me." He flicked his gaze between Lorcan and me, understanding and something like humor twitching his mouth. "I see things have changed a lot since our time in Greece. You have grown in power."

"I have," I declared, not letting him see he still scared the crap out of me. "And I know you need me to break the spell on the sword. I am the last Druid. I am the only one who can, am I right?"

Lorcan's head snapped to me, but I kept my eyes on the King.

Lars's eyebrows raised up in disbelief. He leaned his head and gave a slight nod. "You are."

"Then allow Lorcan and his clan in. No harm will come to them. And we will help fight. I have seen what is coming. You need every one of us. Especially me."

Lars stared wild-eyed as if he wanted to laugh or strangle me.

A noisy crashing of brush revealed Cole, Eli, Cooper, and Gabby running into view, where they stopped at the property line. Their eyes narrowed on their old kin, muscles tightening around their necks. Dax, Sam, and Dominic moved next to Lorcan. Low, threatening rumbles bounced between the groups. This could go ugly fast.

"Kennedy!" My name rang out, full of happiness and disbelief.

Ember came racing up to the line next to Eli, Cal hovering close to her. I thought my anger had dissipated over these last few days. Yet seeing her brought it back to the surface, like burning stew. Part of me wanted to run to her, but another part was indignant, holding its ground in the soft dirt. I couldn't forget she had lied to me about Ryan. She had no right to keep it from me. Good intentions or not, I had every right to know.

Lorcan needed me more. We had to behave like a united front. If I had to step between the groups, I would do it in a second.

Ember's head tilted, looking so much like her "Uncle" Lars, confusion turning to fury. She fisted her hand, anger bristling her features. "Lorcan, I swear to god if you harmed her..."

Lorcan glanced at me, then back to Ember with a smirk. "Does she look hurt to you?"

"Simply because I can't see—"

"I'm fine, Ember," I cut her off. My voice was much firmer than I intended. I felt so different from the girl who'd been taken in the caves in Meteora months earlier. Stronger. More secure. Definitely not the innocent, sweet one anymore.

215

"We heard you were recruiting people for your war. Thought we'd come and offer our services." Lorcan's alpha tone was back. He was on and playing the part of a bastard perfectly. It frustrated me to know I was one of few who knew the truth about him.

"You're kidding me, right?" Ember gaped.

Lars's gaze moved back and forth between Lorcan and me. It hung on the dark dweller for a moment. Anxiety squeezed my gut. He knew our terms. He could turn us away or accept it. There was no middle ground. Lars took in a tiny breath, then gave us a firm nod.

Holy crap times ten. The Unseelie King agreed to my terms.

"W-wh-hat? Are you serious?" Ember exclaimed, her eyes round. "But he killed Aisling."

"This is war, Ember, and we have to sacrifice." His gaze drifted off Ember to me, his words firm. "I may not like it, and when the war ends, some alliances may end. Until then, we must work against our common enemy." Lars pulled at his cuffs and curved away from the property line. He stopped, his stare locked on Lorcan. "Our personal feelings have to come second if we want to achieve our goal. We cannot win unless we are all willing to compromise in some way or another. You are welcome to join; however, if you make one move out of line, I will kill you myself."

I felt the weight of Lars's sentiment land on Lorcan. He held up against it, giving the King a slight nod of understanding.

Lars and his men turned and went back toward the house, leaving the two groups to deal with his verdict. By the expressions on the other side, this was not going to go well. But with the King's permission, we crossed onto his land and entered the circle surrounding the compound.

Ember's burning gaze itched my body. It felt wrong not to immediately run to her, to let her know with an embrace I was all right. I felt pulled to remain at Lorcan's side, but my presence would soften the aggression pointed at him. They would not attack him if I stayed glued to his hip. At least I hoped so.

I turned to Ember, holding her stare. Confusion strained her two different-colored eyes. She saw I was no prisoner. I stood here of my own accord.

Right then she posed the greatest threat to Lorcan. Her hatred for him throbbed off her. For all the crimes she laid at his feet, some true and some not, I understood her anger, but it didn't take away the fact I would stand between them if she tried anything. I would fight one of my best friends.

A hum grew through the two groups, tension scratching and pawing the air. Violence crackled, producing low growls through the party.

I was about to open my mouth and be the moderator before things went south, but Cole cleared his throat, speaking first.

"I don't buy that you are here to help."

Lorcan's eyes briefly met mine, the words behind them crowded my brain like I could understand what he was saying. *This is for you. You know that, right? All for you.*

"I have never been opposed to us working together, remember? You were. I feel we can be stronger cooperating than apart against Aneira," he said to Cole.

Eli's condescending laugh cracked the air like a whip. "This comment coming from the guy who betrayed his family, crawled into bed with the one enemy who banned us to Earth, abducted Ember, turned her over to the Queen, and then kidnapped Kennedy. And you want us to trust you? I don't think so."

Rage sprang up in my arm, to my neck, flaring my nose. They had no clue about the truth. Aneira tortured him. Cursed him. And he was doing everything to fix his mistake. Save the ones he loved. The words simmered in my throat, ready to boil Eli in his own declarations.

Lorcan raised his arm, his fingers brushing my pinkie on the way, before he ran his hand over his head. The brief touch clipped my mouth shut. He was telling me to stay calm and quiet. This was his battle to face.

"Believe what you want about me. What I did was for you guys. You think I wanted to go to Aneira? Eli, you couldn't see straight when it came to her. I knew going to the Unseelie King would only cause a war. And it did. I wanted to avoid combat so I went to the source. *I* tried to keep my family from this. I did it for you."

My feet shuffled over the dirt. He would never apologize or back down, even if he knew he made the wrong choice. He was an old school alpha through and through. Never show your weakness.

But his declaration only hastened fire from the other side. Magic bumped and zapped against my skin, the back of my neck feeling the rise of resentment, anger, hurt, and betrayal.

"Was killing my mother only out of love for your family?" Ember stepped forward, each syllable like daggers pointed at Lorcan.

I gritted my teeth, already knowing Lorcan's response. Another thing he would never apologize for.

"I was doing a job. We were *mercenaries*. It's what we did. We killed for a living, Ember. We have killed a lot of creatures and people who had mothers and families. Your mother was not personal to me."

Rage burned through Ember's eyes. "She was to me."

"If you want to hate someone, hate Aneira," Lorcan replied objectively. "She wanted your death and planned Aisling's murder down to the last detail. I happened to be a pawn she used to do it."

Dominic rumbled, his body radiating the beast inside, the killer wanting to come out. "Too bad Eli screwed it up and you lived. Otherwise, we wouldn't be standing here in this mess."

Crap times ten! Dominic tore the wisp of a treaty between the groups.

Eli's roar echoed and bounced around the forest as he thundered toward Dominic. The dwellers reacted with instantaneous fervor, punching and slamming each other to the ground. A choked scream came from my throat as Cooper rammed into Lorcan, both hitting the ground, sliding through the brush.

Fear slammed at my heart as I heard a tornado of growls and sounds of skin hitting skin. Then it hit me. None were turning into beasts. Even Dominic. This was not a fight to tear each other apart. This was psychological wounds they were fighting. Hurt. Deep down they were still family. They would never actually kill.

Both sides were in the wrong because neither side knew the full story. I stood in the middle, the glue putting these two sides back together, even if it was a crappy job. Anger zinged up my spine as I saw all them tear at each other, focusing on the wrong enemy. My hands went up in the air, a chant already spitting my lips.

Crack. My defensive spell popped the air like a kernel of corn, expanding the space. Everyone was thrown apart, flung into the air, and tossed back into the dirt with a thud, ripping the air from their lungs.

"NOW STOP!" I bellowed, my voice booming in the stunned silence. "It was my idea to come here today. We will be better together than separate. So get over the past and your issues. All of you!" I snapped, looking directly at Ember, knowing she'd be the first one to fight me on a collaboration. Then I looked to Lorcan. "You will behave. I agree with Lars. Let us deal with the real problem. Right now we need to work as a team. We need to defeat Aneira. You will have the chance to kill each other after."

Lorcan's mouth pinched together, his eyes burrowing into mine. *Sorry.* He didn't have to say it out loud.

The rustling of leaves drew my head forward. Cole got to his feet. "She's right. Our grudges need to go on the back burner for now."

"Easy for you to say." Ember stood and Cal fluttered to her shoulder, still snarling at Samantha sprawled a few feet away. "One of them didn't kill one of your good friends and your mother and turn you over to the Queen."

Cole's eyes flickered to Ember and she stiffened. "But—" She stopped when Cole raised his hand, silencing her.

Wow. I knew Ember had become more of a dark dweller without her powers, but to see my friend respond to her alpha was strange to watch. Her furrowed eyebrows told me she was not a fan of having someone control her in any way.

"Only until the conflict is over, as Kennedy recommends. Then we can deal with each other. Until then, we need a truce between us." Cole dropped his hand and returned his attention to me. He looked at me with his chin up, respectful, as if I were someone to listen to and follow.

My chest expanded with awe and nerves. I wanted to hide behind someone, to take the attention off me. I stood my ground, letting the feeling wash over and anchor me.

"Kennedy!" My name rang out, the familiarity of the voice sucking all the air from my lungs. I shot a look Lorcan. He was on his feet, his gaze on me. It was less than a second, but I saw a single vein pop along his jaw, and he turned away.

My lifeline was cut off, or that was what it felt like. I was stranded in a sea of guilt, fear, and confusion. I gazed at the boy running for me. Jared's muscles strained under his workout T-shirt, sweat lined his forehead. My visions had not been wrong. His body filled out quite a bit since I had last seen him, looking more like the eighteen-year-old he was supposed to be.

But all I saw in his goofy grin was the fifteen-year-old.

"Baby!" His arms engulfed me, picking me off my feet and spinning me around before dropping me to the ground. His hazel eyes filled with emotion as he cupped my face. His lips parted to talk but stopped. Lips crashed down on mine; his hands already eagerly fumbling over my body.

I tried to let myself feel the happiness at seeing Jared. To enjoy his kiss. He was my boyfriend. Someone I loved. And I really had missed him. I was never one for PDA, hating any attention on me, but this time it wasn't the other dozen of eyes on me. It was one pair.

A burning sensation sizzled at the back of my neck, awareness seeping in like acid, scorching holes in my skin. All I could feel was Lorcan watching, his gaze torching me in flames.

"I can't breathe." I pulled away from Jared, forcing a smile on my lips. The guilt strangled any joy I had at seeing the youngest dweller.

"I'm so sorry." His hands continued to move over me. "Damn, I've missed you. Are you okay? Did they harm you?"

"No, I'm fine." I gulped, trying to fight the natural urge to glance over my shoulder. Lorcan's presence pulled on my skin, almost magnetically.

I didn't want to focus on him, but my need to see him overruled my will. My head jerked slightly, my attention flickering behind me. Lorcan stood like stone, his expression blank. It was only in the clench of his jaw I saw any emotion in him.

Jared followed my gaze. His reaction instant. Chest

puffed, he bolted toward Lorcan. "You asshole! How dare you show your face here?"

Lorcan didn't move, not even flinching as Jared's fist crashed into his face. My foot barely scraped the dirt as I lunged between them.

Lorcan's eyes landed on mine, halting me. *No. Stay there*. Then they returned to Jared, allowing his nephew to wail on him. Not once did Lorcan block or retaliate in anyway.

I was only a slice of why Lorcan was taking Jared's wrath. I knew he held guilt for abandoning his nephew, disappointing him for turning his back on the clan. Lorcan felt he deserved this. Especially from Jared.

It was so hard, but I stood there watching Jared's anger grow the more his uncle didn't engage. He wanted Lorcan to fight back, another reason to really hate him.

I couldn't stop the emotion I felt. It was Lorcan's way of saying I'm sorry.

"Jared, enough." Cole finally stepped in, grabbing him by the shoulders.

"Let me go!" Jared wrestled against Cole's grip.

"Cooper?" Cole yelled over his shoulder, flicking his head to Jared.

"Let's take a walk. Cool down." Cooper's large hand wrapped around Jared's neck, leading him away.

"I don't want to cool down." Jared's eyes flickered to mine, his cheeks flushing with embarrassment. Then he returned to glower at Lorcan. "How are you guys letting him come here after what he's done? He kidnapped my girlfriend. Betrayed us."

Cooper kept a tight hold no matter how much Jared squirmed and fought against it. Then they disappeared into the woods.

Tears stabbed at my eyes, and my nails dug into my palms to keep them at bay. The shame I felt at what I did turned to anger. This was all my fault. I made a huge mistake and only caused people pain.

I would never tell Jared what happened. It would destroy him. But keeping it secret would hang heavy on my soul. I would have to stay far away from Lorcan. I would earn Jared's love again, even if he didn't realize I had to.

"I think we need to discuss some matters." Cole broke into my thoughts. I lifted my head and locked away any emotion.

Lorcan dabbed at his bloody lip, intense green eyes on me. Grief crushed my lungs as we looked at each other. But my attention was also pulled to the forest where another piece of my heart had gone.

I was being cut in half. And only one part could survive.

SIXTEEN

Deep in Lars's property we stood by a cluster of tiny, sturdy cabins appearing as though they'd always been here. Most likely they had been built recently to hold the numbers of Dark fae venturing in daily for the war. We had walked past tents, cabins, holes, and strange dwellings on our way here. The land was already infiltrated with fae preparing for battle.

"I know working with each other will be difficult," Cole spoke, his authority captivating every person in proximity. "But we need an alliance between us to defeat our common enemy. I know none of us want Aneira to have control of Earth and the Otherworld. Her powers are already too great. Her ideas of freedom and supremacy have destroyed ours and many other Dark clans, and her dominance over both humans and fae will only get worse. We may not see eye to eye on a lot of issues, but I think we can come together on this one."

"I agree with Cole." Lorcan took a stance next to him, not bowing down to his old leader. He was alpha of his group, and he would not hold a less significant place ever again. Some might have seen it as a jab to Cole, but I saw it differently. He was just as much a leader. He deserved to stand there as one. "We need to let go of the past and focus on the future."

"*You* forget the past?" Eli folded his arms. "I find what you say amusing when all you do is bring it back up and put the blame on everyone else for your actions. You stand there pretending to be alpha, saying we need to fight against Aneira, when it was you who worked with her. Not us."

"I understand your feelings, Elighan. As a leader, you do what you feel is best for your clan. At the time I felt I was doing just that. I quickly realized the choice may not have been the most effective option. I have made amends and moved on. Now you won't let go. Neither you nor Cole can stand here and say you have always made the best decisions for the family. Our divide proves this. How ethical you guys have become here on Earth. Do you think Father would even question me? He understood the true acts of a leader and how far you sometimes need to go."

"Father wouldn't have done what you did." Eli flexed his hand, a growl lacing his sentiment.

Eli held so much anger for Lorcan and had no idea all his brother had done to protect him. If he only knew.

As if he sensed my thoughts, Lorcan's gaze drifted over the group and found me. My head gave the slightest jerk, encouraging him to keep talking. *It's time. You need to tell them. They need to know the truth*, I tried to convey to him with a look.

He bowed his head and nodded as if he really had heard me speak.

"You have no idea who Dragen really was, Eli." Lorcan inhaled, rolling back his shoulders. "You were young and idolized him. I saw what he was capable of. Ask Cole. He knows what I'm talking about. You have a notion of Father that is a fantasy. Mother as well. She was equally cruel and conniving. You only saw what you wanted and only remember what you choose. They were dark dwellers through and through, which is why Cole has tried so hard to raise you differently. He never liked how they led. He hated them. Right, Cole?"

Cole's eyes narrowed on Lorcan, his shoulders bristling, like he sensed what lay below Lorcan's question.

"I was older, already too far into following good ol' Dad's footsteps, huh, Cole? Is it the reason you chose Eli? I was too much like the man you despised?" I could see the resentment Lorcan held on to for so long flare up. It had protected the hurting boy inside him. "On the other hand, Cole could still save you." Lorcan waved his hand toward Eli.

Tension swung amidst the group, winding among them like thick vines. Bodies all around me tightened, ready to act.

"And do you want to know why Cole hated Father so much? The man you looked up to as a hero?"

"Lorcan, don't," Cole warned him, looking over at Eli.

With a pop of clarity I understood Cole's guarded expression. *He knew.* He knew he was Dragen's son.

227

The same realization rushed over Lorcan's face. It was brief, but enough that I caught it.

Lorcan drew air through his nose. "Don't what? Tell the truth? Don't you think it's time he knew?" Now that the ball was rolling, one I started, I could see there was no stopping it. The floodgates had opened and years of pent-up resentment were going to be unleashed. "*When* did you find out you were Father's child, Cole?"

Silence descended over the group, alive and consuming, sucking all the air from the sky. It was out there…and all we could do was wait for the truth to fall where it may.

"What?" Owen exclaimed, disbelief darting his eyes back and forth between Lorcan and Cole, almost like he was begging for it to be a joke.

Cole glowered at Lorcan. "*When* did you?"

In three words, Cole had declared to his pack this wasn't something Lorcan was making up. It was the truth.

Shock swept down, clobbering everyone in its path. Gasps and cries fizzed up like a soft drink, popping and bubbling through the throng of dark dwellers. It wasn't merely a secret from Cole and Eli, but them all. Dark dwellers killed, had sex, and betrayed. But not each other. That was the cardinal sin. The only law they lived by was their bond. But now they knew Lorcan wasn't the first to cross the line. Their old glorified leader had not been the man they thought. The man who could do no wrong had fallen from his pedestal.

It was a harsh blow, but one I hoped they would get over. Watching Eli, it didn't look like it would be soon. But even with his jaw locked down, his shoulders coiled, his expression stone, I could feel the hurt and anger escaping through. What he thought he knew for so long was wrong. Maybe this new revelation would let them see Lorcan in a different light, as the man I knew. Or they could make him more the villain. The one emotion sparking off Eli that gave me a little hope was guilt. For decades he blamed his brother, hated him, when Lorcan had been trying to protect him. Hopefully both Eli and Cole could give their brother a chance. I was happy it was out there now. Lorcan no longer had to carry the burden all by himself. I was proud of him for finally letting it go.

My thoughts wandered thinking about Lorcan mending his relationship with his estranged family. When I heard Eli say my name, my head popped up.

"What did you need Kennedy for? Why kidnap her and talk of your need for her if you could already get through the doors to the Otherworld?"

Nerf herder.

Every head swung to me, then Lorcan, their mouths parting with Eli's revelation. Dax, Dom, and Samantha already knew the reason, but Cole's clan now realized the hiccup in Lorcan's plan. Why need me if they already were granted entrance from their previous dealings with the Queen?

"Holy shit!" Gabby put her hands on her hips. "Why did you kidnap her?"

Lorcan's eyes met mine briefly, a pinched smile lifting one side. "Because the curse is not lifted."

Lorcan told them what I figured he would, keeping the true secret of why he abducted me, to break the blood curse on his brothers, only that. A secret. He only let them in on the fact they couldn't stay in the Otherworld. The curse had only altered, not truly broken.

I took my place next to him, defending what he said was the truth. I knew it was the only way the other group would start believing Lorcan. If they trusted me, saw I trusted him, then in time they would come around and realize he wasn't trying to betray them.

Eventually the newly found brothers separated from the group to discuss the truth of Cole's parentage. I took the moment to slip off into the woods to regroup myself. Seeing Jared and Ember had left a heaviness in my soul.

No one noticed my retreat to the forest close by. I hooked my bag higher on my back, letting the trees hide me under their leaves. My hand skimmed along the bark, feeling the rough textures. Libraries and the woods were always my peaceful places, my sanctuaries even though my parents and sister didn't enjoy the outdoors all that much. Their idea of a family trip was an all-inclusive cruise, while I got seasick and longed to be back on land. It all made sense now. A Druid's lifeline was the earth. It was how we got our energy.

A voice broke my solace, stopping me. "Buddy, take a breath. Cool down." *Cooper.* "Kennedy's back. Simply focus on that."

"Yeah, I know," Jared grumbled. Their footsteps crunched across the undergrowth, getting closer. I slunk back, hiding behind a tree. "But damn, I want to punch him again."

"Get in line." Cooper laughed. I could see their silhouettes walking through the brush close by. All I had to do was step out. Make a noise. Instead, I stayed still, held my breath, my heart thumping.

"I love her so much and seeing him standing so near her like he did nothing wrong, like he *knew* her," Jared grumbled. "I couldn't stop myself."

Absorbed in their own world, they didn't reach out and smell or sense me. With so many strange fae here, it might be hard to detect me anyway.

They breached the forest, sauntering back toward the cabins on Lars's land and disappearing from view. I let out a heavy sigh and crumpled back into a tree. *You just hid from your boyfriend. A person you love.* The thought drilled up from my gut, lodging in my throat. A gloom engulfed me like the fog around the trees. My insides ached with confusion and despondency, anger at myself not knowing which to feel more.

1.) Forget everything that happened in the last couple of months and try to be the girl I was before.
2.) Tell Jared I need some time.
3.) Cut off any feelings I have for Lorcan. Like a guillotine. In one sharp swipe.

The lump in my throat was hard to swallow. I could do none of these. Each one hurt someone I cared about. Whatever had happened, it was over between Lorcan and me. He probably was embarrassed he kissed me anyway. Guys like him didn't fall for girls like me except in those romantic, highly unrealistic romantic comedies. Lorcan would easily move on. Jared wouldn't. He was the person I was meant for. Right? He was convinced. So maybe I needed to focus on what I had with Jared.

It was only fair to give us a chance now that I was back. I had changed a lot, but maybe Jared had too. We could grow together. Feeling reinvigorated, I stomped back to the cabins ready to face my future. Whatever it might bring.

~~~~~

"Roomie," Gabby said snidely, her arms folded. Her purple-and-black hair had grown out from her pixie cut and curled behind her ears. She leaned against a cabin, smoke wafting up from the cigarette in her hand.

"What?" My confident stride faltered.

"You and me, nerd girl." She flicked her head back to the small cottage. "Believe me, I'm not any more thrilled than you are. I was quite happy having it all to myself."

"Seriously?" Words came stumbling out of my mouth, packed with horror. "We are rooming together? Is that a joke?"

In school Ryan, Ember, and I had been the group that was friendly with most cliques, but not extremely close to anyone besides each other. The popular girls lived to attack Em, while girls like Gabby found me an easy target. I was conditioned to start sweating at the sight of her.

"You have a problem with that?" Gabby's tongue tapped at her pierced lip as she stomped out her cigarette.

I shifted my feet together, standing up straighter. "No." It wasn't true, but those were old fears, old wounds. I had to remember I was no longer that girl. I was a Druid and someone like Gabby shouldn't intimidate me. Still, I envied her confidence. Nothing seemed to faze her; no one would ever bully her.

"Well, I wouldn't sleep too soundly." She bumped my arm, strolling away. She turned, walking backward. "See you later, roomie." With a wink, she curved back and headed for the field. A mass of fae were out there training through simulated fight sequences.

I exhaled knowing she was only pushing my buttons because I let her. If I didn't grow thicker skin and step up, Gabby was going to eat me alive.

Stepping into the small cabin, it was clear Gabby was not going to be a neat roommate. Gabby's clothes hung over her bed and mine, pouring out of the open dresser drawers like they were trying to flee.

The one room was only big enough to hold two twin cots with a nightstand between them on one wall and a table, chairs, and a dresser by the door of the other wall.

I kicked a pair of Doc Martens from the middle of the room to her side, flinging the extra garments from my bed to hers, and dropped my bag on the bed.

I had barely unzipped it when a knock rattled the door. I instinctively picked up on magic outside the door, familiar magic. It seeped into the room before she did, laced with expectation and hope.

The hours Lorcan had helped me detect energy honed the ability so now I could tell Ember wanted something from me.

"Come in," I yelled, continuing to unpack, taking out my limited outfits and placing them on the bed.

"Hey," Ember's voice clipped with hesitancy.

"Hey." I dumped the Ziploc bag of tiny shampoos and toothpaste next to my clothes. Only a few months had passed, but it seemed like an eternity. It hurt to feel the wall between us, but I stung with how she'd treated me like a child, keeping Ryan's fate from me.

And if I was being totally honest with myself, it wasn't entirely that. It was Lorcan and what had happened between us. What I had wanted to happen. I kept my wall firmly in place from a mixture of guilt, embarrassment, and protectiveness for Lorcan. I knew she would not approve. And I wasn't ready for her to hate me or look down on me because I'd had feelings for her mother's killer.

I made such a mess of things.

Ember cleared her throat, staying in the entry.

"Hope Lorcan had better fashion sense than Gabby or Owen did." The fake laugh died quickly in her throat, her feet shifting. "Ken...I-I am so sorry."

"For what?" I squeezed my lids shut, the pain in her voice, slicing me.

"For what?" she sputtered. "For not protecting you. For not stopping Lorcan from taking you. And not finding you fast enough."

I swiveled around to face her. "None of that was your fault. You couldn't have stopped him, and you can't protect me every minute of every day. I am not a helpless baby. I can look after myself."

"I know." She looked down at her boots, nudging them into the wood planks.

"Do you?" I countered. She said it, but I knew she didn't really mean it. To her I was tiny, sweet Kennedy Johnson. Someone to protect and shield from truth or violence. Not someone who could stand on her own two feet and fight and who had power of her own.

Lorcan seemed to be the only one who saw me as more. He knew what I could do and pushed me to take on more. He didn't think I would fold under the face of truth, no matter how bad.

"Are you all right?" Ember twisted her hands. "Did he hurt you?"

I almost wanted to laugh at what she implied. Lorcan would never harm me, and if he had it was because I begged him to. But she only saw the evil, cruel man. Not the version I did. She never would. It was hopeless thinking she or any of them might see the real man. It gave me a feeling of defeat. Everything was pointing, no, shoving me away from him. Jared, Ember, Ryan...they were people I would also wound.

"No." I slunk down on my bed, trying to blink the sorrow from my eyes.

"What happened then?" She grabbed a chair and dragged it up to the bed, sitting across from me.

"I don't want to talk about it." *You would never understand. I don't even know if I do.*

"Ken?" She went to gather my hands in hers. She took my mood wrong, thinking I was hiding some trauma when it was nothing like that. It scared me to think being with him was the first time in my life I ever felt truly myself. Like the person I wanted to be: strong, powerful, beautiful, and even sexy.

I walked away from her and gazed out the small window facing the field. Bodies in the distance danced through the late afternoon, slicing blades through the air. Thousands of Dark fae prepared themselves for the battle ahead against the Light.

Two figures rambled by the window, and I grasped my stomach. West and Lorcan. Hope surged at seeing them together, I knew how much guilt Lorcan held because of what happened to West.

As if he sensed me, Lorcan's head snapped up, his green eyes catching mine. Detached coldness stared back before he turned away, muttering something to West, and continuing on like he never saw me.

Knives drove into my chest, flaying me open like a fish.

"Kennedy, talk to me."

"You want me to talk?" I turned. I desperately needed to change the subject of Lorcan to another source of soreness. *You made your decision, Ken.* "Fine. Why didn't you tell me about Ryan?"

"I…" Ember's eyes widened, her mouth not finding an excuse.

"You kept the truth from me," I responded. "Don't you think I had the right to know my best friend, the boy I have been friends with since kindergarten, wouldn't ever be able to return to Earth?"

"Ken—"

"Lorcan told me the truth." He denied it, but I knew he specifically asked Dom to find out about my friend. "Do you know how stupid and betrayed I felt being the last person to know? You of all people should know how it feels, but you were the one who kept it from me. You complain about fae keeping secrets from you, and yet you're exactly like them."

Ember jerked back, sucking in sharply. I felt horrible, my voice softening a little. "I believed all our work was to get him out, and for one of us at least to be free of this mess and the Otherworld. But Ryan can *never* come home. He can never see his family again or move to San Francisco like he dreamed."

"I know. I'm sorry." She bit her lip and lowered her head, her red streak falling in her eyes. "You probably won't care, but I actually thought knowing about Ryan would distract you."

Anger spun on a warped loom, weaving into a taut string.

"You had *no* right to decide for me." My hands rolled into fists. "How little you must think of me that I wouldn't want to help. I also have a stake in the war. Ryan or not, I am going to fight. Aneira killed my entire family and would like to see me dead as well. You are not the only one who has reason to hate her."

Ember watched me and for once I felt like she was finally seeing me.

"You're right," she agreed. "All I can say is I am sorry, and I will never keep anything from you again. You can handle much more than I ever gave you credit for."

"Thank you," I whispered.

Heavy silence came over us before she spoke. "Are we okay?"

I looked at my friend. I loved her with all my heart. We needed a little time. I needed to work out some things. "We will be."

Quiet befell the room, followed by sadness inside me. We never had to fill gaps before, even if no one was talking. We had to earn it back with each other.

I curled my arms around myself, sitting back on the bed. "Lorcan kept me safe. He didn't hurt me. He actually helped me. He's taught me a lot. My magic has grown so much."

"Lorcan?" she replied sharply.

Bam. My defenses shot up, spikes jetting out, feeling the judgment and ridicule in his name.

"He's the only one who has been truthful with me. Cole and Owen never told me the full truth, even though they knew. Lorcan told me about my family and the true power of our magic. He's made me stronger."

"Because he wants to use you." Ember's face lined with pity, like I was too gullible to see it myself.

"I already know what he wants from me." I pushed to my feet. "He never kept it a secret. Can you say the same about Eli? Or Cole? They want me for the same thing. What makes him different?"

"Because it's *Lorcan,*" she exclaimed as if it was the clearest notion in the world.

Rage billowed from me, throbbing my chest. "He's not what you think he is." My voice came out low and fierce.

"Wha-what?" Ember stood, almost knocking over the chair. "Lorcan is the guy who kidnapped you, had Ian killed, and murdered my mother."

"*Samantha killed Ian.*" Every ounce of me bristled. I wanted to shoot down every false idea of Lorcan. "Lorcan did not actually want to hurt any of us. He was bluffing to get you to act." *And he only needed you in exchange for West. To save his brother.*

Ember's jaw dropped as she shook her head back and forth. "Lorcan doesn't bluff. He didn't give a shit if Ian died or not. He doesn't give a damn about anybody but himself."

The gulf between us shook, ripping open even wider. Rage split us so far I could barely even see my friend anymore.

"What the hell is going on?" she demanded, searching the room like it would give her the answer. "Is it the Stockholm syndrome or something?"

Her phrase knocked into me, almost bending me over. It hurt so deep, oxygen fought to get down to my lungs.

"What is this, Ken? Why are you defending Lorcan?" she asked, then halted, horror and dismay creeping over her features. "You have feelings for him."

All it took to crush me was one look. Her face contorted, not with shock or concern, but utter revulsion. Like she would cut off my friendship if she found out. I knew for certain nothing would be the same between us if she did.

"Of course I don't," I snapped, lying through my teeth, hoping it could be true. It would be so much easier if it was. But I knew the moment I answered it was too fast. Guilty. *The lady doth protest too much, methinks.*

Ember's lids blinked. "Oh no," she whispered hoarsely. "But Jared?"

"I may have come to understand Lorcan better, but I love Jared." Her judgment set off my own guilt, writhing in my heart like a worm in an apple. I had made my choice: Jared. "Do not confuse your situation with mine. I am not you, though I don't see how you have room to judge. You fell for a killer. But that's okay because you let yourself believe Eli is different."

I could no longer be in the same room with her. Storming past her, I grabbed the door handle. "You have kept secrets and lied to me. You say you're different from the fae, but you aren't. You claim they only want to use me. I'm not stupid, Ember. I can *feel* you came in here for your own motives. What do *you* want to use me for?"

"I-I..." Once again she was speechless, confirming what I had sensed, which only broke my heart more. She hadn't come in here simply to see if I was all right. She wanted me to help her with something.

"That's what I thought." I tried to keep my voice even, but the aching shook my hands.

Twisting the knob, words boiled between my teeth, moving my jaw without my control. *"What has been done cannot be undone, not by my hand. His death will come by yours."*

I shook off the dizzy sensation and the obtuse meaning of the phrase. I wouldn't let myself dwell on it. I bolted through the door, away from my best friend.

And myself.

SEVENTEEN

Twenty steps. That was the farthest I got before I heard my name. I stumbled as I fought to stop when I wanted to run.

"Kennedy!" Jared jogged up, a smile brimming over his face. "I was just coming to see you." His arms went around me, pulling me against his newly pumped-up physique. "Damn, I've missed you." His smile and utter joy were contagious. He was so different from his family. They were gruff, dark, secretive, and hostile. Jared was the sun in their night. Happy, open, and innocent.

"Missed you too." I smiled back. It was the truth. I had missed him. The goofy computer geek I could talk comic books and *Star Wars* with. "Working out I see."

"I know, right?" His face lit up as he stepped back, flexing an arm. "Look at your studly boyfriend now.

Packed on fifteen pounds and can bench over three hundred. You should see me with a sword now. You'd be impressed."

"I was impressed before." I laced my fingers with his, pulling him closer. I wanted him to kiss me, to push me up against one of the cabins and make me forget everything. Formerly, I would have been too nervous or insecure to even think I wanted him to be aggressive with me. We had been loveable with each other, always kissing, but in a sweet, innocent, young-love way.

Something in my body had switched. I no longer wanted to be timid and chaste. An ache had started, one Lorcan had awakened, and I wanted to ease it. Maybe if it was Jared, I would forget all about Lorcan. Although the thought of sex still scared me, there was a hunger there. One which desired more than it feared.

"I have so much to tell you. I can't believe it's been, like, three months," Jared continued to talk, his voice excited and fast. I tried to push back the feeling I was with a friend's younger brother.

He rambled about his training when I went up on my toes, stopping his mouth with my own. I needed to feel the connection between us again, to have all the doubts taken from my gut and crushed.

His lips responded. Eagerly. He cupped my face, deepening our kiss. It was like getting back in your PJs. Comfortable, easy, and enjoyable. Did my blood boil? No. But it was nice. Familiar. Safe.

Jared's hand moved down my side, his thumb brushing the side of my breast. A tiny zing of heat ran up my body, and my mouth moved more frantically against his. I tried to shut up the voice telling me having sex with Jared wouldn't stop the confusion I felt.

Jared noticed the intensity change, sucking in a sharp breath and pulling back enough to look at me. Whatever expression I had on my face crinkled his brow.

"What?" I tipped into him, kissing his jaw. "Don't you want this?"

A snorted laugh came from him. "I'm an eighteen-year-old boy. Hell yeah I want it…but *you* never have before."

"Well, I want to now." If I stopped kissing him, my mind would break in and tell me all the reasons I shouldn't. I was tired of thinking. Tired of being scared.

"Just…wasn't expecting this right now," he rumbled as I nipped at his ear. "Are you sure?"

"Yes." Irritation forced a sigh from my lungs. I didn't want him to ask me questions or be considerate. I wanted him to take me so I didn't have to think or do anything but get caught up in the passion.

"What about protection? I don't have any." He pulled back, his face going serious. Rational. "Maybe one of my uncles or someone around here does…"

The common-sense tone and the mention of an uncle was like a cold shower to my system, jarring me out of my desperation to not ponder anything. *What am I about to do?* My anger from the fight with Ember and my feelings for Lorcan and myself bulleted me down a one-lane road with determination.

"Shit," I hissed, moving around Jared, rubbing my face.

There was a beat before Jared spoke. "Did you swear?"

"Yeah." I rounded back on him. "So?"

"No, it's just I've never heard you swear before. It sounds strange coming from you. Not like you."

"I'm twenty-two, Jared. I swear, drink, and want to have sex."

A blush hinted at Jared's cheeks as he looked around to see if anyone heard.

"No longer the naïve girl anymore," I said, turning back around, pushing my glasses higher on my nose.

He strolled up, his arms wrapping around my middle. "And I'm not the scrawny, pathetic, half-dweller anymore. I mean, look at me. I've been working out every day. Cole says if I continue to train I can be part of the fight."

"He did?"

"Well, not exactly, but he will. He has to." He squeezed his arms around me as if highlighting his newly gained muscles. "And I can show my mate how badass I am."

I cringed at hearing him use "mate." It made me feel as if I had no say or control. "Is that what this about? Proving something?" I pulled away to face him. "Why?"

"What do you mean why?" Bewilderment struck his face. "I'm not sitting back while they treat me like a kid. I've been working hard. Let those fairy pricks try to challenge me now. I can totally take any pansy Light fae down."

My mouth gaped. Was he really this naïve? To misjudge how devastating and brutal wars could be? He had no idea how trained and pitiless the Queen's soldiers were. How little he was prepared compared to them.

"Jared, I—" Blinding white light streaked through my head and snatched me from awareness. The flashes came fast and furious, crowding my head painfully.

Flash.

Aneira. Her long red hair tumbled down her back. She wore tight leather pants, a silky top, and heeled boots and was surrounded by her people. Maps of places I couldn't decipher lay on the table in front of her. High nobles and upper crust Fairies lined the walls like she was a one-woman play, hanging on her every word. My eyes scrolled quickly past the blur of faces, but the feel of eyes twisted my head to the side.

My lips parted and my chest clenched. An albino man with light violet-blue eyes stared right into me from the back of the room, like he really saw me there. It was as if the crowd parted and I could only see him. And him me.

Can he see me? Is that possible?

"Ready, my dear boy?" Aneira's voice snapped my head back to her. She curled her finger, beckoning someone. A boy no older than fourteen or fifteen walked up to her. He was skinny and tall but strikingly beautiful with dark hair, tan skin, chocolate brown eyes, dressed in cream pants and button-up shirt. "Come, Asim."

He stood in front of her, his eyes staring at her as if she was a dream. "Yes, Majesty." He bowed his head.

"It's time to show them what I really can do. I want them to fear me, to understand they are all going to die." Her eyes glinted. "Do not hold back, my pet."

"I won't, my Queen." Asim reached out, wrapping both hands around Aneira's wrists.

Flash.

People screamed. The earth quaked under their feet with fierce jolts. Tall buildings crumbled, large chunks fell into the water. A tower bridge with a British flag swung before it collapsed into a river. Bodies were crushed underneath dropping debris. Metal squealed as a sixteen-story Ferris wheel full of tourists tipped and plummeted toward the dark water. Lightning bolted down, blazing buildings. Colored flames bloomed off the structures.

Magic crackled the sky.

London Bridge was truly falling down.

Destroyed by magic.

By Aneira.

Flash.

More people shrieked and ran. The ground slid under them; chunks of skyscrapers shredded and tumbled to the ground. I looked up and saw the famous Empire State Building wavering under the harsh shaking.

No! My scream vaulted around in my head as I watched New York bend to its knees. Magic danced and crackled in the air, and I knew this is not natural either.

Aneira.

Figures spread out in all directions; their wails pierced my heart. I could feel the terror wafting off them, curling over me. I tried to shut my eyes, to leave the scene, but when I reopened them, New York was still crumbling around me. My back hit rough concrete as I stumbled back into a building. The texture scraped my skin, making me feel as if I was actually there. *No. No. I shouldn't be able to feel it.* I shook my head. *Wake up, Kennedy!*

"Light locked in here." A squawk sounded next to me, and I jumped. Grimmel was perched on a newspaper stand, staring at me. "Lost forever."

"What?" The darn bird never made any sense.

"Trapped in box. Lost." He tilted his head. "Key help find you."

"What do you mean? I'm trapped in here? In my vision?" I leaped as a piece of a building crashed near my feet, splintering into dust. A person's shoulder rammed into me, knocking me to the ground.

"Ooofff." I hit the pavement, my palms scraping cement. The man looked back but kept running down the street. A stinging lured my attention down to the blood and cuts over my hands.

Oh. God. No.

My visions had never interacted with me like this. Pain. It was the one thing that kept me grounded in the real world and helped me separate the two.

"Control light. Or vanish," Grimmel squawked.

"How?" I pushed up, glancing back at the raven. "I don't know how."

"Dark anchors light."

Boom!

An explosion sounded a couple of blocks away, whipping through the buildings. A gush of heated wind blew my hair off my face, the smell of dust and fire filled my nose. *This is not real. This is not real.*

Not yet anyway.

I have to get back into my body. Break free.

"Ken-ne-dy." A whisper of my name whistled down the corridor of deteriorating buildings, jerking my head around. *"Ken..."*

"Heed light."

"Grimmel. Help me. Please." My limbs trembled with oppressive fear.

"Grimmel no help." He cranked his neck to the side.

"No kidding." A frustrated cry broke over my mouth, and I rubbed my face.

"Observe. Find tether. Inside and out."

My arms wiggled around me as I tried to push anxiety from my body. *This is not real. This is my mind. I can get out. I just need to relax.*

In the distance another blast broadcasted debris, icing my veins. The horror these people would go through if I didn't have time to stop it. I had to get back. Talk to Lars. He was the only one with enough power and connections to at least warn someone.

My soul was heavy with responsibility.

Again my name rang out from the distance. I could feel my soul wanting to latch on, follow it out of here.

A tether.

I exhaled, shutting my eyes, focusing on the voice.

"Wildness inside must be tamed. Or light will be consumed," Grimmel said before I heard his wings beating in the air. I parted my lids. He was gone.

All alone. A ball of trepidation coiled in my stomach, fluttering into my lungs. *Calm down, Ken. You need to center yourself.*

Wildness inside must be tamed or light will be consumed. Grimmel's words rang in my head. I was still so green, so new at this, but I pushed out the commotion around me and drew into myself. My body relaxed, the screams lost in a sea of my chant.

"Kennedy. Wake up!" A voice skewered me, dragging me like a hooked fish. I surrendered, letting myself rush to the surface.

Flash.

〰〰〰

A face over me. Familiar green eyes. Safety.

My gaze darted around, my head swirling. Another figure hunched over me, his hazel eyes round with worry.

"Ken! Shit! You scared me. You totally went zombie on me." He moved closer, his hands reaching for my face with hasty movements.

My body reacted like a snake was striking. I wheeled back, crawling back on the ground, my mind too full of the images I saw. Rotating so fast and furious, reality like a thin bubble ready to burst. The devastation. People's screams beat in my head on repeat.

The hazel-eyed boy came forward again.

"Don't!" The man held up his arm, shoving the boy back on his heels. "She needs a minute."

My tether.

"A minute for what?"

I scanned the line of buildings near me, forms in the distance going through battle moves.

Lars's compound.

Lorcan.

Jared.

Lorcan ignored Jared's frown, keeping his eyes locked on mine, helping me anchor myself to earth.

"You're here, Ken." Lorcan's voice was soothing to the frantic mess inside. Sometimes coming out of a vision was an easy switch, but sometimes it felt like a monster clung to my leg, trying to pull me back. Today it was wrapped around my middle, dragging me under.

London.

New York.

Screaming. Death. Fear.

"Kennedy, listen to my voice. You are safe. I am here. Real."

I shook my head, tears hazing my view through my glasses. The pictures in my head sharpened into a horror movie.

"What's wrong with her? I've never seen her like this." Jared stood, stomping toward me.

I flinched. Lorcan was on his feet. "Back off!"

Fury rode over Jared's chest, huffing it out. "Don't tell me to back off. She's *my* girlfriend." He closed his hand. "You're the one who probably caused this. I mean, you kidnapped her. You should be the one to back off."

His anger pumped off him, slamming into me, adding to the abundance of sensations running through me. I hunched over, my head hitting my knees, my arms around my legs, a wail pushing from my mouth. The images flashing faster and faster.

"Fuck," Lorcan swore, dropping down to his knees in front of me. "Breathe, li'l Druid. I'm here."

"It won't stop." Desperation rang in my voice as I lifted my head, needing him. The feeling of being out of control was one of the worst sensations for me. And it seemed to come a lot with my visions. "Death. Earthquake. Pain...so much pain and fear."

Lorcan ran his hands down my arms. "Concentrate on me. On my voice."

"I can't tell the difference anymore." I turned up my palms. Scrapes covered them, amplifying the panic in me. "Oh god. Th-they can hurt me now."

"Kennedy, stop," Lorcan demanded, snapping my attention to him. "I said focus on me. Nothing else."

"What the hell? Get your hands off my girlfriend." Jared tried to pull Lorcan away, but Lorcan didn't budge. His green eyes lasered on me.

"I hear. I smell. I feel. Tell me, li'l bird."

His gaze on mine blotted out everything else. "I hear your voice. Deep and soothing. I smell dirt. Tangy and damp. I feel the chill of the wind."

The intensity of the scenes in my head eased, letting me get a handle on them. Lorcan's hands started to pull away, but I grabbed them, still needing a moor.

"Show me," I practically begged. Even though the vision had interacted with me, I needed the ritual Lorcan and I had to bring me to the earth. Like a checklist.

Lorcan's gaze intensified, his hand reaching up, brushing over my ear. His fingers skimmed the top of my ear and traced down to my earlobe. He pinched till a sting hit my nerves.

A rush of air folded out of my lungs. Like it was my trigger, my feet felt grounded in the earth. My head gave Lorcan the tiniest of nods. He stood, easing me to my feet with him.

"Lars. I need Lars now," I uttered to him.

He nodded, about to turn away, but I held on to his arms. I wasn't ready, my legs still wobbly underneath me.

Lorcan looked away, his tongue skimming his lip. "Jared, stay with Kennedy. I will go get Lars."

No. Don't leave me. The thought almost punched out of my mouth before I ground my teeth together. Peering around Lorcan, I saw Jared's twisted features, his gaze darting between Lorcan and me. I dropped Lorcan's arms, stepping back. Confusion, hurt, anger.

"No. I will go. I need to see him immediately," I said, already moving for the house.

I was almost across the field when Lars came out the side French doors of his office. Cal zoomed out past me toward the buildings.

Lars's yellow-green eyes met mine, and I knew.

I was too late.

EIGHTEEN

"Jared, go retrieve Cole and anyone else you see and send them to my office," Lars ordered the moment he got to our group.

Jared sputtered, his glare still on Lorcan, mouth crimped as though unhappy about being asked to leave the group.

"Now," the King yelled. Jared looked like he was about to rebuff the request, which you did not do to the monarch of the Dark.

"Jared. Please," I cut in before his teenage attitude could get him in trouble. What was with him?

"Fine," he grumbled and loped off, jogging for the cabins.

"It's already happened, hasn't it? I'm too late." Sorrow clipped my throat. "New York and London."

"You foresaw this event?" Lars jerked his head toward me, his gaze so intense I felt my skin might burn beneath it.

"Yes. Just a moment ago. I was coming to tell you. I saw everything." The cries of the people still resonated in my ears. "It was Aneira. She's using Ember's powers. A little boy stood next to her. Asim?"

His fingers wiped at his brow. "The boy is an amplifier. His touch triples the power behind the magic. One finger from him and she can level a town."

My stomach churned with acid. "I have visions, but they happen too close to actual events. I can't do anything about them or stop them from happening."

"That will never be in your control, Ms. Johnson. But you are too new, too inexperienced to be getting such full visions like this." Lars tightened his mouth. "You are a lot more powerful than I first thought." His gaze drifted over my head, his lids narrowing. "What the hell?" He started to move around me. I followed his line of sight. Three Dark fae were breaking into a small stone building across the field. "That room is off limits," he growled, already storming for the building. "Wait in my office. I will be back."

Lars took off, his long legs eating up land.

I turned back and headed for the office, Lorcan by my side, my only source of strength.

Once again, I failed. Thousands of lives lost. Every one of those screams came true.

⁓⁓⁓

Lars had the TV on, which revealed a sea of bloody faces screaming and crying. Cars crushed between fallen buildings, fires lapping up whatever damage hadn't been done by the quake. The monitor split between London and New York.

I put my hand to my throat, felt my pulse beating wildly beneath my fingers. The exact images I had seen were displayed on the screen, taunting me. The headline was fastened to the screen at the bottom.

9.0 EARTHQUAKES HIT
NEW YORK AND LONDON.
FIRE DAMAGE DESTROYS CITIES,
KILLING HUNDREDS OF THOUSANDS.

Lorcan didn't try to give me words of solace. There were none. His hand slipped to my back, pressing against my spine. No one could see but his touch was a lifeline.

By the time Lars returned his office was full, people flooding in by the groups. Dark dwellers—Eli, Ember, Cole, Owen, West, Cooper, Gabby, and Dax—stood near Lorcan and me against the wall. Lars's demon family consisted of Alki and Koke in the middle. Rez made an appearance, but as the person in charge of the constantly ringing phone, she quickly stepped outside fielding calls. I was surprised to see Torin and Simmons enter. I had heard rumors Torin was staying in the Otherworld with Ryan, Lily, Mark, and Ryan's boyfriend, Castien, the fay soldier who protected us in the Queen's castle. Word must have traveled fast to the other realm.

Torin shifted, watching the door.

Lorcan's hand drifted up my back. My gaze went to him and quickly snapped back on the screen. *Not the time, Kennedy.*

"Oh my god," Ember gasped, horror deep in her eyes. I could picture her thoughts: *Not again.*

This wasn't the first time Aneira had displayed her power while trying to send a warning to Ember. She had taken out Ember's hometown of Monterey, California, in one surge of water, a monster tsunami that killed thousands. And Aneira didn't even possess Ember's powers then.

It was terrifying how much devastation one fay could cause. Aneira had grown too powerful and cruel. She needed to be stopped, and Ember was prophesized to do it.

Tears ran down my face, my body frozen in agony. Only a few people here knew this was the second time I had to watch this horror Aneira brought to Earth.

Lars's eyes flicked to me, then back to the room. "My sources say she used Ember's powers, magnified by Asim, to cause this devastation. With the power of earth and fire along with her own power of air, she caused several huge earthquakes and the destruction after. Earthquakes plus fire with massive winds are all she needs. The heart of both cities will burn in a matter of hours. She has all the elements she needs to destroy."

"We have to do something," Ember exclaimed. Simmons flew over to be near her. The pixies had bonded with the future Queen, and I doubted they would ever leave her side.

"What do you want us to do, Ember?" Lars inquired, as if he were testing her.

Ember stepped closer to him, as though challenging him back.

"Something! Anything! We can't let her get away with this. She can't be allowed to kill and destroy again...with *my* powers. We have to stop her."

"What do you suggest?" Lars strolled around the desk, coming toe to toe with her. "Go to the Otherworld and fight her right now?"

"Yes," she responded, gazing around the room, appearing to seek our approval.

"Then she will win. The Queen on her own land is too powerful." Disappointment coated Lars's words. "Neither myself nor any Dark fae will be able to fight there for long."

"What do you mean? You fought her when you rescued me."

"Only for a brief time. I could not have stayed for much longer without feeling the effects."

"What effects?"

"Dark cannot fight too long on Light's land and vice versa." Lars slid his hands in his pockets. "The Dark takes Light's energy and the Light depletes ours. It is why all our battles take place during Samhain. It equalizes the energies of all land, Earth and the Otherworld."

"What do we do? What's our next step?" Ember's shoulders slumped, her hysteria dissolving.

"We will fight her, Ember." He leaned back into the desk. "And we are going to defeat her. The prophecy *will* be fulfilled. As the Light's future Queen, I want to know what *you* would do next."

Ember's mouth parted, her eyes blinking furiously. I recognized the look. Ember was extremely smart, but she'd never done well on tests in school; anxiety emptied her brain. I lived for that kind of pressure, as if my mind sharpened on the facts and nothing else.

Ember didn't take the time to see the trees; she reacted first. I saw one tree at a time and the steps leading me up to the whole forest. I could see everything so clearly, could understand the situation and the list we needed to follow to succeed.

"We need to strategize every move, every role people will be playing." My mouth opened, spilling out the phases in my head. "We do a few practice runs so we all feel comfortable with what we are doing. Familiarity with our roles will keep us on target instead of letting fear take over."

Lars whirled around to me. I realized the entire room stared at me. I automatically stepped back, wanting to hide from the attention, but Lorcan's hand pressed firmer into me, holding me in place.

"Exactly what I was thinking." Lars nodded in approval. "Aneira is attempting to weaken us. I have received an influx of calls from Dark fae who survived and are fleeing London and New York. They will be heading here. Magic caused the destruction, so it not only killed humans, but hundreds of Dark fae have perished as well. The stakes have been raised, and we must be prepared for what is ahead. Merely training is no longer enough. With Cole's help, I have started planning the best approach for war."

Lars's gaze darted back and forth between Ember and me. "Ember and Kennedy are the most vital. When we locate the sword, we'll need them there."

"The sword hasn't been located yet?" Cole asked.

"No. Not yet. I have informants searching. I do not doubt we will have the information before the battle begins," Lars's report draped the room with heaviness. I could feel the spikes of anxiety darting off the crowd like porcupines. Everything relied on us finding the sword. The only way to truly win this war was to kill Aneira. It couldn't be done without the sword, and if we didn't find it, our chances were minimal. Bile gurgled in my stomach, thinking about the possibility we wouldn't locate it in time. *No.* That wasn't an option.

"As you all know, Ember does not have her fay powers. At least she is no longer affected by iron while Aneira is. My spies have told me she is trying to test herself daily around iron, which leads me to believe she thinks she has the dark dweller's powers in her along with Ember's. She is frustrated as to why Ember could push through the iron and she cannot."

It was crippling enough to know Aneira contained the power of fire along with her own power of air. I couldn't imagine it if she also encompassed dark dweller abilities.

"The sword will be protected with spells and guarded around the clock. The critical plan is to get Ember, the sword, and Aneira all in the same room," Lars continued. "I will be sure to always have eyes on the Queen. When she heads back for the castle, I will follow. Until then, I have to be with my men. Aneira has to be sure of my presence on the field. Yet I understand in lieu of Ember not having her powers, I am the only one strong enough to help contain Aneira long enough for Ember to kill her with the sword. Just in case, Cole and I have developed a plan. I want us to be prepared for all circumstances which may arise."

Lars pointed at Cole. Cole pulled an object from his pocket, the metal glittering under the lights. I squinted, pushing up my glasses. A bracelet?

"Ember, you will carry an iron bracelet. This is the only one of these armlets in existence, and it is extremely powerful. It's goblin made, and it will help debilitate Aneira."

"Is that...?" Ember gaped.

"Oh, I've missed your doggie collar. Can't take you for walks like I used to," Eli snickered.

Ember elbowed his stomach, only making him laugh harder. It reminded me so much of Lorcan I had to rub my temple to keep out dangerous memories.

Ember took the bracelet cautiously, slipping it through her fingers as if it were a snake. She relaxed when nothing happened.

"Don't you love the idea of locking it around Aneira's wrist and using it to restrain and deplete the bitch of her powers?" Cooper folded his arms and leaned against the wall.

"If you don't, can I, darlin'?" West lifted his lip in a snarl. "I have a few complaints about the dungeon I would like to file with her."

I knew West less than all the dwellers. Aneira had held him prisoner for my entire time at the dwellers' ranch. Our paths never crossed, though I experienced enough of Aneira to imagine the horror he must have gone through while held captive by her. The turmoil bounding off him was dark and foul, and I pulled back from him, scared of what was beneath the surface. The hate and...shame. No one seemed to see the southern-talking charmer's soul was caked black as tar under his smile, hiding the torment beneath his skin.

"We hope you will not have to use the bracelet, but I want you to be prepared." Lars's fingers brushed his desk as he moved back around it. "And now you can carry it without repercussions." He shut off the TV, swallowing my come-to-life vision from the screen. I hated I felt relieved. But for a moment I needed to breathe without drowning in the pain of so many. "We have a lot to discuss; everyone get comfortable."

Two hours later, I sat in the family room in the basement of the house watching TV. Most had retreated here after we were dismissed, stuck watching the loop of the footage. The only thing new was the rising body count.

Lars requested Ember and Eli to stay back. As I sat there watching the devastation, hearing the people cry for their loved ones, it hit me how stupid I had been earlier. How wasteful my resentment at Ember had been. What was happening to these people might soon be our own future. Did I want to waste my last moments being upset with my best friend? I couldn't go to the family who raised me. Not till the war was over. *If* I lived. But my chosen family was here. I could wrap my arms around and hold them.

I missed Ember. And I really missed Ryan.

The thought of my friend in the Otherworld tugged at my heart. Ryan and I had been through so much together. Though Ryan realized he enjoyed the thought of kissing the lead singer in our favorite boy band more than kissing me, he was still my first kiss at age ten. We both gagged then started laughing.

We'd been there for each other when his father had screamed at him for dressing up as a princess for Halloween at eight. And when a mean girl had pushed me into the mud. When his father hit him. When my parents fought and my mother threatened to leave. So many nights we had comforted each other, taking turns when the bullies came after us. When Ember came along it was like we had been waiting for her. She completed our group.

I wanted nothing more than to hold my friends close. Death was coming. If my visions were true, then most likely for me. The chilling thought only confirmed my priorities: my friends came first.

Ember entered the room and settled on the other end of the sofa, Eli stood behind her. Her attention remained on the television, despair clear on her pinched features.

I felt numb to the pictures. The only sensation I could let in was the heat of Lorcan's eyes on my neck from the back of the room. Dax had left to get away from Cole's group, leaving Lorcan alone with his ostracized family. He wouldn't let me out of his sight, no matter how uncomfortable it was. At first it made me fidgety, but soon I almost forgot he was there.

The screen sucked in my emotions and spit them back out on my lap, empty and ragged. The media tortured us with blood-soaked children and wailing mothers. Ember made a sound and stood, rushing from the room.

"Em?" Eli and I turned, calling her.

"Let me," I said to Eli when he went to go after her. I hurried out of the room, following Ember's stomps as she ran up the stairs, heading for her room on the second level.

Muffled sobs drifted up from the other side of the room when I entered. I moved around her enormous bed, finding her huddled on the other side, her back against the bed, facing the doors to her private balcony.

"This isn't your fault." I kneeled down next to her, my voice soft. She sat on her knees, bent forward, heaving with sobs, shaking violently, and breathing too rapidly. This had been me a few hours earlier, and only one thing had helped me. One person. "Breathe. Concentrate on me. On my eyes." My words echoed Lorcan's as I quietly muttered my relaxation mantra I did most mornings.

Ember blinked, her shoulders and chest falling with relief as she exhaled. Then she paused, her brows crunching together. "Did you work your Druid mojo on me?"

"Yes." I reached out and patted her leg. It really wasn't a spell, but more a suggestion, calming energy transferring to her. "You were having a panic attack. I could see it coming, and it was not going to be pretty. I understand why you feel what Aneira did is more on you than anybody else, but it is not your fault. You did not wreak the destruction we saw. Don't let Aneira get into your head. We need you to be at your best. Aneira took your powers, but she did not take away who you are."

"I feel like those powers are who I am."

"No," I stated. "They add to you, but they are not you. You are much more than your abilities. You are the girl I befriended in junior high, who is strong and feisty, loves deeply, and will fight to the death for those she cares about. That is who you are. You are the person I love and have missed so much." My voice cracked and I looked down.

After a few seconds, Ember flung her arms around me, squeezing me in a tight hug.

"I've missed you so much, too. I hate you being mad at me. It's something I hadn't experienced before and never want to again. I love you so much."

"Today gave me a huge dose of perspective." I held her tight, relishing her comfort. "I was being silly. Right now all I care about is both you and Ryan are alive and in my life. All the rest can kiss my ass."

"Kennedy." Ember jolted back, eyes round, her eyebrows up in her hairline. "You swore."

"Yep, I mean it that much." I smiled. Lorcan was rubbing off on me.

"Shit suddenly got serious." Ember leaned back against the frame, a smile hinting on her mouth.

Then we started laughing. It was like someone pulled the plug on a drain, letting all the icky feelings bleed away. The weight I had been holding since our fight lifted, and I touched the spot on my chest where it had constricted. Now feeling unrestricted, the giggles came out in liberated bursts until my stomach and cheeks hurt. I slid down to sit beside Ember, my shoulder bumping hers.

"Today made me realize I want to do something." I pulled my legs to my chest. "Even if it's really foolish."

"What?" She looked at me with narrowed eyes. I never did foolish. The old Kennedy didn't anyway.

Now I seemed to be throwing myself recklessly down any ravine.

"See Ryan." I let my legs drop, my hands twisting in my lap. The thought had just come to me, but the moment I uttered it I knew nothing would stop me from going. "I know Lars will deny me, but I need to see Ryan. To hug him." *One last time.* "He can't come back here, so the only thing I can do is go to him."

"Ken, I did and was almost killed by the strighoul. It's too dangerous." Ember blinked like she couldn't believe those words came out of her mouth.

"I know, but when did it ever stop you before?" I peered at her.

"Uhhhh...good point."

"Em, please." The more I thought of Ryan, the more desperate I was to see him. I was no fool, I understood going to war meant I might not come back. If I were to die in a few weeks, I needed to say goodbye to Ryan. See him, hug him…one last time.

"Fine. Fine." Ember leaned her head back onto the bed. "I don't have the right to tell you not to do anything." Then a smile glinted at her eyes. "Let's do it."

I let out an excited yelp.

"One problem." Ember's smile dropped. "There is no way I can go without Eli knowing. He will have me chained down in the basement faster than I can blink. And not in the fun way."

"Yeah." I stared into the night, campfires creating ghostly outlines in the landscape. Somewhere out there I felt Lorcan's eyes on me. He no longer had to babysit, was no longer obliged to watch me. But the thought of him walking away left an empty ache in its wake. "Those dark dwellers make it hard to get away with anything."

Ember's gaze burned into me, but I did not meet her eyes. "They are a pain in the butt."

I nodded, my attention pulled to one part of the field. He was there. I knew it.

"My birthday is tomorrow..." Ember spoke, sitting up higher.

Uh-oh. Her expression was all too familiar and had gotten me in trouble with my parents more times than I could count. But this time I was all for it. "The birthday girl should get to do what she wants." I grinned.

"And I want to have a party with my friends and parents in the Otherworld." She met my smile with her own.

"Good luck." A voice came from the door. I peeked up over the bed as Gabby strutted into the room and flung herself across Ember's bed. Her chin landed between us.

"Come on, Gab, it's not like you are a rule follower." Ember shifted over to look at the dweller.

"No, but I like my life, and Eli would kill me if he found out I knew and let you girls go."

"And Eli knows I do what I want. No one *lets* me do anything."

Gabby rolled her eyes, snorting. We all knew Eli could stop Em if he really wanted.

"Besides," Ember continued, "I'm planning to tell Eli. I can't get far without him knowing anyway."

"You think he'll be okay with it? After last time?" Gabby exclaimed. "I thought we were going to have to commit him. You are about as dumb as an imp if you think he will agree to your leaving."

"I have my ways of persuasion." Ember grinned mischievously.

Gabby stared at Em, her brows peaked.

"Okay, they're called blackmail and guilt." Ember shrugged.

"Now, that is a true fae answer."

NINETEEN

The next day was somber, footage of Aneira's wrath still rolling over and over again on the TV. Unable to do anything, I had to turn away from the horrors on the screen and focus on what I could do.

Magic.

With the need for more practice I started toward Lorcan's cabin without a second thought. A twist of awareness stopped me. I didn't even think—I went to him instinctively. Not Jared, who used to stand out in the field with me for hours. Or Cole or Owen, both who had spent weeks helping me.

Lorcan.

Maybe because we had been working so hard on my spells together the last few months, but the sensation under my skin spoke the truth. He was the anchor pulling me. My body yearned to be in close proximity to him. I couldn't keep going to him. It wasn't fair to him, Jared, or me, especially when nothing could be between us.

I reversed my direction. Few steps. And ceased.

But...it was about magic. Lorcan was a great teacher and pushed me more than anyone. I needed to be my best.

Switched direction and continued on to his cabin.

Who are you fooling, Ken? You are creating reasons to see him.

Pause. Walk. Stop. Turn.

"Shit!" The curse word flew from my mouth like it had been waiting behind a starting gate.

"Kennedy?" The sound of his voice came from behind me, jolting my spine into a rod. I squeezed my eyes shut. *Holy-crap-squared.* "What are you doing?"

"Uh." Gradually I turned around, words dissolving from my vocabulary altogether. Lorcan stood there in running shoes, shorts, and a thin sweat-soaked T-shirt clinging to his torso, his chest heaving with exertion. Perspiration glistened on his arms, his muscles flexing as they cooled down.

Uhhhhh… My tongue tried to curve around words. None came. My composure was snatched from me. I pushed at my glasses, stared at the ground, my foot rubbing over the dirt.

Would that be what he looked like after sex? The thought burst into my brain. Blood rushed through my body like a storm as I stood there embarrassed and turned on. *Kennedy!* I chided myself.

"Kennedy." His voice was raspy and low, making my heart bang against my rib cage. "Look at me."

I couldn't.

"I-I saw you with West..." My boot carved deep tunnels with my toe, desperate for neutral territory or anything to break the intensity between us.

He huffed, shifting his feet. "Yeah. We're far from being close like we once were, but it's a start."

My head still down, I nodded, watching my hair tumble around my face. I was so happy Lorcan was taking these steps to repair the broken relationships with his clan.

Silence weeded around us, wrapping around my legs heavy with all the things neither of us were saying.

"Look at me, li'l bird." Lorcan took a single step toward me.

I lifted my gaze to meet his eyes. Green eyes zeroed in on me, flickering with so much intensity they directed another swell of nerves to tighten in my belly. Who was I kidding? The clenching was going on a lot lower.

Seeing the hunger in his stare rattled my muscles, forcing my legs to feel weak. He knew. He was a beast. He could sense pheromones. I knew it was simply biology, but that didn't take away the humiliation or the need pumping through me.

We humans, with our high-level thinking and rationalizing, like to believe we are different from animals. Yet if everything was taken away from us, those instincts would rise to the forefront. Survival and sex were high on the list.

I understood the science of it. But it didn't seem to help calm my heart as he watched me. We were yards apart, but I could feel the pulsing of his body against my skin. My mind filled with an image of him grabbing me, wrapping my legs around his waist as he kissed me hard and pushed me back against one of the cabins.

A barely audible growl rumbled from Lorcan, but he didn't budge. My limbs trembled and itched to move forward. Fear kept me held in place. Desire moved through me like a conscious entity.

"Ms. Johnson?" A voice broke my trance, jolting me harshly. *Oh no.* My head jerked to the side to see Owen standing there, his neck swiveling between Lorcan and me. "Are you all right?"

"Uh." I shoved at the bridge of my glasses, turning to him. "I'm fine."

Owen's gaze narrowed on Lorcan for another beat before he cleared his throat. "The King would like to see you in his office."

Lorcan snorted. "Went from doctor to fetch dog?"

I planted my hands on my hips, glaring at Lorcan. He winked back. I internally groaned. Lorcan couldn't seem to help himself. Always provoking. The bridge between the groups was extremely fragile, but instead of helping his cause, he poked and jabbed, like a little boy who liked a girl. Too fearful if he put his heart out there it would be rejected.

Owen didn't take the bait. "We had a meeting earlier and he asked me, since I was heading to see my *son*, to request *you* to come see him. But I find you here." Owen's implication shamed me, curling around my chest like fog.

"Thank you, Owen." My feet already moved. "I will head straight there." I needed to get away. From Owen. From Lorcan. From the guilt constantly coating my insides with thick tar. I could feel Lorcan's gaze boring into my back, but I kept my head forward.

My new to-do list.

1.) Stop all interaction with Lorcan and turn all attention on learning more spells. This should be your only focus.

The list was short, but I had to follow it. From now on I would ignore these stupid hormones raging inside and only concentrate on my mind. I had done so for eighteen years. It really should not be a problem.

Right?

~~~~

"Ms. Johnson, please sit." The Unseelie King motioned to a chair in front of his desk. Today he was dressed in casual attire: boots, cargo pants, and black T-shirt, his uniform he had for trekking through Greece.

Power filled the room even as he sat in his chair, his eyes on me. He still made me nervous. I didn't think he'd do anything to me because of Ember, but I always felt an underlying threat around him. Even when he was relaxed, you always knew he could cut off your head in the next moment.

"Thank you, sir." I perched at the end of the chair, my hands in my lap.

He watched me for a few more seconds while I stirred in my seat and touched my glasses. He inhaled and glanced away.

"I do not think I have to remind you what is at stake in the war. Samhain is coming, and you are not where I'd hoped you be."

"Not where..." I stumbled over my words, growing defensive. "I am three times better than I was in Greece. And I broke the hiding spell there." I was on my feet, standing my full height. "I will have you know I have been working hard the past few months. I have grown a lot. So before you assume I haven't advanced any, you should ask."

It was about a full ten seconds of Lars staring emotionless at me that it fully sank in what I had just done. Mouthing off to the Unseelie King was not smart. Actually, it was the stupidest thing you could do, but instead of cowering, I held his gaze, forcing my shoulders back.

Ten more seconds passed.

Crapping nerf herders.

Then in a snap, Lars's green eyes glinted and humor twitched at his mouth.

"Have a seat, Ms. Johnson." He let out a chuckle. "If you had let me finish my sentence, you would understand you are still far more advanced for someone at your level."

"Oh my god," I mumbled, my legs bowing back into the chair. "I am so sorry."

"No." He shook his head. "Don't be. I appreciate someone who knows who they are and won't back down." Lars sat up, leaning his arms on his desk. "You are exceptionally powerful. And I know you would have made an exceptional leader of the Druids someday."

"I thought I was the last Druid?"

"Your parents were not the only ones to hide their children from Aneira."

I gulped, feeling a heavy sinking in my stomach when the tense of his previous sentence settled on me. Somewhere in my gut I already understood, had already foreseen but did not want to accept.

"What do you mean 'would have'?" my voice strained.

Lars cupped his hands. "I think you already know the answer to that."

My teeth clamped together, my lids blinking, keeping the tears at bay. I sucked in a huge gulp of air and pointed my chin up.

"I'm going to die, aren't I?"

The softest, most empathetic expression I could imagine on Lars's face was like a sucker punch to my gut. It was worse than if he was nonchalant about it.

"Yes, Ms. Johnson," he said quietly. "There is a very good chance." He shifted in his seat, breaking his gaze from me. "I have tried to come up with any other way. But the only one who will be able to break the curse on the sword is a Druid."

"You know that for sure?"

"Yes, my sources have confirmed the deepest magic set by Aneira is bound around the sword. Only a Druid can challenge it." Lars huffed in frustration and leaned back in his seat. "This admission will never leave this room. I cannot help you. Her magic may not be stronger than mine, but it is different. You are the only one who has a chance to break the spell."

"And you think I can do it?"

He compressed his lips before he brought his fingers under his chin. "You will have to."

The wave of tears threatened to crush down on me, but I bit my lip till they receded.

"I've had visions," I breathed, trying to steady my voice. "Just tiny glimpses, not anything really substantial. But I knew about the sword. I knew I would die in the war."

"You understand, Ms. Johnson, how important you are to this mission? Ember's fate cannot happen without you. She will not succeed if you do not. The world is counting on the two of you. I understand it is a lot for you both to carry, especially two so young. However, you above anyone, including Ember, can handle it. Like I said, you would have made an outstanding leader of the Druids."

I nodded, rubbing my temples.

"The curse surrounding the sword will fight back. It will attack and fight to the end. No matter what, you cannot give up. You are our only hope."

A twisted snort rose up my throat.

"What is so funny, Ms. Johnson?"

"That I'm Obi-Wan and you're Princess Leia."

A frown creased Lars forehead, his lips firming in a strained line.

"Never mind." I cleared my throat, looking down. *Ryan would get a kick out of it.* The thought of him sobered my mind. I had to see him. Even more now.

"Do you understand what that means, Ms. Johnson?"

"Yes." I lifted my head, staring him in the eye. The fear and sadness vanished. I did. I understood my fate in this war.

Lars stared at me again. "People never seem to notice the quiet ones." Rising from his seat, he placed his hands on his desk, leaning in. "In my experience they are always the strongest. The pillars." He walked around his desk. "And you are a true leader, Ms. Johnson."

I had no retort. Lars giving such a rare compliment silenced me.

Then the mood changed, his shoulders hitching back into King mode. His expression hardened to stone, his voice grew even.

"I do not want Ember to know. She has a tremendous burden already weighing her down, distracting her from what is truly important. I hope you understand I cannot have her crippled over what will likely happen to you." Lars did not sugarcoat things. "If she knows about your fate, she will not go forward. You will be the last straw. I already see the cracks. She is a strong woman, but everyone has their limit. The two of you will undo her."

"Two?"

He waved his hand, brushing off my question. "Ember will not know. Are we in agreement of this?"

He was right because if roles were switched, and Ember were the sacrificial lamb, I would not be able to do it. There'd be no way.

My life could not stand in the way of millions. "We are." Sorrow still flooded my response. The moment it was out, magic slammed me down with its weight, curling through my throat. I grabbed at my neck, bent over and gulping for air.

"I apologize for this, Ms. Johnson. I will not leave it up to chance Ember will find out. Even if you slip and say it to someone else and she hears that way, I cannot risk it."

His spell coiled in my throat, like it was knotting itself around my vocal cords.

"The spell will keep you from speaking, writing, signing, or any other method of communication about this. It will break when it is no longer needed." He folded his arms. "And you are nowhere near powerful enough to even contemplate breaking it."

The pressure built, forcing a squeak from me before it broke, dissipating like mist. I heaved in air and sat up in my chair. A part of me felt angry and assaulted, but all too quickly I understood his overprotection of Ember. As a leader he had to be certain we were at our best to be the winners in this war.

Lars took a step closer, his voice softening only a little. "And I know perfectly where your abilities are at this moment. You have improved a great deal, and I have to commend Mr. Dragen for cultivating your skills. Nevertheless, you still have a lot to develop. This is a crash course, and we need to triple your abilities and confidence in an exceptionally short time. You will be working with Maya and Koke every day till Samhain. They are waiting for you now in the training room."

I stood, responding to his order, scrubbing my neck. It didn't hurt, but I still felt the magic rubbing against my throat like a hairless cat.

"Now it is my training time. I must go." He peered down at his watch.

"You train?" I trailed after him to the door.

He stopped, turning his head around. "A good leader knows you never stop learning. Only way to advance and stay a great leader is to never think you know all or can't improve. This is why Aneira will someday fail."

I hoped so.

Lars exited and disappeared down the hall. I headed for the back door, slipping past Marguerite. Her back was to me, busy with whatever she was cooking. Cal stood on her shoulder pleading with her to turn the sink into his distillery, which made me smile.

The smell of her baking and the feeling of her warmth followed me out the back door. I took one step outside and felt overcome with the sounds of metal clanking and the cries of battle as the fae went through drills with Alki out on the field.

The two contradictions of Marguerite's food and battle practice collided, bringing the realness of what Lars and I had talked about to the surface. Realization rammed into me like an avalanche. I gasped and my knees buckled to the ground. My hand went to my chest, feeling my lungs flutter as I tried to draw in air. Darkness lined the rim of my vision, bending me over farther.

I *was* going to die.

Even though I had foreseen it, it hadn't felt real. I could brush away a dream. Lars had just made it actual, something I could no longer deny. For the greater good or not, I didn't want to die. So much remained I still wanted to do. Experience. More time with my friends, the people I loved. To know what it felt like to be with someone. Feel love that made me lose myself.

Grief wept from the depths of my soul, mourning all the things I would never do. The memories I would never obtain. The experiences I would never have. A sob vaulted from my heart, grief and fear so overwhelming I felt like I was drowning. My arms wrapped around my belly, the choked cries racking my body.

And I grieved for what it would do to Ryan. Ember. Jared.

Lorcan.

His image flashing across my mind and drove the knife deeper. I felt a loss so deep it hollowed out my bones. But something about him made the tears stop.

I sat up, wiping my face. "Okay, Ken. Get up. Concentrate on what you can change. Live in the now."

I climbed to my feet, looking over the swarm of people on the practice field. So many of them were going to die too. They knew it but still got up and kept training. Because what we were fighting for was more important.

A.) Do not let them down. Train. Give everything
    you have.
B.) Appreciate what you do have.
C.) Take every opportunity. You're not dead yet.

With a determined step, I headed to the training room where Maya and Koke waited for me. One advancement in my powers might be the difference between life and death.

Training with Maya and Koke was horrendous. Ember had warned me, but until you were the one experiencing their relentless drive, you didn't fully comprehend. My brain was mush, and my body was something even more pulverized. I collapsed ten times, but each time they both yelled till I got up and we started over. When we were done, I turned back to my cabin wanting only to nap, eat, and then nap again.

"Babe!" Jared found me halfway back, loping up to me with a huge grin on his face. I couldn't help but smile back, his energy contagious.

"Hey."

His goofy smile altered into a sexier expression the closer he got, his body pressing into mine. "Hey yourself." He touched a strand of hair falling out from the headband holding back my messy bun. "Love when you wear your hair like this. So cute. Like Gwen Stacy."

My nerd boy and his Spider-Man references. Not one I ever really liked. "Wait, wasn't she the one who dies?"

"Yeah." He shrugged, his lips skating my jaw.

A jolt of irony came flooding out of me, bursting laughter from my lungs.

"What?" Jared stepped back. "What's so funny?"

The dark humor hit me so hard I wasn't sure the tears coming out of my eyes were from laughter or pain. Or a little bit of both. I had shut my brain and emotions off, not letting myself think any more about what Lars and I talked about. Probably in defense, keeping me sane. Or it was something I had already known and was now reconciled to it.

"What? Why are you laughing?" Jared puffed up, his hackles rising. "Are you going through one of your episodes or something?"

"No." I wiped at my eyes. "Sorry, it had nothing to do with you."

"Then who? Tell me." He stepped closer again, but his eyes still held suspicion.

"I can't."

"Why?" He prickled. "Why can't you tell me? I am your boyfriend. *Right?*"

I leaned back, my mouth gaping. "Jared..."

He held up his arms. "Because lately it hasn't felt that way. Since you've come back, you've been different. You've changed."

"That's what growing up is...changing," I responded. "Hopefully together."

"No. This is not the same." He shook his head. "What happened with you and Lorcan?"

My head jerked, face flushing, a shielding wall popping up. *Oh god, did he know?*

"Please, if he hurt you or tried anything against your will..."

"What?"

"You're so little. You couldn't defend yourself against him."

"Are you serious?" I exclaimed. "I can take care of myself. I may be small but do not underestimate me, Jared. I do not need to be shielded anymore. With one word I can flatten you all to the ground. Don't make me demonstrate here."

His lids widened, then he turned his head, his shoulders falling. "You're right. I'm sorry. I just get *so angry* at the thought of Lorcan taking you, and I wasn't there to protect you. You're mine," he growled.

My back stiffened. I didn't want to say he probably couldn't have done anything anyway; his ego was so sensitive lately. I was tired and didn't want to fight with him.

"Have you had lunch yet?" I changed the subject.

His bad mood died, jubilance bouncing his feet in a half of second. "No! I'm starved. Need to fill up before I go back on the field. Alki has us doing these roundhouse kicks." Jared simulated some of the moves.

"Come on, let's go get some lunch." I reached out and grabbed his hand. He laced his fingers in mine and pulled me closer, heading toward the food tent.

"Oh wait." He stopped, spinning me into him. "This first." He grabbed my face, his lips meeting mine. His mouth was so familiar and nice. I opened up to him, deepening the kiss. It wasn't consuming, but desire tingled along my spine. My sexual awareness was increasing every day. My body was ready. I was ready. Jared would be the best to have the first experience with. He was a virgin as well. We'd both bumble around and figure it out together. Someone like Lorcan would be far too advanced. Just those two kisses had shown me that. He was already past the black diamond course, and he would find it boring and a waste of time to come back to the bunny hills.

Ken, why are you even bringing him into this?

No. My first time would be with Jared. He wanted to. I wanted to. I merely needed to be sure I was protected and ready physically as well as mentally. The dark cloud of death hanging over me pushed me to do things I had been scared of before. I would not die a virgin. But how did you get birth control when you were stuck in a camp full of fae? Did they even use normal protection? Did their bodies work differently? I was a Druid but still human. One of the few here.

It was something I was determined to figure out. I could not ignore what was going on inside anymore, and I needed to face it before I did something reckless. *Like attack Lorcan*, the voice in my head spurted out.

I needed to silence that voice for good.

TWENTY

Finding a family clinic or being able to even leave this compound was never going to happen. Talking about this with Owen, even if he were a doctor, was completely out of the question. That would be humiliating beyond words.

So, I could:

    A.) Ask Ember...which I really, really didn't want to do. She would have too many questions.

    B.) Talk to Rez. She could order what I needed, but it might take too long.

    C.) Find one of the staff Lars had helping doctor the soldiers. A stranger.

    D.) Or Gabby, who was in the same room...with me...right now.

My clean clothes were folded neatly, but I shook out each one, refolding them with nervous energy, looking over my shoulder at Gabby every few moments. *Just ask her, Ken.* If you're too embarrassed to talk about it, then you shouldn't be having it. My mouth opened, then snapped shut. I turned back to my pile, trying to gather strength. I was ready. I knew that, but I still had a hard time with people knowing.

"Oh. My. God." Gabby flung her arms out. "Just spit it out already so I can nap."

I spun to her, pressing one of my shirts to my chest. "Wh-what?"

Gabby peeked through one open lid, annoyance creasing her forehead. "Don't you think I can tell you are prancing around like a nervous freak? Jesus, girl, anyone would be able to sense the tension coming off you. You've refolded that same top four times. I know you're anal, but either you need to be committed or you want to talk to me about something."

Shoving at my glasses, I plunked down on my cot, still struggling with the exact words.

Gabby's watchful eyes glinted as she sat up, her boots hitting the floor. "Shit, this must be good. You really do want to girl-talk with me." She was as shocked as I was to be looking to her for advice. "Clearly if you are not running to Ember, you don't want her to know."

Teeth tugged at my bottom lip. "It's not I don't want her to know...but..."

"You don't want her to know."

I exhaled, rubbing the space between my brows.

"Damn. You have me completely intrigued now."

Oh god...she was making a bigger deal out of this than it was meant to be. Going to Gabby was absurd; she loved gossip and drama. She'd spread this faster than a computer virus.

"Never mind." I shook my head, standing back up. "It's nothing."

"Oh no." She leaned over, grabbing my arm and spinning me to her. "Spill, nerd."

I rolled my eyes at my "pet" name. I wore that badge with honor. It had never bothered me. But uncreative bullies thought it was a huge insult to be called "nerd" or "geek." As if being smart and studying were something to be embarrassed about.

I'd learned Gabby rarely intended to be mean. She was merely brusque. In Greece, I got the feeling she longed to belong. To be part of the "girls," but she didn't know how to interact with us, having been raised with almost all men. Samantha didn't count. Those two probably never spoke more than a few sentences to each other over the years.

"I can tell you want to."

Heavy exhale as I peered down at her. "You have to promise not to tell anyone."

"Fae don't promise shit. Especially me, and not before I know what it is."

Now I was making a bigger deal out of it. "Fine." I backed away from her grip. "I don't know how to ask, so I'm just going to say it..." I sucked in strength. "What do you fae do for birth control?"

Gabby stared. Blinked. Then burst into laughter.

All the things I feared. "Forget it. I knew I shouldn't ask you."

"No. No." She waved her hand, trying to speak through her amusement. "Sorry, I thought it was something *really* big."

I folded my arms protectively across my chest.

Her chuckle died, and she cleared her throat. "Really. I'm sorry to laugh, but to fae sex is so much a part of us I forget you humans have such hang-ups about it, like it's something to be embarrassed of."

"If you knew my parents, you wouldn't be so surprised."

"Well, you came to the right girl." Gabby clapped her hands, a look of pride settling on her lips as if she was honored I came to her instead of Ember. "You want to boink my nephew…without more rug rats filling Earth. I can help you with that."

I groaned and fell back on my bed, curling my arms over my head.

"Awww, don't be embarrassed." Gabby snickered, patting my head. "Would've it been better if I said bury the bone, the lust and thrust, feed the kitty…?"

"Stop."

"Thumping thighs, stuffing the turke—"

"Ugh! Pleeease shut up." I lifted my head, pleading.

"You take the fun out of everything, nerd."

"Can you be serious?"

"I can but don't really want to."

"Gabby!"

"Okay. Fine. Fine." She leaned back on her hands.

"What do you want to know?"

"What do you do for birth control?"

Amusement dropped from her face.

"You know, female dark dwellers really don't have that problem. We can only reproduce like two times a year and the chances of human sperm impregnating us is slim to none. That's why I almost always sleep with humans. We also don't get venereal diseases...so sex is great...for me. You, on the other hand, are a walking baby oven."

"A what?" I sputtered with a laugh.

"You are a Druid. Still human, but you have the power to carry any fae baby to term. You are like the prime candidate for a male fae looking to farm a few love children."

Another groan fell from my mouth, and I rubbed harder at my temple.

"For you, human birth control pills would be like taking sugar cubes. You are lucky you came to me before you found out too late."

"What do I do then?"

"Stay a virgin?" She shrugged.

My shoulders dropped and disappointment plunged into me with crackling force.

"Jesus, nerd. You take everything soooo seriously." Gabby sighed, dropping her head back dramatically. "I was just kidding."

I tipped my head to the side, glaring at her.

"Tree fairies and nymphs are experts in this department. They have the strongest method known to human and fae, made with some tree or plant root shit. And lucky for you, we have a group only feet away. We need to take a little trip to our local nymph clinic."

~~~~~

What I imagined as birth control was nothing like what I got. The fairies mixed up a smelly, gag-worthy brew. The moment they poured the thick, lumpy concoction in a cup, they forced me to drink it. Several times I retched, but I finally got it down.

Gabby never left my side and actually ended up drinking one of her own. I shot her a raised brow as she did.

"Never hurts to be prepared." She winked over at me.

I knew she had a crush on Alki, Lars's lead instructor who ran the daily training sessions. *A fae.* It took little thought to understand she was hoping her "mostly human" enjoyment was expanding to a certain hot demon fighter.

"Is that it?" I rubbed my stomach, feeling queasy. "Please don't tell me I have to drink it daily. Then I might stay a virgin."

The stunning redheaded tree fairy who had made it up for me laughed. "No. That is it. You should feel the magic settling in. It will nauseate you for an hour, but it should last you till you are ready to undo it."

"What?"

"Magic." She grinned. "We don't mess around here. When you want to breed, you can come back and we will undo the potion."

Wow. I didn't realize when Gabby called it the strongest stuff known to man and fae, she really meant it.

"Great. Thank you." I nodded. "How much do I owe you?"

The throng of tree fairies behind their leader all pealed with laughter.

"I got it, nerd." Gabby grabbed my arm, addressing the horde of gorgeous women. "I will be sending some lucky victims your way this evening, ladies." Then she dragged me back toward the cabin.

"Does that mean what I think it means?" I jogged to keep up with her.

"That they take payment in sex?" Gabby crooked one eyebrow. "Why, yes, it does. I told you, fae *enjoy* sex. And the women are even more open about enjoying it than the men. Nothing to be ashamed about. And sending a few of my brothers or horny fae men over there to reap the benefits is the kind of payment I can get behind."

We reached the cabin, and I tugged her to a stop. "Thank you, Gabby." I never imagined being close to her. Not that we were buddies, but I felt this had bonded us. This was something no one else shared with me. "Really. I appreciate you doing that for me."

"Yeah, well." She shuffled her feet. "Limiting the population isn't something we need to get all girly and sappy over."

I grinned at her, seeing through her thin wall.

"Don't smile at me. We're not going to be all chummy now and braid each other's hair or anything."

"Of course not." I grinned wider.

"Oh crap...I need to go punch or stab something now. Get this gooey feeling off me." Gabby huffed and marched toward the training field.

"Bye, roomie." I waved.

Without turning she flipped me off.

I got the warmest fuzzy from it.

Life was crazy. And more and more I was enjoying the crazy.

TWENTY-ONE

My hands trembled as I buttoned my jacket. I was meeting Ember in the forest in five minutes for our visit to the Otherworld.

Ryan. My heart beat his name in an excited rhythm. I missed him so much. This was the longest we had ever gone without seeing each other since we were five. We'd never gone more than a few days. One summer his dad sent him to a month-long camp, hoping he'd come back straight. Three days later I found him on my doorstep. My mom phoned his mother, and they decided to let him stay with us till the month was over. His dad was never the wiser.

Now I slunk out of my cabin, not wanting anyone to see me as I slipped into the forest, keeping to the shadows darkening the earth. The sun had set; the fall air nipped my skin. I felt so rebellious, dangerous…and sexy. After the confirmation of my future, or lack thereof from Lars, I felt I had nothing to wait for anymore. This was my life, and I had little of it left. I needed to live. Do all the things I was afraid of.

"Where do you think you're going, li'l bird?"

"Ahhh!" I jumped, spinning around to the figure leaning against a tree. "Dammit, Lorcan."

He smirked, his green eyes blazing in the dark. Damn, why did he look so good? No matter what he wore *or* didn't wear, he carried himself like a model from a magazine. One dedicated to motorcycles and sexy bad boys with tattoos. Jeans, T-shirt, boots, jacket. Nothing I hadn't seen, but my stomach twirled like a drunken ballerina.

"I asked you a question." He pushed off the tree, stalking up to me, getting so close I could feel his presence invading me, as if he were skimming my skin with his fingers.

A blazing warning bell went off in my head, and I took a step back, folding my arms. "A walk."

"Don't believe you, little bird." His gaze moved down my body, taking me all in.

"Stop calling me that."

"Why?" A knowing grin hinted at his mouth, his gaze drifting to where my heart was. He knew it was beating exactly like a small bird's.

"Because."

"Not a good enough reason." He stepped even closer, his breath trickling down my neck.

"You know why." I tightened my folded arms, pulling them painfully into my chest.

"No, I don't think I do."

Damn him. "Don't play with me." I glowered. "I asked you to stop. Please respect that."

He slanted his head. "No."

"No?"

"No," he said matter-of-fact.

"Arrrr." I fisted my hands. "You are so frustrating."

"I could say the same about you." He lifted an eyebrow, hinting at another meaning.

The idea of pushing him against a tree and kissing him rippled through me, first pleasurable, then painful. I wanted it but it could never happen.

"Lorcan." At the tone of my voice he nodded and stepped back.

I started to step forward, then stopped myself. My body reacted to the loss of his. It moved primally, disconnected from consequences or logic. I needed distance from him to think clearly. "I have to go." I turned, but his hand latched around my arm, pulling me back to him.

"Where you are going, I'm going." He looked down on me, his face so serious and intense I couldn't snap free.

I didn't know if he merely meant tonight or in general. I didn't care. "Okay." I realized it was not only all right, but I *wanted* him there.

He let go of my arm, his gaze still heavy on me. I cleared my throat and turned around, not letting him see me gather my strength.

"We're going to the Otherworld."

"Wait," he replied. "Miss Rules is breaking one of the biggest ones?"

"Yes." I glanced over my shoulder, almost challenging. "Have a problem with that?"

"Not at all." His grin widened. "I like this rebellious side of you."

I filled him in on the basics of why we were heading to the Otherworld as we waited for Ember. It wasn't long before Lorcan stiffened next to me, his nostrils flaring. "Eli," he muttered to himself.

I wasn't surprised Eli was joining Ember. For one thing, it was her birthday, and she'd want him to come. Second, he would never let her go without him. Like Lorcan, if she was going to go against Lars's orders, Eli was going to be right by Em's side when she did.

A low growl vibrated from across the forest. I could see Eli's outline puffing up.

"Easy, little brother." Lorcan kept his eyes locked on his brother. "I am not here to cause a problem."

"Then why are you?"

"I'm here to keep Kennedy safe if anything happens."

Ember and Eli stopped, standing opposite us, making it feel like some strange couple-off.

Eli's hands flexed. "I can take care of it."

"I am not saying you can't, but if a group of strighoul comes after Emmy again, who will you protect?"

"Hey! I am not a damsel here and neither is Kennedy. We can take care of ourselves." Ember glared at them.

"I never said you were a damsel. I've heard you are quite the tiger." Lorcan's implication was clear. "But without your powers, you can't help as much as you'd like. And Kennedy's powers aren't for hurting people. Hers are to heal and protect."

Wow. Either he was extremely fast at bullshit or his brain had already formed these scenarios on our short walk. Knowing him, it was most likely the latter. As an alpha, he was always on, ready for any attack or the worst case.

"I said he could come," I declared and forced my voice to stay strong. "Lorcan's right. I can't fight like you guys can, and if something did happen, I trust he will have my back."

"What about Jared?" Ember shot at Lorcan and me.

His name filled me, and likely Lorcan, with tension.

"He was training and seemed quite happy there." My hands went to my hips, letting the white lie slip out. "I thought it would be better if he stayed. If we do come across trouble, I know he can't change like you two can. I don't want Jared to get hurt. I could not live with myself if anything happened to him."

Ember rocked on her feet, clearly fighting her feelings about Lorcan's appearance. I had not thought those things through when I agreed for Lorcan to join, but they were all true. I could do some magic, but I hadn't thought about strighoul or extreme threats coming for us. I had only thought about Ryan.

"I understand your wariness of me, Ember," Lorcan acknowledged. "I killed Aisling. It is a plain and simple fact. It might seem cold and heartless to you, but it's how we were then. Even your boy here cannot be excluded. Eli killed a lot of people, too. Someone's mother or father. I'm not going to ruin your night and go inside. I know Lily would have my head served as the entree. I plan on staying outside, keeping guard like the good, little obedient beast I am."

Ember scowled, her pupils flickering black, but Lorcan did not back down. He stood his ground, holding her glare.

"Fine." Ember glanced away. "But you stay far away from the house. I don't want my mother to get even a whiff of your foul scent. I will not stop her if she tries to kill you."

"Agreed."

Eli moved swiftly and grabbed Lorcan's collar. "You try anything or do anything I don't like, and I will kill you this time, Lorcan. I will not hesitate. Got it?"

"I get it. Lorcan farts too loud, and he is a dead man. Memo received."

Ember grimaced, but she nodded and turned to the trees. "All right, Cal, come on out. You can show us the way."

"H-ho-how did you know I was here?" A tiny voice came from above.

"Because I know you," she replied. When he didn't respond she called again. "Cal?"

"You are wrong. Cal is not here right now. You can leave a message at the beep. *Beeeeep.*"

"Cal, get your little pixie butt down here now." She pointed at the ground.

As Ember argued with Cal, my mind wandered a little. I stared out into the forest, then back where I knew the training session had ended for the evening. I had lied. Jared wasn't training. Nor did I even think to ask him. What kind of girlfriend was I? For every encounter I had with him, I wanted to avoid the next. A flush of disgrace crept over me.

The truth was sitting on my gut ready to screech. I kept swallowing it down, convincing myself everything was fine. We were simply going through an adjustment period. The sinking sensation in my belly told me it was easier for me to refuse than accept what was really forming underneath.

~~~~~

The trek through the woods following Cal was like some warped version of Red Riding Hood and Hansel and Gretel, which the boys argued with us that leaving crumbs in the forest was the stupidest idea ever. And the children deserved to be eaten as the main entrée since they led the monsters in the woods right to them.

It was the first time I had seen Eli and Lorcan come together and act somewhat like brothers. It actually warmed my heart, giving me hope Lorcan could someday be seen as more than the villain in the story.

The optimistic feeling was snuffed out the moment we got to the cave. On the other side was the protected cabin holding our family and friends.

"So...I figure I will be staying right here." Lorcan moved to a boulder next to the cave entrance, a twinge of bitterness laced in his statement.

"It will be best," Ember said as she tucked Cal under her hood.

Lorcan's lips pressed together, a smirk on his face. I hated this. I couldn't stand him having to be left outside like an animal. I wanted him with me to be part of the party. Maybe let his guard down and show people the man inside. The one I really cared about.

But it couldn't be. "Thank you, Lorcan." My fingers grazed his arm, a punch of energy zinging my hand. "We'll try not to be long."

His eyes met mine, went to my hand, and then glanced away, his jaw clenching. I dropped my arm, feeling my heart plummet with it.

"I am watching the moon." He resettled on the rock, his voice distant. "If it moves past the trees there, I am coming after you."

"I'll watch it, too." Eli glanced up at the moon, then moved toward the entrance of the cavern. "We have to be extremely careful about the time we spend here." He gazed at Lorcan, touching his temple. "Let me know if anything happens. Or use our warning call."

"I will," Lorcan concurred.

"Warning call?" I queried, following Eli into the cave.

"It's a specific howl our dad taught us if he couldn't reach us through our link." Eli batted at the string of cobwebs draping the cave entrance.

Caves. Greece had cured me of ever wanting to go in one again. I wasn't claustrophobic like Ember, but I still hated them. An insect not daggered and displayed on a board for a project was a live bug too many. Bats fascinated me, but not when they were flying through your hair pooping. I liked wildlife under a microscope, in a textbook, or on TV. Unfortunately, that was not the case here.

"At least you don't look like a prime steak to them," Cal bellowed from under Ember's hood.

"Meat that's been marinated in alcohol since birth." Eli led the way, his flashlight bobbing along the ground.

"Exactly. One bite and they'd be hooked. I'm scrumptious!" Cal peeked out.

"They'd be drunk," I quipped.

"Only adding to my point. Tasty beefcake full of juniper juice. Who wouldn't want to eat me? Suck me dry!" Cal giggled.

"Oh. God. Please don't ever say that again." Ember snorted.

"Damn, I was gonna ask you the same question of me later." Eli winked back at Ember. "I'm open to either."

I smacked my head, half groaning and laughing, when two notions hit me.

1.) The topic of oral sex was not mortifying to me. At all.
2.) I no longer wanted to just hear about it. The idea actually slithered a tingle down my spine, waking me up inside.

But only one person seemed to be featured in the fantasy.

Multiple crap.

I was going to have to get my hormones in check. Was this normal? Lately I had become obsessed. Ember told me she went through a "growth" period, when her hormones and magic went through the roof. The fae version of coming of age. Maybe Druids experienced the same. Or a watered-down version. Damn. If this was watered down, then I was really starting to understand Ember and Eli more.

I was relieved once we got through the cave and came out on a breathtaking strip of land.

"Wow," I muttered, gazing around. At the bottom of a gully a mountain soared up into the sky, surrounding the stone cabin protectively. A gushing waterfall cascaded from the high ridge into the small lake nearby, pristine as a movie set.

"It's only me." Ember tossed up her arms, waving at the two men who rushed onto the porch, weapons in hand. Torin and Castien were poised to fight off any intruders.

"My lady?" Simmons whizzed past the men, zooming for Ember.

"You said you wouldn't call me that in public!" Cal quipped back, crawling out from under her hood.

"Cal!" Simmons yelped with joy, flying straight into his best friend, knocking them both off Em's shoulder, laughing and jabbering so quickly I couldn't understand them.

"Ember?" A woman stepped out of the house. Lily. She was gorgeous—about my height, toned but curvy, with waist-length auburn hair, huge orange-brown eyes—a fox shape-shifter. I spent time with her at the dwellers' ranch after we escaped Aneira's clutches. I instantly adored her. I could easily imagine her in the vacant spot I always felt at Mark and Ember's house, where I spent so many weekends. Even though Ember found out Lily was not her biological mother, there was something to be said about the influence of the one who raised you. They were so much alike—strong, fierce, and stubborn. "Ember's here?"

"Yeah, Mom. To celebrate my birthday with you."

Lily knocked Torin and Castien out of the way like a miniature linebacker and sprinted to her daughter. "It's your birthday today?"

"Yep."

"Oh, my baby girl. Happy birthday!" She engulfed Em in a hug. Then her eyes lifted, spotting Eli next to me. Her entire demeanor altered, her tone strained. "Elighan."

"Lily," Eli acknowledged her.

"Kennedy?" a voice cried out, directing my attention to the porch. At the sound of him, seeing him, his voice so familiar to my soul, tears pecked at my eyes. "Oh my god. Kennedy!"

"Ryan!" I screamed, sprinting for him. I was heading home.

We hit hard, our arms encircling each other. Sobs already wreaked havoc in my chest. There were people in your life who made up part of you, made you the person you were. Ryan was that to me. He was my other limb. My comfort, my pain, my love, my joy, my sadness. What he felt I felt.

My soulmate.

It had only been Ryan and me for years. Then Ember found us or we found her; it didn't matter. My heart extended. But I couldn't deny Ryan was my core.

"I-I can't believe you're here." Ryan pulled me in tighter, stroking my head, his tears spilling onto my cheeks. "You're safe."

I gulped in air between my sobs, pulling away enough to see his blue eyes. "We made a pact in third grade we would be friends forever and we'd always be there for each other no matter what. I took the promise seriously. There isn't anything that would keep me from you."

"Except when kidnapped by fae."

"Except that." Joy ballooned in my heart while my tears flowed. I hadn't realized how much I'd missed him. I had erected a wall so as not to feel or think about how empty my heart had been without him.

Ryan sighed melodramatically. "Teaches us not to read the fine print in our pact." He pulled me back in, tucking his chin on my shoulder, sighing with a deep contentment. Like he had come home too. "Hey," Ryan yelled behind me, turning my head. "Get your salty ass over here and join our reunion. You're part of us, too."

"But I didn't sign any best friend contract." Ember bobbed nervously. Did she think she wasn't as important to us?

"Your contract was signed in blood. Now get your butt over here." Ryan and I were obviously riding the same thought train.

A grin spread over Ember's face and she ran to us. We held each other for dear life, laughing and crying over our reunion. Did they feel what I did, that these might be our last moments together?

After the talk with Lars, my future felt predetermined so I only held on to hope with the remnants of my naïve optimism. I squeezed my friends again, trying to burn this moment into my memory. It would be a good one to have at the end.

Ryan being Ryan couldn't handle the emotion without trying to break it with humor. "Now, get the smoking-hot Happy Meal over here so I can slyly squeeze his ass," Ryan stage-whispered to Ember, forcing us both to laugh.

"All you have to do is ask, Ryan." Eli raised his arms in invitation

"Holy shit," Ryan muttered into my ear with mortification.

"He has exceptional hearing." Ember stepped back, looking over at Eli. "And a firm ass. I highly recommend feeling it at least once tonight."

Ryan harrumphed and glanced back at his boyfriend on the porch. "Do you mind, honey?"

~~~~

After greeting Lily, Castien, Thara, Torin, and giving Mark a huge hug, most of us moved into the cabin. Lily and Eli took off to "discuss" their past, trying to get on neutral ground for Ember's sake.

Torin stormed off, reacting to Eli like a scorned lover, which he wasn't. I knew Ember really well, and Torin was never for her. The moment Eli entered her life, it was over. I knew the instant we picked her up from school and he was sitting on his bike across the parking lot. I just didn't realize it was my seer powers talking.

Ryan led me to the sofa in the cabin. It was a nice place that reminded me of the cabin Lorcan took me to before heading to Lars's compound. It was a lot bigger inside than it appeared. Fireplace, overstuffed sofas, open kitchen and dining area, bedrooms on one side and stairs leading up to the rest. It felt homey. A place I could easily spend time on the sofa reading or catching up with my friends as the fire blazed.

Dinner cooked on the stove while Mark and Thara started baking a cake for Ember. We talked incessantly, going from serious to laughing so hard tears spilled down our cheeks.

It was easy to forget everything when I was with my best friends, but Lorcan nipped at me. The idea he was waiting for us, not allowed to join, was like a splinter in my finger. You could ignore it, but it was always there, constantly dragging your attention away.

He would never be welcome. My best friend, the opinion mattering most to me in the world, would never approve. Ryan still blamed Lorcan for the death of his cousin, Ian. No matter what I said, if I explained Lorcan didn't want it to happen, that it had been Samantha's bloodthirsty way, Ryan would never accept it. Here was another influence driving me away from the dweller waiting outside.

We poured alcohol through dinner and dessert, and I grasped my stomach in pain from laughing so hard at stories old and new. I could have stayed happily forever, but my head kept moving to the window, my body growing restless. Lorcan was out there.

Eli shifted in his seat, his knee bobbing up and down more by the minute.

The curse.

Lorcan told me it would take a while before it became painful, but the steady movement of Eli's leg said it was time for us to go. He was fidgety, reminding me of when I was a kid with growing pains. Your bones ached, your muscles constricted, never relaxing. It hurt.

You couldn't sit still. Many nights I woke up crying, wanting anything to ease the pain.

Saying goodbye was agonizing. I tried to keep the tears at bay, hoping Ryan wouldn't see through them and know I was keeping other secrets from him. But how did you say goodbye when it was for good?

I clung to Ryan, biting down on my lip. "I love you so much."

"We're past that." Ryan took my hands in his. "I don't want to let go."

"Me neither."

"I know I can't be part of the war. And I really hate you have to be." He swung our hands like when we were kids. "I'm scared. For you. For Ember. Please promise me you will come back to me. Both of you. You are my home, Kennedy. The other half of my heart goes with you."

My throat thickened, and I struggled to swallow. "I will try," I whispered.

"Don't try. Do. I can't live without you. It's not even a possibility in my world. I don't exist without you. Do you get that?"

Don't cry. Don't cry. "Same, Ry." I nodded.

"Now, do me a favor and go get laid. Going into a war a virgin is really sad."

I spurted a laugh. My best friend could still read my mind.

"And the two of you both being is beyond tragic. Like pity-parade level." Ryan patted my hand. "So grab that edible snack of a boyfriend and take him to the mattresses."

I no longer wanted a snack. I wanted a full meal.

Ryan crushed me in one last hug, kissing my temple, then he jerked back, wiping at his eyes. He cleared his throat and looked over at Ember saying goodbye to her mom.

"This spice needs his sugar and salt." He choked, pulling away. "Just come home to me. Both of you."

He turned toward the house, passing Castien on the deck. Castien and I exchanged a look and he smiled, following Ryan into the cabin. We both knew how Ryan handled emotion. His dad tried to beat it out of him growing up; it was still hard for him to let go. But I understood Castien's expression—he would take care of him. Ryan would never be alone again. All I had wished for Ryan was for someone to love him as completely as Castien did.

I made my way to Eli by the cave. Cal hovered next to the dweller. Hot tears burned the back of my throat.

Tears streamed down Ember's face as she approached us. Mark held a sobbing Lily behind her. Eli swabbed her eyes with his thumbs. "You will see them again."

I grabbed Ember's hand. She and I held this battle on our shoulders. Both of us might not make it out.

"We will all be with each other again," I said. Even if it wasn't true in this life, I hoped we would all find each other again someday.

Some souls always found their way back to each other.

TWENTY-TWO

"What the hell took you so long?" Lorcan barreled toward us the moment we stepped out of the cavern, irritation slanting his eyes. His gaze drifted over me, then quickly jumped to Eli and Ember. "I actually thought about coming in and getting you guys."

"Your presence would not have gone over well," Ember replied from behind me.

Back in his company my heart sped up, and I felt jittery and hot. What was it about him?

"Like I give a shit." Lorcan thumped his hand against his leg in a frantic repetition. "You guys were there much longer than you were supposed to be." He was agitated. Off. He didn't seem to notice his hands flexing while they tapped against his jeans.

I moved to him without a thought, driven by the need to soothe him. My fingers softly grazed his arm with the tattoo. The one I had traced so many times in my mind. "Sorry, we had a lot to catch up on. Thank you for waiting."

"Not like I had a choice." His words came out sharp, but when his eyes caught mine, I sucked in a breath. Penetrating. Wanting. Fierce. It was like fire to my veins. The heat under my skin burned along my nerves. My memory burst with images of the times we kissed. The feel of his lips on mine. I wanted it now. The consuming fire.

Ember pushed past me, jerking my head away from Lorcan's burning gaze. "What's that noise?"

Lorcan stepped away from me, shaking his head slightly. "Not sure, but in this forest probably nothing good. Let's get out of here."

Ember, Eli, Lorcan, Cal, and I trekked through the forest. I stayed slightly behind Ember and Eli, Lorcan's footsteps trailing mine. He kept his distance, but it didn't seem to matter. My entire back sizzled with awareness of his presence with the feel of his eyes on me.

Stop. You are with Jared, I chastised myself. *Someone you love and who loves you more than anything.*

I was so lost in my thoughts, I wasn't paying attention and almost slammed into Ember when she came to a stop.

"Holy shit," Lorcan's words snapped me out of my trance.

My gaze halted on the sight in front of us, and my mouth dropped open.

"Lamprog," Lorcan whispered under his breath.

They resembled ladybugs but were the size of a rhinoceros beetle and glowed. The entire forest moved with the flying insects. Thousands of them, lustrous and flickering, lit the night, making the air pulse. They hummed like an air conditioner on high. They were magnetic to watch. Beautiful.

"I remember these things from when I was a kid. We avoided the forest on nights they were procreating. Mean little shits."

I was so entranced with them I barely took in what Eli said. Light danced under the dark canopy of trees, crafting a hypnotic show. I couldn't pull my focus off them. My hand lifted, wanting to become part of the live art. I took a step.

"Kennedy!" I heard Lorcan scream, but it was too late.

I stepped off the ledge. My stomach plunged first before I registered my body had curled forward, slamming into the ground far below, my bones cracking as I hit. I tumbled down the hill, slapping into the throng of huge bugs. Wings and bug bodies hit me as I rolled through.

The buzzing consumed my ears, vibrating with insect anger, telling me my unwelcome intrusion set off their defenses. I remembered a boy I played with when I was a kid who poked a stick at a hornets' nest one time. I was stung so many times my parents had to take me to the emergency room. Thankfully, I wasn't allergic.

But these were no hornets, and their irritation swarming down on me was like a million hornet stings at once. The lamprog bit. Their tiny piranha-like teeth tore into my flesh. The toxins burned through my veins. Welts popped out on my skin in retaliation of the poison.

I screamed as hundreds more dived at me, covering my flesh as they nipped in fury. A tingling throbbed at my muscles and I couldn't run. All I could manage was to sit up. I could no longer feel my toes or fingers as the numbness moved up my legs and arms. Paralyzed. Panic rocketed over me, my blood pumping faster through my system.

"Ken!" Lorcan bellowed. Through the swarm, I saw him growing near. He was covered with them. His legs buckled, but he kept heading for me.

I wanted to scream back, but they crawled over my mouth, getting into my hair. My arm gave out, my head cracking back against the terrain. I rolled tighter into a ball, trying to hide my face. Sleep swirled around my head, causing me to drift unconscious.

"I got you, li'l bird," Lorcan slurred in my ear, his arms curling under my body, picking me up. "I got you."

I felt hot breath down my neck, then my body was jostled, but I couldn't open my eyes. I drifted in a surreal dream, as though floating on clouds, soaring through the sky.

Then my cloud evaporated, dropping me back to the earth with a slam. I hit the ground hard, popping my lids open with a gasp. Rocks, water, and twigs scraped my skin as Lorcan stumbled, crashing us into an embankment.

"Shit." Lorcan edged back off me. "You all right?"

I tried to nod, but my muscles wouldn't obey.

He sat back, his face and arms covered with welts. He appeared woozy and limp, but not as bad as me. Probably a fae thing. Their immunity to things was exceptional.

My gaze drifted past him. On the other side of the creek the wall of lamprog hovered close to the water but didn't cross it. Water was our safety.

An outline broke through the mass of pulsing bugs.

Ember! I tried to call her name but nothing made it past my lips. She staggered through the creek, falling to her hands and knees next to me on the wet dirt, breathing in long pulls.

"Where's Eli?" Lorcan glanced behind him at the barricade of insects, then back to Ember.

"He went to get Cal. He should be right behind me." She turned herself to sit facing the creek.

Tension grew as we waited for Eli to break through. My only thought was if something happened to Eli, Lorcan was dead because of Aneira's curse. Fury at myself not for being able to break the blood curse raced over me. I was still too weak and new to save the brothers from Aneira. If I couldn't break this, how was I going to break the spell around the sword?

Ember bit her lip; I could feel the worry billowing off her. Every second Eli was on the other side, the harder it would be for him to keep upright. He was strong, but could he push through that much poison in his system? Could Cal?

Lorcan pushed himself up and traipsed back through the creek, anxiety creasing his forehead. "Eli?" he shouted, pushing himself back into the curtain, disappearing into the horde.

Ember rose up as though she was about to follow him, but then sank back down with a groan. She rubbed her head, smearing mud across her forehead, and then turned to me.

"Are you all right?" Her hand squeezed mine. Pins and needles pricked my nerves like it had fallen asleep. Sensation was slowly coming back into my body.

My mouth would not work, so I rolled my head in what was the closest to a nod as I could make.

"That was a yes, right?" She brushed back hair from my face. Her attention fluttered back to where Lorcan had vanished, her body fidgeting and growing restless with every second that passed. They had been gone too long.

Without a word, our fears seemed to bounce off each other and grow. Time ticked by. What would happen to them if they passed out there? We were in the fae world. Could they die from these things? Cal was so small he certainly would. He couldn't take in that much poison.

Enough feeling had come back into my fingers to roll them in dread. Ember pushed herself up, clenching her shoulders.

Her anxiety only made mine skyrocket. There was good reason to be afraid if she was. *What if they were already dead?* My heart thumped in my chest.

Ember trudged into the creek, stopping right before the swarm.

"Eli?" She hollered his name, terror lacing every syllable. "Lorcan?"

Only the hum of the insects answered back.

She took a step, about ready to leap back into the gathering of fanged flying cockroaches, when I saw a massive figure coming straight for her. I tried to scream for her, but it only came out a garbled slur over my lips.

Lorcan crashed through the fortification, Eli over his shoulder, and collided into Ember. Their bodies hit with a fleshy bang. Ember flew, landing on her butt a few feet away. Lorcan crashed face-first into the rocky creek, Eli falling on his back in the stream with a harsh grunt, spraying liquid up like a fountain as their frames formed new paths in the creek. Lorcan didn't move while water poured over his mouth and nose.

What if he was unconscious? He could drown. Adrenaline coursed through my muscles, which flexed as though to act. I had to get to him. I barely got my head to lift when Lorcan groaned and rolled over, lying flat on his back next to Eli, staring up at the sky.

Relief sliced through me. The desire to be near him, to really see if he was all right, kept me pushing through the pain and limp muscles.

Ember crawled between the brothers, leaning over Eli. A small groan rumbled from his chest.

"Oh, thank god you're okay." She tipped her forehead onto his chest.

"Yeah, I am fine, too." Lorcan spoke slowly, but the sarcasm was thick in his voice. "No, really, it's sweet of you to ask. Thanks."

She pushed off Eli. "I had hoped you were in there long enough they would at least numb your mouth for a while."

"No such luck," Eli muttered.

"Nice, brother, see if I save your ass again."

The rumble of Lorcan's voice drew me like a magnet. A fish caught on a line. I rocked back and forth to get enough force to push to my hands and knees. I probably looked like a baby learning to crawl for the first time, but I didn't care.

"Where is Cal? Did you get him?" Ember searched the area, looking for her friend.

Eli struggled to move, but Ember seemed to understand what he was trying to tell her. She leaned over, lifting his shirt, a hefty sigh escaping her lips.

"If you..." Eli struggled over his words. "Ever tell him. He was this close to my dick...I will chain you up."

"Hmmmm... foreplay," she muttered, kissing his forehead.

My knees hit the water, moving painfully over the rocks in the stream, but the jabs of pain kept me going, shocking me into movement. Lorcan stayed still, but I saw his fingers curl, as though they were beckoning me to him.

I couldn't fight his summons if I tried. My instincts were on autopilot. Where he was—I would go. My hazy, drugged mind would not let me question or think. Only act. I flopped next to him. He tilted his head to look at me, our eyes locking. The light from the bugs and the moon above sparked off his eyes.

He didn't speak a word, but he lifted his fingers to my mouth, his thumb tracing my bottom lip. Air hitched in my lungs, but I did not look away. I only plummeted deeper into his stare. Tonight he had been the man, the brother, I knew was there. No matter the strain between him and Eli, Lorcan loved him more than life. He wanted to make things right. This incident showed me once again the true man beneath. The one who would fight for his brother. For all of us.

Emotion churned in my chest. I wasn't ready to examine it but knew I could no longer pretend it wasn't there. I let out a small sigh. His hand dropped between us, lacing his fingers through mine, pulling me into him. The heat of his body and the coolness of the water felt like heaven on my throbbing skin.

I leaned my head into his shoulder, my lashes fluttering closed. He felt so good next to me. I couldn't fight snuggling into him more and letting the hum of the bugs serenade me into a deep sleep.

Flash.

"Rouse. Light." A familiar voice growled over my shoulder. I whirled around.

"Grimmel?" I was back in the castle's dungeons, and I followed the rows of cages down to where the dwarf was wheeling out dirty hay. The raven sat on his shoulder.

"Aid baby fire. Treasure hidden below. You will see truth in false night."

"What?" Grimmel was cryptic on his best days. Today he was downright nonsensical. "I don't understand."

"No time. Tick. Tick. It goes by. Must wake and see pass of days."

I felt my body being shoved out, air being robbed from my lungs as everything went black.

Flash.

~~~~

With a gasp, I shot up and slapped my chest with my hand. It took me another beat to suck in more oxygen, calming my hammering heart.

Then my gaze took in my surroundings. Lorcan's hand lay over me, still holding on to my thigh, his face twisted as he twitched in his sleep like he was in pain. Ember and Eli lay next to us. The creek gushed around our bodies. The forest, where the bugs had congregated the night before, was clear, the early morning sun glistening off the dew of the bright green leaves.

Otherworld. Morning. If it was morning in the Otherworld... *Tick. Tick. It goes by.*

Holy-crapping-moly!

"Oh no!" Panic bloomed inside my nerves. The reality of how much trouble we were in fully awakened me. "Guys!" I shoved Lorcan. He groaned, batting at my hand. "We fell asleep. Get up. We have to go."

Ember's head jerked up first, her lids blinking, then they opened wide with horror, finding mine. We needed no words; we both understood our little secret field trip had turned into our worst fear.

She jostled Eli frantically. I shook Lorcan again.

"Lorcan, wake up. Now," I hissed. He moved slowly. His skin was white and sickly, a yellow tint coating under his eyes. He looked unhealthy.

Aneira's curse.

He shouldn't still be here in the Otherworld. This place was tearing apart his magic, taking away his beast.

"Lorcan. Please, wake up." *It can't be too late.* The thought brushed my mind and dropped like a rock into my gut. Horror, fear, and anguish filled me like cement, blocking all logical thought from my mind.

I shook harder, a whimper breaking from my lips. He moaned but still wouldn't open his eyes. Eli stirred next to him, and Ember helped him to his feet. He peered over at his brother, then kicked Lorcan's foot hard.

"Hey, Lorcan, wake up!"

Lorcan's lids fluttered open, struggling to fully rise. He lifted his head, his gaze roaming quickly around before meeting his brother's.

"Not a dream." Eli didn't even give him a chance to wake up fully before he grabbed his arm, yanking him to his feet.

"Hell." Lorcan waggled his head, rubbing his temple. He stared at me, still sitting in the water and muck—my hair in muddy strands down my back, welts covering my body, and my glasses smudged with dirt. I was a sight. Lorcan's hand came down for mine, he watched me carefully, rolling over me as if checking I was in one piece. He drew me to my feet, not letting go even when I secured my feet in the rocks. Then his hand tore from me and he bent over, wrapping his arms around his middle and hissing.

"What's wrong?" I put my hand on his back, instinctively wanting to take care of him. I knew what was wrong, but I didn't know exactly how the curse worked. If it hurt more in a certain area. If I could do anything. I felt so helpless.

His face scrunched up but with a ragged inhale he straightened up, pushing through the pain. "We got to get out of here."

Ember met my worry with the same frown of anxiety. If we didn't get these guys out of here soon, the curse placed on the dark dwellers would tear them up from the inside out.

And the one thing I understood that Ember did not: if anything happened to them, Cole was also dead.

TWENTY-THREE

It took a long time to reach the door to Earth, or it felt like forever, because the boys struggled with every step. Cal spent most of the time sleeping, his little body still not recovered from the trauma of the night before. I was so relieved he was all right. His head popped up a couple of times out of an empty sheath Ember was wearing. The brothers leaned and depended on each other to keep going. If it wasn't so dire, my heart would have been full of happiness instead of worry. They had shifted into protectiveness of each other. I hoped they would find their way back to each other.

Reprieve didn't last long after we stepped through to Earth, the boys sighing with relief. But the moment we neared Lars's compound, two of his guards stepped out, stopping us.

"Sir, they've returned." Goran spoke into his walkie-talkie.

"Crap," Ember mumbled next to me.

"Crap multiplied by a thousand. Ah, screw it. Shit."

"Oh, I think you will be saying a lot more when Lars gets a hold of you. I don't think I've ever seen him so pissed. Right, Rimmon?" Goran smirked. "Come on. Boss is heading our way now." Goran took us over the property line, the four of us following like we were about to be executed.

"How long were we gone?" Ember asked as we waited for the King.

"Five days."

Five days? Three days until Samhain.

We were so in trouble.

※※※

"You must have been put here to test my patience." Lars's eyes were pitch black and pointed on Ember.

My body trembled under the weight of his anger. To say the King was upset with us was an understatement. When he had stepped out, sending everyone else away, his fury snared us like a net. I had seen him turn semi-demon several times in Greece, but this was not semi. His body vibrated with rage, barely concealing it under the designer suit.

His skin was like wax paper, the bones in his skull sticking out. Black pools filled his eye sockets, giving him a petrifying soulless gaze as if he could gut us and string us by our entrails without a thought. Daggered cuspids I had never seen protruded from his upper and lower jaws. His hands were bony and long, like he could reach out from where he stood and wrap his fingers around my throat.

As sunken in as he looked, his body filled the space, bumping into the molecules in the air to give him more space. A growl vibrated the ground and I swallowed.

We might deserve to be reprimanded, but I was terrified of his punishment. Ember and I seemed to be the only two who took it seriously.

"Funny, it's what I think too." Eli smirked and responded to Lars, his gaze darting between the King and Ember.

Lars's black eyes snapped to Eli. In an instant Eli flew up in the air, his hand scratching at his throat like he was being choked to death.

"Oh my god," I muttered to myself and stepped back, my hand covering my mouth. Terror thumped in my chest as I watched Eli fight to breathe under Lars's invisible hold.

"You find it a joke, Elighan?" Lars's deep voice twisted with rage. Eli's fingers continued to scrape his throat, his eyes going blurry.

"Stop it!" Ember screamed at Lars, her face pinched with grief and fear.

Eli made a choking sound, his body losing the battle of oxygen deprivation. I moved to him instinctively with the need to protect him from the bully Lars had become. The protection chant was on my tongue. I didn't care how Lars would react. My friends were my first priority. My mouth opened.

Lars's attention snapped to me, his head tilting like he sensed what I was about to do. Lorcan flew up in the air, then quickly collided with the ground feet away. A cry came to my mouth, then stopped there. Pressure surrounded my neck, like a noose was tightening around it. It yanked down hard, my knees collapsing to the dirt, my lungs twitching as panic blotted out reason. I clawed at the magic wrapping around my throat. Lack of oxygen made me dizzy, ripping away understanding of what was going on between Lars and Ember. My vision tunneled black at the edges. A loud ringing pierced my ears as I dug fruitlessly into my throat. I knew it was pointless, but survival was a primal instinct. I tipped forward, curling over.

As fast as it happened, the magic vanished.

My lungs flexed, taking in hungry gulps of air. Eli landed on the ground next to me. He was only down a beat before he rose to his feet, his green eyes turning red.

I felt a rushed movement next to me, Lorcan crawling to my side. He kneeled next to me, hands cupping my face, eyes seeking me with concern.

"I'm fine." I placed my hands over his, fixing on his eyes. My touch seemed to ease his worry. He nodded, letting his hands drop.

"Enough." Ember moved between us and Lars. "Our disappearance was my fault. I wanted to spend my birthday with family."

"You put yourself in danger and disappeared for five days so you could have a birthday party?" Lars blinked in astonishment, color returning to his face slowly.

"Yes. I wanted one night when I didn't feel helpless or scared." Ember stood strong in front of him. "One night I could forget all I am destined for, all the people

I might lose, and simply have fun spending time with some of the people I love."

Lars's black pupils returned to chartreuse. He first seemed perplexed by the idea, but then a softness loosened his pursed lips. "I want the four of you in my office in ten minutes." He spun around, leaving us in a tense silence.

"Eli, are you okay?" Ember rushed to him.

"Yeah. Fine." Funny, he sounded anything but.

Lorcan helped me to my feet. "Fuck." Lorcan massaged the back of his neck, his head waggling.

"And he was just irritable. You should see when he really gets upset." Ember sighed.

"That was just *irritable*?" Lorcan shook his head.

"Believe me. If he were truly angry, none of us would be breathing right now."

Ember and Eli moved closer, talking privately to each other. Lorcan turned back to me. "You sure you're okay?"

"Yeah. Shook up. Mad. But all right." I brushed a strand of crusty hair off my face. "Are you?"

"Being thrown into the dirt and choked?" A mischievous grin hooked his lip. "That's third base for me."

I chuckled and smiled. With one sentence Lorcan had the power to change my mood. And the way his eyes moved down my body, as if he wanted me to be the one to try it next, burned in my blood, making me forget about anything else but him.

He watched me; our silence was filled with words we could not say. Desire we could not act on.

"Guys, come on!" Ember called over her shoulder. Lorcan and I lurched away from each other. Lorcan motioned for me to go before him. I rushed to catch up with my friend, following her and Eli to the house where I was sure our true penance was coming.

Five days in the Otherworld, against his word, would not go unpunished. For some reason it didn't bother me. The safety I felt in Lorcan me gave me courage to face anything. The notion rammed down on my chest, and I swallowed, trying to ignore the feelings it stirred.

I was not being fair. I needed to talk with Jared. I had felt the distance even before I came back. We were no longer the same people. I loved him, and I always would, but I wasn't sure I was in love with him anymore. The moment I returned, I had been fighting the sensation he was simply a very good friend.

"Ken!" At the sound of my name, guilt soured my gut. I hadn't even noticed we were near the field. Of course Jared would be there.

Jared ran up, his forehead beading with sweat; his face flashed with elated joy at seeing me.

Oh crap...I am a horrible person.

"Where have you been?" He reached me, frowning down at me, like he suddenly realized he should be upset with me. "I was really worried about you." Then his attention went over my shoulder. Lorcan. Jared's shoulders coiled, his chest bucking up. His temper flared. "What the *hell* are you doing here?"

Jared's rage boiling under the surface was always on simmer, ready to be set off. I needed to calm him. The conversation Jared and I needed to have would not happen right now.

"Calm down. It's not what you think."

Jared ignored me, zeroing in on Lorcan. I'd seen that look before with the dwellers. They set on their prey and locked on.

Defuse this quickly, Kennedy.

I grabbed Jared's chin, forcing him to look at me. "Hey."

Jared took me in, his physique relaxing under my touch. Then he grabbed my neck, pulling me in for a quick kiss, his hazel eyes going warm and buttery. "Where were you? You've been gone a *week*."

Every inch of my skin burned with awareness that Lorcan was behind me, watching. I placed my hands on Jared's face, using it to actually lean away from him and keep him from kissing me again.

"I'm sorry. We went to see Ryan. We were only supposed to be gone a day, but some bugs attacked us...and...we were extraordinarily lucky to get out."

Jared yanked out of my hold. "You went to the Otherworld without me?"

"You were training, which is more important than you coming with me," I rushed to explain. "I wanted to see Ryan and spend time with him. You needed to stay here and practice." In my desperation to have him believe me, to get through this till I had time to talk with him later, I kissed him. It worked. And I hated myself more for it.

Anger dropped away, his face breaking into a huge excited grin. "You should see what I learned." He jogged backward then did some flips, kicks, and punches.

"Impressive." I smiled. It still was nowhere near the level to fight highly trained soldiers.

"Think you can fight me now?" Eli's hand engulfed the back of Jared's neck, dragging him closer.

"Oh, I can take you, old man." Jared elbowed his uncle and bounced away, his arms punching out like a boxer warming up.

In a second, Eli dropped Jared to the ground. "You sure?"

I was sure Eli didn't mean to, but in that one move he showed how unprepared Jared was for a real war. He would be killed. I was so happy Cole and Owen still refused to let him be part of it. No matter what Jared hoped for, the rest of us seemed to know he would not be allowed to join.

But now Jared's gaze darted to me, then back to Eli, embarrassment narrowing his lids. He was pissed that Eli had so easily shown him up. He leaped up and slammed a fist into Eli's gut. Eli didn't even flinch.

"We need to go." Ember frowned as though she'd had enough of this sad display of testosterone. "Lars is furious enough with us."

"Keep working on those moves." Eli pulled Jared into a headlock. "I'll come out later and practice with you."

"Where are you guys going?" Jared asked eagerly.

"Lars wants us in his office." I pointed to the house.

"I want to come." He pushed away from Eli and bounced to me, swiping my hand into his, and put it to his chest. He kept darting glances at Lorcan while he clutched me close. I wanted to scream. I felt trapped in this caveman standoff, even though only Jared was playing.

Ember's gaze caught mine. Whatever she saw in my eyes turned her to Jared. "No, sorry, J. But I am saving you from getting strung up by your intestines with the rest of us."

I squeezed his hand then dropped it, stepping away. "I'll come find you after practice."

His lips brushed mine, his eyes still watchful of Lorcan, then he loped back toward the field. My shoulders sagged. With relief, with sorrow, with torment? All of the above.

TWENTY-FOUR

Rez led us into Lars's office. All of us turned as she shut the door, like we had just watched the last chance of escape slip away from us.

Lars leaned back in his chair, observing us. His silence thickened the air in the room. The disappointment in his voice finally broke the strain. It all fell on Ember.

"As the future Queen, I expect you to act a certain way, especially after recent events in London and New York. You need to stop thinking of yourself and start thinking for the kingdom."

Ember flinched.

"You will have obligations, people to lead, and an entire court looking to you to guide them through the aftermath of the war. Start acting like you are the ruler of these people and not like a spoiled, selfish little girl.

You are an adult now. Behave like one."

Ember marched to his desk and slammed her hands down on it.

"That is why I needed to do it. If, and it is a strong *if*, I live long enough to become Queen, my entire life is all wrapped up in a bow. I will have my existence planned out for me, down to when I go to the bathroom. I will do it so the Light does not suffer. Because they need a ruler, and they need someone to get them out of Aneira's mess. I know I am her blood, so if it is meant to be me, then I will do it. But it is not because I *want* to. You know better than anyone what I am giving up to do the right thing. Aneira's massacres and destruction made it exceptionally clear I needed one last night with my family and friends. Don't make me feel bad for wanting to be with them."

Lars and she stared at each other in a standoff, their stubbornness battling against each other. I was shocked when Lars relented. "Tell me everything the raven said and where the sword is."

Raven? What raven was he talking about? Grimmel? Was it possible the same bird visited both Ember and me? I read they were dream-guides. Did he show her the sword as well? When? I didn't get to ask before Ember went into a spiel about the sword being locked in a room in the castle. The coincidences, the way she described the room, I knew it was the same bird.

Lars took in our appearance, grabbed for his phone, and waved us off. "You all look and smell horrendous. Get cleaned up, and then I would like the four of you to go through different scenarios and strategies of getting into the castle. All of you must be ready for every situation thrown your way. I have set up a mock battlefield downstairs in the family room. No one will interrupt you there. I do not want you to leave until you have fleshed out a dozen plans to infiltrate the castle. And even more for how you will escape. You are dismissed."

~~~~~

The shower was heaven. Nothing worse than walking with wet, chafing, or stiff drying pants. My skin felt itchy and tight from the dried mud. I washed my hair twice to get all the grime out of it. The shower floor turned dark brown for the first half of the shower, then it cleared.

Once my damp hair was tied back in a ponytail, my clean clothes snuggled me against the slight chill, I headed down to the basement.

Eli, Ember, and Lorcan were already there when I arrived. Lorcan smiled when I approached, my own smile meeting his. His hand went to my back as he led me to the source of Em and Eli's focus.

The mock battlefield Lars had mentioned stood in the middle of the large family room. An exact replica of the Seelie castle and grounds covered an entire ping-pong table. My mouth fell open taking in the painstaking details. Each room of the castle was decorated and even the white plastic figures, piled on the field, wore the Queen's insignia. Another heap of figures, black ones, lay scattered on the grounds, some with initials on them.

Eli snickered, picking up the one that was head first in the moat, the initials EB stenciled on it. "Looks about right."

Ember glared at him, grabbing another figure, and tossed the one with ED on it into the painted lake.

"Nice," Eli snorted.

"All right." Ember waved Lorcan and me closer. "We need to start. Let's say we get to the bridge but it's blocked. What are our other options?"

We moved to the opposite side, taking in the scene. Lorcan picked up figures LD and KJ and passed mine to me, his fingers grazing mine. Staring at the table, I took it from his hand, my teeth gnawing on my bottom lip as I studied all the scenarios and options. I was grateful to be doing this. Planning and research were catnip to me. Something to focus on and turn my attention from how Lorcan's arm brushed mine, or how I could smell soap and his sexy guy odor.

"The bridge is our only way in and out, unless..." I pointed at the structure.

"...we come from the water," Lorcan finished my thought, his finger tapping at the blue lake.

"Right." I grinned, taking his figure from him and placing them together in the lake.

"This is how I got in before. There are sewage tunnels here." Ember circled a section of the forest with her finger close to the water. "Let's hope no one told Aneira how I entered last time, or she hasn't thought of it."

"Someone will think of it." Eli folded his arms, scanning the table.

"I don't know." Ember pursed her lips. "Torin would have, but Josh is her First Knight now. He would have no idea they are there."

"Her other soldiers would." Eli's eyebrows furrowed.

"Probably, but it's an option. It might be our only way."

"I agree. *On* the water, we are too exposed." Eli assessed the board.

"Not if we're *in* the water," Lorcan and I said in unison. We turned to each other and started laughing, his shoulder bumping mine. "We need to stop doing this."

"I know." I knocked into him playfully. My smile was so big it cracked my dry lips. I knew I was being obvious, but I couldn't seem to stop myself, giddiness bubbling over. "Dax wanted to kill us one night, remember?"

"Oh yeah, I remember." Lorcan chuckled, tipping his head back as he recalled the night of our food fight, when he got pinged with a muffin. Dax had stormed out pissed and disgusted at our playful banter. He didn't like me, but Dax was pledged to guard me, to fight to the death to save mine, and I knew he would not hesitate.

Lorcan turned his head, humor still dancing in his eyes. Then they lost all humor. They searched mine, stealing breath from me, as if he sensed a difference in me.

Heat sizzled under my skin, my eyes not able to look away from his, letting him read me.

"There you are. I've looked everywhere for you guys." Jared's voice echoing down the stairs was like ice down my back, wrenching me from Lorcan.

"Oh, cool." Oblivious to the tension and silence as he trotted up to the table, Jared's eyes grew big and excited seeing the pieces like it was a game. "Where's mine?"

"You don't have one." Tightness strained Lorcan's vocals, clipping his words.

"Why not?" Jared glared at Lorcan, the muscles along his neck coiling. I saw Jared's temper rising, recognizing the red patchy skin spotting his neck and cheeks when he got upset.

I had to defuse this. "Because you won't be going with us. You know that." I reached over, gently touching Jared's arm. My voice calm and soft.

"Right." His glower shifted to me. "I am to stay here with the women and children."

"Excuse me?" Ember and I both reacted. Women in the fae culture were just as much warriors and leaders as men and were never treated like the weak ones. That was a human notion, one which Jared seemed to be picking up.

"You know what I mean," Jared grumbled, looking away.

"You're staying here and protecting people like Marguerite and Rez, which is a huge job," Ember said, not appeasing him in the slightest.

"Dude, my girlfriend gets to go into battle, and I have to stay home with the babysitter. It's not fair." Jared's hand curled and banged into the table, the pot hitting boil in a few seconds.

"When has life ever been fair?" Lorcan replied. Lorcan's words were the fuse to Jared's bomb.

"Fuck off," Jared seethed, rancor slicing at Lorcan.

"Jared, stop it." I had enough. He was like a little boy we constantly had to pacify so he wouldn't throw a tantrum. Why did he want this so bad? Did he think any of us actually wanted to do this? "You know if I could stay back, I would, believe me." I reached out for him.

"Yeah, but they *need* you." Jared knocked my hand away, his resentment building. "You are 'special' in a good way. I'm only a nuisance and a liability, but they can't do without *you*."

"Hey!" Lorcan bellowed, stepping around me. His hand touching my arm as he moved. "That's enough, Jared. You're mad at the situation, at me. Don't take it out on Kennedy."

Jared's eyes fell to where Lorcan's hand rested on me. Lorcan dropped his arm, but it was too late. Jared's shoulders grew, fury filling him like a stuffed turkey. Rage turned his cheeks a deep shade of red. The room surged and thumped with his anger.

A guttural roar thundered out of Jared. He flung himself at Lorcan, his pupils vertical and bursting with wrath. A cry broke from my lips as Jared sprang. I didn't even see Eli move, but suddenly he was there, snatching Jared back.

"Whoa." Eli had a death grip on Jared's shoulders, holding him.

"Get out of my way, Eli." Jared growled and struggled against Eli's grip.

"You need to calm down, J," Eli said low into his ear.

"How about you fuck off, too? You are really no different. You also treat me like a kid. I am almost nineteen," he screamed at the two brothers, his face beet red, his limbs trembling. His head snapped back to Lorcan as he lunged again for him, but Eli held him in place. "And you keep your hands off my girlfriend. Why are you touching her? She is *mine*. Not yours!"

Mine. If I heard it one more time from him I was going to scream. I belonged to nobody. And every time he said it, I felt less his than anyone's.

"Jared. Stop." I stood in front of Lorcan, trying to block the red cape from the bull.

"Why in the hell are you even here anyway? Shouldn't you run back to the Queen like the trained lap dog you are?" Jared yelled over my head. "Why don't you leave, Lorcan? No one wants you here. No one likes you."

"Please, Jared." My calm demeanor was slipping. His attack on Lorcan set my belly ablaze, but I tried to keep composed.

"You want him to go, too, don't you?" Jared's blazing gaze hit me, his chin flicking at Lorcan. "I know you can't stand him any more than the rest of us. Tell him."

"Jared..."

"Dammit, Ken, tell him!"

My mouth opened and shut. I couldn't. My heart wouldn't let me.

Jared blinked, taking in my silence. He stumbled back like I slapped him. Understanding crossing his features. Utter agony flicked through Jared, slicing me in half to see the pain on his face I caused. A ball of grief lodged in my chest.

"Jared, I..." I lifted my hand, the reaction to comfort so powerful.

"Don't," he hissed, stepping away from my touch.

I yanked back my hand, tears leaking below my lids, blurring my vision.

"I get it now." His cold anger fired at me.

"No." He didn't understand. This wasn't something I wanted. I never wanted to fall for Lorcan. I tried to fight it, be *his* girlfriend. "You don't."

"I must have been blind not to see it." He lashed out, each word filled with disgust and venom. "Did you enjoy making a fool of me? Leading me on? Pretending you cared?"

"What are you talking about? I love you..." My sentence trailed off, shocked by his statement. Did he think I had been playing him? Faking it? Was he serious? I had loved him so much. I never wanted to hurt him, never wanted to be a cause of his grief.

"Him?" Jared was no longer listening, his rage on its own stage. "Really? You'd rather be with him?"

"No." It wasn't about rather, as if it were a contest. That's not how it ever felt to me. Lorcan simply got me in ways Jared hadn't, but it didn't take away from what we had together.

Lorcan moved up, his head shaking. "It's not what you're thinking."

To hear him say that twisted the knife in my gut even though I knew he was trying to save me. But I realized how fake it sounded. How untruthful. Who were we kidding? It was exactly like that. I just didn't want to think myself capable of it.

"Shut up!" Jared spit out, pointing at him. "You don't get to talk." Jared inhaled, his body pulsating. His nostrils flared like he was debating if he wanted to go for Lorcan again. His glare hung on me then returned to Lorcan.

He jerked away from Eli and turned for the stairs, his expression twisted with grief.

"Jared?" I shuffled after him. He didn't look back, his feet pounding the steps as he left the room, taking two at a time. "Jared..." He disappeared, and I started to follow him.

"Let him go. He needs to cool off." Eli touched my shoulder, halting me. "He's got the hot Irish temper like the rest of us. He'll be fine once he calms down."

I nodded, hearing Eli but unable to speak. The ball in my chest burst open. A sob rocked my chest, and I covered my mouth to keep the moan from coming out. But it would not obey. Hot tears spilled down my face. I had just hurt one of my best friends.

I swiveled around and ran down the hallway leading to the bathrooms and extra bedrooms. I didn't know or care where I went, I needed to get out of the room. But the guilt, judgment, and hate trailed behind, curling around me, sticking to my skin.

I didn't go far, my legs buckling once I rounded the corner. My back hit the wall as I sobbed silently till I was folded over myself.

"Shit." I heard Lorcan swear. "Maybe I should go talk to him."

"No!" Eli and Ember yelled together.

"Tell him it's not like that," Lorcan continued.

"It's not?" Eli replied dryly. "Jared would see through the lie."

My lids squeezed together, more tears spilling out. They had seen the truth. Even if I had been planning to end things with Jared and never act on my feelings for Lorcan again, it didn't matter. They all knew.

"You will only cause it to be worse right now," Eli said. "I'll go."

"And I'll check on Kennedy." Ember sounded like she was moving across the room. It only took her a few seconds to round the corner and find me sitting there. I lifted my head but stared at the wall across as she settled next to me, her shoulder bumping mine.

"You all right?"

"Not really."

"I am so sorry, Ken." Em put her head on my shoulder, her love soothing the hurt inside just a bit. "You didn't deserve that."

"Don't I?" My voice cracked.

She picked up her head, her eyes watchful. I knew she wanted me to confess, to tell her what she feared deep down. That's what made it so hard. Her reaction.

"Did...*something*...happen with you and Lorcan?"

My head bowed forward, a tear rolled down my cheek, splashing on my hand.

"I am a horrible person, aren't I?" I said quietly.

Ember couldn't hide her shock; it popped off her, leaking all over. She tried. For my sake.

"No, of course you're not." She hugged me close to her. "You're human, Ken...well, mostly. We all make mistakes, but we get up, brush ourselves off, and try to learn from our mishaps. Or so I've heard."

"That's the thing, Em..." How did I explain the man she despised was not a lapse in judgment? He was my lifeline. He pushed me to do better, be better. He didn't treat me like a fragile creature. I was strong, smart, and sensual around him. I woke up wanting to be near him.

Ember gulped. "You don't feel it was a mistake?"

"No. Yes. I don't know." I hit my head against the wall. "I love Jared, but there's a huge gap between us now. I've changed, and maybe he has too. But in whatever way we have changed, it is pulling us apart. I've been feeling it for a long time now, but I've been trying to ignore it. I thought if we could get through it we could make it work."

"So what happened with Lorcan?"

"I don't want to talk about Lorcan. What's going on has nothing to do with him."

"Nothing to do with him?" Ember exclaimed, twisting to face me. "It has everything to do with him."

"No." I wiped at the last of my tears. "This situation has to do with me being honest with myself. The last thing I want to do is hurt Jared, but I can't lie to myself either."

"No." Ember sighed. "You can't. It wouldn't be fair to either of you."

Whatever she felt about Lorcan, she was letting it go. For me. I covered her hands with mine, my appreciation expressed without a word.

"You're not going to tell me what happened?" She peered at me.

"I need to figure some things out on my own first." My hands returned to my lap. "Okay?"

"Yeah." She sighed and nodded. "Okay."

I rose to my feet. "There is no doubt I love Jared. I simply don't know if it is enough to keep us together as a couple." Actually, I was sure it wasn't, but that was between us. I needed to talk to him before I decided anything.

"Lorcan?" Ember stood, a knowing smile hinting on her mouth.

"I care for him." I leaned against the wall. Ember did not give up. "A lot. I don't know what it means yet. I won't deny I am drawn to him, but I will try to work it out with Jared."

It wasn't a lie. I really wasn't ready to throw us away yet, but my feelings for Lorcan were a huge blockade. One I was no longer sure Jared and I could get over.

TWENTY-FIVE

The crisp breeze brushed over my skin, and my shoulders relaxed as I took a deep breath, letting nature calm my frazzled nerves. My walk in the forest stilled my mind and emotions. Despite growing up in a family of people who weren't big nature fans, I was adapting to it like it had always been part of me. I guess it was in my blood. I had ignored it before, but now the earth's energy pulsated over my skin.

My magic was different from Ember's, but we both used nature's energy. While Ember was part of it, nature seemed to treat me more as a visitor. It was accommodating and gracious to let me borrow it, but it still had its limit and always drained me. It gave Ember endless power to tap from, though too much magic pouring in could make you insane or kill you.

Maya had found me earlier saying physical training would start at dawn, then our strategic training in the late morning. Neither were fun, but I knew how important they were. I had gone five days without practicing or advancing.

The farther I walked, the more my shoulders sagged, feeling the weight of my fate and my future. Would I be able to do it? I didn't want to fail. I didn't want to die, but defeating Aneira was a must. Whatever it took.

"Is this pity party for one or can I join?"

"Shit." I swung around, my hand going to my chest.

"Wow, you're getting a mouth on you, li'l bird." Lorcan leaned one shoulder against a tree, with a slightly cheeky grin, but humor did not reach his eyes. Sadness etched along the corners of his lids and brow.

My fingers rubbed my temples, and I exhaled. "Lorcan, I can't deal with this right now."

He glanced away, licking his lip. "I didn't come to add more pressure on you. I know you have enough." He tapped the tip of his boot at a rock. "I'm not going to ask anything from you, Ken. I'm not here to declare anything or demand you to choose. I'm going to step aside. Jared deserves you."

A jolt shot up my spine, and I crossed my arms, feeling protected by their barrier. Was he giving up? Did he not care enough? How could he give me up so easy? Dread wedged in my throat, expanding in my chest. I thought all my tears had been shed, but my eyes pricked with their urgency. *No. No. No.* The words never came out, but I shook my head.

"I *am* here for something."

"What?" Hope sucked in briskly, swirling around my lungs. I didn't know what he wanted, but in my gut I had no doubt my answer would be yes.

"Your magic." He cleared his throat, standing up, his demeanor stiff. Formal. "You said you would help me break the blood curse. I followed through with my end. Now it's your turn."

"Of course." I looked down at my feet, my lashes fluttered, keeping back the disappointment. *What were you hoping he'd say?* It was clear by the hole in my heart what I wanted.

When we made the deal, I had been the one to say there wouldn't be any more between us. In a few weeks the roles had reversed. He was the one telling me no.

Lorcan and I worked for a couple of hours. Actually, he stood there, letting me toss him into the dirt over and over, while I practiced the breaking curse Maya and Koke had worked with me on. My spells were improving, but I could feel the curse fight against me, holding strong.

Lorcan was actually a great test subject for me to work on. With him, I began to really feel what Lars said about it fighting and attacking me.

The spells Maya had made for me to work on didn't originate from Aneira. Each person had their own signature in magic, a different feel, taste. It was good for me to understand Aneira's, learn if she had a weakness somewhere. Lorcan provided firsthand experience with Aneira's curses and magic.

When I was covered in sweat and blood from a nosebleed, my head throbbing, Lorcan finally called it quits.

"No." I rubbed my head. "I can try again."

"No. You've pushed yourself too much today."

I shoved off my knees, getting to my feet again, my jaw grinding. "I. Can. Try. Again."

Lorcan scrutinized me but relented at my determination. Shuffling back to his spot, he rolled up his sleeves, displaying the bruises and knots the day had left all over his battered body. "All right, bring it on."

My boots moved wider as I braced myself, the Latin words coming off my tongue in a growl. Concentrating on the third eye, I sucked back deep into my mind, almost not feeling myself anymore. The pulse of Lorcan's curse kicked back, pushing against me. My mind felt around it, trying to find any way in.

I'm useless! How do I expect to break the one on the sword if I can't break this one? I was going to fail. And millions of people would die because of it.

No! Kennedy Anne Johnson did not fail. Frustration and fury rolled down my spine and crawled over my shoulders. I felt it build in my chest. Pain slashed through my head and dots formed behind my lids. I pushed through. I was mad as hell. I never failed a test or an assignment. I was not going to start now. Spitting the words, wrath vibrated me. The magic grew shrill till I felt like I might shatter.

Then everything went still. Quiet. Like a spaceship passing from Earth's atmosphere to outer space. I floated. Weightless. Only the curse and me. All the forest elements were fuzzy and gray. I could barely see Lorcan's outline over the spell. The magic was vibrant and throbbed with life, swirling and curling around. It sensed me. Tasted me.

Without knowing how it happened, I felt it jerk back. Like it feared me.

For one moment, I touched a different plane.

And then I fell. Hard.

I crashed to the ground, my body falling into a heap on the rocky forest floor.

"Kennedy!" Lorcan bellowed. "Fuck." I felt his hands run over my arms.

I groaned, lifting my head. Lorcan was on his knees next to me, wild panic in his eyes.

"Are you all right?"

I nodded, but I wasn't quite sure. I touched the tickling under my nose and came away dripping with blood. He helped me sit up and used the hem of his T-shirt to stop the bleeding. We sat there in silence as he pinched the bridge of my nose, waiting for it to stop.

Slowly sensations returned to my body. My hip hurt where I landed on rocks. My leg muscles felt like I put them through a pasta maker, and my head thumped like a jackhammer, but I was okay. I felt strangely exhilarated.

"I did it," I whispered, my head pulling away to face him.

"What?" He dropped back on his heels, his eyes widened with hope. "You broke it?"

"Oh no. Sorry." I bit my lip, seeing his expression fall. "I meant I finally broke through to the next plane."

One of Lorcan's eyebrows hitched up.

"I reached it." I curled my legs under me, getting on my knees. "It's what Maya and Koke have been trying to get me to do but weren't able." Jubilance filled my chest. "It was brief, but it was amazing…I mean I've never felt anything like that. It feared me."

"What feared you?"

"The magic." I motioned around. "When I hit that level, it finally took notice of me. And it *feared* me."

"I'm a little afraid of you right now as well."

I tried to glare at him, but the smile on my face wouldn't stay away.

"This is a great thing. It means I have hope of breaking the protection spell and your curse. I mean, I have to stay there longer than a few seconds, but it's a start and—"

"Kennedy." Lorcan grabbed my face, obstructing my rambling words. "I watched you. You were literally only floating for seconds, and I could already feel it killing you. I could smell death and sense your life draining away, and it was scarcely for a moment. What will happen if you stay there longer? What if you have to fight it on that plane?"

I knew what would happen. "I can do it," I said softly, my eyes going back and forth between his. "There's no other choice."

"Yes, there is." His fingers slid a little behind my jaw, holding me tighter. "Don't do it."

"I have to."

"No…not if it means it's going to kill you. I couldn't live with that."

"I couldn't live with myself if I didn't." I stared up at him, allowing him to see my truth. I couldn't tell him I was most likely not walking away from the castle in three days, but I didn't need to. He seemed to understand.

He squeezed his lids closed, his forehead pressing into mine. We breathed together, his fingers curling into the base of my scalp. His breath trailed down my neck. My heart exploded into thousands of pieces, churning emotions inside me like a turbulent sea.

"I won't lose you," he spoke low, but every word slammed into me like a drum.

I leaned in, my mouth finding his. I sighed at the pressure of his soft lips against mine. I started it, but a brush of my lips and his mouth crashed down on mine, inhaling me with a hiss of air. My mouth opened, begging him to deepen the kiss. My hands slid up his neck, trying to bring him closer.

Desperate need consumed us with its own hurricane. My head spun, no longer aware of up or down. My teeth tugged at his bottom lip, knowing perfectly well what it did to him. He growled, and he kissed me deeper. The kiss ignited my body in flames. I grabbed the back of his head, laid myself back, and he followed, lowering himself over me.

I wanted him. The way he made me feel. The way my body reacted to his touch. Nothing else seemed to matter.

My hand clutched the wet blood-soaked spot on his shirt from my nose, trying to pull it up. For some reason I liked it, even on his clothing, I was marked on him. *Mine.* The thought came from the trenches of my subconscious, the deep-rooted animal in my DNA. And I wanted him to bury himself deep in me. The need filled me, spilling out of my skin.

Lorcan inhaled sharply. "Stop," he whispered against my mouth. He sat back, pulling me with him, his hand cupping my cheek. "You're just acting from extreme emotions. This is not really what you want. Not like this. You'd never hurt Jared."

I looked away, shame cooling my desire. I didn't know what I wanted anymore. I had told Ember I would try everything I could to work it out with Jared. But only a few hours later I was desperately pawing at Lorcan, needing him to fill me. I realized the best thing was to let Jared go. I should not want someone else so bad and still think I was committed to making it work with him.

Jared deserved better. But even if I ended it with Jared, it didn't mean I could happily skip off to Lorcan. It would be the same whether or not I stayed with Jared or not. Lorcan and I could never be. The history with his family, my friends...my history with his nephew was all too complicated. My heart twisted with grief at the thought I could never have Lorcan like I wanted.

I should have pulled away from him, but I couldn't. Nor did he seem able to let me go. He drew me closer, our foreheads together, his thumbs stroking my jawline.

"We have to stop," I whispered. He seemed to understand I meant totally. Just not right now.

"I know, li'l bird."

I looked in his eyes, aching. "You can't call me that anymore." The pet name was too much of a reminder. Painful.

He exhaled and drew away. Rising to his feet, he helped me to mine. His eyes lingered on me for a moment then he turned, walking away, the evening shadows quickly swallowing him up. I hated the void I felt when he disappeared.

It's lust, Ken...not love, I repeated in my head, hoping the sentiment was true. Lust I could get past. Love was something else entirely.

And that was not something I should *ever* feel for him.

~~~~

"Come in," Jared's voice grumbled from inside the cabin. I wobbled, tempted to run, but I would not let myself be a coward. Once I understood what my next move was, I headed straight here, feeling relieved. Not for what I had to do, but that I was doing the right thing. The fair thing for all.

I stepped into the place he shared with his father. Owen's side was neat like the man himself, the bed so tidy you could bounce a quarter off it. Only one pair of shoes under the bed even revealed his side was occupied. Jared was orderly for a teenage boy, his comic books in a descending order piled on the nightstand. One thing neither he nor Owen seemed to like to do was laundry. A huge pile of dirty clothes, a mixture of both of theirs, was bundled on a chair.

Jared lay on his bed but jumped up the moment he saw me. Then he seemed to remember he was upset with me, a scowl forming on his face.

"Hey." I stood by the door, not able to look him in the eye. He was only dressed in his running shorts. I noticed his bare chest quite quickly, despite myself. These past few months had completely renovated his physique.

"Hey," he responded, his voice curt. He sat back on the bed, not looking at me either.

Tension writhed between us, caught in jumbled snares. I shifted on my feet, wrapping my arms together.

"I'm sorry." The words tumbled out of my mouth with a need to relieve the buildup of all the other apologies waiting behind.

Jared stared at his hands.

The floorboards creaked underfoot as I moved to Owen's bed, sitting across from him.

Jared leaned his arms on his legs. "What's going on, Ken?"

My stomach dropped like lead. Even knowing what I had to do, I found it almost impossible to get it out. My emotions whirled with confusion for both him and Lorcan.

"I don't know," I whispered.

He lifted his head, hazel eyes peering into mine. Pain, grief, longing, love—his feelings broadcasting like on TV. Unlike the rest of his family, Jared didn't hide his emotions. He was an open book, which could be a good or bad thing.

Tonight it was like shooting my heart out of a cannon. Right onto a spike.

"Tell me honestly. What happened with you and Lorcan? Did you sleep with him?" His mouth twisted, spitting out the last words.

"What? No." I shook my head wildly, my ponytail brushing my arms.

"So what is it?" Jared burst up to his feet. "You got to know him, care about him now?"

"Jared..."

"He kidnapped you, Kennedy!" Fury spurted from his mouth as he threw out his arms. "He's a traitor to his own family. He killed your friend...killed another friend's mother. Got West locked up by the Queen. How can you defend him? Even stand being near him?"

"He's not—"

"Don't..." Jared growled. "Don't tell me he's not like that or it isn't what I think. I've known him my whole life. You have only known him for a few months." Jared moved away from the beds, pacing in the small space. "He played you, Ken. Like he's done to a thousand others before you."

I gazed down at my lap and tried to ignore the stab of doubt painfully working its way to the surface.

"You only want to see the good in people, I get it, but even you have to see what he's done." Jared's shoulders dropped, his anger softening. "You aren't that gullible. I know *my* woman is smarter than that."

I bolted to my feet, rage flaming at the back of my throat, ready to lash out. "Stop talking like you own me."

"But you're mine. I've claimed you."

I clenched my hands in frustration. I could feel that piece of myself, the part that never wanted to hurt anyone's feelings, who kept the peace, slipping. I inhaled, mustering calmness.

"You say it so much I feel like you are trying to force something, more than you actually feel it."

"You don't think I love you?" His face pinched tight.

"I didn't say that." I pushed at my glasses, glancing at the floor. "I just think we are trying to force something, which might not be there anymore."

"What?" Jared sucked in, his foot taking a step back like I punched him.

"Jared, I love you..." I moved up to him, my heart already fraying at the seams. But I knew I had to do this. It was the only thing that felt right anymore. It still made me want to drop to my knees bowed over in agony.

"But," he choked out.

My throat swelled like it could stop me from getting the next words out. "I don't know if it's the way you want. The way I should."

Jared's shoulders flattened in a rigid line; his nostrils spread, drawing heavily through his nose.

"We've both changed. And what made us work before isn't working anymore. We've grown apart instead of together." Stone faced, I pressed ahead, unloading my guilty conscience. "I know you've felt it too. You said it the other day."

"This is because of him, isn't it?" Jared's lids narrowed, his hands going to his hips.

"What?" I jerked back. "No, Jared. This is because of *me*. How *I* feel." I motioned to myself. "Lorcan has nothing to do with you and me. If everything was good, then no outside force in the world would deter it. But all we do is fight. And if we aren't, I feel anything I say will lead to one."

"This is my fault?"

"No. No." I shook my head. "That's not what I was saying."

He snorted.

"I think we should focus our energy on the coming war."

"You mean the war you're a crucial part of," he snipped, running a hand through his hair. "Cole will change his mind. He sees how strong and good I'm getting. You guys need me."

He stepped closer, looming over me. His hands captured my face, tilting it up to his. "I'm in love with you, Kennedy." His gaze searched mine. "You say you don't feel the same about me…and that might be true *right now*. But I know we are meant for each other. You are mine. You have been since the day we met."

"Jared…"

"No. I'm not giving up on us. I'm not letting you, either."

I closed my eyes against the sincerity of his words, my will torn from all sides. What I felt for Lorcan didn't take away my feelings for Jared. They were shifting but hadn't disappeared. And the boy I fell in love with stood in front of me, wanting to give us another chance.

"I'll give you some time, if it's what you need, but also know I'm not giving up." His thumb brushed away a tear that escaped from beneath my glasses. "I'll win you back. Whatever I have to do."

"This isn't merely a separation, Jared." I needed him to understand we weren't in some gray area.

"Call it what you want." He dropped his hands away, folding them in set determination. "Pretend we are over. But I will never be done with you. You're my mate. I will never let you go."

TWENTY-SIX

The days leading up to Samhain were the toughest I'd ever experienced. Lars ran endless drills, mock fights, and simulations to get through to the castle. Then Maya and Koke drained what was left of me. My body and mind were shattered and no matter what I did, I never reached the plane I had with Lorcan where I could see the spell like a separate entity. Every time I didn't reach the next level, more fear bounded me firmer to the earth with its thorny presence.

Training distracted me from knowing Lorcan was avoiding me at every turn, while Jared was in my face more than ever. He had never been clingy or overbearing before, but our "breakup" seemed to make him more determined. If I doubted he would try to get me back, I was sorely mistaken. He followed me everywhere, bringing me food and drinks at every break. He became so overly attentive a few times I had to tell him to back off, which caused us to fight in front of others.

The more I pushed away, the more he came close. So I stopped, letting him do what he needed to. From a distance, I knew it looked like we were trying to work it out. In reality, his actions were only settling the truth I felt inside.

The day before Samhain, Lars pulled Eli, Ember, Lorcan, and me back to his property, away from all the other fae, putting Ember in charge of running a mock drill. He didn't say it, but I knew he was testing her. He wanted the future Queen to start acting like one.

Seeing her wiggle under the leadership role, I went to her side. The seer in me helped her pick the teams, assessing their strengths and weaknesses. We made a good team, and I was getting more comfortable with the focus on me.

A few of us were going into the castle: Torin because he knew every inch of the place; Ember and me, of course; and Eli because he was the best guard to protect her. She would be the prime focus of the other side, the one to kill. Plus, Eli would have followed her anyway.

"Lorcan?" Ember sucked in, like it was hard for her to say his name. Lorcan stepped out of the crowd, his gaze on Ember. "I want you to join Cole. You will be our last line of defense before we get into the castle. Cole will be lookout. Your main job...keep Kennedy safe."

My stomach flew into my mouth. I gritted my teeth trying not to react to Ember's directive. Lorcan looked at me with no feeling, then back at her, and nodded. It was silly but pain swept through my chest, and I looked away.

"All right. Everyone in position," Ember called out.

I grabbed her arm as the fae moved to get into place, turning her toward me. We had been friends long enough for her to understand without a single word from me.

She placed her hand on mine. "I need the best of the best, no matter what I feel about him. I may not trust him with my life, but I *absolutely* trust him with yours. He will die protecting you...that's all I need to know right now."

In the evening we enjoyed a grand "final" dinner for the family. Technically we would have another evening, waiting for midnight tomorrow, but this was for the group of us to relax and enjoy. A last party before we went off to battle...some of us to die.

Sorrow sprang behind my lids, and I blinked away the urge to cry.

No. Live in the now. I had no room to think those sad thoughts. Because if I did, it would cripple me, and I wouldn't be able to go forward. I knew that was the one thing I had to do. So many lives were counting on me.

Rez and Marguerite went all out, so I borrowed a dress from Gabby's limited selection. She was the closest to my size. It was a simple formfitting, black skater-type dress designed with dozens of safety pins down each side appearing to hold the dress together. Not something I'd usually wear, but it fit my mood. It appeared respectable from the front, but from the sides it was barely together, bursting at the seams. I left my hair loose and flowing down my back, then slipped on a cardigan and borrowed flats and stepped out of the cabin.

I paused at the door.

"Jared..." I couldn't stop the exasperation from seeping in at seeing him leaning against the bungalow across the way, waiting for me.

"I thought we could go as friends. Hang out." He shrugged, an adorable shy grin on his face, reminding me of the boy I used to know.

My irritation floundered, a softness skimming through.

"You look gorgeous."

"Thank you." I brushed absently at the front of the dress.

"May I escort you?" Jared held out his arm for me, wiggling his eyebrows up and down.

I laughed. "You're such a dork."

"Takes one to know one." He grinned wide, winking at me.

I shook my head, taking his arm. We strolled across the property to the main house. We scarcely made it to the door when I felt a burning prickle gnaw at the back of my neck, slipping down my body.

Li'l bird.

I peered over my shoulder, swearing I heard it whispered through the air. I searched into the night. Fires and outlines from the fae camping in the field flickered across my view, but not the person I sought. He was there. I sensed him. It was strange, but I recognized the feel of his eyes on me. Like he had his own signature, which my body responded to.

"You okay?" Jared asked, holding the door open.

"Yeah." I turned back. A part of me wanted to spin around and run into the night. To him. But I didn't. I did what was right and let Jared take me into the house, shutting the door behind me.

~~~~

The dinner was delicious. Marguerite's home cooking was amazing, as usual. Her chicken molé and fresh tortillas were better than ever. The enormous dining room was filled with the fae who lived here and most of the dark dwellers. Of course Lars excluded Lorcan's group.

Ember and I sat opposite each other in the middle of the table, the referees between the two disgruntled sides. Centuries of bad blood were in temporary suspension, some because of the common enemy and war ahead, but mainly because of Ember. Thankfully their love for her forced them to get along, or at least be tolerable of each other.

I could feel an undercurrent of melancholy, knowing tomorrow night everything would change, but for the night joy and alcohol flowed freely. Lars gave a moving speech, Gabby and Eli started a food fight, and the pixies—okay, Cal—proceeded to get hilariously drunk.

It was strange to admit, but I was having fun. Jared was sweet, making me laugh reminiscing on stories.

"Remember…" He started to laugh, tapping my arm. "Remember in Greece…" Jared inhaled, trying to control his mirth. "When you whacked me in the face in the middle of the night, and I woke up, flying out of the sleeping bag, and smacked into the tent wall." Jared slapped his face with his hand, mimicking himself hitting the tent. "I bounced back on my ass."

"Oh my god, I was laughing so hard. It was like watching a cartoon." I giggled, recalling the incident. Jared was not even fully awake, his beast side in reaction mode.

"Dude, I flew!"

"I asked if you were okay. And you looked at me, rolled over, and went back to sleep." A peal of hilarity rocked my stomach, and I gripped my torso, which ached from laughter.

"That tent was made out of some flexible shit. It flung me back like a rubber band." Jared jerked out his arms in dramatic motion, knocking into me. I hit Gabby's shoulder next to me and bounced back. Smacking into Jared, I grabbed him, trying to stop myself from falling. But he came down with me, crashing to the floor in a heap.

The entire room burst into laughter at us. Tears leaked from Jared's eyes; we faced each other in giggles. Then his mirth altered. His eyes glinted with a smoldering warmth. Love.

"See." Jared's eyes softened as his hands reached for my face, his lips brushing my forehead. "This is how we are supposed to be. We belong together." He pulled me closer, kissing my head again. "I've missed you. You. Are. *Mine*. No one else's."

My enjoyment died, sobering me. For one second we'd been having a good time, being the friends I hoped we could be. But it was never going to be. He'd never let it be just that.

All eyes were on us, the good humor in the room held in suspension.

"I am not yours, Jared. We've been through this." I sat up and scooted away. I spoke low, not liking to say these things in front of his family. "I am not something you own. *Especially* now."

Jared glanced around and back to me, taking in our audience. I saw his eyes flash, then something changed. He didn't get angry like I thought, but he leaned back, crossing his legs.

"And how many times have I explained to you I am a dark dweller? You are mine. I claimed you. It's how we work."

"You seem to easily forget you are also part human." I rose to my feet, disgusted by his behavior. "What is it with you lately? You're trying so hard to be something you aren't. I thought we could still be friends..." I wrapped one hand on my waist and pushed my glasses up with the other. I was tired of this same fight over and over. Of feeling guilty and awful. "Yes, you are a dark dweller, but you are also human. You used to be simply Jared, the boy I loved, which doesn't seem to be enough for you anymore."

"Funny," Jared responded as he climbed to his feet, his attitude shifting to irritation. "I seem to be the one who is not enough for *you* anymore," he spat. "Plus, why the hell do I want to be 'just Jared'? It's weak and pathetic. Everyone treats me either like I am going to break or I'm stupid."

"I am human also. Would you say I'm weak or stupid?" I yelled back at him, no longer seeing anyone around us.

"No."

"Then why would you say those things? You are anything but."

"Really?" he exclaimed, his tone mocking and vicious. "*You* of all people are asking me why? When you are the one who treats me the most like an idiot. You don't think I can see the truth, but I do. I am not blind."

I stepped back, putting a hand protectively to my chest.

Jared twisted toward the room, holding out his arms. "You are all about me accepting my human side. Then fine. I'm eighteen. An adult. I make my own choices."

"Jared, you lost a few years in the Otherworld." Owen shoved back his chair, rising, his face strained with disappointment. "You are not emotionally eighteen yet."

Cole got up too and stepped between us.

"I know you're upset with my decision, but I'd rather you hate me than get killed. We talked about it. I can't afford for you to be rash or reckless. Not with something this serious. You are young, and you think you're invincible. As much as you hate it, being half human does cause you to be more vulnerable. I will not risk losing you because you are careless and untrained for what lies ahead."

"You think I *want* to be half human?" Jared yelled, striking his torso. "An embarrassment to the clan? I want to be full dark dweller so I can be treated like one of you."

A clatter rang across the room, Owen's chair

smacking the wood floor as he stormed for Jared. "Don't say that!"

The room went still. Owen was the kindest, most compassionate of the dark dwellers. You could almost forget he was a beast, which was a mistake. You should never forget what they were, but it was still startling to see the dweller merge from the gentle doctor. The fury running through him turned his eyes vertical, his shoulders hunched. Jared stepped back a few feet at his father's approach.

Owen got in his son's face. "You are half your *mother*. One of the strongest people I have ever known. Do not be ashamed of what she was. Do *not* insult her memory."

Jared swallowed, his eyes darting away. "But I've done all the training. I thought you'd change your mind when you saw how good I am. And I *am* good."

Owen stepped back, pinching his nose, taking in several deep breaths. His shoulders eased. "You are, but it's not enough."

Rage tainted Jared's skin; his body trembled.

"I lost your mother. I will not lose you, too," Owen choked, turning away from Jared.

No one spoke. No one moved. The dining room clock chimed seven times.

"You are anything but an embarrassment to us." Cole finally broke the silence. "You are the glue keeping our family together. You are our lifeblood, and if anything happened to you..."

"You can't keep me in a bubble forever," Jared rasped, his hands still in balls at his side.

"I know. But this is not the time. I would prefer if Kennedy stayed too, but she has to go. She's a vital piece in the war."

"Yeah, yeah. Not wanted." Jared spun for the door, his body tense, but his shoulders slumped. "Message received." He stopped right in the doorway, let out a soft cry, smashed his fist into the wall, then stomped out of the room.

I stood there reeling from what had transpired. His tantrum broke me. So many of us were going to die, and he was throwing a fit like a toddler. Ember and I bore so much weight, but did he once ask me if I was doing all right or if I was scared? It was always about him. About being jealous.

I needed to get out of this room before I exploded over everyone.

TWENTY-SEVEN

I burst through the glass doors, which opened up onto the patio and gardens. I needed air. What had happened to us? At one time we were inseparable. Merely seeing his face had sent tingles and happiness flowing through me. I thought I was in love. The forever kind.

It hurt to think those clichés about young love were right. Had I been naïve and full of idealism? Jared and I spent hours laughing and talking; it wasn't deep or all consuming, but it was enough. Then.

"No." I gripped my fist, hitting them against my legs, mumbling to myself. "I loved him. I will not belittle what we had."

"Do you still?" A deep voice came out of the darkness.

My hand flew up to my mouth as I jumped back. "Dammit, Lorcan, you scared me."

"So skittish." His huge silhouette moved from behind a tree, almost blending with the deep shadows.

"Sorry, I don't have superhero hearing." My eyes narrowed in on the figure slipping soundlessly through the night onto the path. "Plus, it is rude to eavesdrop on someone else's conversation."

"You were talking to yourself." He was suddenly in front of me, his body only inches from mine. His voice was low and sultry.

"It-it-it's still…" I stuttered, pushed my glasses up the bridge of my nose, and glanced at the way the moonlight flickered off the pool. I felt frozen, unable to look at him. The intensity of his eyes burned into me.

"Calm down, li'l bird." He reached out and brushed his hands down my arms. "Breathe."

A quick, sharp laugh burst out of my mouth. Calm down? When he was touching me like that?

"Easy for you to say," I mumbled. My eyes rushed over him and then went back to the pool. His proximity was enough to cause my breath to stumble and clog my thoughts. The best thing was for me to move away. To get as far away from Lorcan Dragen as I possibly could. My body ignored my pleas to vacate and run.

"Look at me."

I sucked back my bottom lip, biting it, and shook my head.

"Kennedy? Please." His fingers slipped under my chin, his thumb brushing my mouth.

My lids pressed together trying, wishing, to block him out. His voice, his touch. The way he caused my skin to tingle and the blood to roar in my ears.

Leave, Kennedy. Walk away.

I was about to step back when his hand tilted my head back, and I opened my eyes. Oxygen dissipated in my lungs. Green eyes lit up the darkness around us. They searched mine with desire, setting me on fire. I wanted him so badly my body shook with need.

"You didn't answer my question." He was so close, the vibration of his voice tickled my ear, sliding silkily down my neck. All rational thought had ejected my brain.

"What question?" My throat was dry. The words struggled to find their way out.

Lorcan frowned and glanced at the ground. "Do you still love him?"

His question drilled into my head, down my throat, and into my heart. I sucked in a breath and stepped away from him. What kind of person was I? Jared and I had only been broken up a few days.

"That is none of your business." I tucked my arms underneath my rib cage, taking another stride back.

Lorcan's mouth gaped. "None of my business?"

"No, it's not." I forced my chin to stay high.

Lorcan's eyes flashed brighter, his head tilted to the side. "Are you serious?"

On the outside, my body was tight, my shoulders rolled back defiantly. Inside I was a quaking mess. He would only have to touch me, and I would crumble.

"I see." He ran his hand over his head, turning away from me. "Is this what you want? Last time, li'l bird, I will *never* ask again."

It seemed a simple enough question, but it was not. My world, my happiness, others' happiness—all weighed on one word from me. Yes or no. People would be hurt. Either choice would break me.

Tears filled my eyes, and I blinked rapidly to keep the dam from exploding. "Yes," I whispered. It would be easier this way.

A guttural grunt came from deep within Lorcan. He moved his palm up to the tree and leaned into it. He stayed silent and the tension in the air swelled, thickening into something I could almost taste. Bitter and tangy. No matter what I chose I hurt someone I cared about.

"All right." He sighed. I couldn't hear any anger or resentment, merely resignation in his voice. "I will leave you alone."

He pushed off the tree, arms rigid at his sides as he walked away from me. He had said that before, but this time he meant it.

The war began tomorrow. The probability of either of us surviving was a low percentage. Especially me. Putting all the statistics aside for just getting to the castle, the level of magic I was going to have to use to break the protection was going to kill me. I understood what I was getting into. My sacrifice would be well worth it if it saved people, most of all my friends and family.

But I didn't have to sacrifice my happiness now.

Live in the now.

Every step he took from me, my heart thumped louder in my chest. Pain swelled my heart. Words fought and wiggled their way up my throat. Panic froze me in place as I watched his figure distance himself from mine, until the moment the shadows engulfed him, taking my last chance with him.

If my life was to end tomorrow, how did I want to spend my last night?

An abundance of emotion moved me to seize my opportunity. Everything in my body wanted him—heart and soul. It was like someone smashed a book into my face, waking me up.

Oh. My. God.

Recognition of something I had been fighting for so long was in my face, bobbing around my chest like a submarine had surfaced. The clarity of my feelings was like a pristine lake. I could see all the way to the bottom.

I was in love with Lorcan.

My legs moved before I even realized it. My flats struck the damp grass with a gushy slap as I ran forward. "No. Wait!" The words broke through the barrier and released themselves into the night. I hurried up to where I saw him disappear. "Lorcan?" My voice was desperate and raw. It was not a tone I was used to hearing from myself. "Lorcan!"

Crickets and the soft wind broke through the trees, circled around my words, and consumed them. They stole the syllables, leaving only their vacant empty rebuttal.

"Lorcan?" A strangled cry came up as I circled around, searching for any sight of him. Nothing. My hand came up to my mouth, thinking it could keep the raging emotions back. "LOR-CAN!" He was gone. I missed my chance. "No…" My shoulders fell forward.

"Scream my name any louder and the entire camp is going to hear you," he rumbled behind me.

My arms flailed as I jumped in the air, spinning around. "Dammit, Lorcan!"

He laughed at my exceptionally ungraceful response.

Hands on my hips, my chest puffed up in agitation. "It's not nice to sneak up on people."

The smile slid from his lips, his gaze growing more intense. "You forget, li'l bird, I have exceptional hearing. I heard you call me the first time."

My lids narrowed. "Then why make me keep calling you and stand out here like an idiot."

He took slow prowling steps toward me. "Because…" His tongue skimmed over his bottom lip, while his body came so close I could feel the heat pulsing off him. "I like hearing you scream my name."

A lump lodged in my esophagus. I couldn't move or breathe. My arms were stiff, my back rigid with fright. But this fright cooked my blood and boiled all logical thoughts. Every nerve came alive and they were fully aware of his proximity.

"Why did you call me back?" He leaned down closer to my face but did not touch me.

"I-I don't know." All I understood was the need for him to touch me, which sent my brain into a whirlpool leaving me dizzy, confused, and wanting to throw up.

"I don't buy it." He moved in even closer, our mouths only centimeters away. I could feel the energy radiating off him, like a dozen tiny fingers lightly skimmed my skin. "I want to hear you say it, Kennedy. You need to tell me. What do you want?"

I tried several times to swallow, the words smashed up in my throat.

"It's up to you, but you need to admit it to yourself."

Why couldn't I say it? Confess what I felt? With Jared "I love you" came out soon and easy…almost too easy. Yet the notion of putting my heart out there and having Lorcan not feel the same caved my throat in on itself.

Lorcan leaned back. "I am not someone who wants to be a maybe." His jaw set in a firm line. With conviction, he tramped past me, heading for the forest.

Urgency to stop him finally melted my limbs. I grabbed his arm, swinging him back around.

"I know Jared said he claimed me. But I never felt that was true. Never knew when he was near." I swallowed. "I feel you. Everywhere. I want you… I've wanted you for a long time, Lorcan."

I didn't let myself acknowledge my declaration or wait for him to respond. I pushed onto my tiptoes and grasped his face, pulling him down to me. My lips found his and an inferno exploded within me, burning and consuming. It took him only a moment to respond. His hand curved around my head, bringing me in closer. I had only kissed three people in my life, but nothing compared to this. Lorcan kissed me with such desire and hunger time and space disappeared. My body dissipated into a zillion molecules exploding into the galaxy.

"Jared only claimed in words. His beast didn't. It can't be forced," he mumbled against my mouth. "He has no idea what it means for the beast to really claim someone."

"Do you?" My fingers brushed over his scruff, my breathing panting.

He didn't answer but seized my mouth with his, dipping his tongue into my mouth, tracing my bottom lip. A slight moan escaped from my chest, and Lorcan groaned back, pressing me firmer against him. It didn't matter, it would never be close enough. With his free arm, he cupped my backside, picking me up. My legs circled low on his waist as he set me on his hips, my dress riding up. This time I gasped. Every bit of him throbbed hard against me. Only his jeans and my underwear blocked him from entering me. My body responded with a violent, desperate need. Before I knew it, my fingers were acting, tugging off his jacket, wanting to free us of the obstructions. Lorcan pushed my back against the pool shed, his mouth opening mine farther, his tongue discovering the depths of mine with a fury. The animal in him was always at the surface, always on the verge of coming out. It frightened me, but the fear only heightened the deep thrill.

When the tips of my fingers slid in between the buttons of his jeans, popping them one at a time, he stilled and leaned back.

"What?" I gasped for air, my chest heaving with exertion and excitement. "Why did you stop?"

"We are about to cross a line here. One I might not be able to stop if you touch me there again." He took in a steady drag of breath. "I'd rather take the blue balls now. It will only get worse if we keep going."

A smile curled my mouth. A boldness I never thought I possessed spoke through me. "I want to cross the line."

He slipped my body back to the ground and stepped away from me. "Kennedy, I think you need to take a moment."

What? Lorcan Dragen, the ruthless arrogant dark dweller, was telling me to *think about it*?

I shifted against the metal of the pool shed and adjusted my glasses. "I have taken years to think about it. Sex has been dangling over me since I was sixteen...mocking me." Fury rushed up to the surface, covering my embarrassment. "I am now twenty-two, and I've only kissed three guys total in my life, one of those doesn't really count since it was Ryan. There is a war tomorrow and most likely I am not going to survive." I hit my fist against the tin, stressing my point. "So what exactly do you want me to think about?"

Lorcan's hand rubbed the back of his neck. "You want to have sex with me because it may be your last opportunity?" His eyes darted up, pinning mine. "That is not a good enough reason."

Rage seethed over the top of my head. "You think I want to give up my virginity because you are here and available? And I am *that* desperate?" My fists came out and hit his chest, shoving him. "You don't think I could go to Jared right now if I wanted? Or..." I motioned to the moonlit field. Campfires sprinkled the vast countryside, outlining the thousands of tents and cabins sprawled across the acreage. "I couldn't find some hot fae wanting to sleep with me?"

"I know you could." He grabbed my floundering hands, clasped them together, and pinned them to his chest. "Easily."

"But you don't want me?" my voice squeezed out, barely audible.

"You think I don't want you?" Lorcan choked, fighting back a laugh. "Come on, you are smarter than that. All you have to do is look at my pants to know that is about as far from the truth as you can get."

"Then what's the problem?" When I dragged my eyes back up to his, he had moved closer to me, leaning in. His thumb absently rubbed my hands, still trapped against his chest.

"Me," he whispered. "I don't deserve to be your first."

My mouth dropped open. I sensed Lorcan had changed quite a bit since I first met him, but I didn't comprehend how much. To the outside world, they might not see the drastic change, but I did. The fact he let me in, see who he really was...

He let go of my hands as I pushed off the wall. "Yes, you do." My neck craned back, peering up at him. "Do you want to know why?"

"Why?" he responded. His voice and face were unemotional. Defensive.

"Because I am in love with you." It came out strong and sure.

He stood motionless, his face like stone. His eyes were the only things that moved. They searched mine, seeking a falseness in my sentiment, a lie somewhere in it. He could keep searching, but I knew it with every fiber in my being. It was not something I could research, study, or analyze. Everything on paper said he was wrong for me. We were opposites. Logically I should not have been attracted to someone like him, nor him to me. But the moment you put us together we proved every theory wrong.

Finally Lorcan seemed to grasp the sincerity of my words. He turned his head, shaking it back and forth. His eyes were closed as he licked his bottom lip. Then slowly he reopened them and turned his face back to mine. A grin inched up his face; his eyes blistered with light. "I was hoping you'd say that."

My feet lurched off the ground as he picked me up, wrapping my legs back around him. There was no wall, no fear. A huge smile stretched my lips; my hands were braced on either side of his shaved head, tilting his head back. The prickles of growth tickled my palms. I leaned down, forgoing any more words. When his lips found mine this time, it felt different. If someone bet me a long time ago I would not only fall in love with Lorcan, but want him to be my first, I would have lost my entire collection of first edition *Wonder Woman* comics.

Our kisses started off gentle but quickly changed. He had awakened my desire. No, this was not quite true. I felt desire with Jared, but Lorcan stirred the sexual creature in me, and it made me ache. I was normally so timid and shy, especially with guys. He made me want to do things I once blushed over and covered my ears merely hearing Ryan and Ember talking about them. When I looked at him, the chagrin evaporated. Once again my fingers found their way to his pants, the first two buttons already undone.

"Not here." His voice was gruff in my ear.

I didn't want to wait any longer. I freed the next button. It would have been two, but his hand pulled mine back. He dropped my feet to the ground, clutching my hand tighter in his. Without a word he hauled me toward the field, in the direction of his cabin.

"What about Dax?"

"Don't worry. He's taking advantage of the night before a big war with some tree fairies. And I told him not to return tonight." Lorcan tapped at his head as he continued to drag me through the field, weaving around large, boisterous, drunk groups of Dark fae.

I could feel the heat rising in my cheeks. "Oh."

Lorcan smirked. "Don't worry, he doesn't know who I'm with. You don't need to be embarrassed."

"I'm not." I so was. Then another thought hit me. I also didn't want Jared to hear about this. It would crush him.

Lorcan went far around the dark dwellers' camp, ensuring no one would see us. He slammed through the door of his cabin, pulling me in with him. The door closed behind us, swallowing up any evidence of my presence. He dropped my hand and turned his gas lamp on low.

Suddenly I felt shy and awkward. Fear started eating at my confidence, faltering my assurance. I wrapped my arms around myself, one finger pushing at the bridge of my glasses. It was a nervous tic of mine.

"Hey." Lorcan widened his stance to come down closer to my height. He still towered over me. He brushed my long chestnut hair off my shoulder; the loose strands tapped at my lower back. "Look at me."

I sucked in a breath and forced myself to meet his gaze.

"We don't have to do anything. I just didn't want your first time to be on the ground with rocks and sticks cutting into your back. Believe me, it's not as romantic as you first think it's going to be." His finger circled my ear, tucking my hair back securely.

Ember and Eli seemed to do fine, I thought, but it was another word he said which tripped up my thoughts. "Romantic?" I chuckled. "I didn't peg you as a romantic."

The side of his mouth hitched up in a barely there grin. "You're right. Dark dwellers by nature aren't. I certainly have never been. Hell, I used to make fun of the saps." He leaned in, his lips tentatively touching mine. "But you deserve more than that for your first time. We can try the elements next time."

"The next time, huh?" I laughed.

"Yeah," he said against my mouth, opening my lips with his. "Next time."

"Thought you said we didn't have to do anything?" I teased.

"You want me to stop?" His teeth skated down my neck, his soft, firm lips trailing the sensitive place behind my ear.

Oh hell no, I thought. The nervousness fell away, slithering back under the door to the outside world. I wrapped my arms around his neck, my fingers skating up the back of his head. Lorcan took my mouth in his and breathed me in with a kiss. It was like he unleashed the pent-up, sexually terrified, uncomfortable Kennedy. The good, proper girl my mother always tried to instill in me just got shoved to the side, bound and gagged. Nothing in me wanted to be good.

His hand moved down, reaching the hem of my cotton dress. He pushed it up, letting his finger trail over the band of my underwear to my backside and slipping under the fabric. His hand caressed the naked skin and moved around to my hip. His touch electrified every one of my cells. My breath was rapid and uneven. His other hand slipped beneath my underwear on the opposite hip. Very slowly he dragged my panties down. His touch all the way down left a trail of sensitivity between pleasure and pain. It took a lot to keep myself standing. I stepped out of them, along with my flats. The sudden freedom was exhilarating. Except now that I was not covered and hidden, I felt so exposed as if a beacon of light shined on me, letting everyone know it was out and free. My instinct was to snatch the cotton shield and put it back on, but his hand drifting up my leg shattered that idea. He paused on his way back, his lips pressing into the fabric of my dress between my legs. The heat from his mouth soaked through the material. He kissed the area again. Quivers sprinted down my body. I made a guttural moan.

"When you make sounds like that it makes it almost impossible to be good," his lips mumbled against me. My head fell back with the vibration and movement of his mouth. At the moment, I would do anything he asked, the war could start and I wouldn't care. "I want to throw you on my bed, open your legs, and take you."

"Then do it," I whispered hoarsely. Pleading edged my voice.

He gave me one more soft kiss before standing up. "Not yet. I'm taking my time with you."

"If it's going to be anything like this, I don't think I will be able to handle it."

He smiled, retaking the hem of my cotton dress, and pulled it over my head, dropping it onto the floor, leaving me only in my bra. "You are going to lose your mind," he teased me. "Over and over again." His hands moved to my back and within a second my bra joined my dress. He was still fully dressed. I felt small and extremely exposed standing before him naked, but the way he looked at me made me feel sexy. I understood a woman had power over a man, especially a naked one, but I never imagined the man I wanted to seduce would be Lorcan.

I forced myself to stand steady under his gaze. I would not hide or feel ashamed. I could feel my Druid blood stirring, wakening.

"Now your turn." He let me undress him. I pulled his shirt over his head. My fingers glided over his bare chest, discovering every muscle, before I moved to the last two buttons of his jeans. "I'll warn you, dark dwellers aren't into wearing underwear." He winked.

"Good. One less thing I have to take off." Where was this boldness coming from? I couldn't believe those words came out of me. I felt brave and daring. Though I did falter a bit when I pushed his jeans over his hips, spotting his V-line and patch of hair. I had seen him before, even touched him, but this was different.

Holy crap this is happening. Did he get bigger? He was at full salute and...there was no way. My mouth parted.

"We'll take it slow," he spoke, but my attention was on his massive size. "We'll *stop* if it's too much. But we have to be *safe*. Careful."

The word "stop" jerked my head up in attention. We—I—was way past being able to stop. A seductive smile toyed at my mouth, my hands still clutching the side of his pants. "No, we don't. Gabby took me to see the tree fairies." I had never been with anyone, and fae didn't get STDs.

Lorcan shot me a mischievous smile back, grasping my meaning. He kicked off his shoes, letting me yank the pants down the rest of the way. Again a boldness took over me, and I leaned in and kissed his inner thigh.

A deep growl vibrated through Lorcan.

TWENTY-EIGHT

The light of early morning slid between the curtains, splintering my lids apart. My blurry vision gave the room a dreamlike quality. It always made me feel unsettled and off, instantly wanting to slip my glasses on, reassuring me the world came in details.

Today was different. The obscurity of things kept what happened last night in a bubble. Not that I could forget one second of it, the feel of his hands, his tongue, him inside me. The pain turning into unbelievable pleasure as he rocked into me over and over. I never wanted to forget it.

The other part of me wanted to see everything in crystal clear detail. Remember each moment like it might be my last. It very possibly would be.

I stretched, my body sore and highly aware it had been used in a new way. Multiple times during the night. Each time only making me eager for the next.

Raising my head from his arm, I looked over my shoulder. Lorcan slept mostly on his back, though our legs were entwined to stay in the small bed. His free arm lay across his chest, his other propped below me as my pillow. I wanted to run my hands over his bare torso ripped with muscles, and then follow the lines of his tattoos with my tongue.

My teeth sank into my bottom lip with a rush of desire. Damn, he was beautiful in a scary, sexy way. He had done some awful things in his life, yet all I could see was the man I fell for.

A gulp of air hissed through my lungs. I *was* in love with Lorcan Dragen. When did that happen? *How* did I let it happen? He was the exact opposite type of man I liked. He was everything wrong, bad, and dangerous. The exact combination I would roll my eyes at when other girls came back crying their guy was a jerk to them. Yeah, duh? How did you not see it coming?

Now I was that girl. I wanted to slap myself for being a cliché...because I wanted nothing more than to spread my legs open for him again.

My head jerked back at my bold thought, heat rushing up my neck. The twin cot groaned, and I halted as he stirred behind me. My heart thumped in my chest, and I felt suspended in place, like an animal frozen in headlights.

Why was it so easy to let go in the dark? To be the assertive, confident girl who wasn't afraid to express herself and reciprocate? My cheeks grew hot at the memory of the things I said and did. How I cried out. How that drove him wild.

In daylight, I was unsure and apprehensive. What if he changed his mind? What if he realized this was a huge mistake?

What if I did?

I waited for regret to set in, the self-loathing and guilt. But instead all that came was the realization I wanted more. A lot more. *What did he do to me?* My body trembled with the need to be touched, to have him take me again till I screamed.

My breath caught when a hand slid up my hip to my stomach, pulling me onto his body. His skin brushed mine with heat. I slammed my eyes closed. The length of him pressed into my lower back.

"Morning, li'l bird." Lorcan's lips grazed my temple. Chemistry was such an interesting thing. Lorcan's very makeup, his smell and structure and touch, produced a chemical reaction in my body. An instant response. My body flooded with it.

"Relax," he muttered into my ear, his hand skating down my hip. "I can feel and hear your heart beating like a hummingbird. You're freaking out."

I sucked in a deep breath, trying to calm. Normally I would have hated him knowing I was freaking out, but he soothed me with his voice and the way he pulled me in closer to his body. But now my heart sped up for different reasons. His length grew harder behind me.

He propped himself up on his arm, and I lay back flat underneath him. His green eyes blazed into mine.

"You all right?"

I nodded.

"Why are you flipping out?" A quirky smile twisted

up his mouth. "Staging a breakout? Thinking up the best way to flee?"

"No." I stared up at him, wishing I had my glasses. I felt bare and vulnerable without them.

"Then what?" He brushed strands of hair away from my face. "I know fear. It has an especially sharp odor. Remember you can't hide emotions from me. I can sense and smell them. Even more now…"

"Why even more?"

Something flashed over his face and then it was gone. He moved over me, placing his arms on either side of my head, pinning me under him. My legs opened without a thought, letting him fit better into me, his cock throbbing against my stomach.

"Are you sorry?" Lorcan whispered, his voice gruff. "Do you wish it never happened?"

I stared up at him, my mind losing coherent thought as he slid himself over my entrance.

"You can't lie to me, Kennedy," he growled. "You are so fuckin' wet I can feel your desire for me. I can smell nothing else. Don't be afraid of it." He licked his lips, ground into me more, spreading my legs farther. "Is this what you want?" He palmed himself and wiggled the tip a little more into me. My back arched, my body hungry for his. "Tell me." His breath heavy as his eyes sparked red. "Tell me you want my dick in your pussy."

I could not help blushing. I never used words like that, and I certainly would have never imagined them turning me on. Dirty talk in movies or books either made me cringe or laugh. When Lorcan said them, desire was an ocean crashing inside me.

"What do you want, Ken?"

I pushed against him, desperate and frantic. "Please..." I begged.

"Please what?" His thumb rubbed me in exactly the right spot. My hips bucked against him. "I don't want you afraid or uncomfortable with sex. Enjoy it. Know what you want. Go after it. No barriers between us, got it? With me it's safe to let go. Completely."

I nodded, already too far gone to hold back. No longer Kennedy the shy, embarrassed, human girl. I was Druid. Powerful and strong. And now a girl who immensely enjoyed sex. And with Lorcan I didn't want to be insecure or timid.

He pushed into me a little more, his thumb working harder.

"Oh my god," I breathed out.

"Tell me," he demanded. "Need to hear it. Tell me what you want."

"I want you inside of me," I gasped out, almost screaming the last part. "I want you so deep inside me...fucking me." The words felt so foreign and strange coming out of my mouth, like it wasn't me at all, but every one of them was true.

"Shit." Lorcan's eyes shifted to a deep blazing red. "I don't think I've ever been so hard," he growled.

I reached down for his ass, pushing him into me, my voice barely above a whisper. "Fuck me, Lorcan. Please."

A feral rumble in his chest vibrated the bed. Energy slammed into me as he entered me. I inhaled sharply, my body trying to adjust to him.

Our hips crashed together, our movements growing more desperate. He grabbed my arms, pinning them above my head, and shifted higher above me as he pushed deeper inside me. My neck curved back into the pillow as I made sounds I didn't think a human could. Once they started, I couldn't keep them inside any longer.

Lorcan's words grew dirtier, heating my already boiling blood. He clamped my wrists with one hand, and drew up one of my legs to his shoulder with his free hand.

I belted out a gasp as he went even deeper.

"Jesus, Ken." Sweat dampened his body, his voice sounding more like a growl. "You are so tight...you feel so un-fucking-believable."

"Harder!" I could feel myself starting to go over the edge of ecstasy, clenching around him.

"Shit!" He hissed through his teeth but moved deeper and faster. His hand slid down my body. "Come with me." He pressed his thumb into me, finding the exact spot.

I heard people say having an orgasm felt like they left Earth. I thought it was simply a phrase. When mine hit, I lost my sense of reality and didn't even feel like I was in my body anymore. I knew the scream tearing through the room was mine but couldn't recall myself doing it. He thrust in once more and a roar eclipsed my cry, and I felt him release inside of me; my own body greedy, draining him of everything.

He collapsed on me, pushing up to his elbows to keep from crushing me. But I didn't mind. I liked his weight on me.

Panting, we both came down from the high, sweaty and in total bliss. He leaned over, kissing me deeply. "Damn," he muttered against my lips. "That was..." He kissed me again. "Seriously un-fucking-believable."

I nodded in agreement, still trying to catch my breath.

"You are amazing." He nipped at my lip. "I've never had an orgasm like that. I think I almost passed out."

"Please. You've slept with how many girls? *Experienced* girls—"

"We're not having this discussion," he cut me off. "Especially when I'm still inside of you."

I blushed and turned my head. I could already feel him starting to get hard again. So, the rumors about the dark dwellers were true.

"Hey." He grabbed my chin, turning my face to his. "I'm not one to sugarcoat or say things I don't mean. You should know that by now. I'm not a nice guy. I've kicked more than one girl from my bed after I got off, but that is not what this is."

He held my chin, so I looked away.

"You think, on the last night before the war, possibly my last living night, I was looking to stay sober and try to screw my nephew's virgin girlfriend because it sounded like a cruel, screwed-up Lorcan thing to do?"

"I'm not his girlfriend." My eyes snapped back to Lorcan.

"Good thing." He smirked. Wow, it was strange to feel him grow hard inside me. A good strange. "Nor are you a virgin...now."

Heat once again flooded my cheeks.

"I love I can get you to blush so easily." He kissed the tip of my nose. "Today everything is going to change if we get through this..." He licked his lips. "I want you. Not for only a night or quick screw...but in my bed all the time, screaming my name and fucking me relentlessly forever."

I gasped. My heart swelled with joy and fear.

The slight movement drew him in and just as suddenly we were both ready to go again. I couldn't seem to get enough of him, and I heard dark dwellers were continuously ready to go. This might become a problem.

"Okay?" He cupped my head.

"Yes." My throat felt thick. I was scared of how Jared was going to respond to this, but nothing would keep me away from Lorcan now. As always, he seemed to know what I was thinking.

"I don't want to hurt him either. It's the last thing I want." Lorcan looked away. "I love him more than anything. I tried to fight you..."

"I know." I ran my palm up his stubble, drawing his face back to me. "I tried to fight you, too. To deny what I felt. But I couldn't. If I die today, I'm exactly where I want to be."

Lorcan closed his eyes for moment, his face scrunching in pain before he opened them again. "You are not going to die. I will not allow it."

"Some things even you can't control." I smiled thinly, my throat tightening. Lars's spell on me strangled my ability to speak the truth. "If I do, I want you to know..." Trepidation gripped my chest, but I pushed through. "I'm in love with you. Hopelessly."

His forehead hit mine; his face twisted again. "I don't deserve it."

"Doesn't matter. It's not how love works."

He lifted his head off me, his eyes drilling into mine, swirling with emotion. But he didn't say the words back, he only said one. "Mine," he growled, his lips crushing mine, his hips slowly rocking forward.

Every time Jared had made that statement, it angered me. I hated the possessive ownership. With Lorcan it made me feel safe, alive, and I was tempted to utter it back.

⁓⁓⁓⁓

"Holy shit! You're crumbling the foundation out here, Lorc." Dax pounded on the door. "And if you think I'm kidding, I'm not."

I was still coming down from another earth-splitting orgasm, drawing in deep gulps of air. Lorcan spent the rest of the morning showing me just how exuberant dark dwellers really were. I kept up with him more than eagerly, each time growing more secure and open with my body. We had discovered every part of each other, thoroughly.

The one thing I was still nervous about was taking him into my mouth. I don't know why it felt more intimate than sex. I was so scared of being bad at it or doing it wrong. He picked up on my reluctance immediately.

"It's about you today, li'l bird." He winked, kissing his way down my stomach. "Believe me, I've dreamed about your lips around my cock, but it will give me a reason to survive. And also doing this again." His tongue found my core, stealing my breath.

"So you'll live merely because I owe you a blow job?" I grabbed his head, pulling him close.

"Seems like a good enough reason as any."

"We'll make sure you do then." I writhed underneath him. "I want you to show me what you like."

"Is that a promise?" He nipped at me and my hips bucked. "Didn't hear you."

"Yes! Yes... God, yes!"

He chuckled against me, only making me crazier. Then he grabbed my hips and lifted me, sending me out into another realm, until the sound of Dax's voice again crashed me back to reality.

I frantically searched for the blanket to cover myself. Lorcan sat back on his heels, pinning the comforter underneath him, a smug grin on his face as he licked his lips and fingers.

Oh geez.

"Hey, Lorc, Cole and Lars want to see you." More knocking. "Plus, I'd like to get some of my stuff. Take a shower. Get the smell of tree fairies off me."

Lorcan batted my hand as I reached around him for the comforter.

"Lorcan," I hissed. "I'm naked."

"Fully aware of it." His eyes grazed over my body, not moving an inch off the bedspread.

I sighed, letting my head fall back. He would always push me out of my comfort zone. "Shit, Lorcan. We're gonna have to burn this place after we leave." Human sex left a strong residue, but fae sex was ten times more pungent. Sweet and intoxicating, and heady with lust.

"Tell Cole I'll be right there," Lorcan yelled over his shoulder, his gaze never leaving me.

"Seriously, bro, she's still there?" Dax exclaimed. "They're usually long gone by now. It's almost noon."

No doubt everyone nearby heard us.

Lorcan stayed silent. It was strange, but I felt a buzz. I knew they were communicating through their link.

"Yeah, fine. Going," Dax grumbled, footsteps breaking across the dirt and grass.

I opened my mouth, then slammed it shut, knowing Dax could still hear me.

"He knows it's you." Lorcan grinned. "He can smell you...*our* smell is drenching this room."

I slapped a hand over my face. How close did you have to be to smell us?

"Great." I sat up, putting my feet on the floor, hunting for my glasses and clothes. I stood and found my dress tossed near the door as reality seeped up my shoulders, tensing my spine. *What if Jared heard? What if he smelled us? What kind of person are you, Kennedy? How cruel is that?*

I ground my jaw and slipped the dress over my head. My bra and underwear were lost somewhere in the cabin. "Where are my glasses?" Panic rose along with my voice.

"Ken?" Lorcan stood, climbing off the bed.

"Where are my glasses?" I rolled my hair back into a messy bun, my blurry eyes scouring for the lost item.

"Kennedy." Lorcan blocked my way.

"I need to get out of here. Now." I tried to move around him. "Help me find them."

"Kennedy, stop." He grabbed my arms, pinning me in place.

"No! I simply want to leave. So let me find my glasses so I can do that."

He exhaled slowly, reaching one hand over my shoulder to the table, grabbing my glasses. He unfolded them, sliding them gently onto my face. Everything around me snapped into a clear picture. His face was sharp and strong.

"You didn't do anything wrong."

"Are you serious?" I scoffed. "You don't think sleeping with my ex-boyfriend's uncle is not wrong?" I wanted to turn away, but he held me in place; his massive figure was so close to me I felt unsteady on my feet. I rubbed at the sour spot forming in my stomach. "I know my actions are going to come back and punish me. I let desire rule, didn't care who I hurt, what it cost."

"So you'd forgo your happiness—mine—for someone you didn't love?"

I jerked from his hands, anger burning through me. "Don't tell me I didn't love him, because I did."

"Not the kind of love I'm talking about."

"What? Because I didn't sleep with him means I didn't love him?"

"Ken, you know that's not what I mean." Lorcan moved his hands from my arms to my face. "But there is a difference between puppy love and when you find it for real."

"You think you're real?" His touch disarmed me, ripping the anger out from my vocals.

He sidled closer to me, his breath hot on my neck as he leaned in. "I know I am."

His lips met mine, and I couldn't even pretend for a moment I didn't feel the electricity zap between us, melting me into him. He slid his hands through my hair, unraveling my bun, pulling me into him, deepening our kiss.

He withdrew, but I wasn't ready to end it, grabbing his neck, bringing him back to me. He was so hard and ready for me.

He shot me a twisted smile. "You're gonna have to stop, or I'm going to throw you back on the bed and fuck you till there's no one who hasn't heard us."

Fire bloomed in my body. I wanted him to do exactly that. I never thought I'd be the girl who liked it rough or dirty. I was so wrong. At least with Lorcan.

He grabbed my arms, peeling me away, grimacing. "Seriously, walking a thin line right now. I need to go see Cole, and you need to go get ready for tonight."

I nodded, stepping away, trying not to look at his body. Seeing him eager for me sent a new kind of thrill through me. It gave me confidence.

"I will find you later, li'l bird. I promise you." He grabbed his jeans off the floor, tugging them on.

"Okay." I slipped on my shoes and cardigan. Turning for the door, I grabbed the handle. It opened a crack. Suddenly the door was yanked from my hand, slamming shut, my body whipped around. Lorcan picked me up, my legs wrapping around him as we crashed back into the door. His kiss was rough, almost like he was marking me. And I kissed him back with equal need, demanding all of him.

"Shit, I love feeling you bare against me," he muttered, sliding my dress a little farther up my leg. I wore no underwear, and he still had no shirt. His mouth took mine, inhaling me. Devouring. I was about to rip his jeans off again, when he dropped me to the floor. "See you later?"

I couldn't talk, only nod dumbly.

"Okay." He pulled me off the door, opened it, and peered out. "All clear." He patted my butt on the way out. "Try not to look like you just got thoroughly fucked." He shut the door with a chuckle.

Jerk. He knew there wasn't any hope of that. I was still spinning from the kiss, and my body ached everywhere. My hair was a mess, and I was still dressed in last night's clothes, minus undergarments, and probably had an expression on my face clearly displaying I had more orgasms than brain cells left.

And all I could think was: *Is it later yet?*

I was so in trouble.

TWENTY-NINE

"Kennedy?" My name came from behind me as I reached for my cabin door. My stomach dropped and halted me in place. *Oh no. Oh no. Why is it always him?*

I slowly swiveled around to face Owen. "Yes?" I couldn't meet his eyes. Jared would have been worse, but running into my ex-boyfriend's father came in a close second.

"We've been looking for you everywhere. Gabby said you never returned last night." Owen's hazel eyes went from my head to my feet, a frown creasing his forehead.

"Uh-no...I..." I babbled, clueless how to respond. Why didn't I know any spell that would make the earth swallow me up?

Owen's nostrils flared, and I recognized the instant he picked up my smell—sex and sweat. Not his son's. His chin lifted, his eyes narrowing.

"Ah." He glanced away. "I see."

Three words and my heart was ripped out of my chest. I felt so dirty. Loathing injected into my skin, filling me with self-hatred. I forced back the tears filling my eyes. There was nothing I could say.

"Lars would like to see you immediately." Owen's response was stiff and detached.

"Can I take a shower?"

"I suggest you don't keep the King waiting." He clasped his hands and turned to go. "He and Cole are in the office."

My gut twisted, my chest sagging with weight. I felt sick. It would take everyone in the room only a second to know what I did last night. And if Lorcan were in the room, it wouldn't take a genius to figure out with whom. I was getting better at not being embarrassed, but this was too much. Humiliation I could survive, the hurt I would cause...

Please say Jared is not there.

My feet led me to the house by their own accord, while I tried my best to smooth the wrinkles in my dress and untangle my long hair. My heart thumped, my nerves strangling my throat when I knocked on the door.

"Come in," Lars's voice boomed through the door.

I inhaled and stepped into the room.

Lars loomed behind his desk, with Cole in front and Lorcan between the two guest chairs. All heads turned to me when I entered. Green eyes locked on me with such intensity my body tingled wildly. I directed my gaze at Cole and Lars.

Blood boiled in my cheeks, dotting the back of my neck with perspiration. The fact I was standing in the Unseelie King's office not wearing underwear embarrassed me, but only because I felt a strange thrill of it. I could feel Lorcan's eyes on me, scalding every inch of my skin, burning the area he knew was bare and desperate for him. This was not like me, this sensation of feeling turned on simply because I forgot my underwear. Well, it wasn't the old me. But something changed, and it all had to do with the man standing next to me.

"You needed me?" I cleared my throat, trying to ignore my bodily awareness of Lorcan.

"Yes, Ms. Johnson. We've been searching for you most of the morning."

"I apologize, sir." No matter how many times I swallowed, my throat felt dry and thick.

"We want to go over the plan with you one last time, before your final training with Maya." Lars stuffed one hand in his pocket. "Everything hangs on the five of you getting into the castle, especially you and Ember." Lars's gaze bored deep into mine. "I need to know you can handle this, Ms. Johnson. No doubts or ideas of running. I need to confirm you are quite clear about your role."

"I am." I nodded, feeling numb to the idea I would most likely die. "I have no illusions."

A hint of a smile tipped up Lars's mouth. "Good answer." He grabbed a few files off his desk. "Now, I will leave you with Cole while I speak with my men about tonight."

Lars gave us a curt nod and left the office. Tension filled the space where Lars had been standing.

Cole had stayed quiet the entire time, his eyes darting from Lorcan to me. "You're freakin' kidding me," he growled, folding his arms, his attention locked on Lorcan.

"Cole—" Lorcan started.

"No," Cole cut him off. "What the hell, Lorcan? Tell me this is a sick joke."

My cheeks flamed with chagrin.

"We didn't mean for it to happen."

"That doesn't matter. It has." Cole swore under his breath, rubbing his scruff. "You planning on telling him? Or letting him find out like I did? He might not have senses like ours, but he'll eventually suspect it. This thing between you and Kennedy will only strengthen, not dim."

"Of course," Lorcan replied. "I just don't think today is the best day. Hell, we all might be dead by tomorrow and not have to worry about it."

Cole lowered his eyes but stayed quiet. I couldn't seem to find my voice. I wanted to believe Lorcan wasn't a mistake, but with every disappointed and hurt look I got, it was harder to stand strong. Did I love Lorcan? Yes, but was it enough? Was the hurt worth it?

My gaze darted over to him and quickly back. Existing around him felt like being thrown out into outer space, dazzling and amazing, but it ripped the air out of my lungs, leaving me floating in a void.

"Never saw this one coming." Cole palmed his face and raked his hand roughly over it.

"Nothing you can do to change it. And believe me, it was not something I wanted. We can't control it, Cole."

Cole nodded, lifting his head. "Shit. This is gonna kill him. The poor kid."

I gripped my stomach, feeling the tears burn my eyes.

"I want you two in the training room in thirty." Cole exhaled. "Last opportunity to work on Kennedy's basic fighting techniques. Go. Please take showers so no one else, especially Jared, has to smell you two."

Oh geez...floor, please open and take me away from this.

Lorcan snorted. "You know that won't help."

"No." Cole sighed. "But let's hope his dark dweller sense doesn't suddenly kick in. So far he doesn't seem to have it, which right now is a small blessing."

The way they spoke I started to feel like I was missing something.

Lorcan nodded and turned for the door, his hand grazing my shoulder. I quickly moved away from him, bolting for the door.

Lorcan got to it first and paused, turning to Cole. "Thank you, Cole. I know this is not the ideal situation." Lorcan licked his lips, his Adam's apple bobbing, his voice cracking with emotion. "And I'm sorry for all the years I took my anger out on you. I hated my father, but it was easier to take it out on you."

I think both Cole and I froze, our mouths gaping. Did *Lorcan... apologize*?

Cole stared at him for a moment then looked briefly at me before turning back to Lorcan. He gave him a small nod. An acceptance of his apology.

Wow. I just witnessed a monumental event. If we survived this war, maybe they had a chance to reconcile. At least to try and mend their broken relationship, rediscover each other as true brothers now.

Lorcan nodded, then opened the door, motioning me through.

~~~~~

Lorcan and I walked back toward our cabins, with me keeping a pace a few feet ahead of him. I spotted Jared, Eli, and Ember on the training field going through moves.

I curved the opposite way, wanting to hide. I didn't even realize I was running till I heard Lorcan's voice calling for me. I didn't slow till I was deep in the brush, hidden from the world.

"Ken?" He jogged after me, following me into the forest. "Hey." He grabbed my arm, swinging me around.

"Dammit, Lorcan. What did we do?" I bent over, feeling my lungs constrict. "What kind of person am I? How could I do that to him?"

He cupped my face, turning it up to him. "I won't lie and say what we did was right. But it wasn't wrong either."

"Then what is it?" I threw out my arms. To me, things usually fell in one or the other category. Right side of the law or the wrong. No in between. Lorcan didn't feel wrong in my heart, but it certainly wasn't right. "I've always been analytical. I worked hard at school, always studying and being responsible. I like facts and lists. Logically working out a formula for an answer makes sense to me. But this…" I motioned between us. "This I can't solve, I can't figure out."

"Life isn't black and white. Some things aren't meant to be figured out. They simply are."

I pulled away from him, turning around. "I don't know how to deal with that."

"We'll figure it out."

Who was this guy? Was he the killer who took Ember's mother away from her or the man wanting to comfort and touch me? "What's going on?"

"What do you mean what's going on?"

"I mean with us. What were you and Cole talking about in the office?"

Lorcan glanced away. "As many times as you came last night and this morning, I'd think you'd figure it out by now."

"What? That you are great at sex? Congrats, you are. Well done. You snagged yourself a virgin." I folded my arms, feeling prickly and defensive.

"Whoa." Lorcan lifted his hands. "This just took a wrong turn."

I was being irrational. I had always been reasonable and sensible. The moment Lorcan and I first kissed, I had started to roll down the hill with no brakes. And it only ended up hurting people I cared about.

"I think we need to end this now." The words came out of my mouth but felt empty on my tongue.

"What?" Lorcan's eyebrows hitched up.

"We made a mistake. The best thing to do is back away and pretend it never happened." My fingers curled into my arms, cutting into my skin.

Lorcan tilted his head. I expected him to yell or even agree, but instead he smiled, amusement glinting in his eyes.

"What?" Irritation picked up my shoulders.

"You." His smug grin turned feral.

I glared at him, which only made him smile wider. "You don't think I'm serious?"

"I think *you* think you're serious." He took a step toward me, rubbing his jaw.

I took a step back. "I'm not kidding."

"Me neither." He continued to move toward me. I already felt my body betraying me, desiring the feel of his hands sliding up my thighs. The out-of-control sensation Lorcan produced in me scared the hell out of me. I couldn't control him or how I felt. With Jared everything felt so safe, at all times. Lorcan tipped me off solid ground, severing me from everything I understood. But the closer he got, the more I wanted to let go.

"Lorcan. Don't." I held up my hand, backing up. My legs and back thumped into a large boulder, stopping me from getting to a safe distance.

"Ken, if I truly believed you wanted nothing to do with me, I'd walk." His boots flushed with my shoes, a hand running through my hair, tugging on the ends. "Remember you can't lie to me. I can taste your desire on my tongue. How much you want me to be inside you right now."

I inhaled sharply, still shocked by the bluntness of his words. And even more embarrassed because they were true.

His thumb ran over my bottom lip and my heart pounded. I could hear the training on the field nearby. They were so close. Jared was so close.

It should have stopped me from wanting Lorcan. Yet my breath went ragged as his hand slid up my leg, finding me. "I wanted to do this the entire time we were standing in Lars's office. Knowing you weren't wearing any underwear... I don't think I heard a word they said."

I made an involuntary moan, arching into him.

"Shit, Ken. You are so wet..." He slid his fingers into me.

I moved against his hand, desiring more.

"What do you want?" He moved in closer, his voice low, eyes buzzing with desire.

"You." I grabbed at his jeans, unbuttoning them, shoving them down his hips. Seeing him so ready for me almost gave me an orgasm on the spot.

He growled, picked me up, and wrapped my legs around his waist. "I'm not saying we don't need to tell Jared, or figure us out, but right now I want to feel you come. We can worry about it after the war. Today is ours, all right?"

I nodded. There might not be a need to ever tell Jared. One or both of us might be dead by tomorrow. And I couldn't deny I wanted this. Badly.

I had no idea what happened to the old Kennedy, but she had disappeared, taken over by the woman who

Stacey Marie Brown

knew what she wanted...and took it. Up against a rock.

〜〜〜

After showering, training, and showering again, this time not alone, my stomach ordered me to the buffet Marguerite set up on the deck for us. I hadn't spoken to Ember all day, but I knew in a few hours we would be heading into battle together. My stomach twisted with nerves, but I had to eat. I grabbed a plate, peering at the dishes. They all smelled amazing and my mouth watered.

"Kennedy?"

My knuckles whitened, the grip on my paper plate wrinkling it. *Oh. No.*

"Can we talk?" Jared spoke again from behind me. I squeezed my eyes shut, my appetite gone. *Please. Please, don't let him pick up on anything.*

I slowly turned to face him. His hair was wet from a shower, and he wore jeans and a "Geeks do it better" T-shirt. Even his shirt mocked me. Science would say guilt didn't actually have a physical weight. It was an emotion, not something tangible, yet I felt it in my body, like wet cement.

"Ah. Sure." I set my plate back on the table, my eyes never fully meeting his. I followed him off the crowded patio, walking past the pool, the creek bubbling and rushing near us.

"I want to apologize for last night."

Last night? My brain struggled to get past my hot-and-dirty night with Lorcan and remember the mess dinner turned into because of Jared's temper tantrum.

"It's fine, Jared." I laced my fingers together.

"No. It's not. I was a jerk. And I'm sorry." He ran his hand through his hair with a huff.

"Apology accepted," I said quietly. Soon I would be asking for his apology in return, and I knew I would not get the same response. Not that I deserved it.

Jared breathed out, turning to me with a goofy smile. My heart shriveled as I took in his childlike grin, his happy hazel eyes, his bouncing movements as if he were constantly pumped on caffeine. I cared about him so much. Even now I only wanted to hug him. But I didn't want more. He now felt more like my friend's younger brother. One day he would grow into an amazing man, and I'd probably kick myself for letting him go, but I had to follow my heart.

"Jared." I licked my lips. "You know I will—"

"Let me say something first." He grabbed my hands, twining his through mine. "I was a jerk, but it doesn't mean I didn't mean what I said. You and I will be together. I will win you back. I will prove myself, you'll see. You are mine, Ken. You *always* will be."

I lowered my jaw in disbelief, wanting to say something, to tell him he was wrong, but he never gave me the chance. He grabbed my face before I could even react. I couldn't deny the familiarity of his lips, the way his mouth moved over mine, the comfortable reaction to want to kiss back. I didn't, but I didn't stop him either.

He broke away, keeping his palms firm on my cheeks. "I love you and will prove it. You'll see. I'm no longer the boy you fell in love with, but the man you'll want a future with." He kissed me again, then turned away, disappearing into the evening shadows, leaving me standing there, feeling gutted, confused, and guilty.

My head fell forward, my hair curtaining my face. I stared at the creek, the water tumbling and bashing over the rocks. Like my heart.

Prickles spread up my back, tickling the back of my neck. I knew why. My body was coded to pick up on him, to know when he was near, and to sense what he was feeling. It felt as if his emotions were radio waves being directed at me. It was strange, but not unnerving.

"You can't be mad." I curled my arms around my biceps, still watching the water.

"I'm not mad." Lorcan stepped out from the shadows, his dark clothes blending him in with the approaching night.

"Really?" I snorted. "That's not what I got."

Lorcan stopped, jerking my head to look at him.

"What do you mean? Could you feel me?" He watched me with a guarded expression.

A nervousness twitched in my belly. "I could sense you were irritated. It was like a freaking Bat-Signal. "

Lorcan blinked, then twisted away, swearing under his breath.

"What?"

He shook his head. "Just not something I was expecting."

"What are you talking about?"

He stared at the ground, blowing out of his mouth. "I wasn't mad at you." He raised his head, stuffing his hands in his jeans. "Just feeling possessive."

"Well, stop!" I dropped my arms, hitting my legs in frustration. "I swear Jared would pee on me if I gave him the chance. I don't need it from you too. I am not anyone's."

"If you want to believe that."

I narrowed my lids. "I'm. Not. Anyone's."

"You sensed me? Knew I was here and what I was feeling without even seeing me?"

"Yes." I felt my defenses rising, trying not to think what he was hinting at.

He smirked, and with a nod he turned round, walking away. The night swiftly engulfed his silhouette.

"I'm not!"

I could have sworn I heard him chuckle softly, but the sloshing of water from the creek also sounded like it was laughing at me.

Many times in my life I'd seen my mom win a case with solid evidence against the accused while the guilty party still spouted their innocence all the way to jail, holding on to the last shred of hope.

That's what I felt like. And I knew there wasn't any hope. No last appeal to save me from plummeting.

THIRTY

The midnight sky sparked with deep hues, kindling the atmosphere like fireworks through the thin wall, the castle and the Seelie waiting to attack.

Here was my vision come to life.

Lars perched on a bird-shifter in the sky, dressed in armor, tantalizing his soldiers with words of freedom and liberation. The Dark fae gathered on a hill, dressed and banging weapons, sounding our own battle drum.

Loud, piercing battle cries tore through the air from both sides, raking chills over my skin. I struggled to swallow, my body shaking with fear. We had talked about it so long. Now it was here.

A piercing horn signaled the start of the war.

The battle had begun. Tonight I would die.

"Kennedy, stay close to me." Ember glanced over her shoulder at me, unaware of what I had been thinking. I gulped and nodded, my trembling hands re-gripping the gun attached to my waist, reassuring myself it was still there. They loaded me with a gun, ammo, and a sword. I could handle the gun, but the sword was there more for decoration. If I had to use it, then all hope was lost.

Torin, Thara, and the pixies mingled around me, all dressed and ready for combat. Some of the dark dwellers were in their beast forms, ready to assault anyone who came at us. Eli, Cole, Lorcan, and Owen had not yet shifted. They were our A-string, the group going to get us all the way to the castle.

A crack of lightning rippled over the night, pushing more waves of vibrant colors through the air. The intensity of Otherworld magic pumped through the thin veil between worlds and clawed at my lungs. My muscles buzzed with vigor.

"You're stronger than you think," a voice rumbled behind me. My neck shivered. His nearness slowed my racing heartbeat. "You will survive this war."

My eyes darted to the man standing at my shoulder, and I had to stop myself from leaning back into the warmth of his body.

"Plus, I'm owed a blow job, and I plan on collecting."

A tiny snort swelled from my nose, and my face broke into a grin. It quickly dissipated, terror filling my lungs. "I'm scared."

Lorcan moved closer, half his body pressing into mine. "I don't plan on leaving your side," he murmured into my ear.

I gasped at the sudden shrill of clanging metal, screams, and howls from monsters down on the field.

"I'd tell you to list what you hear, see, and smell, but I think it will make things worse right now."

He was right. All I could hear was the clanking of swords, screams of death, see thousands of fae running to kill us, and smell blood in the air.

His hand brushed mine, squeezing it briefly. He couldn't do anything to take away the terror and what was ahead of us, but the simple act of taking my hand felt like enough in the moment. I clasped his back before letting it drop.

Then it was time. Lars swooped overhead, still riding one of his bird-shifters, and yelled for his forces to attack.

"Let's move," Cole called out. "You know the plan. Let us see it through."

I took in a deep breath and jogged along with my troop, knowing how much the fae and humans were counting on us, even if they didn't know it. Unbeknownst to human children dressed in costumes of monsters and ghouls tonight, the real ones were fighting for dominance only steps away from their front doors.

Ember and I were the thread between life and death. If we failed, Earth fell.

～～～

Our selective group moved down the field, not following the rest of the Unseelie army, and separating to make our way to the castle. We skirted the back, but death was already soaking the earth near us. The crunch of bones and armor played in the air like out-of-tune violins.

Above us electricity discharged, illustrating Aneira's control over Ember's powers. The rod struck the Otherworld's shield with a splintering crack. Energy blasted into the air, tossing our bodies back onto the ground with a thud. The charged bolt crackled over the barrier, shredding a cavity through the thin surface, allowing magic to leak through with a rush. Cries came through the open wound as a group of Light fae with weapons in hands rushed straight for us.

"Come on!" Eli screamed at us as he jumped up, tugging Ember with him. Lorcan yanked me to my feet as hundreds of gnomes and wolf-shifters gushed in waves toward us.

"Oh my god," I mumbled, freezing with fear at the figures moving toward us, licking their lips in anticipation of our blood.

Lorcan swore, his grip tightening around my wrist, yanking me with him as he started to run. Torin stood a little ways away motioning for us to follow, the pixies winging close to the ex-Seelie soldier.

The group of wolves was narrowing in on us, already nipping at our heels. My heart batted against my ribs, my boots trying to keep up with my fae companions. *Damn these little legs!* I was going to slow my friends down. Get them killed.

Two dark dwellers I was pretty sure were West and Cooper suddenly stopped, their backs curling, the blades lining their spines, mirroring the lights embellishing the sky. They roared and dived for the enemy, moving together after the largest wolf. I ran faster at the sound of bones and ripping skin.

"Shit!" Lorcan muttered next to me. I followed his

gaze and was about to repeat his sentiment. More troops surged over the crest, cutting off our route.

"Go. I will stall them." Cole yelled at the five of us to keep going.

What was he thinking? One of him against hundreds? I could sense the protests building off every one of us.

"I can help you, Uncle." A form emerged from the brush, sprinting to Cole.

I whirled around, and my stomach clenched with a gasp. Time stopped.

Jared came running through the trees to Cole, a sword in his hand. He wore only cargo pants and a shirt, with one other knife hanging from his belt. No other weapons or protective gear.

"Jared. No!" My feet moved toward him, my arm outstretched. Owen's cry resounded near me.

Jared glanced from his father to me, our eyes connecting, excited determination set fiercely on his face. It expressed what I feared, what he had warned me of earlier: *I will prove it. You will see. I'm no longer the boy you fell in love with, but the man you'll want a future with.*

He was here to prove himself. To his family. To me.

"What are you doing here? Go back, Jared. It's too dangerous," Cole exclaimed, pointing back to where his nephew had come from. Anger and fear widened his eyes.

"This is my fight too. I'm a dark dweller! Let me act like one." Jared gripped the sword he was holding, puffing up his shoulders.

"No. This is not pretend. People are going to die, and I will not let you be one of them." Owen grabbed his son's bicep, shaking him. Jared clicked his jaw together, stepping out of his father's grasp.

The Seelie were getting closer every second.

"Go!" Eli stalked up to him. "We can't worry about you also."

Jared's head snapped to me, his face flushing, his eyes shifting with burning rage. "Then *don't*! I can fight." His mouth clenched in a strong, defiant line. With every second we stood there, our opponents gained ground on us. We had no time to fight over Jared's arrival.

"Guys?" I pointed ahead of us, the wolves and gnomes almost upon us.

"I will stay. You go with them." Owen prodded Jared toward Eli, his body already shifting into his beast form. Owen and Cole took off, trying to distract the horde coming for us.

"My lady, we are surrounded!" Simmons came zooming back for Ember, Cal on his tail. Right then Torin bellowed, and I jerked my head toward the commotion. More fae crashed through the trees, cutting off our exit.

"Crapping cupcakes, there is a mess of them coming our way." Cal wrenched his swizzle swords from his belt.

"Let's lessen their numbers, boys." Ember followed suit, pulling her blade.

I gazed around with a terrible sense of dread. A flash of my friends lying dead at my feet. Me, covered in their blood. The vision careened into my thoughts. Not one of my friends survived. Everyone dead, staining the grass deep shades of red with their blood.

No! I could not let this happen. The chant started forming in my mouth before I could even think, terror saturating each word.

"Kennedy, don't!" Lorcan called to me.

But it was too late. Magic lurched off my tongue, the power forced into each syllable blasted energy from my body. Like a bomb detonating, everyone within a fifty-foot radius of me went sailing back, tumbling and crashing to the ground.

It took them all to the ground, putting my friends closer to harm.

Shiiittt!

They scrambled to their feet, trying to regain the space between our enemies.

"I'm so sorry. I was only trying to help." My hands went to my mouth. I still struggled with controlling my magic. I could easily hurt as much as assist.

"Please, don't *help* again." Lorcan glanced over his shoulder at me, my eyes latching to his, feeling the unspoken connection between us.

Shrill roars from our assailants brushed the back of my neck, frosting my blood. They came from all sides, promising death. And all we could do was try to take theirs first.

My fingers wrapped around my gun, pulling it out of its holster and taking aim. It was the one thing I was not afraid of using. My dad had taken me out target practicing and hunting when I was younger. Though I never liked killing animals, I held no such compassion for the ones attacking my friends.

The booms from my gun echoed through the air, volleyed back down, and fused with the slashing sounds of ripping flesh and crunching bones. I reloaded twice, my bullets ticking off more and more Seelie soldiers. Eli and Lorcan kept Jared close as he bounced and jabbed his sword into a stream of gnomes.

"Ha! Another baker's dozen." Jared sliced into a barrage of gnomes, his gaze darting to mine. I could see the rush of adrenaline, the pride he got off each kill. To him this made him a man, a dark dweller I would choose. All this proved was how young he really was.

"Good, J, but don't get too cocky." Lorcan cut the head off a wolf leaping for him without even looking.

"Yeah, you're the one to teach me not to be an arrogant prick," Jared scoffed.

It was strange to watch the two men I cared about fighting next to each other. Of course there were similarities, but all I could see were differences. The happy, nerdy, sweet boy who was so impatient to prove his manhood. He was comfort and fun. The other was bad, dangerous, and broken. He was everything that scared and thrilled me.

"Mine." A low growl broke me away from watching Lorcan, turning my veins to ice.

Ember was on top of a fae, her eyes black, pupils vertical, and locked on him like he was prey, oblivious to the one behind. A sword raised, swinging down for her head.

"Ember!" I screamed at the same time my fingers took over, tugging back the trigger. Gunfire sang through the air, the bullet shredding the fae's chest. His eyes widened as blood pooled out of his mouth before he dropped, crashing down on Ember. She blinked her eyes, which returned to her normal two different colors.

She jerked her head to me. "Thank you," she mouthed.

Ember rose and behind her I could see Cole and Owen heading back, their bodies sleek and shimmering with blood and open wounds.

"Dad!" Jared yelled for his father, spotting the blood gushing from Owen's side. But a rustling of the bush near Jared stole my attention. A gasp tore from my throat. An ogre about seven or eight feet tall broke through the foliage. The axe he was carrying was aimed for the youngest dark dweller.

"Jared!" A shriek raced up my chest, flooding over my lips. He jerked his head back and gaped at the ogre, frozen in place as the axe sliced downward for him.

A roar ricocheted in my ears as Owen's beast leaped for Jared, shoving his son away. The axe sank deep into Owen with the sickening crunch and squelch of flesh and bone splitting apart as the blade dived into the ground, severing Owen in half.

Screams spiraled out of me as Owen's top half fell on Jared, pinning him underneath, his final act to protect his son from danger. My brain couldn't take in what was happening, shock held me in place on the grass.

The noise that came from Cole chilled my bones. His beast leaped for the ogre, and his scythe claws slashed at the giant's neck and ripped his head clean off. The creature's head thumped to the ground like a hollow pumpkin, rolling to my feet, its eyes open and staring at me.

"Retreat!" The few Seelie still left around us went running, afraid of the executioner. Cole howled, tearing after them, his eyes blazing the deepest red I had ever seen, blood dripping off his teeth, wanting more death. More revenge.

All of us stood in shock. Horror.

Torin finally broke into the grief, panic dancing him around. "We have to go. More men are coming." He motioned to more figures in the distance heading for us.

My feet still hadn't budged, my head swimming with disbelief.

Wails swelled from the figure below the dead dark dweller.

"Jared," I heard Eli say softly. He was crouched next to his nephew, dragging him out from under Owen's dead body, holding him up on his feet. "Jared, we have to go. We can't stay. Owen would not want you to."

"No!" he wailed, struggling against Eli's hold.

"Do it for your father. He did not save your life for you to forfeit it." Eli wrapped his arms around him tighter, pressing him to his chest. "I need you to stay alive, kid."

Something snapped me awake, seeing the grief ripping Jared apart. He needed me. My feet rushed to Jared. I touched his arm, and his body went rigid, wiping the tears from his cheeks before he faced me. I didn't want him to pretend, to act like he couldn't show his feelings. I wrapped my arms around him. There was nothing I could say. No words that would make it better. Instead I kissed his forehead and hugged him tighter. He sighed deeply, his arms circling me, holding on for dear life. "I'm so sorry," I muttered in his ear.

A choked sob hiccupped in his throat, his body trembled, and he then pulled back. His hazel eyes showed so much grief it gutted me. "Ken..." His jaw clenched, trying not to cry. "It's my fault."

I shook my head and drew him in again, my gaze landing on Eli and Lorcan over his shoulder. They bent over Owen's body, mumbling something I couldn't understand. They stood, expressions cold and hard.

"Let's go," Eli ordered.

Lorcan's eyes met mine and quickly snapped away, but I sensed his anguish. And I could not comfort him.

I gave Jared another kiss on the forehead then drew back, squeezing his hands in mine. The shock of Owen's brutal death, the fact we had to leave him behind, hung heavy on us. Disbelief and heartache stiffened our joints and locked our emotions underneath the surface. We had to move forward. The only way to do that was to pause our pain and stumble ahead into the unknown.

Torin and the pixies guided us into the depth of the forest, all eyes constantly roaming the terrain, searching for unseen threats or followers. The sewer tunnels, where we would enter the castle lay at the edge of the forest. So close, yet still so far away.

The woods were like a doorway. The moment we entered and Owen's body was no longer in view, our moods became even more somber and quiet. Except Jared. It was like a switch had flipped in him. Anger bristled around him like explosives ready to ignite.

I didn't hear Ember say anything, but I saw Eli reach up and put a finger to his lips, slanting his head to her.

"Let them come," Jared barked, stomping through the woods, hacking at brush. "I will kill all of them."

"Jared." I reached for him, trying to soothe him. He'd masked his grief in fury. It hurt my heart to see him like this, but he was being reckless. Loud.

His gaze darted to me, his hazel pupils reshaping into diamonds. "Don't tell me to be quiet. I recently lost my father. They. Killed. Him. I'll tear them limb from limb," he bellowed.

"Jared. Be quiet," Lorcan's voice was low with warning.

Jared's eyes flashed red, his muscles contracting with rage. "Don't tell me what to do! Why are you even here, Lorcan? You don't care about anything but yourself. Oh, except stealing my girlfriend. Or should I say ex-girlfriend."

This was not the time for our personal drama. We were being pursued and hunted. Every life, human and Dark fae, was on the line. "Jared, stop." My fingers grazed his elbow, and he jerked away from me like I was the foulest piece of garbage.

"No, I will not stop it. I don't give a shit about any of you right now. My dad was sliced in half in front of me." He waved his arms around, his voice going high with emotion. "Come out, you fuckers. You want to kill us? Come get me!" He circled around, calling out into the forest. Then he dropped his arms to his side. "He died trying to save me. And it's his own damn fault. It's all of your faults. If I had trained more, been treated as an equal, this never would have happened."

"Jared." Eli took a step toward him.

"I was never good enough." Jared sprang, getting toe to toe with Eli. "You guys always thought of me as less than you, as your weakness."

"*Stop!*" Eli boomed, my skin prickling with the power of his voice. "You *are* our weakness, but not in the way you think. You are the one we all love more than anything." Eli grabbed Jared's arms. "We protected you too much because we could not fathom how we would carry on if something happened to you. You made our exile to Earth the best thing to happen to us. You were our glue when most of us wanted to kill each other." Eli's gaze darted to Lorcan and then back. "You are the reason we still try to be a family."

"He's right." Lorcan nodded. "I never stopped loving you, kid. Never."

Jared stared at the two brothers, his shoulders sagging. The anger behind his eyes pooled into sadness, but I also saw love and awe in his hazel eyes. I knew how much he looked up to his uncles, especially Eli. Lorcan had hurt him when he left, so I imagined it meant the world to him to hear Lorcan's kindness now. The tension between them broke.

The dark dwellers' heads snapped to a spot behind us. Lorcan and Eli stiffened, growling.

The scene before me bored into my gut. It was so familiar. Like I had seen it before. My mouth parted, the realization coming too late.

An arrow zipped through the trees. Heading for me. My scream echoed in my head like a banshee. Seeing death a moment before it was supposed to hit. In my dream I had been frozen, unable to move, watching the arrow come straight for me. *Move!* I shrieked in my head.

I heard the whistle of the arrow hurtling through the air. My legs let go, and I fell to the ground, my knees slamming into a broken stump, zapping pain all the way up into my spine. The air rushed over me as the weapon grazed my head and flew past me. Relief surged through my limbs, and I wrapped my arms around my middle, my lungs gulping for air.

Then I heard Eli cry out, screaming Jared's name.

His tone was pure terror, as if a sea of anguish had broken the dam and flooded the world. My stomach burned with acid as I twisted my head over my shoulder to where Jared had been. A scream warped the air with a bone-chilling sorrow echoing off the trees, ripping at the air. My throat shredded with more cries as my mind reacted to the horror.

The metal barb meant for me stuck out of his chest, pinning him to a tree. Blood squirted like a fountain from his heart, where the arrow dug in.

His eyes, wide with fright, met mine. I saw his fear, his sadness, his shock.

Voices shouted, metal clanged, but it sounded distant as I pawed my way to Jared's body, my jeans tearing as I crawled to him.

"Jared!" I cried as I reached him, clambering to my feet

"Ken..." He choked, his body rattling.

I was about to tell him not to talk to save his energy when he spoke again.

"I know...I know...you and Lorcan." Blood

sputtered from his mouth, dribbling down his chin. "Saw you come from his cabin. You love him." He gulped, struggling for air. "But I will always love you. You'll always be mine..." Then like someone pulled a plug in a sink, life slipped from his body, emptying his eyes. His head sagged to the side, the last bit of air leaving his lips in a small, sad sigh.

He was gone. The boy who had been so full of life and energy, the one who painted the world with it and touched everyone near was now a shell.

Dead.

Neither my brain nor my heart could take it in. I didn't even realize I was wailing, desperate to be wrong. Hoping against hope, he was still alive and still the exuberant Jared I loved.

Nothing made sense anymore. Agony shut down my brain. I moved purely on instinct.

Red liquid dripped onto his boots like rain and pattered against the leaves around him, soaking the earth. His name spurted from my lips over and over in a chant, my hands moving over his body, trying to feel any sense of life. I chanted over and over. No energy bounced against my palms, only a vacancy under his skin. Nothing left. Why hadn't I tried the moment I walked up? Why did I not think of it till it was too late?

The blankness in his eyes, the slack in his jaw, finally snapped something in me. I collapsed to the ground, screeching with pain till my throat gave out, not caring about anything else around me.

"Kennedy," a voice came into my ear, warmth nipping where he touched me. "Ken?"

I felt Lorcan touch my back, but I didn't respond.

His arms circled around me, picking me up and moving me away. Stepping up with Eli, they both moved around their nephew.

Jared was dead. Because of me.

I tried to recall the original visions of the arrow heading for me. Why had they not showed Jared? I could have stopped his death. Maybe I could have stopped him from coming out here to prove he was good enough for me. He didn't understand I wasn't good enough for him. He was innocence and light. At one time I had been too. Not anymore.

Eli's fingers wrapped around the end of the bolt and yanked it from his chest. Lorcan grabbed Jared's body, easing it down to the ground.

My body bent over, acid sizzling up my throat.

The brothers kneeled over his body. Eli let out a soft sob, his hand brushing over Jared's face as he closed his nephew's eyes. Their abyss of grief and shock was palpable; sharp spikes of black and blues from their auras stabbed at my skin and expanded my own agony.

I'd watched Jared sleep before; it was the only time he was still. For a moment hope twisted reality, making me want to believe he was just recharging. Soon his lids would pop open, and he would bound around like a puppy again, full of wonder and life.

A gasp tore through my throat, jerking Lorcan's attention to me. I could not meet his gaze. The chasm Jared left was filled with guilt and anger.

"Where is Ember?" Torin came bounding up behind us, blood staining his clothes and hair. Simmons and Cal fluttered around him, looking like the devil and angel on each shoulder.

"She was there and then when I looked again, Girlie was gone." Worry lined Cal's face.

"My lady needed me and I failed her," Simmons berated himself, his head low.

Eli shot up, his head swiveling around in search for her. Anxiety strained his muscles, his body jerking more frantically with every second that passed.

My gaze darted wildly about, my heart hammering in my chest. We all knew Ember would never leave us. She would have been in the middle of the fight. But she was gone.

"Fuck!" Eli ran his hand through his hair. "I can feel her. She's close enough, but there is so much blood and bodies, it's hard to decipher where. No one saw where she went?"

Lorcan stood, his nostrils flaring as he sucked in air. "Shit."

"What?" Eli's gaze burrowed into Lorcan.

"Take a deep breath, brother."

Eli tried to still himself and took in a deep breath, his eyes widening. "Samantha."

Lorcan nodded. "She's always been obsessed that you two were meant to be. Samantha is going to kill her."

"Don't underestimate Ember." Eli's eyes flared, but I saw his shoulders rise, trepidation coiling them.

"Sam's one of mine. I can track her the best," Lorcan said.

"We need to find her." My voice came out strong and demanding. "I will not lose Em too."

It was like I had kicked on the start button. We all jerked to move, each of us giving one last look to Jared's slumped body. A sob broke through my heart. Each step tore a fissure in my heart. Leaving him here felt wrong.

Jared had been my first love. At one time I thought I would spend my life with him. We'd spent hours laughing, talking, and discovering the innocence of first love. Now that love lay in the dirt. All alone. Never to laugh or talk again.

For Ember I moved forward, but most of me stayed behind, curled up and dead next to Jared.

THIRTY-ONE

I kept up with the boys, although I was completely numb. A ghost in my own body.

"That way." Lorcan pointed to a small stone building in the distance, straight out of a Grimm's fairy tale with a flesh-eating "grandma" waiting for us to enter.

Eli halted. He bobbed on his feet, his body still pointed toward the cottage. "You guys continue on. Get into the sewer system. We'll catch up."

"Are you sure?" Lorcan's eyebrows scrunched down.

"Yeah." Eli nodded. Torin opened his mouth as though to protest, his worry for Ember apparent on his face, but he nodded at Eli. Cal and Simmons frowned at Eli's order too. All of us wanted to follow. "This is personal. I need to deal with Samantha, like I should have a long time ago."

With that Eli was gone, his body moving so swiftly my eyes lost track of him.

Ember. My heart pounded her name. She and Ryan were my family. My foundation. Without her, my world would stop. No doubt Eli felt the same about her. I had to trust he would get our girl...bring her back safe. She was eminent in our plan. The future Queen of the Seelie.

"Come on." Torin touched my shoulder softly. I sighed, turned, and followed him to the passageways leading us to the sword. To the final stage in our plan.

And most likely to my own death. The idea no longer bothered me.

Jared, I'll be with you soon.

~~~~~

The rancid stench of the tunnels assaulted my nose as we entered. Darkness engulfed us the deeper we went. I pulled out the flashlights in my bag, handing one to Torin.

"Wait here." Torin flicked on his light. "I'm going to continue down and see if there are any traps."

"I will help, Sir Torin." Simmons flew to him.

They both turned to head down the dark channel.

"Cal?" Simmons called to his friend.

"I'll stay. I've got a bag full of *make-me-forget*." Cal patted the carrier attached to his belt full of crushed juniper berries.

"Cal! Remember it is not for you. My lady specifically said not to eat it."

"Just a little. No one will notice."

"You really want to disappoint my lady? After all she's done for us?"

"All right, all right, biscuit-nipper. You are a pain in my ass," Cal grumbled, flying down the path behind Simmons and Torin.

It wasn't long before the silence filled the cavern, my body becoming highly aware of Lorcan near me. His breath slid over my skin, without even touching me.

And all I could see was Jared's face. Blood oozing from his mouth. *"I know...you and Lorcan. Saw you leave his cabin. You love him. But I will always love you. You'll always be mine..."* Guilt grew, strangling my vocals and choking me. My breath stuck in my chest, my lungs seeking air to fill them.

"Ken?" Lorcan moved to me. "The arrow was goblin made. No human or fae would have survived. There wasn't anything you could have done."

"I could have tried!" I cried, gulping more air.

"Li'l bird." Lorcan fingers wrapped around my wrist.

One touch. A brush of his skin. That was all it took.

Rage. Disgust. Guilt. The emotions were so vivid and raw they burst behind my eyes, coloring everything in front of me crimson.

"Don't!" I wrenched out of his grip. "Don't you dare touch me!" Coiled fury sparked under my skin like a storm. My body vibrated. Hate, blame, agony, and grief punched at each vertebra and exploded in my body, the flames consuming me. There were no logical thoughts in my head, I was simply one giant nerve reacting to the excruciating pain.

"He came here because of me." I jabbed at my chest. "He told me he wanted to prove himself. Be the man he thought I wanted. He's dead because of me. Owen's death is because of me. If Jared never came…"

"It's not your fault." Lorcan's green eyes blazed. "Nothing would have stopped him from coming. If anything, it's our fault. We protected him too much."

Grief continued to pour down on me, engulfing me in waves. Sobs hiccupped up my throat, and bile burned the back of my throat.

"Kennedy," Lorcan said my name softly, his hand stroking my back.

"He knew, Lorcan!" Each breath was a sledgehammer to my heart. "That's what he whispered to me."

"What?" Lorcan jerked back.

I couldn't hold back the guttural sobs ramming up my throat. "And he told me he still loved me."

Lorcan moved to me again, pulling me into his arms, wrapping me up against his chest. My body rocked with pain, drowning in it. I wanted to disappear and let Lorcan's embrace hide me from the world, guard me from the unbelievable agony. But being in his arms was the reason Jared was dead. If Jared didn't feel the need to prove himself to me, if he believed he was more like his family, then I would pick him. I would fall in love with him again.

Jared was everything good, pure, and innocent. He made me laugh. I felt light and joyous with him. But it hadn't been enough. I ruined what we had over the cliché experience with the bad boy. I was that girl. The stupid one who saw her mistake way too late.

Lorcan would only hurt me, ruin me, and throw me away when he got bored. He was not capable of love. Not the love that lasted past lust. I shoved out of his arms

Lorcan tilted his head, confusion lining his forehead, then understanding tilted his head up. "Ken—"

"Shut up," I hissed. "There is nothing you can say. Nothing will make this right." I motioned between us. "We were selfish and cruel, and Jared is dead because of our actions. We. Killed. Him."

"No. That's not—" He tried to reach out for me again.

"Don't!" I screamed. "When you touch me, my skin crawls."

Lorcan's body jerked like I slapped him.

Whatever Lorcan and I had the night before was tainted, like tar in my blood. Ugly and dirty. "What we did, I hate myself for it, for making such a *huge* mistake. I will never forgive myself...and I will never forgive you."

Lorcan's lids lowered. "You don't think I feel as guilty? That I'm not devastated?" he exclaimed. "I just lost one of my brothers and my nephew..." Sorrow etched his face. "But what we did? It was not wrong or a mistake."

A strange crackle came from me. "You screwed your nephew's virgin girlfriend, knowing he was still in love with me."

"I was not the only one there. I never forced you." A nerve twitched in his jaw.

"No, you played it well. Made me beg for it. Good for you."

"You think this was all a ploy?"

I felt possessed—rage and hurt influencing every word, making me say things I didn't even know if I meant. "But why should I be surprised? Lorcan Dragen, the bastard who murdered Ember's mother, betrayed his own brother and family, worked with the Seelie Queen, had one of my best friends killed, and kidnapped me. I'm the one who should take the blame."

Muscles along Lorcan's jaw popped and twitched, his chest heaving with anger. I could feel it radiating off him, his fists rolling into balls.

"That's what you think of me after all the time we spent together?"

"You mean the time you held me captive?" My surging breaths matched his. "You mean when I was tied to a pipe?" His fury was laced with pain and grief. I was hurting him. But it was like I was watching myself from outside my body, unable to stop.

We were silent for a moment, our ragged breaths filling the cavern.

"I'm in love with you, Kennedy," he whispered hoarsely, almost accusatory.

My entire world crumbled under his statement, tearing a sob from my throat, obliterating my heart. In a few words he destroyed me. Hollowed me out into an empty shell. Because no matter what, Jared was dead. His death changed everything.

My head slowly lifted, my gaze meeting his. My voice was low and controlled. "Remember when you said if you truly believed I wanted nothing to do with you, you'd walk away?"

His jaw clenched, his face turning to stone.

"Do you believe me now?" The emptiness in my voice reverberated off the walls.

Lorcan held my gaze, his jaw locking up.

"Yes." He jerked his chin, then turned away, walking out of the tunnel.

And out of my life.

~~~~~

I thought Jared's death killed everything inside me, but the moment Lorcan walked away, my heart split into tiny fragments, bleeding out anything left.

I moved down the tunnel like a zombie, then stopped. My back hit the wall, and I slid down, unable to do anything but breathe. The loss of Lorcan felt like the third death of the night, a hollowness my heart could not handle. It only increased the guilt over Jared. My heart longed to fill the chasm with Lorcan's touch. The cause and cure of my pain.

I had no clue how long I sat there when a face appeared in front of mine.

"Kennedy?" Torin's voice cascaded over me like velvet. "Are you all right?"

Was I all right? Nowhere near it.

"What's wrong with her? Did she lose her marbles too?" Cal's voice hummed near Torin.

"Cal!" Simmons chided. "Be nice. Ms. Kennedy just lost her mate. And she still has more marbles in her head than you do."

"That's because I *play* with mine." Cal wiggled his eyebrows then landed on my knee. I didn't feel anything. "Troll farts, I've seen this look before." Cal folded his arms. "Cracked like an ogre's ass. This one has malfunctioned. Went kaput."

"Ms. Johnson?" Torin's warm hand cradled my cheek, his eyes full of worry.

I couldn't even open my mouth. Nothing remained inside to say or feel. Only a void.

Torin bit down on his lip and frowned more deeply. Then, unexpectedly, he pulled me into his chest, folding his arms around me. Cal flew into the air, grumbling, but otherwise didn't talk.

I could hear Simmons fretting about Ember, but it all felt like a dream. I closed my eyes, giving in to the warmth of Torin's embrace.

The sound of pounding feet reverberated down the tunnel, alerting Torin. He let me go and stood, pulling his sword.

"Cal, Simmons?" He nodded in the direction of the sound. Simmons saluted him, and both pixies darted around the corner, investigating our intruders.

Ember. Please be Ember.

If anything happened to her... A surge of fresh anguish flushed to the surface, ripping away my breath.

My shoulders sagged with relief when I saw Ember and Eli jogging around the corner, covered in blood and scratches, but otherwise fine. Cal and Simmons had settled on her shoulders.

"Where have you guys been?" Torin demanded, still standing over me.

"Sorry." Ember frowned. "I was trying not to become a meal of vengeance served with a side of loathing."

Torin huffed and whipped around, heading down the dark corridor.

Ember rushed over, crouching down, then took me in her arms and held me tight. When she let go, her gaze held deep sorrow. She didn't have to say anything. Our grief was mutually understood. But she would never know the depth of mine.

In Ember's expression, I understood what she was saying. *Get up, Ken. Jared would not want you to give up. He'd want you to fight.*

I gave her a nod and let her pull me up to my feet. I would do this for him. For every life we lost today and to protect the ones who survived. The world was counting on Ember and me. I could not give up now. Inhaling, I rolled my shoulders back and followed the group toward our fate.

THIRTY-TWO

Torin knew almost every inch of the castle and how to get to it. There were secret doors and tunnels hidden everywhere.

"Here." Torin pressed his hand over the wall, shoving at it. Nothing happened. "Dammit. She's blocked me from entering the passages."

"What do we do?" I pulled at my ponytail.

"Find another way in." Eli gazed down the long dark path in front of us.

"Another way?" Torin spun around, his hatred for Eli clear on his face. "We don't have time to find another way."

Eli stepped up to Torin's face. "What do you expect us to do? Stand here and wait for it to open? Sorry, but I forgot my garage door opener."

"What is *your* great plan?" Torin matched Eli, their noses inches apart.

"Stop it, both of you." Ember got between them, pulling them away from each other. "We don't have time for the testosterone crap."

"No. You don't," a boy's voice rang out. The secret door swung open.

We all froze. Reality dawned on me with an eerie feeling of *deja vu. This has happened before.*

"Josh?" Ember exclaimed, rounding to face her old friend. Josh was dressed in the First Knight attire: leather pants and a long-sleeved shirt with a special crest of the Queen over his breastplate. His long arms and legs were now corded with muscle.

"You seem surprised," Josh replied, keeping his gaze on Ember. "You actually thought I'd turn my back on the only person who ever cared about me? I'd actually fall for the Queen's tricks? I know you don't trust me, but I swear I never planned to betray you."

Eli gritted his teeth, looming over Josh. "You're right. I don't believe a word coming out of your mouth. How do we know it's not a trap?"

"You don't." Josh's lip hitched as he glared at Eli. "But Ember, you know me. I mean really know me. *Believe* me. I am on your side."

"You turned me and the sword over to the Queen. How can I possibly trust you?" Ember shook her head.

"I had to. She watched my every move. I needed her to believe I was faithful." Josh tried to move around Eli, but the dark dweller blocked his every advance. "Believe me!"

"Trust the night," Grimmel had squawked. *"Fire needs light. Needs night to burn."* Oh crap. He wasn't talking about night, as in evening, but *the Knight.*

Ember ran her hand over her ponytail.

Josh glanced at Torin. "I'll admit I fell for the idea of her and what she could offer me at first, but after what she did to you I saw her for what she truly is. I could easily be the next guy she tortured. By the time I realized this, it was too late. She was in my head. I had to do what she wanted, or we would all be dead. But I swear to you, Em, I always planned to help you in the end."

A buzz of energy came over me. I heard the truth ring sharply in each of Josh's words. "He's telling the truth." The words floated out of my mouth, no longer in my control. *"The false Knight will guide the way."*

When I opened my eyes I saw the hesitation leave Ember, a small smile twisting her mouth, like all she needed was my confirmation to trust her friend again.

"It's about freakin' time you got on the right side, Josh. We have so much to talk about, but right now we are kind of in a hurry here."

"Hey! I've been standing here waiting for you. Do you know what it took to slip away from 'my men' unquestioned? At least Aneira is too distracted by Lars and the battle to be in my head." Josh tossed up his arms.

"Wait. What?" Eli's mouth dipped open.

"I knew it." Ember ignored Eli, throwing her arms around Josh.

"I am so sorry, Em. It was necessary. She was in my mind every single second, compelling and threatening me. I had to play like I actually was betraying you. She needed to believe she had me completely under her spell. I didn't know she would be in Greece. I freaked out, and in overplaying it, I almost got us killed."

"Are you fuckin' kidding me, Brycin?" Eli bellowed. "Whatever Kennedy says, are you actually going to trust him? Are you insane?"

Ember let Josh go, facing Eli. "Yeah. I guess I am. I believe him. And I need you to have faith in me. What other choice do we have?"

Eli gazed up at the ceiling like he was counting to ten, then he took several deep breaths before looking back at Em.

"Fine." Eli stepped closer to Josh. "But if you betray us, I will tear you to pieces before you can even blink. Do you get me?"

Josh's swallowed nervously. "Yes. I understand."

We followed Josh down the private passageway, leading us directly into the castle. There was no pleasure being back here with its familiar scents and the powerful pull of magic lapping at my skin. I hated the time I was held captive here. But as scary as it was, this was where Jared and I met. Where we first fell in love.

Ember sent the pixies ahead of us as we entered the main part of the castle.

Dread. I felt it in my bones. Fate had something in store for us and played with us like insignificant pieces on a board game. It had given me only slight glimpses of things, dreams that made no sense until it was too late.

"There." Torin pointed at a set of large wooden doors, dragging me out of my thoughts. Enchantments encircled the area, crackling the air. This was where the sword was held, the only weapon in the world that could end this war, kill the Seelie Queen, and protect the humans.

My thoughts briefly went to my sister and parents, wondering how they were and what they were doing. *Please keep them safe.*

"Guys, what the hell...?" The tone of Ember's voice wedged an equal fear between my ribs. My skin prickled, realizing far too late the eerie quiet settling over the space was not normal. No guards watched the door. No pixies waited for us.

Nothing.

Eli's growl sent goosebumps down my arms, and his back curled as he stared deep into the shadows. Torin pushed me behind him, unsheathing his blade.

"You shouldn't send pixies to do a man's job." A figure of a man stepped from the shadows. Even though fairies' voices were smooth as chocolate, this one rang with disgust and cruelty.

A gasp rebounded in my throat.

Quilliam.

The fay moved closer to us, his hand curled at his side, something protruding from his fingers. A tiny body.

"Cal!" Ember tried to rush forward but Eli snatched her arm, tugging her back into him. "What did you do to him?"

"He got a taste of his own medicine. A lot of it. Poured it down his little bitty throat until he gagged." Quilliam chuckled.

I nearly choked on my own horror. Cal and Simmons were friends, no, they were part of my extended family. I wanted to protect them, guard them from evil. Cal was still alive but struggling to breath, his body trying to burn off the abundance of condensed powder in his system.

Torin stirred in front of me, lifting his sword. "Let him go, Quilliam."

"I don't think so, Torin. This guy seems strangely important to you. How many times did I beat you at cards? You know I don't give up a good hand. I'll keep him safe, right here." Quilliam jammed Cal into his pocket with a pat.

"You play cards the same way, by slipping some in your sleeves and pockets to cheat with later." Torin gripped his blade more tightly.

"You are such the hero, aren't you? You pick right and wrong, while I pick the winner." Quilliam's voice was full of scorn. "I think the Queen will prefer my way."

"Speaking of Aneira..." Eli kept his hand on Ember, her body still leaning toward the lump in Quilliam's pocket. "Where is your owner?"

"She is kicking the ass of the Unseelie King right now. Soon he will be dead and so will you."

"You think you can take all of us?" Eli scoffed, his shoulders tensing.

"I do." He nodded. As if on cue, a rush of fae men dressed in the Queen's uniform descended like ants into the room, amassing behind their leader.

My neck prickled with magic that hung heavily in the room. I inched closer to Torin, my heart slamming into my chest. When I glanced over my shoulder at Josh, fear slammed down my throat, choking off the warning scream there.

A sword lay edged across Josh's throat as a guard slunk up behind him, yanking him back away from our group. Josh's eyes shot to mine, a gasp rippling like shock waves from his mouth.

Torin bumped into me, automatically taking a step toward Josh, but stopped. "Quilliam, let him go. The argument is between us." Torin glanced between Quilliam and the man holding Josh.

"You're right," Quilliam sneered, barring his teeth. "My real hatred is directed at you."

"Does having to play second fiddle still eat at you?" Torin turned to his old comrade, a smirk hinting at his face. "Must have hurt when the Queen passed over you again, especially for a human."

Quilliam swallowed hard. Torin had hit a bullseye.

"At least I didn't disgrace myself for a dae." He glared at Ember.

"Looks like your nose has healed. Though I have to say it looks crooked. Suits you." Ember lifted one eyebrow in a taunt.

Torin chuckled and kept his gaze on her. An intimacy, a shared moment passing between them. A flicker of pain flashed so quickly in Torin's eyes I almost missed it. He jerked his head away from her and focused on his old friend.

"You used to be something, Torin. You had everything. I looked up to you. Now you are nothing. And it seems you didn't even get the girl." Quilliam flicked his head at Ember. "So was that *thing* worth it?"

"Yes." Torin's voice clenched along with his grip on his blade.

Quilliam bellowed a deep laugh. "Seems both *First Knights* have a weakness for daes," Quilliam commented, then smiled with smug abandon as he strolled over to Josh.

With no warning, white blinded my vision. It slammed into me. My body was torn from reality, freezing my limbs as images consumed my mind, seizing my senses.

Flash

"I am still the First Knight. Back down." Josh ordered the men, but his voice wobbled with fear. "You have to obey me."

"Do I?" Quilliam tilted his head, standing before the human boy.

"Yes. It is Fay law. You obey your First Knight without question." Josh's Adam's apple bobbed, a trickle of sweat dampening his forehead.

"You're right, I do." In a blink, Quilliam yanked his blade from his belt, the metal tip driving into Josh's throat. Blood spurted in a long stream onto Quilliam's face and gushed down Josh's neck.

"Now you are no longer the First Knight."

Death. Blood.

The visual of Josh's empty eyes reminded me so much of the boy I just lost.

Flash.

~~~~

With a strangled cry, my mind tossed me right back into the present. Terror gripped my lungs so tightly I bent over, gasping for air. My head spun, but this time I was aware of my surroundings. My Pavlovian reaction was the need to see Lorcan, to hear his voice, feel his touch, smell him. He was my anchor.

I lifted my head, my gaze catching the glint of Quilliam's blade, already pulling out his weapon. He had already moved beside Josh.

I knew what came next.

"No." My voice came out strangled and low, barely heard in my own ears. *Oh my god, it's happening.* I froze with the horror watching the exact thing transpire I had just seen but was unable to stop.

I was too late...again.

The sword pierced Josh's airway. Sound was never as clear in my visions as it was in real life. A slurping sound of skin and cartilage came with a gurgling cry slick with blood. Josh sagged and collapsed down on the stone to his knees, the sword twisting deeper into his neck as he grappled for air, his eyes wide and full of terror.

"Josh!" A scream shredded from behind me as Ember's cry splintered my heart. I could have stopped this. Why didn't it hit me sooner? Why did I see it if I couldn't do anything about it?

"You never really were her First Knight. You were nothing to her and even less to us." Quilliam spit on Josh before ripping the blade from his neck. Blood surged out of the gap. "The Queen was looking forward to killing you herself. She could not stand the sight of you, human. But she will have to forgive me. I couldn't bear listening to your irritating voice for one more moment." He kicked him, sending Josh's body to the ground, where red blood pooled mercilessly below him.

Josh's gaze shot toward Ember, full of fear and heartbreaking grief. Then the glaze of death coated his eyes as he stared blankly into the void.

All I could see was Jared's sweet hazel eyes staring at me. Blaming me. Hating me.

Everything followed in a hazy whirlwind. People talking, yelling, inching toward us, a flutter of Simmons's wings from the ceiling, but my brain had shut down, locked on the body on the floor. I was frozen in my guilt. I'd left the boy I had loved in the woods, an arrow through his chest. Discarded and alone like he meant nothing.

"Elighan, get her out of here!" Torin's voice snapped my head up. He moved towards the encroaching group of Seelie soldiers.

What was he doing?

Suddenly an arm came around my waist, tugging me away. Ember struggled next to me, crying out, but Eli's firm grip on both of us didn't budge as he shoved us through a door.

The last glimpse I got before Eli slammed the door and locked it was Torin sparring with his sword, holding the men back from reaching us. Simmons buzzed over Torin's shoulder as more of Quilliam's men ran for him.

Sacrificial lambs.

The two of them couldn't hold off eight men.

"Eli! We can't leave them. There are too many guards. Torin and Simmons will die," Ember shouted, her expression swathed in panic.

"It's his decision. Simmons's too." Eli stepped up to her, tilting her face toward him. "They are doing it so you can finish your quest and others may live. Torin understands your mission is bigger than his life."

She fell onto Eli's chest, a small sob escaping her throat. The loss hung heavy over all of us. We all understood Torin was forfeiting his life for us to continue. Another one on the list of people we would lose tonight. And none of us wanted to admit that probably meant Cal and Simmons as well. Eli engulfed Ember, his strong arms giving her a safe place to mourn for a moment.

In spite of the consuming guilt I felt over Jared, seeing Eli's concern for Ember only made me miss Lorcan. To feel his arms around me. The weakness of my need for him only caused more hatred. For myself and for him.

Ember sucked in, straightened her shoulders, and stepped back. "Let's finish this."

We slunk down the hallway, the possibility of soldiers coming for us from front or behind keeping us on guard. We turned down a hallway and Eli's arms shot out, halting us at the corner. He peered around quickly.

"Two guards. Asleep," he whispered back to us. The pixies did their job, sprinkling powdered juniper berries over the guards, which put them to sleep.

The moment I rounded the corner, magic slithered up my arms, leaving bumps behind. Dense air clogged my lungs and pulsed against my skin like a heartbeat as we slid past the guards. It was waiting for us.

For me.

Kennedy...

As if pulled by an invisible cord, my feet shuffled forward into the room, my eyes locked on the object in front of me. The spell surrounded us, tasting our skin. The sword floated in the center of the chamber, shimmering with the heavy protection spell.

The idea of my death had been discussed, but only when I stood before this object of great power did I understand the truth. I was not ready for this level of magic. If we had any hope of breaking it, I would have to give it all I had. Even if I won, I lost.

I stepped up to the glittering spell, mesmerized by its beauty. The blade was etched with Celtic symbols and decorations. The carvings swirled, intertwined, and infused in a gorgeous design. The pulse of life inside the sword flickered, and I felt it in my own veins.

Kennedy. It called to me, drew me to it. To my end.

"I don't usually say this, but *fuck.*" I exhaled, my fingers tapping at the wall of magic.

"I'll second it." Eli came up beside me.

"Yeah, but when she says it, I know we're screwed." Ember stood on my other side, all of us staring in awe and fear at the object before us.

"The spell is quite powerful and complex," I said with more confidence than I felt. The magic slamming off the protective field was way above my ability. I was still so new to being a Druid. "The magic protecting it is beyond my capabilities. I don't know if I can break it."

"You have to." Ember turned to me.

"What if I can't, Ember?" My legs wobbled underneath me, my body trembling under the pressure of the world. "What if we got all the way here and I'm unable to break it?"

Hands grabbed my arms and turned me. Bright green eyes pinned mine. The familiarity of them forced the world away. All I saw in my mind was Lorcan. Heard his voice.

"Jared believed in you, and I have faith in you. Close your eyes and take a deep breath," Eli ordered me.

Panic simmered at the edges, ready to explode, but I closed my eyes, letting the idea of Lorcan soothe me. I understood my role in this world, and I would not back out. My parents, little sister, friends—everyone human needed me as much as the creatures of the fae. Ember needed to fulfill her destiny. I was part of it, and I would step up. There was no nobler way to die than for the ones you love.

"Ignore everything outside of you." He released his hold and turned me toward the sword. "Forget the room exists or anybody else is here. Only concentrate on what's in front of you. Feel the magic and let go. You can do it, Kennedy."

I took in a deep breath, pulled my head up, opened my eyes, and nodded at Eli. I was ready.

The moment the chant peeled over my lips, Aneira's curse pushed back with a force that felt like walking into a hurricane. My breath caught in my lungs as it slammed into me, and my lids shut against the force. Magic poured down on us, each syllable getting harder to say, like blocks were stacking on my tongue.

The battling energies grew deafening, buzzing and crackling in my ears. Energy whirled around us, blowing my hair back, tangling it into knots as my muscles quivered under the density.

You have never failed a test, and you will not fail this one.

I could feel the sword quivering, eager, but the enchantment was getting angry. Both the sword and the hex clawed at me in different ways. My legs wavered, dipping toward the floor, but I locked them as more pressure filled the room. It swirled in the room like angry bees, stinging and slapping against my skin. I cried out, shoving each word out, putting more force behind them, my chants growing into bellows, stripping my vocals raw. Tears slid down my face along with sweat as I fought the invocation. It hurt, like someone crawled inside and was trying to rip me out of my own body while the magic ate at my flesh from the outside.

It still wasn't enough. The spell held strong against my anti-charm.

Come on, Kennedy.

You're stronger than you think. Lorcan's voice filled my head.

My toes curled in my shoes and with a guttural cry, I shoved my incantation at the wall.

Crack.

Something broke. Inside me or the spell, I wasn't quite sure. I could no longer feel. No longer hear. The pressure vanished, and I felt my soul start to float, rising to the next level. I lost all sense of my body, time, or space. The world went gray, except for the silver of the sword and the colorful magic wrapped around it. Aneira's signature was carved deep into the hex.

The spell seemed sure of itself. The more my words punched against it, tearing at its flesh, the more it grew, a whirling, angry vortex. Even scared, it was stronger than me. My energy and life seeped out too quickly, blood gushing from my nose and eyes. I was dying.

Suddenly pictures flickered in my head. Ryan, Ember, and I hugging each other the last time. The many movie nights we spent at Ember's, laughing, happy. Reading to Ryan in the fort we built to keep the bad monsters away. My family eating dinner together. Jared and I curled up talking. When I did my first spell. The moment in the bathtub with Lorcan. How alive I felt. The way he grinned. Held me. Kissed me...made love to me.

My friends and family were everything to me. They gave me power. Strength. Happiness. With a last push, I screamed out the words, the power of my friends' names under each letter.

Crack.

Like a rushing river, pain crashed into every fiber of my being. A sharp pop burst in my head, igniting firecrackers behind my eyes. From the distance I heard a blood-curdling scream and then nothing.

Death claimed another victim.

~~~~~~

"Kennedy?" A woman's voice called to me, strong and deep, but beautiful, like an orchestra had put my name to music. My eyes blinked open. A woman leaned over me. Her long red hair fell in in waves down to her waist, framing kind violet-blue eyes.

I knew her. The awareness of who she was came like a fact I read in a book. It was in the familiarity of her aura, in the resemblance to her daughter.

"Aisling?" Her name flowed off my tongue. She was so beautiful it was like staring at the stars. Instantly I felt the draw to her, understanding why so many loved her.

"You must get up, my dear. It's time." Her hands gently helped me sit up.

"Time for what?" Even in death I did not get a break.

"Your role is only beginning. Death cannot stop the prophecy," she said. "My sister's time must end."

"What are you talking about?" I stared, her statement constricting a knowledge I held in my gut.

"It's you. You are the destined one." Her hands clenched mine, holding firmly. "You are the one to end it all and save her."

"Save who?"

"Please..." Aisling's grip constricted. "Please save her. I will try to help. But you are the only one who can." One hand left mine and went up to my third eye. The moment her fingers touched my skin everything went black. Her voice filled my head.

"By one of the Light, Darkness will take its revenge.

A bloodline that cannot be repressed will rise to power.

A descendant will take the throne. Blood will seek to kill you.

She who possesses the Sword of Light will have the power."

THIRTY-THREE

My eyes shot open, air forced down my throat as if through a hose. My mind felt like it had been electrocuted. Mushy and dazed. I had been dead. And Aisling brought me back.

Voices slithered their way into my ear. I turned my head. My gaze landed on the Seelie Queen. Aneira stood over my friend, holding a sword.

"Well, Aisling...do you hear me?" Aneira's voice sounded crazed. "Your bastard daughter is following you to the dark pits of the underworld. You will finally have some time together."

Ember grunted and wiggled like she was pinned down, unable to move.

"Aisling?" Aneira's eyes widened as she stared down at Ember, mumbling frantically, her eyes wide. Then Aneira straightened, her voice rising. "Aisling, I know you can hear me. I won, little sister. You did well at trying to best me, but I prevailed. Daddy always said you were the smarter, stronger, more magical one. It looks like he was wrong. I survived you all. And I even won against a prophecy. At the end I outsmarted everyone."

My eyes were slow to track the figure on the floor. I blinked. It was no longer Ember there, but the same woman from my dream. Aisling.

"I loved you, Aneira, even when you made it impossible," Aisling spoke to her sister, sadness tinging her words.

"You betrayed me! You left me. You did not love me. You loved those demons more," Aneira screamed wildly.

Then in another blink the woman with long flaming hair was gone. Ember was back.

"Please save her. I will try to help. But you are the only one who can." Aisling's words came back to me. She was helping. Stalling Aneira.

Aneira jerked, her spine straightening at the change. She snarled in disgust. "I have been waiting for this day. It should have been you who died, not my sister. I cannot believe she would betray me for a demon and a bastard child. A DAE!"

Ember lifted her head, her eyes rolling briefly to the sword on the floor before returning to Aneira.

I pushed myself slowly up to sit, following Em's gaze to the sword, noticing a man's body crumpled on the other side of her.

Eli. No! My seer could sense no life in his body. Eli was dead?

Then Lorcan was dead, too...

I drew my feet underneath me, standing on shaking legs with the sheer power of my fury and despair. There had been enough loss, enough grief, enough heartache. This woman had taken my real family from me, had slaughtered every Druid because of her own fear.

I inched closer to the Sword of Light, which rested between Eli and me.

Your role is only beginning. Save her.

I came back for a reason. I knew exactly what I had to do. Protect Ember.

"You will not be leaving here. Alive anyway." Aneira gripped her blade and shoved the tip at Ember's throat. "Now it is your turn to join your mother and father. Aisling gave her own life to save you...all for nothing." With a sweep, Aneira drew up her sword, preparing to swing it down on Ember's neck. "You failed, Ember. Even the prophesied one could not kill me."

Wrath filled me, and my body moved without thought. I was pissed.

My fingers grasped the handle of the Sword of Light, Nuada's sword. The moment I touched it I felt a wave of familiarity, a knowing so deep it was almost intimate. Energy ignited, zinging up my arm in almost painful waves. Magic rushed through me, hurling me toward the woman about to kill my best friend, leading me to where it wanted to sink in.

Aneira cut her weapon toward Ember's neck. I did not think or question but simply reacted to protect my own.

The weapon pulsed in my hand, giving me more strength than I normally had. I bellowed and swung the blade in my hand through Aneira's spine with every emotion I held inside: fear, anger, grief, revenge, and fierce protectiveness. My arm vibrated as the sword ripped through her body.

A piercing shriek wrenched out of Aneira's throat, her weapon falling to the ground in a clatter. Her body stiffened at the invasion, blood oozing from her back, catching on the fabric of her dress.

I twisted the sword in deeper. Aneira's body jerked with a violent shudder, and then she fell with a slurping of her innards against my blade as she crumpled to the floor.

"Daes weren't the only ones whose bloodlines were repressed." I stared down at the woman, revenge for my family on the blade. The sword throbbed with magic and light in my hand, illuminating the room.

Ember pushed herself up, her eyes wide. My gaze fastened on hers and whatever fiery rage I'd felt a moment ago evaporated. All I saw was my friend. The person who had always been the stronger one, staring up at me in awe.

"Ember!" I dropped the sword, scrambling to her. I tried to help her up, my arms shaking with the excess energy still flooding my system. She stumbled, but I grabbed her, raising her to her feet. "Are you okay?"

"I think so."

A moan slid from the body at my feet, causing me to jump back. Ember instantly kneeled down next to her, rolling Aneira onto her back. "She's still alive."

I stared at Aneira then at Ember. Killing her wasn't my job, it was stopping her from slaying Ember. Right?

As if reading my thoughts, Ember shook her head. "Kennedy, it has to be you. It glowed for you." She nodded at the sword lying on the floor. "You are the prophesied one, not me. You are meant to kill her. And as long as Aneira lives, the curse is still on me. I cannot touch the sword." She pinned her lips together, her eyes boring into me. "You have to chop off her head. It's the only way to kill her."

"What?" The word shot from my mouth. "I can't chop off her head."

"You have to." Ember stood. Each word sounded certain, like she finally understood something. "It must be you. You were meant to be Queen."

Your role is only beginning. Death cannot stop the prophecy. It's you. You are the one destined. Aisling's words came back to me.

Holy nerf-herder.

A bubbled scoff came from Aneira, her eyes fluttering to us. "You both are pathetic. Even the all-powerful dae and Druid can't kill me ..." Coughs seized her, cutting off her sentence.

Ember twisted me toward her. "Kennedy, you and you alone have to fulfill the vision. Remember all she has taken from you: your human family, Ryan, and Jared. Your whole clan died because she wanted to break the spell on the sword. This sword was always meant for you to avenge your family."

The woman had taken so much from all of us. I would never know my blood family because she massacred them.

Aneira lurched for her own sword.

My mind shut off. All I could hear were the screams of my dying friends and family, the dead eyes of Jared, the lifeless body of Eli in the corner. Lorcan was also gone. And Cole. My adoptive family would become slaves under her control.

Instinct took over and I swiped the fated sword off the ground, brilliance bursting into the room. Aneira cried out as she struggled to her feet, rage siphoning all the beauty from her face as she leaped for me.

Nuada's sword exploded with power, and I swung my arm with everything I had. A deep bellow filled my ears. The blade found her long neck and slashed through the bone as though her neck were a fresh fruit. Moisture freckled my face as her blood spurted. In one breath her body caught up with what happened and dropped to the floor like a rag doll. Red hair flew like a kite in the wind as she fell. Her head landed on the stone with a fleshy crunch then rolled underneath the Queen's throne. Her dead eyes stared back at us with horror.

A whoosh of magic shot through the room. Ember fell to her knees with a cry, energy directed at her, filling her.

I could not move as I gaped at the headless Queen. I had no idea how long I stood there watching blood trickle from the dead Queen's neck and mouth, but I finally heard Ember's voice next to me. "Holy crap."

My gaze still would not leave Aneira's.

"Are you all right?" Ember asked. "Kennedy? Are you okay?"

I nodded slowly, feeling the trance break free. The sword slipped from my fingers, clanging on the floor. A cry crawled up my throat and pushed out over my teeth without warning. I thrust my hand to my mouth, my legs shaking.

Ember's arms were suddenly around me. Feeling my friend's embrace broke through my shock. Sobs hurled from me. She only tightened her hold on me.

"Shhhh! It's okay."

"She's dead." I gasped for air.

"You did it." She squeezed me. "That took a lot of balls, girl. I am so proud of you."

I lifted my head and stepped back. Ember grabbed for me again when my legs dipped. But I felt her shaking as much as I was. A powerful pulse of magic throbbed off her. She had her powers again. The curse was broken.

We actually fulfilled our destinies. I had no idea what lay outside these walls and how bad the damage was, but we killed Aneira.

"*We* did it." I grabbed her hand in mine.

"Yeah. We did." Tears filled Ember's eyes, pain shot through her small smile. "*Together.*"

She bent over and picked up the sword, laying it flat in her hands, and held it out to me.

I stared at her, not fully understanding.

"She who possesses the Sword of Light will have the power." Ember placed it in my hands, and it instantly lit up at my touch. "A bloodline that cannot be repressed will rise to power. A descendant will take the throne."

Oh holy crap squared.

I had done what needed to be done without thinking of what it meant.

"The prophecy was about both of us." Ember curled my hands over the weapon with her own. "You were always supposed to be the Queen, Kennedy. Not me. I never wanted it. Nor did it feel right to me. But you...it makes sense."

She moved back, her eyes glistening with more tears. "Queen Kennedy." She dipped her head.

My mouth hung open. I wanted to deny it, to say there was no way I could be Queen, but the words wouldn't come. I suddenly knew. She was right.

Neither of us could say if the loss was worth it. All I knew was the world would never be the same, and neither would I.

I was a ruler.

Kennedy Anne Johnson.

Queen of the Light.

EPILOGUE

I stared out over the glistening blue lake, the sun sparkling off the waves. It was a chilly but beautiful winter day. Christmas, which the fae called Yuletide, was only a week away.

Lars thought it best to have things set, giving the unstable world something to hold on to, traditions they recognized, and security in their monarch.

"You look gorgeous." I turned toward the voice, my dress swishing against the floor. "Seriously, Ken. You are breathtaking."

I glanced down at the delicately beaded and embroidered dress. It was heavy and uncomfortable, but I only had to wear it for a few hours. "Thank you."

Ember walked up to me, claiming me in a hug. "Are you nervous?"

I let out a humorless laugh.

"Stupid question. Sorry." She stepped back, brushing her hair off her shoulder.

"Look at you." I motioned to the exquisite long black dress she wore. The shimmery fabric hugged every curve. "I was sure you'd come in sweats with ruffles on them."

She snorted, pressing a hand to her mouth, recalling the last time she wore a dress and wished she was back in her sweats. Our school dance, senior year. "That feels like lifetimes ago." She dropped her hand, a look of sorrow creasing her lovely face.

"Yeah, it does." I felt I had aged years in the last few months.

"But don't think this won't come off the moment it can. Along with these torture devices they call shoes." She slipped out of the heels, groaning in delight at being liberated from them. "That's how much I love you. I wore these instead of my chucks."

We did this for Lars, who demanded we all look the part. She knew I wouldn't have cared.

It had only been a month and a half since the war. We may have won, but so had Aneira. We had been too late to stop the worlds from colliding. The walls between the two collapsed and magic flooded in like a tsunami, destroying buildings, bridges, and homes across the world.

So many lives were taken due to the devastation, including my family. Ember had found out for me soon after the war they were all dead. My mourning didn't end, but my new role did not allow me to grieve when so many others needed me. It was easier to push away and delve into work.

Humans could now see the monsters that once only lived in the pages of fairy tales. Every day I got reports of humans reacting to fae like they were terrorists, killing and attacking them in hordes. And fae used this time to capitalize on the weakness of humans, doing the same in return.

We were in darkness, and I didn't see how I could light the way. Could I bring stability to the new world, especially when so many hated the fact a Druid was their queen? I was technically not their leader yet. It had been too busy after the war to take a moment to breathe, let alone do a ceremony.

Today I would be formally crowned.

There had been so many threats against me Lars had quadrupled my guards. I couldn't even pee without someone practically following me in.

"Lars says everything is set. They are trying a new device to see if it will record and broadcast out, even to Europe. He wants everyone to see you being crowned and take the throne. I believe he is hoping it will ease people's fear."

Or increase it.

Lars's response to my accession to the throne stunned me. After he reconciled it would not be Ember leading alongside him, he treated me like an equal and helped me with the rough transition, teaching me the basics of ruling, especially the business stuff, and how to deal with the nobles. I had a lot of haters and being by my side, showing his support, he hoped others would follow his lead and accept me as their Queen.

"I doubt it will ease anything." I brushed at the traditional cream-colored dress. I knew my rule would be anything but traditional, but I wanted to give the fae a little bit of familiarity. "They are too scared and grieving."

Ember sighed, and I sensed a change in her aura. In the new world, with magic heavy in the air, auras were actually harder to see now.

"What?"

She gazed down at the floor. My heart heard her, knew what was coming.

"You're leaving, aren't you?" I said quietly.

She sighed, her head bobbing. "We have to." She lifted up her face. "Eli has agreed to come with me. Cooper's already taken the role of second. He doesn't want to be here either. It's too hard."

It was extremely hard because of the ghosts haunting the dwellers' house. Owen, Jared, and even Samantha prowled every silence and empty seat there.

Jared left not merely a hole, but a chasm in all our hearts. He didn't just haunt his family. Jared roamed my heart and mind, waking me at night crying and gasping for air.

"I'm sorry, Ken." Ember grabbed my hand in hers.

Tears strangled my throat. I had already foreseen this, but it still hit like a bulldozer. I was happy she and Eli would be together.

When I cut off Aneira's head, every curse she ever placed had broken. Eli's life had dangled in the gray until Ember was able to save him, pouring her magic into him. Eli's first gasp of air had also returned Cole and Lorcan from the dead.

Not that I had seen Lorcan. He had kept to his word and stayed far away from me. Ember said he was visiting the dweller camp on occasion, spending time with his brothers, bonding. But she said he appeared exhausted and sad, almost like he was a shell.

Like me.

Time only made it worse, tearing at my heart. Yet each time I thought about Lorcan, pain and anger reared up and reminded me why I had driven him away. It was for the best. My life was no longer mine, I had to give everything to my people. Even if they didn't want me.

"Hey, my salty sugar. The spice is in the house." Ryan's voice boomed from the doorway as he strutted in wearing a fitted dark navy suit, a light pink shirt, bright fuchsia tie, and a chevron-patterned handkerchief poking out of his breast pocket. His shiny shoes squeaked on the stone floor as he twirled in, showing off his hip attire.

Ember let out a low wolf whistle. "Damn, hot stuff."

"I know, right?" He grinned, twisting his body as if he were a runway model.

"Not supposed to show up the Queen," I tsked him, trying to keep my smile at bay.

"I'm the arm candy. I'm supposed to show up everyone." He winked, rubbing his hands over his body. "They're obligated to be envious of *all* of this. Desire one of their own."

Ember and I snorted.

He opened up his arms and I dove in, needing to feel the security of his embrace. The one good thing coming out of the worlds fusing was Ryan and Mark were free.

They could come home. Ryan chose to not find his family, saying all he needed were his friends. He and Castien lived with Lily and Mark, near Dark Dweller House, but I had plans to get Castien back as one of my soldiers. If he came back, Ryan would follow. The idea of Ryan being under the same roof made me extremely happy. I needed him.

"Your coronation awaits, my dear." Ryan bowed and held out his arm. "Even though technically we all know I'm the true queen here."

I laughed, took his arm, and headed for the door. Ember shoved her feet into her heels with a groan and caught up with us. I held out my arm for her, she wrapped hers around it, and the three of us walked down the corridor.

Our lives were about to be in turmoil again, the future scary and unknown. But I knew in my heart as long as I had these two, we could handle whatever was to come.

Like I said, some souls always find their way back to each other.

~~~~~

"I present to you, Kennedy, your undisputed Queen," Lars boomed through the vast room. "All hail the Queen!"

The room exploded in unison. My limbs shook under the weight of the crown and the robe. Both symbolized the weight of responsibility on my head and shoulders.

Standing before hundreds of people, which represented a fraction of how many were now under my reign, terrified me. Scratch that. Terrified wasn't a strong enough word. I was one unsettled breath from throwing up.

I kept glancing at Ember and Ryan in the front row, and Castien and Eli who sat with them, beside Mark and Lily. They grounded me, but I still felt as though I were adrift in the ocean, about to go under with no life preserver.

"Your Majesty, congratulations," Torin spoke in my ear. He stood to my left, right behind me. Torin had not only survived that night, but killed Quilliam and his men. He was in intensive care for a week, but the fact he lived was astonishing.

A warrior I wanted beside me.

I had immediately reinstated him as First Knight, without any of the first Queen's job description. I knew he was the best for the job and would protect me unquestioningly. When I asked him, he gave me the first genuine smile I had seen from him in a long time. A new lightness glowed under the darkness. Maybe there was hope for him to find happiness again.

"Thank you, Torin." I looked back at him.

"Whatever you need, my lady, I am here for you." His eyes twinkled as he bowed, his gaze never leaving mine.

I nodded and smiled back.

A monitor on the far wall recording the ceremony mirrored my image back. This version of me held her chin up high and strong, but fear pooled beneath the façade. It was like staring at a stranger, someone else who had my face and looked the part. Royal. Regal. I did not feel like she looked.

My gaze drifted over the people until my head was pulled to the corner of the room like it had been tugged there. Air caught in my throat, and I sucked in with a sharp hitch.

Green eyes pierced mine, even from the shadows. My heart crawled up my throat like it wanted to escape, strangling my airwaves as it tried to flee. My body instantly became aware of his presence. Lorcan's energy skated over me like stroking fingers. My gaze was fastened to his, not able to break away, falling into the depth of them.

A strange humming filled my head. *Li'l bird.* It was as if his eyes spoke the words into my head. Heartache, anger, loss, and sorrow crashed into me. The intensity of his energy snapped my view to the other side of the room, but the magnet was too strong. I peered back.

The spot was empty. No sign he had been there. *Did I imagine him?*

My hands rolled into fists up under the sleeves of the gown, and I inhaled deeply. *Get it together, Ken. You have to lead the world...get it back on its feet. Lorcan does not fit in.*

Before the exhale departed my lips, a buzz crackled the monitor, yanking my head back to it. The feed of my coronation flickered and disappeared, the room gasping in unison.

A man took over the screen, a smug smile widening his face. A gasp hiccupped in my throat. I knew him, had seen him before, but my mind could not recall from where. He appeared to be around his mid-thirties and was extremely striking, but in a disturbing way. His hair, beard, and skin were void of pigment, blending almost together. Albinism, most likely. I had researched it for an assignment once. An inherited disorder, resulting from a lack of melanin. His violet-blue eyes were so light they almost looked white, but the trivial ounce of color surged off the screen.

"Sorry to interrupt." His accent had a Scandinavian tinge to it. He was tall and built in the shoulders with a chiseled jaw. Dressed in a nice suit, he sat back in a leather chair at a desk. Everything about him screamed money and power.

Lars went rigid next to me. "Luuk," he snarled, his eyes darkening. Clearly the King knew who this man was. Even on the monitor, I could sense the albino man held power. He was not someone to ignore. Lars's reaction only confirmed a right to the fear parading down my veins.

"You think you can growl and I will quiver under your pathetic excuse of authority? Your brother was a better leader of the Dark by far." Luuk chuckled. It was slightly high-pitched and chilled my blood. "And that's saying a lot since I despised the bastard too." He sat up, folding his ghostly hands. "Aren't you curious how I broke in? Here are the unfathomable Seelie and Unseelie leaders, and it takes only one mid-level hacker to hijack your feed?" A white eyebrow lifted as he cleared his throat. "Foolish people, these leaders want you to think you are safe, in capable hands to lead you." Luuk sneered, the red from his gums contrasting sharply with his skin, looking like he recently drank a vat of blood.

"But it's all a farce. They dress up a pretty girl and put a crown on her head, but does that give her the power, experience, and right to rule? No!" He hit his fist on the desk. "I know I am not alone in thinking our leaders are unfit to reign. Especially a Druid! She is not true fae and no prophecy should dictate unequivocal devotion to a *human* girl." His unnerving eyes latched on to me, his lip rising in disgust. I couldn't move; I was locked in his gaze like a laser beam. His eyes, the way he stared straight into me felt so familiar. Trepidation battered against my spine, holding me prisoner in my own body.

"I am here to call forward those who do not want to follow like sheep and be led by the incompetent, weak, and subservient. Convenient for the Unseelie King, is it not, to put into power someone so incapable he can control her...and us?"

The men behind the camera frantically tried to shut off the display. Lars didn't move or respond to Luuk. His face stayed expressionless as Luuk ranted on, but the energy leaking from Lars was heavy and sparking with fury.

"We finally have Earth again. Our true home," Luuk declared. "Now we will decide who gets to rule."

His image scrambled before the screen went black. The man behind the fae-made video device in the back of the room stomped on it, breaking it into pieces.

It took a moment before the whispers of the room reached me. I was still glued in place.

Lars made a sound so strange, like a vibration in his throat. I twisted my neck to look at him. His expression blistered with rage.

"What happened?" I croaked.

"A revolt," he gritted through his teeth.

"What?" Panic butterflied in my chest.

Lars tugged at his cuffs, taking measured breaths. "Luuk manages almost half of the European Seelie. He was a favorite of Aneira's. He would not pronounce a revolt unless he knew he had backing."

I licked my lips, terror burning the back of my throat.

"I will send men to squash this quickly." Lars turned, storming off the raised platform. Goran, Rez, and Rimmon waited for him in the doorway.

I struggled to swallow, feeling about an inch tall, keenly aware of eyes on me from every corner of the room. I couldn't deny much of what Luuk said was true. I was inexperienced and too trusting of Lars's help.

I felt lost, as though floating out to sea, the waves crashing down on me. But I would not let my people down. I would not cower or hide.

I had no idea what was ahead, but America had gotten a taste of their own medicine, like when we revolted against the English crown to be our own country. Europe was taking one from our handbook. Europe just tossed tea into our harbor with a big middle finger pointed at me, revolting against me.

They wanted me, the Crown of Light, to fall.

Thank you to all my readers. Your opinion really matters to me and helps others decide if they want to purchase my book. If you enjoyed this book, please consider leaving a review on the site where you purchased it. Thank you.

Want to find out about my next series, *The Lightness Saga*? Sign up for my newsletter on my website and keep updated on the latest news.

www.staceymariebrown.com

Nothing on a list or in books will prepare her for what's ahead.

Even her own feelings.

Lightness Falling

Lightness Saga #2

In gaining the crown, Kennedy lost friends, her first love, and her heart.

And now her throne is being threatened.

In this time of turmoil, radical groups surface trying to kill her and take down the kingdom. Kennedy is forced to go undercover and penetrate one of these groups with the help of the one person she has sworn against ever seeing again.

Lorcan Dragen.

The one man she let in, but cannot have.

What she has to do to save her falling reign is dangerous, foolish, and impossible. That doesn't even come close to the truth she discovers along the way.

Kennedy's world is flipped upside down with heartbreaking discoveries, betrayal, secrets, lies…and a darkness Kennedy won't be able to fight.

Herself.

When lightness falls, darkness rises. Which side will win? Find out in the conclusion of Kennedy's story.

Acknowledgements

I was going to end the Darkness Series at Book 4 and move on. Between the characters and my amazing readers, this did not happen and I couldn't be more grateful. Kennedy exist only because of you guys, for falling in love with these characters as much as I have and demanding their story. Thank you again for wanting me to bring her story to light!

I am a very lucky girl. I get to work with the best of the best in this business! A HUGE thanks to:

Jordan, the woman that can make me fly or bring me to my knees, but always in the end it's a far better story. Thank you. http://jordanrosenfeld.net/

Hollie "the editor", how can I put into words what you have come to mean to me. My friend, my editor…you're like my happy place. You are always there anytime I need. No question. Thank you so much! http://www.hollietheeditor.com/.

Dane at Ebook Launch! Thank you for doing your thing and designing such a beautiful cover, despite all my control issues! https://ebooklaunch.com/ebook-cover-design/

To Judi at http://www.formatting4u.com/: Always such a pleasure. You always got my back.

Mom- Sorry I'm such a pain in the ass and a bitchy boss! You still love me, right?

To all the readers who have supported me: My gratitude is for all you do and how much you help indie authors out of the pure love of reading.

Stacey Marie Brown

To all the indie/hybrid authors out there who inspire, challenge, support, and push me to be better: I love you!

And to anyone who has picked up an indie book and given an unknown author a chance. THANK YOU!

About The Author

Stacey Marie Brown is a lover of hot fictional bad boys and sarcastic heroines who kick butt. She also enjoys books, travel, TV shows, hiking, writing, design, and archery. Stacey swears she is part gypsy, being lucky enough to live and travel all over the world.

She grew up in Northern California, where she ran around on her family's farm, raising animals, riding horses, playing flashlight tag, and turning hay bales into cool forts.

When she's not writing she's out hiking, spending time with friends, and traveling. She also volunteers helping animals and is eco-friendly. She feels all animals, people, and environment should be treated kindly.

To learn more about Stacey or her books, visit her at:

Author website
www.staceymariebrown.com

Facebook Author page
https://www.facebook.com/staceymarie.brown.5

Pinterest
www.pinterest.com/s.mariebrown

Twitter   @S_MarieBrown

Instagram   Instagram.com/staceymariebrown

Made in the USA
Coppell, TX
25 April 2021